PENGUIN BOOK

ICE-CANDY-MA

Bapsi Sidhwa was born in Karachi and brought up in Lahore. An active social worker among Asian women, she represented Pakistan at the Asian Women's Congress held in 1975. She has published two other novels, *The Crow Eaters* and *The Bride*. Bapsi Sidhwa divides her time between the United States, where she teaches, and Pakistan.

PRAISE FOR BAPSI SIDHWA

'Bapsi Sidhwa deals with the partition of India, a subject as harrowing as the Holocaust. Before our disbelieving eyes, she performs the remarkable feat of bringing together the ribald farce of Parsee family life and the stark drama and horrors of the riots and massacres of 1947.

'She has achieved the impossible through one masterly stroke creating a child's world of home and games in the park amidst a motley company. At the center of this world is the child, Lenny. For all that she bears the bitter burden of history on her eight-year-old-shoulders, Lenny is not allowed to become merely the embodiment of an abstract idea. Sidhwa's triumph lies in creating characters so rich in hilarious and accurate detail, so alive and active, that long after one has closed the book, they continue to perform their extraordinary and wonderful feats before our eyes.'

—*Dawn*

'If you wish to relive the Lahore of the '40s and '50s, go no further. In *Ice-Candy-Man* the tale is told with skill and craftsmanship unrivaled in the Sub-continent.'

—*She*

'Sidhwa's humour comes in pungent one-liners and her style is highly visual.'

—*India Today*

'Sidhwa captures the turmoil of the times, with a brilliant combination of individual growing-up pains and the collective anguish of a newly independent but divided country. Sidhwa's work—particularly the dehumanizing effects of communalism she movingly reveals in *Ice-Candy-Man*—is painfully relevant to our present day India.'

—*Economic Times*

'It may be that the atrocities of 1947 are best seen through the innocent, naïve eyes of a child, who has no Hindu, Muslim, or Sikh axe to grind . . . Lenny is free both from the prejudices of religion, and from the prejudices against women, and the constraints she will be subject to as she grows older. The authorial voice (is) a powerful voice of hindsight.'

—Ralph Crane

'Bapsi Sidhwa cannot be easily labeled . . . She cannot be categorized as just a Pakistani novelist, she is much more versatile. 'Lame Lenny' can be related to Oscar of Gunther Grass's *Tin Drum*. There are books about boys growing up (Mark Twain's *Huck Finn*), however Sidhwa's novel is unique as it establishes the girl-child's point of view.'

—R.K. Dhawan

'Sidhwa's evocation of a Lahore childhood, seen through the eyes of a precocious child called Lenny, is as sweet and enticing as the popsicles that the hero of her novel sells. It is a passionate account of Partition told through the cooling mists of Parse humour.'

—*Parsiana*

'Lenny can be compared to the persona that Chaucer adopts in his Prologue to *The Canterbury Tales*, rendering credibility by being almost a part of the reader's consciousness . . . With the wonder of a child she observes social change and human behaviour, her persona a source of sharp irony.'

—Novi Kapadia

'Sidhwa's *Ice-Candy-Man*, is a bold experiment in narrative strategies and time, in which the unspeakable horrors of communal violence are told mainly from a little girl's point of view.'

—*Times Literary Supplement (TLS)*

'In this rich, original novel Sidhwa contrives, without fake naïvete, to tell the story through the eyes of a sharp, inquisitive eight-year-old girl Lenny, who has a crippled foot and is cared for by a beautiful young Ayah. Lenny is established so firmly as a truthful witness that the mounting unease in Lahore, the riots, fires and brutal massacres become real through the child's experience. The colossal upheaval of partition, when cities were allotted to India or Pakistan like pieces on a chess-board, and their frightened inhabitants were often savagely uprooted, runs like an earth tremor through this thoughtful novel.

—Sylvia Clayton

'With skill and sympathy, and a delightful sense of humour, Bapsi Sidhwa shows the small girl Lenny growing up in comfort and tranquillity. The book's many characters all come to exuberant life, exhibiting the odd tastes and unpredictable behaviour of real individuals.'

—*London Magazine*

'Sidhwa's Rabelaisian language and humour are enormously refreshing, especially in the context of modern Indian fiction, which has tended rather towards the prim and stilted. In *Ice-Candy-Man*, as in her previous novels, she succeeds in transmitting into English much of the spirit of Punjabi language and culture, which is nothing if not earthy. But her prose is also both delicate and precise in its imagery and descriptions, with words chosen as carefully as pieces of inlay in a marble wall.'

—*The Literary Review*

'Like all Sidhwa's work, the novel contains a rich undercurrent of legend and folklore. It combines Sidhwa's affectionate admiration for her own community with a compassion for the dispossessed. Her own childhood memories give the novel further depth and resonance.'

—*The Oxford Companion To Twentieth-Century Literature in English*

A fluent, fast moving narrative of wit and wisdom.

—*Irish Times*

A born storyteller, an affectionate, shrewd observer . . . she writes with authority and flair.

—*New Statesman*

'Bapsi Sidhwa is new to me, and something of a discovery. She is writing here about the hatred and terror which accompanied the partition of the Indian subcontinent. The opening sections of the novel set a mood in which continuity is taken for granted, and unfamiliar terrain and complex social relationships are suffused with the melancholy charm of awakening sexuality . . . The girl's beloved Ayah is a Hindu and it is one of the most poignant moments in the book when the girl, trusting the *Ice-Candy-Man*, betrays her hiding place. It is as if her childish innocence is as powerful as a devil, and she cannot help telling the truth.'

—London Times

'*Ice-Candy-Man* is extremely taut, highly sensitive and its heart-rending realism is best brought out with the familiar elements. The treatment, much to the fulfillment of the reader, is not only delightfully different but also inimitably exclusive . . . Sidhwa's somewhat Joycian insight into child psychology and keen observation of child behaviour is what makes the book so compelling and virtually unputdownable.'

—Miscellany

'The brilliantly created Indian characters in this novel are made with a real face, that turns at times into a mask of horror and others into a peal of laughter . . . Of all the marvellous people brought to life in this novel there is one who signifies resistance to change and used the chaos around him for his own malicious ends. And so in the end there is one person who comes out unscathed and no writer from the brutal pain of Indian independence: *Ice-Candy-Man*.'

—Weekly Mail

'As the ambiguities and contradictions residing in the political situation in the Punjab are explored in the course of Lenny's narrative, so examples multiply of Sidhwa's talent for fusing broad humour and trenchant criticism, concrete observation and imaginative insight, the realities of everyday existence and the abstractions of politics and religion.'

—Third World Quarterly

'Without a word of protestation or preaching and without histrionics, Sidhwa has written one of the most powerful indictments of the riots which occurred during the Partition.'

—World Literature Today

The novel is about the slow awaking of the child heroine both to sexuality and grown-up pains and pleasures and to the particular historical disaster that overwhelms her world . . . compulsively readable.

—*Observer*

A powerful and dramatic novelist.

—*The Times*

'Sidhwa, a Parsee living in Pakistan, is a rarity even in swiftly-changing Asia—a candid, forthright, balanced woman novelist. Her twentieth century view of Indian life can only be compared to V.S. Naipaul's. Sidhwa is among the most invigorating Indian writers.'

—*Bloomsbury Review*

'*Ice-Candy-Man* is a novel in which heartbreak coexists with slapstick . . . and jokes give way to lines of glowing beauty ('the moonlight settles like a layer of ashes over Lahore'). The author's capacity for bringing an assortment of characters vividly to life is enviable. In reducing the Partition to the perceptions of a polio-ridden child, a girl who tries to wrench out her tongue because it is unable to lie, Bapsi Sidhwa has given us a memorable book, one that confirms her reputation as Pakistan's finest English language novelist.

—*New York Times Book Review*

'Bapsi Sidhwa has turned her gaze upon the domestic comedy of a Pakistani family in the 1940s and somehow managed to evoke the great political upheavals of the age . . . and I am particularly touched by the way she has held the wicked world up to the mirror of a young girl's mind and caught so much that is lyrical and significant . . . a mysterious and wonderful novel.'

—*Washington Post, Book World*

'Much has been written about the holocaust that followed the Partition of India in 1947. But seldom has that story been told as touchingly, as convincingly, or as horrifyingly as it has been by novelist Bapsi Sidhwa, seeing it through the eyes of young Lenny . . . there is great humanity in this novel.'

—*Philadelphia Inquirer*

'Reading Bapsi Sidhwa's *Ice-Candy-Man* is like foraging through a tableful of discounted Swatch watches, and finding a gold

Rolex . . . it illustrates the power of good fiction: a historical tragedy comes alive, yielding insight into both the past and the subcontinent's turbulent present.'

—*USA Today*

'Bapsi Sidhwa is a writer of enormous talent, capable of endowing small domestic occurrences with cosmic drama and rendering calamitous historical events with deeply felt personal meaning. Her *Ice-Candy-Man* is a lively, compelling novel, ambitiously conceived, skillfully plotted and beautifully written.'

—*New York Newsday*

'Set against the partition of India, this fast-paced, seriocomic saga tracks the daily peregrinations and capricious thoughts of Lenny who unwittingly learns that people and events are not as 'transparent' as she had thought.'

—*The Miami Herald*

Ice-Candy-Man is a masterful creation of another time and place with characters that continue to live and speak long after one finishes reading. Author of earlier novels, including *The Crow Eaters*, Sidhwa's work has been translated into many languages and has won many prizes.

—*Crosswinds*

Imagine a child skipping innocently through the carnage of war. The child's lighthearted presence makes the devastation around her all the more heartbreaking. This is the effect of Bapsi Sidhwa's compelling novel.

—*Milwaukee Sentinel*

Readers soon come to realize that they are seeing 1947 Lahore through a skillful narrator's eyes (as) street scenes, as well as family life, come alive. Sidhwa provides a vivid, realistic picture of Indian family life and human interaction . . . with an introduction to what continues to happen (in the sub-continent) today.

—*Arizona Daily Star*

'*Ice-Candy-Man* is a superb novel, brilliantly and lovingly written. It is also a masterful work of history as it relates political events in the most simple but also most humanly meaningful terms, with comedy and anguish, through the eyes of a child.

—*Albuquerque Journal*

Sidhwa's viewpoint is of someone to whom the scenes she depicts are known with great intimacy. As foreign readers we're invited to learn what it was really like to live as an Indian in those years of violence. Lenny has the privilege of detachment: She gives us the story whole, instead of in fragments.

—Remark

'For one of the most important appealing narrators you will ever come across, for a compelling and illuminating view of a moment in world history, and for clear-eyed insights into human nature, read this book.'

—Reading Woman

'Sidhwa is a superb storyteller, sprinkling the book with tersely-captured vignettes, which increasingly knit together into a story of passion and betrayal, 'the unscrupulous nature of desire' and 'the pitiless face of love'. It's a great, thronging bazaar of a book, bustling with riches.'

—New Internationalist

'This exquisitely written, tightly constructed novel offers an engaging glimpse into Asian life and a vivid record of a dark chapter in history.'

—Masterplots: Women's Literature

Bapsi Sidhwa is technically Pakistani, but literature has no need of partitions, particularly as Sidhwa's novel *Ice-Candy-Man* is one of the finest responses made to the horror of the division of the subcontinent.

—The New Yorker

The originality and power of Sidhwa's splendid novel on the partition of India and the subsequent communal violence derived from her choice of protagonist: Lenny, an eight-year-old Parsee girl from Lahore, a spectator living in the midst of, but apart from, the rising tensions among Hindu, Muslim, and Sikh . . . Throughout, the novel sustains the vitality of Lenny's world with a series of wonderfully comic scenes. Highly, recommended for all libraries.

—The New Yorker Library Journal

Sidhwa's luminous present-tense prose, is laminated with the magic of childish wonder . . . She manages to do justice to the complexity of racial, ethnic, and religious violence that accompanied the partitioning of India . . . Richly layered, both realistic and magically evocative, as well as topical: a novel that brings to triumphant life an India that 'has less to do with fate than with the will of men.'

—*Kirkus Reviews*

The novel's politics are effectively juxtaposed against a lush, sensual center, as the author's prose lingers on the hot, dry Lahore streets . . . A novel to savor.

—*Booklist*

Lenny's honesty is compelling, and the reader, like many in the story, cannot help but trust her. She is alternately thrilled and frightened by the events she dutifully records, and so in the end, is the reader.

—*Publishers Weekly*

Ice-Candy-Man is a multifaceted jewel of a novel. Lenny is as striking a creation as Harper Lee's *Scout*. Who plays a similar role in *To Kill a Mockingbird*.

—*Houston Chronicle*

Sidhwa is the kind of writer who catches you by surprise. In the subtlest of ways, she teaches and edifies as she entertains.

—*Radcliffe Quarterly*

Sidhwa deals with the bloody partition of India through the eyes of a small girl growing up in a Parsee family, surviving through female bonding and rebellion.

—*Ms. Magazine*

Sidhwa is a feminist and a realist. One sees in her women characters the strength of passion, the tenderness of love, and the courage of one's convictions.

—*Belles Letters*

Ice-Candy-Man

BAPSI SIDHWA

PENGUIN BOOKS

Penguin Books India (P) Ltd., 11 Community Centre, Panchsheel Park,
New Delhi- 110 017, India
Penguin Books Ltd., 27 Wrights Lane, London W 8 5 TZ, UK
Penguin Putnam Inc., 375 Hudson Street, New York, NY 10014, USA
Penguin Books Australia Ltd., Ringwood, Victoria, Australia
Penguin Books Canada Ltd., 10 Alcorn Avenue, Suite 300, Toronto
Ontario, M 4 V 3 B 2, Canada
Penguin Books (NZ) Ltd., Cnr Rosedale and Airborne Roads, Albany, Auckland, New Zealand

First published by William Heinemann Ltd 1988
Published in Penguin Books 1989

10 9 8 7 6

Printed and bound in Great Britain by
Richard Clay Ltd, Bungay, Suffolk

For Xerxes

Acknowledgments

I thank Rana Khan for sharing with me his childhood experiences at the time of Partition. He lives in Houston, and still bears the deep crescent-shaped scar on the back of his head, and innumerable other scars.

I would also like to thank my good friends: Nergis Sobani for so painstakingly typing the final (and semi-final) drafts of my novels; Safder Butt, who with his raconteur's gift inspired me to write in the first place; Phillip Lopate for his scrutiny of the manuscript and for his comments; Rosellen Brown and Max Apple for their good cheer and support; Ali Asani, and Noman Haq for assisting me with the selection of the Urdu poems; Reetika Vazirini, my hapless flatmate, for her help; and finally the Bunting Institute and the National Endowment for the Arts for providing me with the time, space and means to complete this novel.

Grateful acknowledgment is made for permission to reprint excerpts from *Urdu Literature* edited by D. J. Matthews, C. Shackle and Shahrukh Husain, published by Urdu Markaz, London, 1985.

Acknowledgments

I thank Reza Khan for sharing with me his childhood experience at the time of Partition. He lives in Houston, and still bears the crescent-shaped scar on the back of his head, and [illegible].

I would also like to thank my good friends [illegible] Sethna [illegible] so painstakingly copying the first (and sometimes [illegible]) drafts of my novels; Sadiq [illegible], who [illegible] inspired me to write in the first place; Phillip Lopate for his scrutiny of the manuscript and for his comments; Rosellen Brown and Mark Apple for their good cheer and support; Ali Asani and Nermin [illegible] for assisting me with the selection of the Urdu poems; [illegible], my [illegible], for her help; and finally the Bunting Institute and the National Endowment for the Arts for providing me with the time, space and means to complete the novel.

Grateful acknowledgement is made for permission to reprint excerpts from *Urdu Literature*, edited by D. J. Matthews, C. Shackle and Shahrukh Husain, published by Urdu Markaz, London, [illegible].

Chapter 1

Shall I hear the lament of the nightingale, submissively lending
my ear?
Am I the rose to suffer its cry in silence year after year?
The fire of verse gives me courage and bids me no more to be
faint.
With dust in my mouth, I am abject: to God I make my
complaint.
Sometimes You favour our rivals then sometimes with us You
are free,
I am sorry to say it so boldly. You are no less fickle than we.
(Iqbal: 'Complaint to God')

My world is compressed. Warris Road, lined with rain gutters, lies between Queens Road and Jail Road: both wide, clean, orderly streets at the affluent fringes of Lahore.

Rounding the right-hand corner of Warris Road and continuing on Jail Road is the hushed Salvation Army wall. Set high, at eight-foot intervals, are the wall's dingy eyes. My child's mind is blocked by the gloom emanating from the wire-mesh screening the oblong ventilation slits. I feel such sadness for the dumb creature I imagine lurking behind the wall. I know it is dumb because I have listened to its silence, my ear to the wall.

Jail Road also harbours my energetic electric-aunt and her adenoidal son . . . large, slow, inexorable. Their house is adjacent to the den of the Salvation Army.

Opposite it, down a bumpy, dusty, earth-packed drive, is the one-and-a-half-room abode of my godmother. With her dwell her docile old husband and her slavesister. This is my haven. My refuge from the perplexing unrealities of my home on Warris Road.

A few furlongs away Jail Road vanishes into the dense

bazaars of Mozang Chungi. At the other end a distant canal cuts the road at the periphery of my world.

* * *

Lordly, lounging in my briskly rolling pram, immersed in dreams, my private world is rudely popped by the sudden appearance of an English gnome wagging a leathery finger in my ayah's face. But for keen reflexes that enable her to pull the carriage up short there might have been an accident: and blood spilled on Warris Road. Wagging his finger over my head into Ayah's alarmed face, he tut-tuts: 'Let her walk. Shame, shame! Such a big girl in a pram! She's at least four!'

He smiles down at me, his brown eyes twinkling intolerance.

I look at him politely, concealing my complacence. The Englishman is short, leathery, middle-aged, pointy-eared. I like him.

'Come on. Up, up!' he says, crooking a beckoning finger.

'She not walk much ... she get tired,' drawls Ayah. And simultaneously I raise my trouser cuff to reveal the leather straps and wicked steel callipers harnessing my right boot.

Confronted by Ayah's liquid eyes and prim gloating, and the triumphant revelation of my callipers, the Englishman withers.

But back he bounces, bobbing up and down. 'So what?' he says, resurrecting his smile. 'Get up and walk! Walk! You need the exercise more than other children! How will she become strong, sprawled out like that in her pram? Now, you listen to me ...' he lectures Ayah, and prancing before the carriage which has again started to roll says, 'I want you to tell her mother ...'

Ayah and I hold our eyes away, effectively dampening his good-Samaritan exuberance ... and wagging his head and turning about, the Englishman quietly dissolves up the driveway from which he had so enthusiastically sprung.

The covetous glances Ayah draws educate me. Up and down, they look at her. Stub-handed twisted beggars and dusty old beggars on crutches drop their poses and stare at her with hard, alert eyes. Holy men, masked in piety, shove aside their pretences to ogle her with lust. Hawkers, cart-drivers, cooks, coolies and cyclists turn their heads as she passes, pushing my pram with the unconcern of the Hindu goddess she worships.

Ayah is chocolate-brown and short. Everything about her is eighteen years old and round and plump. Even her face. Full-blown cheeks, pouting mouth and smooth forehead curve to form a circle with her head. Her hair is pulled back in a tight knot.

And, as if her looks were not stunning enough, she has a rolling bouncy walk that agitates the globules of her buttocks under her cheap colourful saris and the half-spheres beneath her short sari-blouses. The Englishman no doubt had noticed.

We cross Jail Road and enter Godmother's compound. Walking backwards, the buffalo-hide water-pouch slung from his back, the waterman is spraying the driveway to settle the dust for evening visitors. Godmother is already fitted into the bulging hammock of her easy-chair and Slavesister squats on a low cane stool facing the road. Their faces brighten as I scramble out of the pram and run towards them. Smiling like roguish children, softly clapping hands they chant, *'Langer deen! Paisay ke teen! Tamba mota, pag mahin!'* Freely translated, 'Lame Lenny! Three for a penny! Fluffy pants and fine fanny!'

Flying forward I fling myself at Godmother and she lifts me on to her lap and gathers me to her bosom. I kiss her, insatiably, excessively, and she hugs me. She is childless. The bond that ties her strength to my weakness, my fierce demands to her nurturing, my trust to her capacity to contain that trust – and my loneliness to her compassion –

is stronger than the bond of motherhood. More satisfying than the ties between men and women.

I cannot be in her room long without in some way touching her. Some nights, clinging to her broad white back like a bug, I sleep with her. She wears only white khaddar saris and white khaddar blouses beneath which is her coarse bandage-tight bodice.

In all the years I never saw the natural shape of her breasts.

* * *

Somewhere in the uncharted wastes of space beyond, is Mayo Hospital. We are on a quiet wide veranda running the length of the first floor. The cement floor is shining clean.

Col. Bharucha, awesome, bald, as pink-skinned as an Englishman, approaches swiftly along the corridor. My mother springs up from the bench on which we've been waiting.

He kneels before me. Gently he lifts the plaster cast on my dangling right leg and suddenly looks into my eyes. His eyes are a complex hazel. They are direct as an animal's. He can read my mind.

Col. Bharucha is cloaked in thunder. The terrifying aura of his renown and competence are with him even when he is without his posse of house surgeons and head nurses. His thunder is reflected in my mother's on-your-mark attentiveness. If he bends, she bends swifter. When he reaches for the saw on the bench she reaches it first and hands it to him with touching alacrity. It is a frightening arm's-length saw. It belongs in a wood-shed. He withdraws from his pockets a mallet, a hammer and a chisel.

The surgeon's pink head, bent in concentration, hides the white cast. I look at my mother. I turn away to look at a cloudless sky. I peer inquisitively at the closed windows screening the large general ward in front of me. The knocks of the hammer and chisel and the sawing have ceased to alarm. I am confident of the doctor's competence. I am bored. The crunch of the saw biting into plaster continues as the saw is worked to and fro by the surgeon. I look at his bowed head and am arrested by the splotch of blood just visible on my shin through the crack in the plaster.

My boredom vanishes. The blood demands a reaction. 'Um . . .' I moan dutifully. There is no response. 'Um . . . Um . . .' I moan, determined to draw attention.

The sawing stops. Col. Bharucha straightens. He looks up at me and his direct eyes bore into my thoughts. He cocks his head, impishly defying me to shed crocodile tears. Caught out I put a brave face on my embarrassment and my non-existent pain and look away.

It is all so pleasant and painless. The cast is off. My mother's guilt-driven attention is where it belongs – on the steeply fallen arch of my right foot. The doctor buckles my sandal and helps me from the bench saying, 'It didn't hurt now, did it?' He and my mother talk over my head in cryptic monosyllables, nods and signals. I am too relieved to see my newly released foot and its valuable deformity intact to be interested in their grown-up exclusivity. My mother takes my hand and I limp away happily.

It is a happy interlude. I am sent to school. I play 'I sent a letter to my friend . . .' with other children. My cousin, slow, intense, observant, sits watching.

'Which of you's sick and is not supposed to run?' asks the teacher: and bound by our telepathic conspiracy, both Cousin and I point to Cousin. He squats, distributing his indolent weight on his sturdy feet and I shout, play, laugh, and run on the tips of my toes. I have an overabundance of energy. It can never be wholly released.

The interlude was happy.

* * *

I lie on a white wooden table in a small room. I know it is the same hospital. I have been lured unsuspecting to the table but I get a whiff of something frightening. I hate the smell with all my heart, and my heart pounding I try to get off the table. Hands hold me. Col. Bharucha, in a strange white cap and mask, looks at me coolly and says something to a young and nervous lady doctor. The obnoxious smell grows stronger as a frightening muzzle is brought closer to my mouth and nose. I scream and kick out. The muzzle moves away. Again it attacks and again I twist and wrench, turning my face from side to side. My hands are pinned down. I can't move my legs. I realise they are strapped. Hands hold my head. 'No! No! Help me. Mummy! Mummy, help me!' I shout, panicked. She too is aligned with them. 'I'm suffocating,' I scream. 'I can't breathe.' There is an unbearable weight on my chest. I moan and cry.

I am held captive by the brutal smell. It has vaporised into a milky cloud. I float round and round and up and down and fall horrendous distances without landing anywhere, fighting for my life's breath. I am abandoned in that suffocating cloud. I moan and my ghoulish voice turns me into something despicable and eerie and deserving of the terrible punishment. But where am I? How long will the horror last? Days and years with no end in sight . . .

It must have ended.

I switch awake to maddening pain; sitting up in my mother's bed crying. I must have been crying a long time. I become aware of the new plaster cast on my leg. The shape of the cast is altered from the last time. The toes point up. The pain from my leg radiates all over my small body. 'Do something. I'm hurting!'

My mother tells me the story of the little mouse with seven tails.

'The mouse comes home crying.' My mother rubs her knuckles to her eyes and, energetically imitating the mouse, sobs, '"Mummy, Mummy, do something. The children at school tease me. They sing: 'Freaky mousey with seven tails! Lousy mousey with seven tails!'" So, the little mouse's mother chops off one tail. The next day the mouse again comes home crying: "Mummy, Mummy, the children tease me. 'Lousy mousey with six tails! Freaky mousey with six tails!'"'

And so on, until one by one the little mouse's tails are all chopped off and the story winds to its inevitable and dismal end with the baby mouse crying: 'Mummy, Mummy, the children tease me. They sing, "Freaky mousey with no tail! Lousy mousey with no tail!"' And there is no way a tail can be tacked back on.

The doleful story adds to my misery. But stoically bearing my pain for the duration of the tale, out of pity for my mother's wan face and my father's exaggerated attempts to become the tragic mouse, I once again succumb to the pain.

My mother tells my father: 'Go next door and phone the doctor to come at once!' It is in the middle of the night. And it is cold. Father puts on his dressing gown and wrapping a scarf round his neck leaves us. My screaming loses its edge of panic. An hour later, exhausted by the pain and no longer able to pander to my mother's efforts to distract, I abandon myself to hysteria.

'Daddy has gone to fetch Col. Bharucha,' soothes Mother. She carries me round and round the room stroking my back. Finally, pushing past the curtain and the door, she takes me into the sitting room.

My father raises his head from the couch.

The bitter truth sinks in. He never phoned the doctor. He never went to fetch him. And my mother collaborated in the betrayal. I realise there is nothing they can do and I don't blame them.

The night must have passed – as did the memory of further pain.

As news of my operation spreads, the small and entire Parsee community of Lahore, in clucking clusters, descends on the Sethi household. I don't wish to see them. I cry for Godmother. I feel only she can appreciate my pain and comfort me. She sends her obese emissary, Mini Aunty, who with her dogged devotion to my mother – and multiplicity of platitudes – only aggravates. 'My, my, my! So here we are! Flat on our backs like old ladies!' She clicks her tongue. 'We've no consideration for poor Mummy, have we?' As if I've deliberately committed surgery on my foot and sneaked my leg into a cast!

But, preceded by the slave, Godmother comes.

She sits by my bed stroking me, smiling, her eyes twinkling concern, in her grey going-out sari, its pretty border of butterflies pinned to iron strands of scant combed-back hair. The intensity of her tenderness and the concentration of her attention are narcotic. I require no one else.

All evening long Mother and Father sit in the drawing room, long-faced and talking in whispers, answering questions, accepting advice, exhibiting my plastered leg.

When Col. Bharucha makes his house call at dusk he is ushered through the sitting room – hushed by his passage – into the nursery by the officiating and anxious energy of Electric-aunt. Father, cradling me like a baby, carries me in.

The visiting ladies form a quiet ring round my cot as with a little mallet the doctor checks my wrist, knees, elbows and left ankle for reflexes: and injects a pain-killer into my behind. Cousin, watching the spectacle, determines seriously to become a doctor or a male nurse. Any profession that permits one to jab pins into people merits his consideration.

Taking advantage of Col. Bharucha's brief presence Mother reads out her list of questions. Should she sit me out in the sun? Massage like this . . . or that? Use almond or mustard oil? Can she give me Mr Phailbus's homeopathic powders? Cod-liver oil?

'I'm to blame,' she says, 'I left her to the ayahs . . .'

A month later, free of pain, I sit in my stroller, my right leg stuck straight out in front on account of my cast, as

Ayah propels me to the zoo. I observe the curious glances coming my way and soak in the commiserate clucking of tongues, wearing a polite and nonchalant countenance. The less attention I appear to demand the more attention I get. And, despite the provocative agitation of Ayah's bouncy walk, despite the gravitational pull of her moon-like face, I am the star attraction of the street.

When we stop by the chattering monkeys in the zoo, even they through their cages ogle me. I stare at the white plaster forcing my unique foot into the banal mould of a billion other feet and I ponder my uncertain future.

What will happen once the cast comes off? What if my foot emerges immaculate, fault-free? Will I have to behave like other children, slogging for my share of love and other handouts? Aren't I too old to learn to throw tantrums – or hold my breath and have a fit? While other children have to clamour and jump around to earn their candy I merely sit or stand, wearing my patient, butter-wouldn't-melt . . . and displaying my callipers – and I am showered with candy.

What if I have to labour at learning spellings and reciting poems and strive with forty other driven children to stand first, second or third in class? So far I've been spared the idiocy – I am by nature uncompetitive – but the sudden emergence from its cocoon of a beautifully balanced and shapely foot could put my sanguine personality and situation on the line.

I flirt, briefly, with hope. Perhaps, in his zeal, Col. Bharucha has over-corrected the defect – and I see myself limping gamely on the stub of my heel while the ball of my foot and my toes waggle suspended.

I am jolted out of my troublesome reverie when I realise that Ayah is talking to Sher Singh, the slender Sikh zoo attendant, and I have been rolled before the lion's cage. There he lies, the ferocious beast of my nightmares, looking toothless and innocent . . . lying in wait to spring, fully dentured, into my dreams.

Chapter 2

Father stirs in the bed next to ours. 'Jana?' Mother says softly, propping herself up on an elbow.

I lie still pretending sleep.

She calls him Jan: life. In the faint glow of the night-bulb I see him entirely buried beneath his quilt like in a grave. Mother hates it when he covers his face: as if he is distancing himself from her even in his sleep. She knows he is awake. 'Jana?' she says again, groping for his head. 'Don't cover your face like that ... You'll suffocate.'

'So?' says Father drowsily, hanging on to the heavy cotton quilt and unveiling only his eyes. 'You'll be a merry widow. You'll blow every pice I've saved.'

I can almost feel a languorous happiness settle in my mother's flesh. He sounds teasing, affectionate: as she says he did in the first year of their six-year-old marriage.

'Don't say that, Jana. Even as a joke,' Mother says, her voice plaintive, grateful, husky. She rolls over and moulding herself to his back makes small burrowing, yearning movements. Father turns and lifting the quilt buries his head in the breasts she has inherited from a succession of bountifully endowed Parsee grandmothers.

Having polio in infancy is like being born under a lucky star. It has many advantages – it permits me access to my mother's bed in the middle of the night.

'*Baijee?* Wake up.' Ayah taps Mother's hand urgently. '*Baijee?*'

My lids fly open. Mother looks startled and her eyes, still glazed with dreams, stare fixedly at Ayah.

'Something's happened to Papoo ... I've put her in the nursery,' whispers Ayah. 'You'd better come.'

In one starting movement Mother pushes away the quilt and swings her feet to the icy floor. Her calves gleam creamily in the pale light seeping in through the narrow windows. Shanta, my eighteen-year-old Ayah, pushes the red felt slippers towards her mistress's feet and holds out Mother's pashmina shawl.

I sit up, whimpering, and Ayah swings me up and places me on her hip. I know I am heavy with my cast.

It is warmer in my nursery. A thin woollen dhurrie covers the brick floor and the sweeper's daughter is lying on it in front of the glowing rods of an electric heater. She is three years older than me, a bit taller, but she weighs less I'm sure.

Ayah places me in my cot and squats beside my kneeling mother. I feel a sickening lurch of fear – and fury. From the way she lies, ashen, immobile – the right side of her dark cheek and small mouth slightly askew, a thread of saliva stretched to a wet spot on the dhurrie – I think that there is something terribly wrong with Papoo. 'Has Muccho beaten her again?' I ask fiercely.

Ayah looks up at me, shivering in the sleeveless cardigan worn over her cotton sari. Her hair is dishevelled and her large eyes are dilated with anger too. 'Shush,' she says. 'She'll be all right.' The shawl she has flung aside earlier lies in a heap on the floor.

'Papoo,' Mother says, smoothing back her straight, sun-bleached hair, 'open your eyes, child. You're safe. Come?'

But the girl, normally so responsive, lies absolutely still. She looks unbearably ill: shrunken, her small features barely defined, showing milky crescents beneath her lids.

'We'd better get her to the hospital,' Mother says, standing up. 'I'll tell Sahib to mind Lenny.'

Papoo remains in the hospital two whole weeks. She has concussion. Her mother says she fell off her bed but we know she's lying. Muccho maltreats her daughter.

When Papoo returns from the children's ward of the Ganga Ram Hospital she is sprightly, defiant, devilish and as delightful as ever.

* * *

My parents sit on wood-bottomed chairs in Col. Bharucha's consulting room. Mother holds me. I've been inflated to twice my size by knitted underwear, pullovers, a five-foot Kashmir shawl and a quilt.

Col. Bharucha is applying a stethoscope to the emaciated chest of an infant. A woman in a shabby black burka holds the child. The infant coughs so severely that his mother has to hold him upright.

Col. Bharucha removes the stethoscope from his ears and lets it hang from his neck like a talisman. 'How long has he had this cough?' he asks.

The father, standing deferentially to one side, bends towards his wife. She turns her veiled face to him and whispers.

'For a week, doctor sahib,' the man says. His head and neck are wrapped in a muffler and his gaunt face is careworn.

'How often does he throw up?' asks the doctor.

Again the man stoops and, relaying his wife's words, says: 'Quite often, sir.'

'Once a day? Twice a day? Ten times a day?' the doctor booms impatiently. I feel Mother's arm twitch.

This time the woman addresses the doctor directly, looking at him through the netting covering her eyes. 'He vomits every time he has milk . . . five, six times a day.' Her voice is incredibly young. She couldn't be more than twelve, I think, surprised.

'Why didn't you bring him earlier?' the doctor roars.

'I'm sorry, sir,' the man says. 'She didn't tell me.'

'She didn't tell you? Are you a father or a barber? And you all want Pakistan! How will you govern a country when you don't know what goes on in your own house?'

The man, shivering slightly in a short, scruffy jacket and cotton trousers, hangs his head and smiles sheepishly.

His patients understand Col. Bharucha. The more he roars and scolds the more likely he is to effect a cure. They have as much faith in his touch as in his mixtures.

'Take this to the dispenser,' Col. Bharucha says, handing him a prescription. 'He won't charge you for the medicine.'

'Your fees, sir?' The man fishes out a handful of grubby one-rupee notes from his coat pocket.

'No need,' Col. Bharucha says with a dismissive gesture, and turning to us, asks, 'Well?'

The man salaams and shepherds his wife out of the tiny room.

'It's Lenny,' says Mother. 'You said you'd remove her plaster today? She has a cold . . . I don't know if you should . . .' Her voice trails off on a quavering note.

I quake. The news comes as a complete shock. I thought I was seeing the doctor for my cold. Misinterpreting my devotion to the cast which conceals my repaired foot, Mother thinks I'm merely scared of being hurt: and has kept the true purpose of the appointment from me.

'No!' I scream, unable to bear the thought of an able-bodied future. The suspense – although it has given my forehead premature wrinkles of worry – is preferable to the certainty of an altered, laborious and loveless life.

I open my mouth wide and bawl as loudly as I am able and cleave to my mother.

'It won't hurt, *mai*,' soothes Father gently.

'Don't you remember? It didn't hurt at all last time,' carols Mother brightly. 'Dr Bharucha would never let you hurt.'

Father waves a crisp ten-rupee note before my nose as I turn my face from side to side to abjure temptation and establish disdain. It is a touching gesture of extravagance on Father's part. I would appreciate it in any other circumstance.

But trade my future for ten rupees?

Col. Bharucha moves his spindly chair closer and looks eloquently at me, implying: Now what's all this fuss about? I won't tolerate nonsense.

But my terror is genuine: and the doctor compromises. 'I only want to have a look at the plaster,' he says, and displays hands innocent of saw, chisel or hammer. 'See? I have nothing.'

He shifts his eyes to Mother. 'How do you expect me to examine her through all this quilting?' And standing up from his desk, tall and stooping, directs: 'Bring her to the table.'

Mother briskly removes the quilt and hands it to Father. She unwinds the shawl, removes my coat and trousers and lays me on the hard and treacherously narrow table that is covered only by an iodine-stained white sheet.

'Take her clothes off, woman!' the doctor hollers.

'She has such an awful cold and fever . . .' says Mother hesitantly.

'Then take her home and broil her! If you know what's good for her, why bring her to me?'

Mother and Father hastily strip me of my pullovers and knitted underwear, sparing only my cotton knickers.

The doctor applies his cold stethoscope. I'm still trembling from the thunder of his angry roars – and now I shiver also from the cold.

'She hasn't got a fever,' the doctor declares severely. He signals to Mother and she covers my naked and trembling torso with the shawl. At the direction of a swift and secret signal I miss, Father and Mother move to either side of me and firmly stroke my arms and shoulders: and, at my instant alarm, make soothing noises.

'Lie still!' the doctor orders, and petrified by his tone, I lie still.

Col. Bharucha saws, hammers and chisels at my cast, and using both hands, tears it apart.

'See? No pain,' he says, moving his eyes close to mine. 'Have a look,' he offers, helping me sit up. Mother hastily winds the shawl round my shoulders and I examine the doctor's handiwork.

I let go my breath in a massive sigh of relief. My right leg looks dead: pathetically thin, wrinkled and splotched with discoloured and pale patches. The shape of my ankle has definitely changed. It joins my foot at a much more reasonable angle. On the whole I'm surprisingly pleased. My leg looks functional but it remains gratifyingly abnormal – and far from banal!

I am dressed and stood on my bare feet. My heel still clears the floor. Col. Bharucha tries briefly to press my heel down.

'Much better!' he announces, looking up. 'See the difference?'

My parents' twinge of initial disappointment is at once replaced by readjusted expectations. They nod their heads with admiring smiles of satisfaction.

'Mind you, she must wear her callipers for some time,' says the doctor: and turning to me he adds, 'We'll get you new ones.' I could hug him. 'She still needs care . . . Massage, ultra-violet rays, physical therapy.' He raises my right arm and bends my torso to the left. 'Her right side is affected: she will have to exercise and stretch her waist like this!'

Mother's eyes are brimming with tears, her beautiful mouth working.

Col. Bharucha places his arm around her. 'What's here to worry now?' he says gruffly, surprised at Mother's agitation. 'By the time she grows up she'll be quite normal.'

Mother blows her nose in a daintily embroidered cambric handkerchief and taking the doctor's hand presses it to her eyes. Father sniffs and clears his throat.

'What about her schooling?' he asks, masking his emotion. I can't tell if he is inordinately pleased by the condition of my leg – or inordinately disappointed.

'She's doing fine without school, isn't she?' says the doctor. 'Don't pressure her . . . her nerves could be affected. She doesn't need to become a professor.' He turns to me. 'Do you want to become a professor?'

I shake my head in a firm negative.

'She'll marry – have children – lead a carefree, happy life. No need to strain her with studies and exams,' he advises: thereby sealing my fate.

Mother's mouth is again working – her eyes again brimming. And driven by unfathomable demons, again her guilt surfaces. 'I don't know where I went wrong,' she says. 'It's my fault . . . I neglected her – left her to the care of ayahs. None of the other children who went to the same park contracted polio.'

'It's no one's fault really,' says Col. Bharucha, reassuring her as usual. 'Lenny is weak. Some child with only the symptoms of a severe cold could have passed the virus.' And then he roars a shocking postscript: 'If anyone's to blame, blame the British! There was no polio in India till they brought it here!'

As far as I'm concerned this is insurgence – an open declaration of war by the two hundred Parsees of Lahore on the British Empire! I am shocked because Col. Bharucha is the President of our community in Lahore. And, except for a few designated renegades, the Parsees have been careful to adopt a discreet and politically naïve profile. At the last community dinner, held on the roof of the YMCA building on the Mall, Col. Bharucha had cautioned (between the blood-chilling whines of the microphone): 'We must tread carefully . . . We have served the English faithfully, and earned their trust . . . So, we have prospered! But we are the smallest minority in India . . . Only one hundred and twenty thousand in the whole world. We have to be extra wary, or we'll be neither here nor there . . .' And then, surmounting his uncharacteristic hesitancy, and in thunderous voice, he declaimed: 'We must hunt with the hounds and run with the hare!'

Everybody clapped and gravely said: 'Hear! Hear!' as they always do, reflexively, every time anyone airs a British proverb in suitably ringing tones.

'The goddamn English!' I think, infected by Col. Bharucha's startling ferocity at this 'dastardly' (one of Father's favourite words, just as 'plucky' is Mother's) instance of British treachery. 'They gave us polio!' And notwithstanding the compatible and sanguine nature of my relationship with my disease, I feel it is my first personal involvement with Indian politics: the Quit-India sentiment that has fired the imagination of a subject people and will soon sweep away the Raj!

Chapter 3

Ayah and I, arrested by a discordant bugle blast, come to a dead stop outside Godmother's gate. There is a brief roll of drums. The tall tin-sheet gates of the Salvation Army compound open and the band and marchers emerge from the leafy gloam of neem trees fermenting behind the walls.

It is always a shock to see the raw hands and faces of the English exposed to the light of day; and as the column moves away my mind transforms it into a slick red and white caterpillar, its legs marching, marching, its hundred sightless eyes staring ahead.

At startling intervals the caterpillar bursts into sound. Drums, bugles and tambourines clash – and as it curves out of sight round a bend in Jail Road it manufactures a curious vibration, like a unison of muzzled voices raised in song.

I stand transfixed, waiting for the creature's return. Ayah tries to drag me away but I resist, and she leans resignedly – and attractively – against the white-washed gatepost.

When the caterpillar returns, now marching on our side of the road, the red jackets and white saris separate to take the alien shapes of Englishmen and -women. Observed in microscopic dissection the head of the centipede is formed by a strutting Englishman holding the stout pole of a red flag diagonally across his chest. Of its own volition his glance slides to Ayah and, turning purple and showing off, he wields the flag like an acrobatic baton.

Close behind, orifices glued to convoluted brass horns, strut two red jackets: and on their heels, forming the shoulder and chest of the creature, a tight-packed row of red jackets beating drums, cymbals and tambourines, their leaden eyes attracted to the magnet leaning against the gatepost.

The saviours move away and the bits and pieces of Englishmen and -women fit together again to form the elongated and illusionary caterpillar of Jail Road.

* * *

We no longer use the pram to visit Godmother's house: it is a short ten minute walk. But when Ayah takes me up Queens Road, past the YWCA, past the Freemasons' Lodge, which she calls 'The Ghost Club', and across the Mall to the Queen's statue in the park opposite the Assembly Chambers, I'm still pushed in a pram. I love it.

Queen Victoria, cast in gunmetal, is majestic, massive, overpowering, ugly. Her statue imposes the English Raj in the park. I lie sprawled on the grass, my head in Ayah's lap. The Falletis Hotel cook, the Government House gardener, and an elegant, compactly muscled head-and-body masseur sit with us. Ice-candy-man is selling his popsicles to the other groups lounging on the grass. My mouth waters. I have confidence in Ayah's chocolate chemistry ... lank and loping the Ice-candy-man cometh ...

I take advantage of Ayah's admirers. 'Massage me!' I demand, kicking the handsome masseur. He loosens my laces and unbuckles the straps gripping my boots. Taking a few drops of almond oil from one of the bottles in his cruet set, he massages my wasted leg and then my okay leg. His fingers work deftly, kneading, pummelling, soothing. They are knowing fingers, very clever, and sometimes, late in the evening, when he and Ayah and I are alone, they massage Ayah under her sari. Her lids close. She grows still and languid. A pearly wedge gleams between her lips and she moans, a fragile, piteous sound of pleasure. Very carefully, very quietly, I manoeuvre my eyes and nose. It is dark, but now and then a dart of twilight illuminates a subtle artistry. My nose inhales the fragrance of earth and grass – and the other fragrance that distils insights. I intuit the meaning and purpose of things. The secret rhythms of creation and mortality. The essence of truth and beauty. I recall the choking hell of milky vapours and discover that heaven has a dark fragrance.

Things love to crawl beneath Ayah's sari. Ladybirds, glow-worms, Ice-candy-man's toes. She dusts them off with impartial nonchalance.

I keep an eye on Ice-candy-man's toes. Sometimes, in the course of an engrossing story, they travel so cautiously that both Ayah and I are taken unawares. Ice-candy-man is a raconteur. He is also an absorbing gossip. When the story is extra good, and the tentative toes polite, Ayah tolerates them.

Sometimes a toe snakes out and zeroes in on its target with such lightning speed that I hear of the attack only from Ayah's startled 'Oof!' Once in a while I pre-empt the big toe's romantic impulse and, catching it mid-crawl or mid-strike, twist it. It is a measure to keep the candy bribes coming.

I learn also to detect the subtle exchange of signals and some of the complex rites by which Ayah's admirers co-exist. Dusting the grass from their clothes they slip away before dark, leaving the one luck, or the lady, favours. I don't enjoy the gardener's turn because nothing much happens except talk. He talks and Ayah talks, and he listens and Ayah talks. I escape into daydreams in which my father turns loquacious and my mother playful. Or of heroics in which I rescue Godmother from the drooling jaws of her cannibalistic brother-in-law who is a doctor and visits from way beyond the perimeter of my familiar world.

I learn fast. I gain Ayah's goodwill and complicity by accommodating her need to meet friends and relatives. She takes me to fairs, cheap restaurants and slaughter-houses. I cover up for her and maintain a canny silence about her doings. I learn of human needs, frailties, cruelties and joys. I also learn from her the tyranny magnets exercise over metals.

I have many teachers. My cousin shows me things.

'You want to see my marbles?' he asks, and holds out the prettily coloured glass balls for me to admire and touch – and if I so wish, to play with. He has just returned from Quetta where he had a hernia operation. 'Let me show you my scar,' he offers, unbuttoning his fly and exposing me to the glamorous spectacle of a stitched scar and a handful of genitals. He too has clever fingers. 'You can touch it,' he offers. His expression is disarming, gallant. I touch the fine scar and gingerly hold the genitals he transfers to my palm. We both study them. 'I am also having my tonsils removed,' he says. I hand back his genitals and look at his neck. I visualise a red, scalloped scar running from ear to ear. It is a premonition.

Sometimes I spend days and nights with my limber electric-aunt and my knowing and instructive cousin. 'See this pillow?' he asks one night – and as it moves nearer it resembles a muzzle. I scream. Frightened, he covers my scream with the pillow and sits on it. I struggle madly at first and then feebly, and cautiously he allows me to emerge, screamless.

The next day, when we are alone, my cousin's face looms conspiratorially close and he says, 'Come on. I'll show you something.'

He leads me through wire-mesh doors to the back veranda. He drags a wooden stool close to the white-washed wall and climbing on it points to a hole in a small white china object stuck to the wall. 'See this?' he asks. 'Put your finger there and see what happens.' He jumps down and almost lifts me to the stool. He is a couple of years older than me. I raise my hand, index finger pointed, and look down at him expectantly. He nods. I poke my finger into the small depression and an AC current teaches me everything I will ever need to know about gullibility and shock. Though my faculties of reason, deduction and logic advance with the years, my gullibility and reaction to shock remain the same as on the day I tumbled screaming, hair, nerves and limbs spread-eagled, into my cousin's arms.

My electric-aunt is a resourceful widow addicted to quick decisions and swift results. The speed at which she moves from spot to spot – from dawn to dusk – have earned her a citation. She is called, in moments of need and gratitude, *bijli*: a word that in the various Indian languages, with slight variations, stands for both electricity and lightning.

She is also addicted to navy-blue. She and her son share a bedroom. It has navy-blue curtains, navy-blue bedspreads and navy-blue linen doilies on the dressing table. It is, depending on my mood, either a restful or a gloomy room. The night of my lesson in gullibility and shock I find it gloomy. My cousin and I spread mattresses and sleep on the carpeted floor of the cheerful sitting room next to the bedroom.

That night I have the first nightmare that connects me to the pain of others.

Far away I hear a siren. Tee-too! Tee-too! it goes, alarming my heart. The nocturnal throb and shrieking grow louder, closing in, coming now from the compound of the Salvation Army next door. Its tin-sheet gates open a crack to let out a long khaki caterpillar. Centipedal legs marching, marching, it curves, and as it approaches Electric-aunt's gate it metamorphoses into a single German soldier on a motorcycle. Roaring up the drive the engine stops, as I know it must, outside Electric-aunt's doorstep. The siren's tee-too tee-too is now deafening. My heart pounds at the brutality of the sound. The soldier, his cap and uniform immaculate, dismounts. Carefully removing black gloves from his white hands, he comes to get me.

Why does my stomach sink all the way to hell even now? I had my own stock of Indian bogey-men. *Choorails*, witches with turned-about feet who ate the hearts and livers of straying children. Bears lurking, ready to pounce if I did not finish my pudding. The zoo lion. No one had taught me to fear an immaculate Nazi soldier. Yet here he was, in nightmare after nightmare, coming to get me on his motorcycle.

I recall another childhood nightmare from the past. Children lie in a warehouse. Mother and Ayah move about solicitously. The atmosphere is businesslike and relaxed. Godmother sits by my bed smiling indulgently as men in uniforms quietly slice off a child's arm here, a leg there. She strokes my head as they dismember me. I feel no pain. Only an abysmal sense of loss – and a chilling horror that no one is concerned by what's happening.

Chapter 4

I pick up a brother. Somewhere down the line I become aware of his elusive existence. He is four – a year and a month younger than me. I don't recall him learning to crawl or to walk. Where was he? It doesn't matter.

My brother is aloof. Vital and alert, he inhabits another sphere of interests and private thoughts. No doubt he too is busy picking up knowledge, gaining insights. I am more curious of him than he of me. His curiosity comes later. I am skinny, wizened, sallow, wiggly-haired, ugly. He is beautiful. He is the most beautiful thing, animal, person, building, river or mountain that I have seen. He is formed of gold mercury. He never stands still enough to see. He turns, ducks, moves, looks away, vanishes.

The only way I know to claim his undivided attention is to get him angry. I learn to bait him. His name is Adi. I call him Sissy. He is too confused to retaliate the first few times I call him by his new name. At last: 'My name is Adi,' he growls, glowering.

The next day I persist. He pretends not to notice. In the evening, holding up a sari-clad doll I say, 'Hey, Sissy, look! She's just like you!'

Adi raises his head and looks squarely from the doll to me. His jet eyes are vibrant. His flushed face holds the concentrated beauty and venom of an angry cobra. And like a cobra striking, in one sweep he removes a spiked boot and hurls it at me. I stare at him, blood blurring my vision. And he stares back communicating cold fury and deathly warning.

It's not that he doesn't want to play with me. It's just that I can't hold his attention for more than a few seconds. His unfathomable thoughts and mercurial play pattern absorb him. Squatting before corners or blank walls, head bent, fingers busy, he concentrates on trains, bricks, mud-balls, strings. Quickly he shifts to another heap of toys and garbage in another corner; or out the doors into the garden, or vegetable patch, or servants' quarters at the back of the house.

At night he's into his night suit and fast asleep while I'm still soaking my chilblained toes in scalding salt water – or standing on a stool brushing my teeth. We sleep in outsize elongated cots. Like our loosely tailored clothes with huge tucks and hems, our cots are designed to last a lifetime. (My brother outgrew his cot. I still fit into mine.) Ayah tucks in the mosquito-net and switches off the faint light.

Is there anything to compare with the cosy bliss of snuggling beneath a heavy quilt with a hot-water bag on a freezing night in an unheated room? Particularly if you've just dashed from the bathroom over a bare brick floor? And you're five years old? And free to go over the excitements and evaluate the experience of the day and weave them into daydreams that drift into sleep? That is, provided the zoo lion does not roar. If he roars – which at night is rare – my daydreams turn into quaking daymares: and these to nightmares in which the hungry lion, cutting across

Lawrence Road to Birdwood Road, prowls from the rear of the house to the bedroom door, and in one bare-fanged leap crashes through to sink his fangs into my stomach. My stomach sinks all the way to the bottom of hell.

Whether he roars at night or not, I awake every morning to the lion's roar. He sets about it at the crack of dawn, blighting my dreams. By the time I dispel the fears of the jungle and peep out of my quilt, Adi is already out of bed. A great chunk of his life is lived apart: he goes to a regular school.

* * *

Spring flowers, birds and butterflies scent and colour the air. It is the end of March, and already it is hot in the sun. Cousin and I come indoors and see my brother, imbedded in the sag of a charpoy, fast asleep. We gently turn him on his back and propped on elbows scrutinise his face.

'He's put on lipstick,' Cousin says.

'Yes,' I agree.

His face has the irresistible bloom of spring flowers. Turn by turn Cousin and I softly brush our lips and cheeks against his velvet face, we pry back a sleek lick of dark brown hair and kiss his forehead and the cushioned cleft in his chin. His vulnerability is breathtaking, and we ravish it with scrutiny and our childish kisses. Carried away by our ardour we become rough. Adi wakes up and opens indulgent, jewel-jet eyes. They are trusting and kind as a saint's.

'You've put on lipstick?' I ask, inviting confidence.

'No,' he says mildly.

'Of course he has!' says Cousin.

'No, I've not,' says Adi.

'Can I rub some tissue and find out?' I ask courteously.

'Okay,' he says.

I stroke the Kleenex across his lips and look at it. It is unblemished. I moisten it with my tongue and rub harder. Cousin is armed with his own tissue. Adi withstands our vigorous scouring with the patience of the blameless. I notice blood on the Kleenex. The natural red in his lips has camouflaged the bleeding. Astonished, we finally believe him.

'He should have been a girl,' says Cousin.

By now Adi is fully awake. I watch helplessly as mercurial preoccupation veils his eyes. He becomes remote. His vulnerability vanishes. He kicks out, pushing back our hands with the tissues. He is in control.

Passing by, Ayah swoops down on him and picks him up. After hugging him and nuzzling his face she abruptly puts him down again, saying: 'He is my little English baba!'

Last evening Ayah took us for a walk in Simla-pahari and a passer-by, no doubt impelled by her spherical agitation into spouting small-talk, enquired: 'Is he an English's son?'

'Of course not!' said Ayah imperiously. However, vanity softening her contempt, she added: 'Can any dough-faced English's son match his spice? Their looks lack salt!'

Ayah is so proud of Adi's paucity of pigment. Sometimes she takes us to Lawrence Gardens and encourages him to ıun across the space separating native babies and English babies. The ayahs of the English babies hug him and fuss over him and permit him to romp with their privileged charges. Adi undoes the bows of little girls with blue eyes in scratchy organdie dresses and wrestles with tallow-haired boys in the grass. Ayah beams.

* * *

On bitterly cold days when ice sales plummet, Ice-candy-man transforms himself into a birdman. Burdened with enormous cages stuffed with sparrows and common green parrots he parades the paths behind the Lahore Gymkhana lawns and outside the Punjab Club. At strategic moments he plants the cages on the ground and rages: 'I break your neck, you naughty. birds! You do too much *chi chi*! What will the good memsahibs think? They'll think I no teach you. You like jungly lions in zoo. I cut your throat!'

He flourishes a barber's razor. It is an infallible bait. Clutches of tender-hearted Englishwomen, sporting skirts and tennis shoes, abandon their garden chairs and dainty cucumber and chicken tea sandwiches to rush up and scold: 'You horrid man. Don't you dare cut their throats!'

'Them fresh parrots, memsahib. They not learn dirty words yet. I catches them today,' coaxes Birdman, plunging his crafty hands into the cages. 'They only one rupee for two birds.'

His boneless fingers set up such a squawking and twittering among the parrots and the sparrows that the ladies become frantic. They buy the birds by the dozen, and, cooing, 'You poor little itty-bitty things,' snuggle them to their bosoms.

After the kissing and the cuddling, holding the stupefied birds aloft, they release them, one by one. Their valiant expressions and triumphant cries enthral the rapt crowd of native gawkers as they exclaim: 'There! Fly away, little birdie. Go, you poor little things!'

Squatting on his heels Birdman surveys the tearful and spirited mems with open-mawed and marvelling admiration. Conjuring rueful little nods and a catch to his voice, he remarks: 'It go straight to mama-papa.' Or, sighing heavily, 'It fly to hungry little babies in nest.'

And today, foreshadowing the poetic impulse of his future, wiping tears and pointing at a giddily spinning and chirping sparrow, Ice-candy-man says: 'Look! Little sparrow singing, "See? See? I free!" to mad-with-grief wife!'

Ayah, Adi and I watch the performance with concealed glee. Every now and then we heighten the histrionics and encourage sales by shouting, 'Cut their throats! Cut their throats!' We cheer and clap from the sidelines when the birds are released.

Ice-candy-man resorts to his change in occupation only two or three times a year, so his ingenuity works. He usually clears a packet. And if the sale has been quick and lucrative, as on this Saturday afternoon just before Christmas, he treats us to a meal at Ayah's favourite wayside restaurant in Mozang Chungi.

We are regulars. The shorn proprietor acknowledges us with a solemn nod. He is a *pahailwan*: a wrestler. Covering his massive torso with a singlet in deference to Ayah's presence, he approaches. Despite the cold, his shoulders gleam with sweat and a striped lungi clings to his buttocks and legs.

We are directed to sit on a narrow backless bench. Opposite us Ice-candy-man drapes his lank and flexible length on another bench, and leaning across the table ogles Ayah. He straightens somewhat when an urchin-apprentice plonks down three tin plates heaped with rice and a bowl of vegetable curry. The rice is steaming and fragrant. We fall to it silently. Ayah's chocolate fingers mould the rice into small golf balls which she pops into her mouth. She eats with her right hand while her left hand reposes in her lap.

Halfway through the meal I sense a familiar tension and a small flurry of movement. Ice-candy-man's toes are invisibly busy. I glance up just as a supplicating smile on his face dissolves into a painful grimace: and I know Ayah's hand is engaged in an equally heroic struggle.

Meanwhile the mounds of rice steadily diminish. Outwardly calm, systematically popping golf balls, Ayah signals the proprietor for another helping.

After the meal, as we descend the rickety wooden steps into the crowded gully, Ayah tries, tactfully, to get rid of Ice-candy-man. But he hoists Adi on to the seat of his bicycle and persists in walking with us to Warris Road.

At the gate of our house, less tactfully, Ayah says: 'You'd better go. I have chores.'

'What chores?' asks Ice-candy-man, reluctant to let Ayah go.

'A ton of washing . . . And I haven't even dusted *Baijee*'s room!'

'Let me help you,' says Ice-candy-man.

'You gone crazy?' Ayah asks.

Imagine Ice-candy-man working alongside Ayah in our house. Mother'd throw a fit! He's not the kind of fellow who's permitted inside. With his thuggish way of inhaling from the stinking cigarettes clenched in his fist, his flashy scarves and reek of jasmine attar, he represents a shady, almost disreputable type.

'Okay, I'll go,' Ice-candy-man temporises reluctantly, 'but only if you'll come to the cinema later.'

'I told you I've work to do,' says Ayah, close to losing patience. 'And I dare not ask *Baijee* for another evening off.'

'Talk to me for a while . . . Just a little while,' pleads Ice-candy-man so piteously that Ayah, whose heart is as easily inclined to melt as Ice-candy-man's popsicles, bunches her fingers and says, 'Only ten minutes.'

Aware of the impropriety of entertaining her guest on the front lawn Ayah leads us to settle on a bald patch of grass at the back near the servants' quarters. The winter sun is diffused by the dust and a crimson bank of clouds streaks the horizon. It is getting uncomfortably chilly and my hair already feels damp. Ayah notices it and, drawing me to her, covers my head with her sari *palloo*.

'Now talk,' she says to Ice-candy-man. 'Since you're so anxious to talk, talk!'

Ice-candy-man talks. News and gossip flow off his glib tongue like a torrent. He reads Urdu newspapers and the *Urdu Digest*. He can, when he applies himself, read the headlines in the *Civil and Military Gazette*, the English daily.

Characteristically, Ice-candy-man starts by giving us news of the world. The Germans, he informs us, have developed a deadly weapon called the V-bomb that will turn the British into powdered ash. A little later, drifting closer to home, he tells us of Subas Chandra Bose, a Hindu patriot who has defected to the Japanese side in Burma. 'Bose says the Japanese will help us liberate India from the *Angrez*,' Ice-candy-man says. 'If we want India back we must take pride in our customs, our clothes, our languages . . . And not go mouthing the got-pit sot-pit of the English!'

Obviously he's quoting this Bose. (Sometimes he quotes Gandhi, or Nehru or Jinnah, but I'm fed up of hearing about them. Mother, Father and their friends are always saying: Gandhi said this, Nehru said that. Gandhi did this, Jinnah did that. What's the point of talking so much about people we don't know?)

Finally, narrowing his focus to our immediate surroundings, he says to Ayah, 'Shanta *bibi*, you're Punjabi, aren't you?'

'For the most part,' Ayah agrees warily.

'Then why don't you wear Punjabi clothes? I've never seen you in shalwar-kamize.'

Though it has never struck me as strange before – I'm so accustomed to Ayah only in a sari – I see the logic of his question and wonder about it.

'*Arrey baba*,' says Ayah spreading her hands in a fetching gesture, 'do you know what salary ayahs who wear Punjabi clothes get? Half the salary of the Goan ayahs who wear saris! I'm not so simple!'

'I've no quarrel with your saris,' says Ice-candy-man disarmingly demure, 'I was only asking out of curiosity.'

And, catching us unawares, his ingenuous toe darts beneath Ayah's sari. Ayah gives a start. Angrily smacking his leg and smoothing her sari, she stands up. '*Duffa ho!* Go!' she says. 'Or I'll get *Baijee* to V-bomb you into ash!' Applying all his strength, Adi restrains Ice-candy-man's irrepressibly twitching toe.

'*Arrrrey!*' says Ice-candy-man holding his hands up as if to stave off Ayah's assault. 'Are you angry?'

'Then what?' Ayah retorts. 'You have no sense and no shame!'

Grinning sheepishly, grovelling and wriggling in the grass to touch the hem of Ayah's sari, he says, 'I'm sorry, forgive me. I won't do it again . . . Forgive me.'

'What for?' snaps Ayah. 'You'll never change!'

Ice-candy-man coils forward to squat and, threading his supple arms through his calves from the back, latches on to his ear lobes. It is a punishing posture called 'the cock', used in Urdu-medium schools to discipline urchins. He looks so ridiculous that Ayah and I laugh.

But Adi, his face grim, dispenses a totally mirthless and vicious kick to his ankle.

Ice-candy-man stands up so abruptly that his movements are a blurr.

And, my eyes popping, I stare at Adi dangling in the air at the end of his rangy arm. Ice-candy-man has a firm grip on the waistband of Adi's woollen trousers and Adi looks like an astonished and stocky spider plucked out of his web and suspended above the level of my eyes.

'I'm going to drop him,' Ice-candy-man says calmly. He takes a loping step and, holding Adi directly above the brick paving skirting the grass, raises his arm. 'If you don't go to the cinema with me I'll drop him.'

I can't believe he means it.

But Adi does. His face scarlet, he lets out a terrified yell and howls: 'He'll drop me! Save me . . . someone save me!'

'I'm going to drop him,' repeats Ice-candy-man.

Ayah's round mouth opens in an 'O', her eyes stare. Seeing her expression, my wiggly hair curls tighter. I look in horror upon the distance separating Adi from the brick. Adi kicks, crawls and squirms in the air and yells: 'Save me! Save me! *Bachao! Bachao!*'

And Ayah shouts: 'Put him down at once, oye, badmash! I will go to the cinema.'

Ice-candy-man carefully lowers Adi – face down and dribbling spit – on the grass.

Ayah deftly pulls off a sandle and, lunging wildly, strikes Ice-candy-man wherever she can. Ice-candy-man cowers; and gathering his lungi above his knees, snatching up his slippers, manages to move out of her reach. Ayah chases him right out of the gate.

Chapter 5

Rich men's wives and children soar to the Simla or Kashmir Hills in summer. We also soar, but to the lesser Murree Hills at the foot of the Himalayas.

Adi is perched on a tall pony. I am on a donkey. My donkey trots alongside and I perceive just how short it is. My legs stick out beneath the safety ring on the saddle. I grip the ring resentfully. The donkey-man holds the reins. I am not spared even this indignity! My donkey perch is ludicrous.

I am about to shake heaven and earth to set things right when an astonishing tidal wave of relief and frivolity barrels over the world. Shop-keepers on the Murree Mall have picked out a few words from the static of their 1944 radios and happiness strikes all hearts. Men, women, beast, mountain, tall pony and short donkey all exult. Simultaneously we know that the war is over. We have won! Victory! The war is over! Faces around me are wreathed in smiles. Incredibly Father is blowing a whistle that uncoils a foot-long paper tongue. God! I have never been so happy. I who have subversively hoped that the defector Bose and the Japanese enemy win the war. All the same I am swept by a sense of relief so unburdening that I realise I was born with an awareness of the war: and I recall the dim, faraway fear of bombs that tinged with bitterness my mother's milk. No wonder I was a colicky baby.

The gaiety on people's faces is infectious. My mother's face swims up with a smile I never again see; and plucking paper cups, streamers and whistles from the air she gives them to Adi and me.

Father seldom visits Murree for more than two or three days at a time. He returns to Lahore. A week later we catch a bus and follow him down into the plains which the sun has scorched and pulverised into a dusty hell. We pant under ceiling fans. And now the temperatures soar.

Our stay in Murree has been cut short because the Parsees

of Lahore are holding a Jashan prayer to celebrate the British victory.

On the day of the Jashan the temperature is 116°F in the shade. A tonga waits in the porch. Hollow-eyed and dazed with heat we pile perspiring into the tonga. Mother and Ayah in the back and Adi and I up front with the tongaman. We sit back to back on a bench divided by a quilted backrest. A flimsy canvas canopy shelters us from the sun. The tonga is held together by two enormous wooden wheels on either side of the shaft and is balanced by the harnessed horse. Up front we are more secure – unless the horse falls.

Scarcely out of our gate, the horse falls. Adi and I shoot over the guard and spill on Warris Road. Mother and Ayah are suspended high in the air, clinging for all they are worth to the other end of the see-saw. Adi and I get up and scamper to one side. The tongaman picks himself off the horse cursing: and the Birdwood Barracks' sepoy abandons his post and runs forward to render help. Ayah's presence galvanises men to mad sprints in the noon heat. It is a pity she has no such effect on animals though.

The tongaman and the sepoy lift the shafts and assist the harnessed horse to stand upright. Adi pats the horse's rump. The animal swishes his bristly tail and blows wind in our faces. The sepoy makes an encouraging sucking noise with his tongue and pushes one of the enormous wooden wheels to start the tonga. Straining and quivering under the dual burden of passengers and heat, the shaken animal drags us past the barracks, the barricading walls of the Lucy Harrison School for girls next to it, up Queens Road, past the pretty pink spread of the Punjab High Court and behind the small-causes court to the Fire Temple.

We leave the tongaman and Ayah to gossip and doze beneath whatever shade they can find.

The main hall of the temple is already full of smoke. Two priests, sitting cross-legged and swaying slightly, face each other across a fire altar. They are robed in a swollen froth of starched white muslin. They wear cloth masks like the one Col. Bharucha wore in the hospital. Their chanting voices rise and boom in fierce competition and the mask prevents specks of spittle from profaning the fire. They sit on a white sheet amidst silver trays heaped with fruit – grape, mango, papaya – and flowers. And the *malida* cooked by the priest's wife. Adi and I join the children sitting patiently on a wooden bench – our collective mouths drooling.

The priests cannot be hurried. They go through a ritual established a millennium ago. They stoke the fire with silver tongs and feed it with sandalwood and frankincense.

It is comparatively cool beneath the high ceiling. My eyes are getting accustomed to the dark but smarting with smoke. Mother has found a seat in the front row. There is an empty chair between her and Col. Bharucha. He must have grown taller, because his pink scalp thrusts higher above his hair-line than before. Godmother sits next to him, fanning herself and the doctor with a slow, rotary motion of her palm-leaf punkah. She catches my watering eye and winks. Only I ever see her wink. Her dignified bearing and noble features preclude winking. She only relaxes her guard with me. No one sees her as I do. Slave-sister is snatching a few blessed minutes of sleep in the last row. Godmother knows she's asleep. She knows everything. Slavesister sleeps peacefully because she knows Godmother will not mind. Godmother, after all, is not unreasonable.

Both priests stand up, smoothing their beards and garments. Chairs squeak as the ladies greet each other and gradually converge on the fruit trays. Slavesister waddles plumply forward on painful bunions, smiling her patient, obliging smile, securing her sari border to her hair. The women shoo us from the benches and sit down to peel and cut the fruit.

Mother stands talking to Col. Bharucha. She is tense, alert, anxious to please. Electric-aunt joins them, also tense. Her quick, intelligent eyes scan the room. I know she is looking for me. Godmother releases me and I run up to them.

'What is this?' says Col. Bharucha. Copying and exaggerating my limp he lurches halfway across the room like a tipsy giraffe. 'Put your heel down! You must remember to.'

Mother purses her shapely mouth and looks at me sternly. Electric-aunt frowns, her thin lips a tight, anxious line beneath her sharp nose.

Col. Bharucha stoops and pushing down on the contracted tendon presses my heel to the floor. 'Massage the back of her leg down: like this,' he says, kneading and stretching my stubborn tendon.

He straightens, pats my back and dismisses me. I know they are beaming behind my back, pleased with my progress since the operation. Cousin is waiting for me to be free of the grown-ups.

'I want to show you something,' he says, drawing me to a window in the wings. He reaches into the pockets of his shorts and pulls out scraps of cardboard. He lifts off one layer and reveals a pressed butterfly, its colours turned to powder, its wings awry.

'Hold out your hand,' he commands. I withhold my hand. There are certain things I'll hold and certain things I won't. Cousin gropes for my hand and, 'No,' I say. 'Don't!'

'But it's for you,' says Cousin.

'I don't want it!'

Cousin is, for once, confounded.

There is a drift now towards the inner sanctum. Electric-aunt beckons Cousin and Mother signals me. We step into the inner room and I can see through two barred windows and an open archway the main fire altar. It is like a gigantic silver egg cup and the flames are dancing above a bed of white ashes.

I kneel before the altar and touch my forehead to the cool marble step beyond which I cannot go. Except for the priests who tend the fire and see that it never goes out no one can enter the inner sanctum. Mother kneels beside me. I ask God to bless our family and Godmother and all our servants and Masseur and Ice-candy-man . . . until Mother says, 'That's enough! The meeting's about to start. Hurry!'

And Adi hisses, 'Don't hog God!'

We enter the main hall. The chairs have been rearranged. Col. Bharucha is standing before the mike, testing it with practised snaps of his fingers. 'Hello hello,' he says, and knocks on it with his knuckles. He struggles with both hands to stretch the rod. Mr Bankwalla, an officer at the Central Bank of India, his slight body crisp and dependable in sweatless white shirt and white trousers, rushes up obligingly. Between them they adjust the mike to suit the colonel's height.

The banker moves back, fleet and unobtrusive beneath his maroon skull-cap, to his seat in the aisle next to his jolly wife. (His wife is so indefatigably jolly that it is said after the initial burst of grief she even wisecracked at her son's funeral. Later I heard she cracked jokes on her death-bed and prepared to meet Ahura Mazda with jests, and sly winks at the mourners, whose appreciative laughter turned to inconsolable grief when the will was read. She left everything to the Tower of Silence in Karachi.)

By the time Col. Bharucha clears his throat, and it is an impressive throat-clearing, we are all settled in our chairs.

Col. Bharucha tells us: 'We are gathered here, etc., etc. To thank God Almighty, etc., etc.'

The mike has transformed him from a plain-speaking doctor into a resounding orator. But his rhetoric has a cadence that makes my mind wander.

Suddenly I hear him declare: 'Gandhi says, we must stop buying salt. We should only eat salt manufactured from the Indian Ocean!'

The colonel pauses, dramatically, and my loafing mind becomes attentive. The pause, shrewdly timed to permit just that tiny licence so dear to a Parsee audience, is snapped up. 'Who does this Gandhi think he is?' shouts an obliging wag promptly from somewhere in the middle. 'Is it his grandfather's ocean?'

Col. Bharucha, smiling amiably, explains that the British government is charging an unfair salt tax and, as a protest, we should not buy it. Gandhijee plans to walk a hundred miles to the ocean to make salt for us. He is even prepared to go to jail to make his point!

'And what do we do while he's in jail? Walk around with goitres for lack of salt?' shouts the wag.

'Go to jail for us!' snorts Dr Manek Mody. (He is Godmother's brother-in-law, and is here on one of his periodic visits from Rawalpindi.) 'Big deal!' he booms. 'There's such a demand for A-class in jails that there's no room left for folk like us!'

(Even though I cannot see him I can tell it's Dr Mody by the amazing volume of his voice. He is a short, chubby man, with a totally bald and brown head.)

'Yes,' chimes in the first wag. 'The Congress gangsters provoke the police and get rewarded with free board and lodging. It's a shame! I propose that the Parsee Anjuman lodge a formal protest with the Inspector General of Police. Why should we be left out of everything?'

'Hear! Hear!' agrees the congregation, and thumps the arm rests of its chairs and wooden benches.

'Let us march to jail now!' the wag says, jumping to his feet. He is a paunchy man with a very dark skin.

Col. Bharucha raises a restraining hand. 'No doubt the men in jail are acquiring political glory . . . But this short cut to fame and fortune is not for us. It is no longer just a struggle for Home Rule. It is a struggle for power. Who's going to rule once we get *Swaraj*? Not you,' says the colonel, pointing a long and accusing finger at us as if we are harbouring sinful thoughts. 'Hindus, Muslims and even the Sikhs are going to jockey for power: and if you jokers jump into the middle you'll be mangled into chutney!'

Wise heads nod – Godmother's, Electric-aunt's, Slavesister's – although Slavesister's can hardly be called wise.

'I hope no Lahore Parsee will be stupid enough to court

trouble,' continues the colonel. 'I strongly advise all you to stay at home – and out of trouble.'

'I don't see how we can remain uninvolved,' says Dr Mody, whose voice, without aid of mike, is louder than the colonel's. 'Our neighbours will think we are betraying them and siding with the English.'

'Which of your neighbours are you not going to betray?' asks a practical soul with an impatient voice. 'Hindu? Muslim? Sikh?'

'That depends upon who's winning, doesn't it?' says Mr Bankwalla. 'Don't forget, we are to run with the hounds and hunt with the hare.'

'No one knows which way the wind will blow,' thunders the colonel, silencing everyone with his admirable rhetoric. 'There may be not one but two – or even three – new nations! And the Parsees might find themselves championing the wrong side if they don't look before they leap!'

'Does it matter where they look or where they leap?' enquires the impatient voice. 'If we're stuck with the Hindus they'll swipe our businesses from under our noses and sell our grandfathers in the bargain: if we're stuck with the Muslims they'll convert us by the sword! And God help us if we're stuck with the Sikhs!'

'Why? Which mad dog bit the Sikhs? Why are you so against them?' says Dr Mody contentiously.

'I have something against everybody,' declares the voice, impartial and very hurt.

'Order! Order!' says Mr Bankwalla. And Col. Bharucha clears his throat so effectively that the questions, answers, and wisecracks subside.

'I'll tell you a story,' the colonel says, and susceptible to stories the congregation and I sit still in our seats.

'When we were kicked out of Persia by the Arabs thirteen hundred years ago, what did we do? Did we shout and argue? No!' roars the colonel, and hastily provides his own answer before anyone can interrupt. 'We got into boats and sailed to India!'

'Why to India?' a totally new wit sitting at the end of my bench enquires. 'If they had to go some place why not Greece? Why not to France? Prettier scenery . . .'

'They didn't kick us hard enough,' says Dr Mody, with hearty regret. 'If only they'd kicked us all the way to California . . . Prettier women!'

There is an eruption of comments and suggestions. The meeting is turning out to be much more lively than I'd anticipated. Godmother's brother-in-law restores order with his built-in microphone. 'Shut up!' he bellows, startling us with the velocity of his voice.

Col. Bharucha continues as if he's not been interrupted at all.

'Do you think it was easy to be accepted into a new country? No!' he booms. 'Our forefathers were not given permission even to disembark!'

'What about our foremothers?' someone enquires.

'And our foreskins?' an invisible voice pipes up from the back.

'Mind! There are ladies here!' says the colonel sternly. There is a long pause no one dares interrupt. Satisfied by our silence, the colonel continues: 'Our forefathers and foremothers waited for four days, not knowing what was to become of them. Then, at last, the Grand *Vazir* appeared on deck with a glass of milk filled to the brim.' He looks intently at our faces. 'Do you know what it meant?'

Knowledgeable heads nod wisely.

'It was a polite message from the Indian Prince, meaning: "No, you are not welcome. My land is full and prosperous and we don't want outsiders with a different religion and alien ways to disturb the harmony!" He thought we were missionaries.

'Do you know what the Zarathushtis did? God rest their souls?'

Knowing heads nod, and among them I spy Cousin's. I feel annoyed. I am not privy to information that is rapidly being revealed as my birthright. Even if Godmother,

Mother, Slavesister and Electric-aunt did not tell me, Cousin ought to have!

Col. Bharucha, again answering his own question, continues: 'Our forefathers carefully stirred a teaspoon of sugar into the milk and sent it back.

'The Prince understood what that meant. The refugees would get absorbed into his country like the sugar in the milk . . . And with their decency and industry sweeten the lives of his subjects.

'The Indian Prince thought: what a smart and civilised people! And he gave our ancestors permission to live in his kingdom!'

'*Shabash!* Well done!' say the Parsees, regarding each other with admiration and congratulatory self-regard.

'But, as you see, we have to move with the times,' roars the colonel, his oratorical capacities in full form. 'Time stands for no one!'

'Hear hear! Hear hear!'

Even I applauded on cue.

'Time and tide wait for no man!'

Thunderous applause.

'Let whoever wishes rule! Hindu, Muslim, Sikh, Christian! We will abide by the rules of their land!'

A polite smattering of Hear hears! The congregation, wafted on self-esteem and British proverbs, does not want to be brought back to earth.

'As long as we do not interfere we have nothing to fear! As long as we respect the customs of our rulers – as we always have – we'll be all right! Ahura Mazda has looked after us for thirteen hundred years: he will look after us for another thirteen hundred!'

Like English proverbs, Ahura Mazda's name elicits enthusiasm.

'We will cast our lot with whoever rules Lahore!' continues the colonel.

'If the Muslims should rule Lahore wouldn't we be safer going to Bombay where most Parsees live?' asks a tremulous voice weakened by a thirteen-hundred-year-old memory of conversions by the Arab sword.

A slight nervousness stirs amidst the timorous. There is much turning of heads, shifting on seats and whispering.

'We prospered under the Muslim Moguls didn't we?' scolds Col. Bharucha. 'Emperor Akbar invited Zarathushti scholars to his *darbar*: he said he'd become a Parsee if he could . . . but we gave our oath to the Hindu Prince that we wouldn't proselytise – and the Parsees don't break faith! Of course,' he says, 'those cockerels who wish to go to Bombay may go.'

'Again Bombay?' says the man sitting at the end of my bench who had objected to our coming to India in the first place. 'If we must pack off, let's go to London at least. We are the English king's subjects aren't we? So, we are English!'

The suggestion causes an uproar: drowned, eventually, by Dr Manek Mody's remarkable voice. 'And what do we do,' he asks, 'when the English king's *Vazir* stands before us with a glass full of milk? Tell him we are brown Englishmen, come to sweeten their lives with a dash of colour?'

Mr Bankwalla, precise as the crisp new rupee notes he handles at the bank, says, 'Yes. Tell him, we came across on a coal steamer . . . and drop a small lump of coal in the milk. That will convey the unspoken message of love and harmony.'

'As long as we conduct our lives quietly, as long as we present no threat to anybody, we will prosper right here,' roars the colonel over the mike.

'Yes,' says the banker. 'But don't try to prosper immoderately. And, remember: don't ever try to exercise real power.'

The wag at the back, who's been champing at the bit to butt in, stands up and irrelevantly shouts: 'Those who want four wives say aye! Those who want vegetarian bhats and farts say nay!'

There is a raucous medley of ayes and nays. There is nothing like a good dose of bathroom humour to put us

Parsees in a fine mood. It is impossible to conduct the meeting after this.

We emerge into the sun's brassy blast and our faces crinkle in self-defence. Mother reminds us to rub the ash from our foreheads. Ayah looks as if she is melting. The tongaman removes the horse's feed sack and we pile into the tonga.

Chapter 6

I sit on the small wooden stool and Ayah's soapy hands move all over me. Water from the tap fills the bucket. Ayah, squatting before me, rubs between my toes. I'm ticklish. Deliberately she rubs the soles of my feet and, screaming, I fall off the stool and wiggle off the slippery floor. She pins me to the cement with her foot and douses me with water from the tin bucket. By the time I'm dried, powdered and lifted to the bed Ayah is drenched.

Now it is Mother's turn. Ayah calls her and she appears: willing, conscientious, devout, her head covered by a gauzy white scarf and smelling of sandalwood. She has been praying.

Ever since Col. Bharucha tugged at my tendon and pressed my heel down in the Fire Temple, Mother massages my leg. I lie diagonally on the bed, my small raised foot between her breasts. She leans forward and pushes back the ball of my foot. She applies all her fragile strength to stretch the stubborn tendon. Her flesh, like satin, shifts under my foot. I gaze at her. Shaded by the scarf her features acquire sharper definition. The tipped chin curves deep to meet the lower lip. The lips, full, firm, taper from a lavish 'M' in wide wings, their outline etched with the clarity of cut rubies. Her nose is slender, slightly bumped: and the taut curve of her cheekbones is framed by a jaw as delicately oval as an egg. The hint of coldness, common to such chiselled beauty, is overwhelmed by the exuberant quality of her innocence. I feel she is beautiful beyond bearing.

Her firm strokes, her healing touch. The motherliness of Mother. It reaches from her bending body and cocoons me. My thighs twitch, relaxed.

Her motherliness. How can I describe it? While it is there it is all-encompassing, voluptuous. Hurt, heartache and fear vanish. I swim, rise, tumble, float, and bloat with bliss. The world is wonderful, wondrous – and I a perfect fit in it. But it switches off, this motherliness. I open my heart to it. I welcome it. Again. And again. I begin to understand its on-off pattern. It is treacherous.

Mother's motherliness has a universal reach. Like her involuntary female magnetism it cannot be harnessed. She showers maternal delight on all and sundry. I resent this largesse. As Father does her unconscious and indiscriminate sex appeal. It is a prostitution of my concept of childhood rights and parental loyalties. She is my mother – flesh of my flesh – and Adi's. She must love only us! Other children have their own mothers who love them . . . Their mothers don't go around loving me, do they?

* * *

A portion of our house at the back is lent to the Shankars. They are newly married, fat and loving. She is lighter skinned than him and has a stout braid that snuggles down her back and culminates in a large satin bow, red, blue, or white. At about five every evening Shankar returns from work. He trudges up the drive, up along the side of our house, and somewhere in the vicinity of our bathroom lets loose a mating call.

'Darling! Darling! I've come!'

No matter where we are, Ayah, Adi and I rush to the windows and peer out of the wire netting.

'My life! My Lord! You've come!' rejoices Gita, as if his return is a totally unexpected delight.

At his mate's answering call Shankar puffs out, and further diminishing a slender leather briefcase he carries under his arm, breaks into a thudding trot.

Because theirs is an arranged marriage, they are now steamily in love. I drop in on Gita quite often. She is always cooking something and mixed up with the fumes of vegetables and lentils is the steam of their night-long ecstasy. It is very like the dark fragrance Masseur's skilful fingers generate beneath Ayah's sari. Gita is always smiling – bubbling with gladness. She is full of stories. She tells me the story of Heer and Ranjah, of Romeo and Juliet.

Ayah, too, knows stories. Sitting on the lawn in front of the house she stretches her legs and dreamily chews on a blade of grass. Hari the gardener, squatting in his skimpy loincloth, is digging the soil around some rose bushes. He moves on to trim the gardenia hedge by the kitchen. It is the middle of the day in mid-February.

Pansies, roses, butterflies and fragrances – the buzz of bees and flies and of voices drifting from the kitchen. The occasional clip-clop of tonga horses on Warris Road, and bicycle bells and car horns. Hawks wheeling and distantly shrieking beneath a massive blue sky. I think of God, I pick up a dandelion and blow. 'He loves me – he loves me not. He loves me – he loves me not . . .'

Ayah hums. I recognise the tune.

'Tell me the story of Sohni and Mahiwal,' I say.

Ayah's hum becomes louder and she half croons, half speaks the Punjabi folk tale immortalised in verse. We drift to rural Punjab – to a breeze stirring in wheat stalks and yellow mustard fields. To village belles weaving through the fields to wells.

Ayah's eyes are large and eloquent, rimmed with kohl, soft with dreams. 'Beautiful Sohni – handsome Mahiwal . . .'

Their love is defiant, daring, touching. Their families bitter enemies. Sohni is not allowed to meet Mahiwal.

The wide Chenab flows between their villages, separating the lovers. But late one night, slipping furtively from her village, risking treacherous currents and fierce reprisal, Sohni floats across on an inflated buffalo-hide to her lover.

Mahiwal's delight is boundless. He celebrates in rapturous outbursts of verse. But he is distraught when he discovers he has nothing in the house to feed his Sohni.

It is too late to send for sweets – the bazaar is closed, 'But such is the strength of his passion – the tenderness of his love,' says Ayah lowering her lids over her far away and dreamy eyes, 'that he cuts a hank of flesh from his thigh, and barbecuing it on skewers, offers his beloved kebabs!'

Ayah cannot speak any more. Her voice is choked, her eyes streaming, her nose blocked.

'Does she eat it?' I enquire, astonished.

'She gobbles it up!' says Ayah, sobbing. 'Poor thing, she doesn't know what the kebabs are made of . . .'

In the end the doomed lovers die.

* * *

A shout, a couple of curses, a laugh, break away from the hum of voices coming from the kitchen. And then a receding patter of bare feet.

They are after the gardener's dhoti.

Ayah and I jump up from the grass and following the pattering feet run along the side of the house and past Gita's window.

'What's happening?' Gita calls from within.

'They're after Hari's dhoti!' I shout.

We approach the servants' yard and, sure enough, see the ragged scuffle around Hari. Hari's spare, dark body is almost hidden. Ayah stops to one side and I dive into the tangle of limbs yelling for all I'm worth, contributing my mite of rowdyism to the general row.

Yousaf the odd-job man, Greek-profiled, curly-haired, towers mischievously over Hari. Everybody towers over the gardener – even the sweeper Moti. I, of course, am still far from towering. As is Papoo, the sweeper's daughter, who comes galloping and whooping from the servants' courtyard, an infant wobbling dangerously on her hip, and brandishing a long broom. Her wide, bold mouth flashing a handsome smile she plunges herself, the insouciant babe, and the fluffy broom into the scuffle.

Yousaf has a grip on Hari's hand – which is hanging on to the knot at his waist. Yousaf casually shakes and pulls the hand, trying to loosen its hold on the loin-cloth, and Hari's slight, taut body rocks back and forth and from side to side.

Imam Din, genial-faced, massive, towers behind Hari. He is our cook. His dusty feet, shod in curly-toed leather slippers, are placed flat apart. He drums his chest, flexes his muscles and emits the fierce *barruk* cries with which Punjabi village warriors bluff, intimidate and challenge each other. '*O vay!*' he roars. 'I'll chew you up and I won't even burp!' Majestically, good-naturedly, he lunges at the cloth between the gardener's legs.

Hari is having a hard time fending off the cook's hand with his spare arm, and also coping with Moti's sly attacks, and Papoo's tickling broom. The washerman, who has brought our laundry for the week, has also joined the mêlee. We are like a pack of puppies, worrying and attacking each other in a high-spirited gambol.

But we play to rules. Hari plays the jester – and he and I and they know he will not be hurt or denuded. His dhoti might come apart partially – perhaps expose a flash of black buttock to spice the sport – but this happens only rarely.

It is a good-natured romp until suddenly three shrill and familiar screeches blast my ears. 'Bitch! *Haramzadi!* May you die!' And Muccho's grasping hand reaches for the root of her daughter's braid. The gaunt, bitter fingers close on the hair, yanking cruelly, and Papoo bows back and staggers backwards at an improbable angle. She falls sitting on her small buttocks, her legs straight out; still holding the jolted and blinking infant on her hip and the broom in her hand.

'*Haram-khor!* Slut! Work-shirker! Move my eyes from

you, and off you go!' shrieks Muccho in ungovernable rage, raining sharp, hard slaps on Papoo's head and back.

Ayah swoops down to snatch the infant to safety, and with an outstretched leg tries to fend off the blows. We abandon Hari. And the men, Hari included, group around Papoo, setting up a protective barrier of arms and hands, and muttering: 'Forgive her, Muccho, she's just a child . . . You're too hard on her . . .'

They cannot physically restrain Muccho. Handling a woman not related to them would be an impropriety. Her husband, Moti, dares not interfere either. Muccho would make his life intolerable. Submissive in all other respects, Muccho's murderous hatred of their daughter makes her irrational.

Despite the intervening arms, Muccho manages to pound her daughter with her fists and with swift, vicious kicks. Her hands protecting her head Papoo rolls in a ragged ball in the dust, screaming, '*Hai*, I'm dead.'

I hate Muccho. I cannot understand her cruelty to her own daughter. I know that some day she will kill her. From the improbable angle of Papoo's twisted limbs, I'm sure she has already done so.

Papoo lies deathly still, crumpled in a dusty heap. Ayah, holding Muccho's son on her hip, dips her *palloo* into a mug of water and sponges the dust from Papoo's lifeless face. 'I don't know what jinn gets into her every time she sees Papoo,' she declares. 'Even a stepmother would be kinder . . . After all, what's the innocent child done that's so terrible?'

'What do you know?' Muccho screams. 'She's no innocent! She's a curse-of-a-daughter . . . Disobedient, bone lazy, loose charactered . . . she'll shame us. She'll be the death of me, the whore!'

'How can she be your death? You've already killed her!' says Imam Din.

Imam Din rarely shows anger and his harshness intimidates Muccho. Afraid she might have gone too far, she shakes Papoo's shoulder roughly, as if to awaken her from sleep. 'She'll be all right: don't carry on so,' she tells Imam Din.

'Oye, Papoooo . . . Oye, doll,' she says with affected affection. 'Come on, get up.'

She lays Papoo's head on her thigh and pinching her cheeks forces her mouth open. Papoo shows the whites of her eyes as Muccho pours water between her teeth from the mug Ayah brought.

Suddenly Muccho curses – and shies as if blinded. Papoo is spitting a fine spray of water straight into her face. As Muccho raises her hand to lash out Papoo leaps up, miraculously whole. Skipping nimbly from her mother's lunges, Papoo jerks her boyish hips and makes dark, grinning faces and rude and mocking sounds and gestures. All at once she pretends to go limp and, again rolling her eyes up to show their whites, crumples defenceless to the ground; and then spinning like a bundle of rags in a gale, flinging her limbs about, twists away from Muccho's eager clutches; dodging, jeering, now tantalisingly close, now just out of reach. Papoo is not like any girl I know. Certainly not like the other servants' children, who are browbeaten into early submission. She is strong and high-spirited, and it's not easy to break her body . . . But there are subtler ways of breaking people.

'Wait till I fix you, you *shaitan*! You *choorail*!' Muccho screams vindictively. 'You've got a jinn in you . . . but I'll knock it out or I'm not your mother! Just you see what I have in store for you . . . It'll put you right! You'll scream to the dead . . . May you die!'

We laugh at Papoo's feigning – and her funny faces – and her mother's ranting. The men start to drift away and Papoo, followed by a cursing, shrieking Muccho aiming stones at her, imitates my limp – and lurching horribly, runs out on the road.

Papoo, recognising the manipulative power of my limp – and perhaps empathising with my condition, sometimes affects it. She never does so out of any malice. Besides she knows it aggravates Muccho no end.

Chapter 7

Ayah calls Imam Din the Catcher-in-the-kitchen. He sits in a corner on a wicker stool near the open pantry door and grabs anything soft that enters the kitchen. Sitting it, him, or her, on his lap he gently rocks. Ayah, I, Adi, Papoo, stray hens, pups, kittens and Rosy and Peter from next door have all had our turn. Rosy and I are bewildered by Imam Din's behaviour. Adi and Peter, belonging perhaps to the same species, are less confused and more aggressive.

One day I come upon a dazed Rosy rocking dizzily on Imam Din's lap and I pull her off. 'Don't do that, you damn fool!' I say, unleashing my bottled-up fury. 'Why do you do that!'

Imam Din gives a sheepish grin, genially pulls us both squirming on his lap, offers us puffs from his hookah and proceeds to tell us we should not mind. It is what he playfully calls only a little '*masti*' – a bit of naughtiness.

And he tells me, 'Lenny baby, don't swear – swear-words don't become you.'

I know. Adi can swear and it's a big joke. Rosy can curse and look cute. Papoo can let fly a string of invective, compared to which the tongawallah's invective sounds like a lullaby, and manages to appear stunningly roguish. And I cannot even say a damned 'damn fool' without being told it does not suit me!

Imam Din possesses a sixth sense – a sensitive antenna that beams him a chart of our movements. And no matter how stealthily Ayah or I sneak into the kitchen, he is ready to pounce. He knows exactly who it is and he never pounces on Mother or Yousaf or Hari. Or us, if we are followed by any of them.

Imam Din is tolerated because of the grey bristles in his closely cropped hair. They permit him to get away with liberties that in a younger man would provoke, if not the wrath of God, at least dire consequences from Ayah. As it is, God looks the other way and Ayah merely pulls away from him saying, 'Have you no shame? Look at your grey hairs . . . Fear God, at least!'

Imam Din is tall, big-bellied, barrel-chested, robust: he bicycles twenty miles to and from his village once a month to impregnate his fourth wife. Happily he is three times widowed and four times wed. He is the most respected elder in his village; and his benign temperament and wisdom have earned him a position of respect in our house and among the other servants on Warris Road. He is sixty-five years old. Now you see why he is allowed a certain latitude? Indulged even, you might say?

Rocking apart, I like him and take to him my complaints. So does Ayah. He is a fair and imaginative arbitrator – and when Adi grows up a bit, and I grow, and Adi resolutely peeps through a crack in the bathroom door with a single-minded determination that is like an elemental force, Imam Din is the only one who can handle him.

Twice Imam Din has taken me to his village. I have only a vague recollection of pleasurable sensations. I was too young then.

It is not yet winter. I have been badgering Imam Din for the past week to take me on his next junket to his village home.

'Lenny baby, I'm not going to my village,' he says, sighing heavily. 'I need to go to my grandson, Dost Mohammad's, village. It's too far . . . Pir Pindo is way beyond Amritsar . . . Forty miles from Lahore as the crow flies!'

'It may be too far for a little crow; but it's not too far for a strong old ox like you,' says Ayah. She is toasting *phulkas* (miniature chapatties) on the glowing coal fire and deftly flipping them with tongs. 'Poor child,' she says. 'She wants so much to go . . . It won't break your back to take her.'

'Not only my back, my legs too!' says Imam Din. 'I'm not so young anymore . . . I'll have a heart attack merely conveying myself there.'

'Go on with you!' says Ayah. 'You should talk of growing old! I'll know that when I know that!'

'I'll never be too old to bother you,' murmurs Imam Din, sighing, pushing his hubble-bubble away and advancing from his corner on Ayah.

Ayah whirls, tong-handed, glowing iron pointed at Imam Din.

'*Arrey baba* . . .' says Imam Din hunching his shoulders and holding his hands out defensively in front. 'I still haven't recovered from the last time you scarred me. Aren't you ashamed . . . burning and maiming a harmless old man like me?'

'I know who's harmless and who isn't! Go on, sit down!' she commands.

Imam Din collapses meekly in his corner and drawing deeply on the hookah, causing the water in the smoke-filter to gurgle, offers her a puff.

But Ayah is in a determined mood. 'Will you take her with you or not?' she demands, tongs in hand: and Imam Din capitulates.

'*Arrey baba*, you're a Hitler! I'll take her. Even though my back snaps in two! Even though my legs fall off! I'll take her.'

'She weighs less than this *phulka*,' says Ayah turning her back on us and tossing a thin disk of wheat on the fire until it is swollen with trapped air.

The next morning Ayah wakes me up when it is still night. She helps me to dress quietly: wrestling my arms into last year's coat and my ears into a horrible pink peaked-cap Electric-aunt knitted me two years ago. Imam Din and Ayah have a small altercation in the kitchen. Rather, Ayah scolds and Imam Din only protests and pacifies affably. I don't know what the argument is about, but I can guess. Imam Din must have attempted with some part of his anatomy the seduction Ice-candy-man conducts with his toes – with less audacity perhaps: and perhaps with less ingenuity – but, at last, Ayah is appeased – and properly apologised to – and we cycle down our drive with the first faint smudge of dawn diluting the night.

I sit on a small seat attached to the bar in front of Imam Din and his legs, like sturdy pistons, propel us at a staid and unaltering pace through the gullies and huddled bazaars behind Queens Road, then along the Mall past the stately pink sprawl of the High Court, and the constricted alleys running on one side of Father's shop. It is an illuminating experience – my first glimpse of the awakening metropolis of two million bestirring itself to face a new day.

At the crack of dawn, Lahore, the city known as the garden of the Moguls, turns into a toilet. Creeping sleepily out of sagging tenements and hovels the populace squats along alleyways and unpaved street edges facing crumbling brick walls – and thin dark stains trickle between their feet halfway down the alleys.

Cycle bell ringing, Imam Din and I perambulate through the profusion of bared Lahori bottoms. I hang on to the handlebars as we wobble imperturbably over potholes past a view of backsides the dark hue of Punjabi soil – and the smooth, plump spheres of young women who hide their faces in their veils and bare their bottoms. The early risers squat before their mugs, lost in the private contemplative world of their ablutions, and only the children face the street unabashed, turning their heads and bright eyes to look at us.

Past Data Sahib's shrine, past the enormous marble domes of the Badshahi mosque floating in a grey mist, and just before we cross the Ravi bridge we rattle through the small Pathan section of town. Now I see only fierce tribesmen from the northern frontiers around the Khyber and Babusar Passes who descend to the plains in search of work. They leave their families behind in flinty impoverished valleys concealed in the arid and massive tumult of the Karakorams, the Hindu Kush and the Himalayas. They can afford to visit them only every two or three years. The tribesmen's broad, bared backsides are much paler, and splotched with red, and strong dark hair grows down their backs. In place of mugs there are small mounds of stone and scraps of newspaper and Imam Din sniffs: 'What manner of people are these who don't clean their arses with water?'

A particularly pale bottom arrests Imam Din's attention. The skin is pink, still fresh and tingling from cold mountain winds.

'So. We have a new Pathan in town!' he muses aloud.

At that moment the mountain man turns his head. He does not like the expression on our faces. Full of fury he snarls and spits at us.

'Welcome to Lahore, brother,' Imam Din calls.

Months later I recognise the face when I see Sharbat Khan, still touchy and bewildered, bent intently over his whirring machine as he sharpens knives in the Mozang Chawk bazaar.

The sun is up, dispelling the mist. Filthy with dust, exhausted, we roll into Wagah, a village halfway to Amritsar. We have covered sixteen miles. I've stopped talking. Imam Din is breathing so hard I'm afraid he really will have a heart attack. He pedals slowly down the rutted bazaar lane and, letting the cycle tilt to one side, stops at a tea stall.

After a breakfast of fried *parathas* and eggs we get a ride atop a stack of hay in a bullock-cart. Imam Din stretches an arm across his bicycle, and lulled by the creaking rhythm of wooden wheels, we fall asleep. Two miles short of Pir Pindo the cart-driver prods us awake with his whip.

We rattle along a path running between irrigation ditches and mustard fields. As we cut through a corn field a small boy, followed by three barking dogs, hurtles out of the deepening light gathered in the stalks. He chases us, shouting, 'Oye! Who are you? Oye! What're you up to? Oye! Corn thief! Corn thief!'

The cycle wobbles dangerously. Cursing, Imam Din kicks out. A ribby pup yelps, and backs away. Imam Din roars: 'Oye, turd of Dost Mohammad! Don't you recognise your great-grandfather?'

Ranna stops short, peering at us out of small, wide-set eyes. He bends to scrape some clay from the track and throws it at the dogs, shooing them away. He approaches us gingerly, awkwardly. He is a little taller than me. His skin is almost black in the dusk. He already has small muscles on his arms and shoulders. A well-proportioned body. But what attracts me most is his belly-button. It protrudes an inch from his stomach, like a truncated and cheeky finger. (Later, when he sees me walk, I can tell he is equally taken by my limp.)

As soon as Ranna is within range Imam Din ministers two quick spanks to his head; and, the punishment dispensed, introduces us. 'Say salaam to your guest, oye, mannerless fellow!'

Ranna stares at me, his mouth slack. His teeth are very white, and a little crowded in front.

'Haven't you seen a city girl before?' Imam Din raps Ranna's head lightly. Ranna flinches. 'Why aren't you wearing a shirt, oye? Shameless bugger . . . Go tell your mother we are here. We want supper. Tell Dost Mohammad we're here.' Both Dost Mohammad and Chidda are Imam Din's grandchildren. Muslim communities like to keep their girls in the family; so marriages between first cousins are common.

Ranna appears to fly in his skimpy drawers, the pale soles of his feet kicking up dust as he dissolves down the path.

In Ranna's village we dwell close to the earth. Sitting on the floor we eat off clay plates, with our fingers, and sleep on mats spread on the ground, breathing the earth's odour.

The next morning Ranna and I romp in the fields, and Ranna, fascinated, copies my limp. I know, then, that like Papoo, he really cares for me. I let him limp without comment. In return, he shows me how to mould a replica of his village with dung. And, looking generously and intently into my eyes, permits me to feel his belly-button. It even feels like a finger.

His sisters, Khatija and Parveen, barely two or three years older than us, already wear the responsible expressions of much older women. Like the other girls in the village, they affect the mannerisms and tone of their mother and aunts. They are pretty girls, with large, serene eyes and a skin inclined to flush. Painfully shy of me, they are distressed – and perplexed – by the display of my twig-like legs beneath my short dress. (I don't wear my callipers as much now.) They don't know what to make of my cropped hair either. Busy with chores, baskets of grain stuck to their tiny hips, they scuttle about importantly.

Every short while Ranna suspends play to run to his mother. Chidda is cooking at the clay hearth in their courtyard; she feeds her son and me scraps of chapatti dipped in buttermilk.

Later in the blue winter afternoon a bunch of bearded Sikh peasants, their long hair wrapped in loose turbans or informally displayed in top-knots, visit Pir Pindo. They are from Dera Tek Singh, a neighbouring village. The men of Pir Pindo – those who are not out working in the fields – come from their barns and courtyards and sit with the Sikhs in a thick circle beneath a huge *sheesham* standing in a patch of wild grass.

The rough grass pricks my bottom and thighs. Ranna has sidled into his father's lap. Prompted by Imam Din, he wears a buttonless shirt he has clearly outgrown. I sit between Dost Mohammad and Jagjeet Singh; a plump, smiling, bow-legged Sikh priest, a *granthi*. Khatija and Parveen, looking like miniature women of eight and nine, their heads modestly covered, bring us piles of fragrant cornbread fried in butter and a steaming clay pot of spicy mustard-greens. I see the wisdom of their baggy shalwars and long kamizes as I fidget in the grass, tugging at my dress.

The Sikh *granthi*, grey-bearded and benign, beckons the girls, and, shy eyes lowered, they come to him. He strokes their covered heads and says, in Punjabi, 'May the seven gurus bless you with long lives.' He draws them to him affectionately. 'Every time I see you, you appear to have grown taller! We'll have to think about arranging your marriages soon!' He leans across me and addresses Dost Mohammad. 'Don't you think it's time their hands were painted yellow?'

Jagjeet Singh has alluded to the henna-decorated hands of Muslim brides. The sisters duck their heads and hide their mouths in their veils. Ranna finds the suggestion outrageously funny. Slipping from his father's lap, his belly-button pointed at them like a jabbing finger, he jumps up and down. 'Married women!' he chortles. 'Ho! Ho! Married women!'

Already practised in the conduct they have absorbed from the village women, the girls try not to smile or giggle. They must have heard their mother and aunts (as I have), say: '*Hasi to phasi!* Laugh (and), get laid!' I'm not sure what it means – and I'm sure they don't either – but they know that smiling before men can lead to disgrace.

We have eaten and belched. The hookah, stoked with fresh tobacco, is being passed among the Muslim villagers. (Sikhs don't smoke.) In the sated lull the village mullah clears his throat. 'My brothers,' he says. And as our eyes turn to him, running frail fingers through his silky white beard, he says, 'I hear there is trouble in the cities . . . Hindus are being murdered in Bengal . . . Muslims, in Bihar. It's strange . . . the English *Sarkar* can't seem to do anything about it.'

Now that he has started the ball rolling, the mullah raises his white eyebrows in a forehead that is almost translucent with age. He looks about him with anxious, questioning eyes.

The village *chaudhry* – sitting by Imam Din and the mullah – says, 'I don't think it is because they can't . . . I think it is because the *Sarkar* doesn't want to!' He is a large man, as big-bellied and broad-beamed as Imam Din, but at least twenty years younger. He has large, clear black eyes and an imposing cleft in his chin. As he talks, he slowly strokes his thick, up-twirled moustache: without which no village headman can look like a *chaudhry*. 'But all that is in the cities,' he continues, as if he has considered the issue for some time. 'It won't affect our lives.'

'I've not come all this way without a reason,' says Imam Din. The villagers, who are wondering why he is visiting them, look at him attentively. He rubs his face with both hands; as if it pains him to state the reason. 'I don't think you know how serious things are getting in the towns. Sly killings; rioting and baton charges by the police . . . long marches by mobs . . . The Congress-wallahs have started a new stunt . . . they sit down on the rail tracks – women and children, too. The police lift them off the tracks . . . But one of these days the steam engines will run over them . . . Once aroused, the English are savages . . .

'Then there is this Hindu-Muslim trouble,' he says, after a pause. 'Ugly trouble . . . It is spreading. Sikh-Muslim trouble also . . .'

The villagers, Sikh and Muslim, erupt in protest.

'Brother,' the Sikh *granthi* says when the tumult subsides, 'our villages come from the same racial stock. Muslim or Sikh, we are basically Jats. We are brothers. How can we fight each other?'

'*Barey Mian*,' says the *chaudhry*, giving Imam Din his due as a respected elder, 'I'm alert to what's happening . . . I have a radio. But our relationships with the Hindus are bound by strong ties. The city folk can afford to fight . . . we can't. We are dependent on each other: bound by our toil; by Mandi prices set by the Banyas – they're our common enemy – those city Hindus. To us villagers, what does it matter if a peasant is a Hindu, or a Muslim, or a Sikh?'

Imam Din nods. There is a subtle change in his face; he looks calmer. 'As long as our Sikh brothers are with us, what have we to fear?' he says, speaking to the *granthi*, and including the other Sikhs with a glance. 'I think you are right, brothers, the madness will not infect the villages.'

'If needs be, we'll protect our Muslim brothers with our lives!' says Jagjeet Singh.

'I am prepared to take an oath on the Holy Koran,'

declares the *chaudhry*, 'that every man in this village will guard his Sikh brothers with no regard for his own life!'

'We have no need for oaths and such,' says the mullah in a fragile elderly voice. 'Brothers don't require oaths to fulfil their duty.'

Later, when the mullah's voice calls the evening prayer, and the Sikhs have begun to saunter across the fields to their village, Dost Mohammad carries his son to a small brick mosque with a green dome in the centre of Pir Pindo. I stay back with the women.

* * *

We are due to leave in an hour. Chidda has awakened early to prepare breakfast. I sit on the floor crosslegged, eating my *paratha* and omelette. Parveen shuffles closer to me. With extreme delicacy, her face flushed and confiding, she whispers into my ear. It takes me a while to realise, she is asking if my hair was cut on account of lice.

'Of course not!' I say. I don't care who hears me. 'It's the city fashion.' I glare at her. 'Even my mother's hair is short.'

Chidda, squatting by the hearth, summons her daughter. Rapping her on the head she says: 'Who told you to be uncivil? Who told you to ask questions? Haven't I taught you to mind your tongue? Go! Get out of my sight!' she says. Ranna quickly grabs his sister's share of the breakfast.

A bunch of villagers accompanies us for a mile, wheeling Imam Din's bicycle for him as we walk. I leave Pir Pindo with a heavy heart and a guilty conscience.

Chapter 8

When I return from Imam Din's village to the elevated world of chairs, tables and toilet seats, Imam Din continues his efforts to keep on the right side of Ayah. She is the greatest involuntary teacher ever. He plies her with beautifully swollen *phulkas* hot off the griddle, slathered with butter-fat and sprinkled with brown sugar. He prepares separate and delicious vegetarian dishes for her. In fact he is, to a large extent, responsible for her spherical attractions. Where would she be without his extra servings of butter, yoghurt, curry and chapatti? Wouldn't she look like all the other stringy, half-starved women in India whom one looks at only once – and never turns around to look at twice?

He continues to appease Adi and me with dizzying inhalations from his hookah; and chicken giblets and liver, turn by turn, on those occasions when my parents have guests and he cooks chicken.

My parents entertain often: and when guests are expected we are fed early. Adi and I sit across the oilcloth on a small table against the wall, away from the silver cutlery and embroidered dinner cloth. Yousaf folds the starched white napkins into fancy peacocks and stuffs their props into long-stemmed crystal glasses. Flowers blaze in silver vases.

Glitter and glory, but very little food. We know the guests will be served delectable but small portions.

We have already shared the chicken liver, and today it is my turn for the single giblet. I place it on a side-plate, saving it for the end when I can chew and suck on it for long uninterrupted moments. I notice the movement of Adi's eyeballs under his lids as they sneak to the corners, peer at the giblet and slip back. This only enhances the quality of my possession. I am at peace – there is honour even among thieves – and the fear of reprisal. I casually place my left hand above the plate and manoeuvre it to shield the giblet. I don't wish to put undue strain on Adi's honour.

As it happens, the precaution is unnecessary. I raise a glass of water to my lips and Adi's swift hand strikes. The giblet is jammed into his mouth and swallowed whole. His throat works like a boa constrictor's and his face turns red. I grab at his mouth and he opens it wide, saying 'Aaaaaa!'

There is nothing left to retrieve.

What hurts me most is him swallowing my giblet like a pill. Not even tasting it. It is an affront to my sense of fair play. I grab his hair and let out a blood-curdling shriek that brings Mother rushing from the drawing room and Yousaf, Imam Din and Ayah from the kitchen.

Mother spanks Adi, and Adi, cursing and fighting back, is picked up by Yousaf and spirited away into the darkness outside.

Ayah carries me screaming into the kitchen and proceeds to splash my face at the sink. Imam Din pops a chicken heart into my mouth. Yousaf carries Adi back to the kitchen. Adi's mouth is working. It too has had something popped into it. I wonder what? An uneasy truce is contemplated as we scrutinise each other's ruminating mouths. A short while later when everyone is busy preparing dinner we slip unobserved beneath the dinner table, friends again.

We have done this innumerable times. One would imagine that someone might think to look under the table and chase us away before dinner is served.

The table is supported by stands of polished wood. The stands are held to by a beam which runs six inches above the floor. We roost quietly on the beam in cloth-screened twilight, amidst a display of trouser cuffs, sari borders, ankles, shoes and a medley of fragrance.

Rosy and Peter's parents are present: we can tell by their legs. His are crossed at the ankles, smell frankly of cow-dung and are prone to shake in and out at the knees. Hers are planted solidly side by side beneath her sari. Peter's father is a turbaned and bearded Sikh. He is not permitted to cut his hair or shave – not even the hair of his armpits or crotch. Peter has told us this.

Their mother is American. She ties her blonde hair back

in a severe knot and always wears a white cotton sari with wide borders. Sometimes I feel she doubles as one of the marching Salvation Army band-women. She is green-eyed and very white and placid and other-worldly. She carries on with whatever she is doing – which is for the most part a mystery – and pays scant attention to the world. Nothing that her children, or her husband, do can wipe the placid look from her face or disturb her unhurried movements.

Her husband is not a bad man. Mr Singh does not beat her or white-slave traffic in her. But he has habits that would drive Mother up the wall . . . I've heard her say so. He roams on long hairy legs in loose cotton drawers, barefoot. He milks his water buffalo himself. He converses loudly in vituperative Punjabi and he clears his throat and spits around – generally conducting himself like a coarse Jat in a village. Mother expects more refined conduct from a man married to an American woman.

They are infrequent guests.

This appears to be an evening dedicated to neighbourly brotherliness. The other guests are from the Birdwood Barracks: Inspector General of Police and Mrs Rogers. He is tall, colourless, hefty-moustached, pale-eyebrowed; and she, soft, pretty, plump and submissive – with a fascinating proclivity to clean out and around her children's ears with a handkerchief dampened with spit.

Their two children are younger than us. The only reason we countenance them at all is because of their glowing ears.

There are only four guests to dinner tonight, plus my parents – which makes six. Father calculates six portions to a chicken. Hence the single giblet.

Meanwhile Father has launched his emergency-measures joke.

A British soldier and a turbaned native find themselves sharing a compartment. They are travelling by the Khyber Mail to Peshawar. The Indian lifts a bottle of Scotch to his mouth frequently. He does not offer any to the soldier. When the Indian leaves the compartment for a moment the soldier steals a hasty draught from the bottle.

Again the Indian goes out, and the tommy sneaks another swig.

They get to talking. The soldier confides he took a draw or two from the Indian's bottle of Scotch. 'Since you didn't offer it to me, old chap, I helped myself!' he says companionably.

The native is aghast.

'But that is my urine in the bottle!' he exclaims. 'My *hakim* prescribed it as a cure for syphilis . . .'

Poor soldier.

Father and Mother hoot with laughter. Their Sikh guest is in guffaws. And twice, unable to constrain his appreciation, Mr Singh inserts two fingers in his mouth and emits piercing whistles. His American wife, I think, titters.

I cannot see them but I doubt if the Rogers manage even a smile. All I see – and barely escape – is a vicious little kick the Inspector General of Police gives the beam. His boots, smelling faintly of horse-dung and strongly of shoe polish, keep stabbing the wood.

Father adds a postscript: 'You know – I learnt the other day – there was no syphilis in India until the British came . . .'

'You won't be able to blame everything on us for long, old chap,' says Inspector General Rogers. 'That old bugger, Gandhi, is up to his old bag of tricks.'

'We will have *Swaraj*!' declaims Mr Singh in deafening belligerence. As if the Englishman, instead of hinting at the premature departure of the British, has just denied him Home Rule.

'You think you'll be up to it, old chap?' says Mr Rogers snidely.

'Why not?' shouts Mr Singh as if he is arguing with the Inspector of Police across a hockey field. 'I am up to ruling you and your Empire! You recruit all our Sikh soldiers into your World War Number Two and we win the war for you! Whyfore then you think we cannot do Home Rule?'

Mr Singh's broad Punjabi accent and loud voice never fail to annoy Mother. She must have indicated her displeasure with some gesture because Mrs Singh placidly says, 'Don't shout, dear.'

'I am not shouting!' hollers Mr Singh. 'I'm telling this man: Quit India! Gandhijee is on a fast,' he warns the police officer. 'If he dies, his blood will be on your head!'

'That wily Banya is an expert on fasting unto death without dying,' says the heftily moustached policeman demurely.

'And what if he dies?' questions Mr Singh righteously. 'You mark my word. One day he will die! Then what you will do?'

'I'll tell you what I'll do. I'll celebrate!' says the Inspector General losing his patience.

'You will not celebrate! You know why? Because rivers of your blood will flow in our gutters!' says Mr Singh in a sarcastic sing-song. He shakes his knees in and out in an engaging rhythm and bangs his fist on the table. I can tell by the swift little stabs of the Inspector General's shoe on the wood that he too is angry.

'Rivers of blood will flow all right!' he shouts, almost as loudly as Mr Singh. 'Nehru and the Congress will not have everything their way! They will have to reckon with the Muslim League and Jinnah. If we quit India today, old chap, you'll bloody fall at each other's throats!'

'Hindu, Muslim, Sikh: we all want the same thing! We want independence!'

Inspector General Rogers recovers his Imperial phlegm. 'My dear man,' he intones, 'don't you know the Congress won't agree on a single issue with the Muslim League? The Cabinet Mission proposed a Federation of the Hindu and Muslim majority provinces. Jinnah accepted it; Gandhi and Nehru didn't!

'They even rejected Lord Wavell's suggestion for an Interim Government with a majority Congress representation! They're like the three bloody monkeys! They refuse to hear, or see that Jinnah has the backing of seventy million Indian Muslims! Those arrogant Hindus have blown the last chance for an undivided India . . . Gandhi and Nehru are forcing the League to push for Pakistan!'

'And where will this so-called Pakistan be?' enquires our Sikh neighbour with withering and snickering sarcasm.

'They want the Muslim majority provinces: Punjab, Sind, Kashmir, the North West and Bengal,' replies the police officer, as if coaching a backward child. I can imagine the haughty flare of his English nostrils.

'They are only saying that to be in a better bargaining position and you are stringing them along because of your divide-and-rule monkey tricks!' accuses Mr Singh. 'You always set one up against the other . . . You just give Home Rule and see. We will settle our differences and everything!'

'Who will? Master Tara Singh?' It is a contemptuous, curl-of-the-lip tone of voice.

'Yes. He is my leader. I will obey him!' Mr Singh says this so quietly and firmly that for a moment I wonder if someone else has spoken in his stead.

The Inspector General makes a very peculiar sound. Then he says, 'The Akalis are a bloody bunch of murdering fanatics!'

Even I can tell it's a tactless thing to say.

Mr Singh's rhythmically knocking knees grow perfectly still. In one quick movement, drawing his legs to his chair, almost knocking it over, he stands up. Everybody's feet make erratic moves. Adi and I, terrified of discovery, retract our legs and cower in hunched-up bundles.

Father has stood up also. I hear him say in Punjabi: 'Oye, sit down, Sardarjee . . . I say, *yaar*, don't mind the *Angrez* Sahib. He doesn't know . . .'

But before Father can finish the sentence Mr Singh cuts in: 'Oh yes? He knows very well!' and one of his legs completely disappears. There is a clatter of crockery, a heavy thump over our heads, and three variously pitched feminine 'Oh's! Mr Singh must have leaned clear across the table.

'Jana! Take the fork away!' Mother shouts.

'Don't you dare touch him!' screams Mrs Rogers hysterically. 'Oh! He'll blind him!'

'Put that fork away, dear,' says Mrs Singh, her voice quavering in the effort to sound firm.

I realise with a little thrill of excitement running up my spine that Mr Singh has tried to stab the Englishman's eyes with a fork: and since Mr Rogers has not cried out, the attempt has failed. No blood has so far been shed.

Father's legs skittle behind Mr Singh's solitary leg. There is a brief scuffling sound. A piece of cutlery falls clattering on the table top. Mr Rogers remains disappointingly quiet. Obviously Mr Singh has been de-forked. Then Mr Singh's wide butt pounds down on the cane-bottomed dining chair.

'Tell him to apologise!' he roars, almost wailing, shuffling on his seat.

'Go to hell, you fat hairy slob!' spits the police officer, his short breath betraying his jolted nerves.

'Please,' pleads Mother. 'Please apologise.'

I can visualise Mother's hand on the Inspector's arm. None, except Father, can resist her touch.

There is a tense pause.

'Oh, all right . . . I'm sorry, old boy! I shouldn't have said that,' says the Englishman gruffly.

In sandalled feet Father toddles back to his own seat, and Mr Singh's muscular thighs commence their rhythmic twitching with renewed vigour.

Mother and Mrs Rogers chatter excessively about the weather. Suddenly they become quiet.

'You know, old chap,' Inspector General Rogers has just said to Mr Singh, 'if you Sikhs plan to keep your lands in Lyallpur and Montgomery, you'd better start fraternising with the Muslim League. If you don't, the Muslims will throw you off your rich lands.'

'That mother-fucker isn't born who can throw us out! We will throw them out! and you out!' Mr Singh bashes his fist on the table with such force that the cutlery and crockery jangle.

'Who wants pudding?' trills Mother shrilly, loudly banging a spoon against her glass.

In the startled silence that follows, Mrs Rogers enthusiastically warbles: 'Oh, I'd love some pudding!'

And Mrs Singh, mustering all the emphasis of which she is capable, says, 'Me too!'

In a determined effort to flood with oil the precariously tranquillised waters, Mother tells Father, 'Janoo [a variation on Jana], you must tell everybody that joke about the cannibals and the padre's wife that you told me! About breakfast in bed . . .'

Since when did Father start telling Mother jokes? Mother has this habit of voicing her fantasies . . . If she persists in her visions of conjugal bliss, I'm afraid she will lose touch with reality.

There are other jokes. Father and Mother crack up with hoots that I'm sure can be heard by the lion in his zoo. Beneath the table Adi and I mimic their laughter, taking care to time the whoops and blend our voices. Mr Singh is breathless with laughing. He stamps his feet, here and there, unaware of the havoc he is causing beneath the table.

After they are through with the pudding, and the thimblefuls of liqueurs, Adi pinches Mrs Singh's calf and I pinch Mrs Rogers's. Even the imperturbable Mrs Singh shrieks. Their feet fly up to our chests and chins. The tablecloth is raised and six bewildered faces poke under.

We emerge. Mother is angry. Apprehensive. She glances at Father and, taking her cue from his amused countenance, relaxes. She beams at us in that way I have begun to notice and resent: her 'other-people-are-around' way. Father looks pleasant and even makes indulgent sounds. Yousaf gathers us by the ears and propels us to bed.

Father's dinner party jokes never fail. The Rogers have scarcely eaten. Over the years it saves thousands of rupees' worth of chicken, lamb, caramel custard and other party fare.

Half asleep I can still hear them laugh. Was that really Father? that communicative person making 'pooch-pooch' noises with his lips and kindly saying, 'Get along you two!' as Yousaf took us from the room? and that hooting, rollicking woman my remote and solemn mother?

* * *

At about this time I become aware of a second-hand Morris Minor in our midst. It has a crank up front to start the engine, a radiator that consumes countless kettles of boiling water, and a five-man-power crew to push-start the eight-horse-power motor.

The snap of the crank now features as one of the regular noises of the morning. Together with the lion's roar, the bustle of domestic activity to provide Father with his newspaper and cups of tea – and the battle Muccho wages with Papoo – it awakens me. In my nightsuit, barefoot, I go to the veranda. The crank changes hands every five minutes. Imam Din is at it. One hand on the car bonnet, a duster wrapped round the handle for a firm grip, he lurches mightily and the engine burps. He straightens and presses the small of his back.

Hari takes over. Stooping before the handle like a frisky terrier he energetically turns the crank with both hands.

Adi bursts out of the dining room door in his pyjamas, holding his toothbrush, followed by Ayah's shouts and then by Ayah. He too has a crack at the crank.

I help Ayah pry him loose and Moti takes over.

I go to greet Father. He is in the bathroom, enthroned on the commode. With a great rustling of newspaper, preoccupied and mute, he sits me on his bare thigh.

Father is in a good mood. So, Mother too is in a good mood. She gives me a hug. She puts toothpaste on Father's toothbrush. She tells me to take Father's empty cup and saucer to the pantry. But Father latches on to me with such a show of speechless anguish and consternation at the thought of being parted from me that Mother says, 'Let it be. Yousaf will take them.'

She smiles indulgently: as if she could cross my father if she had a mind to.

* * *

Father has a twenty-minute nap after lunch. Not nineteen, not twenty-one, precisely twenty. He knots a kerchief tightly round his eyes and lies down flat on the bed with his sandals on. Mother removes his sandals, his socks if he is wearing socks, blows tenderly between his toes, and with cooing noises caresses his feet.

With a stern finger on her lips she hushes the household, until Father's internal alarm clock causes him to jump out of bed, and within four minutes on to his bicycle.

After lunch on a luminous November Saturday I'm idling on my cot, filling my tedium with dreams, when a hushed rush of sound comes from my parents' bedroom. Not the harsh angry sounds that still me with dreadful apprehension, but the kind of noises signifying Father's frolicsome mood. Father takes a longer break some Saturdays.

I leap from my bed and burst into their room.

Mother and Father are standing at the opposite ends of their joined beds. 'Janoo! Don't tease me like this . . . I know you've got it: I saw it!'

Mother's voice teeters between amusement and a wheedling whine. She is a virtuoso at juggling the range of her voice and achieving the exact balance with which to handle Father. Father has the knack of extracting the most talented performances from us all – and from all those who work for him.

'Jana!' Mother says in throaty exasperation, 'you know I'm going to get you!' and she lunges around the bed.

Father, limber in his striped cotton nightsuit and maroon dressing gown, maintains a strategic distance. 'Don't be foolish,' he says with fake and *sotto-voce* irritability. Conscious of the servants, my parents squabble in low voices and, being a more private person, Father is more particular.

Outside their window Yousaf is shaving the leaves from the trees with a scythe, assisting the half-hearted Lahori fall to complete its task.

Mother clutches the headboard and tries to dodge, taking a step this way and that. Then, climbing on the bed, she scrambles across the mattress on all fours.

Father skips away easily. 'Stop pestering me,' he says, 'I'm getting late for work.'

'I won't let you go, Jana,' says Mother in a voice so tearfully childish that it cannot possibly present a threat to Father's authority. Turning appealingly to me, her bosom heaving, she enlists my support.

'Lenny, catch him.'

'Stop acting like a child,' Father says disgustedly. He spreads his hands to show that he is not concealing anything.

But Mother, an expert at reading his face, says, 'I know you are smiling under your moustache, Jana. I love it when you are this way.' And attuned to the nuance underlying his disgusted voice, she knows she can persist. 'I'll get my hands on the money, or my name isn't Bunty.'

I run round the bed, exaggerating my modified limp, and grab hold of Father's leg.

'One minute. One minute,' he coaxes, loosening my grip and misleading me. The instant I release his leg he vaults through the curtains into the narrow study, and, swiftly shutting the doors, draws the bolt.

'Jana! Let me in, Jana,' Mother cries shaking the door and rattling the loose iron bolt. I bang on it. Yousaf and his scythe have moved to shave another tree and the wintry sun shines through its bared branches.

'You will break the door, stupid twit!' cries Father in a harsh, hushed voice. Uncomfortably aware of the ubiquitous servants, he pulls the bolt and opens the door.

Mother and I rush him excitedly. Expecting the charge, Father staggers back and plonks down on the settee with Mother and me on top of him. Mother's searching hands move all over his dressing gown, and beneath it, probing his pockets, crotch and other crannies.

Knowing now I'm looking for money, I also stroke and pat his clothes.

'You've hidden it, Janoo,' cries Mother in dismay. 'But I'll find it! I'm not about to give up!'

Heaving herself off Father, determinedly and methodically Mother opens and shuts drawers in a rickety old desk and in a steel filing cabinet. Father lounges on the settee looking smug. But when Mother strides towards the large teak cupboard at the far end of the room he bounds forward and, spreading his hands, stands before it. The heavy panels on the top half of the almirah conceal a neat array of narrow drawers, and the lower half is composed of two sets of deeper drawers.

We fling ourselves at Father. My wiry Father is strong, but Mother has the advantage of her voluptuous weight. In the tug of war that ensues we manage to open the door panels – and to keep them open – despite Father's desperate efforts to dislodge us.

Mother, breathing heavily, plunges her hands here and there and with a triumphant cry sprints out of the room, her stubby fingers closed on a large wad of notes.

'*Oye, uloo!*' Father says, rushing after her. 'It's not my money, you crazy! I'll bring you your house-keeping money from the office.'

'I'll take only what I have to,' Mother shouts, locking herself into the bathroom. 'I haven't even paid Lenny's physiotherapist yet . . . I've to buy the children's clothes for Christmas and New Year.' (Christmas, Easter, Eid, Divali. We celebrate them all.)

'Oye, madwoman,' hisses Father through the door, ostensibly mindful of the servants' ears. 'Show some sense. I owe the money. I have to return it on my way to the office. Give it back at once.'

'I'll give it after I've taken what I need, Jana,' Mother warbles and suddenly opening the door shoves the bundle at my father.

Before she's had time to move to her cupboard Father has flicked through the notes and counted them. '*Arrey!*

You've taken far too much!' he exclaims as if shaken to the core and bankrupted by the banditry. But I am also schooled to read between the lines of my father's face. His heart is not in his anguish. Mother must have withdrawn a very meagre and reasonable sum indeed!

'She's bent on destroying us,' Father grumbles, striking his forehead again and again. 'Money Money Money Money! From morning to night. Money Money Money Money! I'm fed up.'

But Mother, with dew in her eyes and a misty smile, blows him kisses. And, having locked the money in her cupboard, goes about her business of picking up Father's clothes and tidying the beds and getting dressed.

Chapter 9

To our left is the Singhs' large bungalow. The compound wall we share is partially broken by the sloping trunk of a eucalyptus tree near our kitchen. This is where Rosy, Peter, Adi and I, and sometimes Cousin, gather to discuss world affairs, human relationships, Mr and Mrs Singh's uncut hair and Rosy's sister's impending baby.

'I'll tell you how babies come,' says Rosy.

'Oh, we know,' I say, 'Ayah's already told us.'

'How?' challenges Rosy. 'The stork brings them?'

Rosy sighs, rolling her eyes. 'I'll tell you how they are made,' she persists; 'my sister's told me everything.'

Rosy is obnoxiously smug and swollen these days. She may walk about with a grown-up air – but her cotton knickers, I notice, remain wet. Her big sister unquestionably pumps her with questionable knowledge.

'If your sister knows so much, how come she could not even pass her Matric exam?' I ask.

Rosy has picked up a reasonable way of talking which

gives me goose bumps. 'Passing Matric exams has nothing to do with having babies,' she explains sweetly. 'She has a husband who she loves – and who loves her . . .'

'She's got to have a husband, stupid! She's married isn't she?' Adi butts in, 'and married people have babies! That's all there is to it!'

'You're much too young to understand such things,' says Rosy.

'I'll show you who's too young,' says Adi, pushing her back and jumping the wall after her and knocking her down and throwing himself upon her. They argue with their limbs and voices, churning dust. How is Rosy to know that just that morning Cousin settled an argument with Adi by shoving him off Skinny-aunt's veranda saying: 'You're too small to know anything, stupid., Scram!'

The kitchen door banging shut, Yousaf emerges to investigate the row. He snatches Adi up and Rosy, dragged to her feet by her hair, emits a bloody yell that curdles the milk in Mr Singh's buffaloes. Yousaf carries Adi kicking and cursing into the kitchen.

For the moment at least Adi has knocked the stuffing out of Rosy's intolerable grown-uppishness. Red-faced, bawling, martyred, wet knicker-bottoms caked with mud and arms outstretched, Rosy totters in slow motion towards her veranda.

Putting on a straight face I jump the wall after Rosy. I place a hypocritical arm protectively round her shoulders and console her all the way up the veranda steps to her room.

'What is it, Rosy? What is the matter, dear?' warbles Mrs Singh in her cool-water-in-a-jug American voice from somewhere in the house.

Rosy bawls something indecipherable and Mrs Singh, apparently satisfied, asks no more questions.

The three miniature glass jars wink at me!

Leaving Rosy to cope with her hurt feelings and bruised flesh, I crouch before them. One by one I lift the fragile jars and remove their tiny crystal stoppers. They gleam, reflecting rainbow hues – insinuating questions . . . What is eternity? Why are the stars? Where do cats lay their eggs? And why don't hospitals have flushing bed-pans built into the beds?

Rosy never even looks at the jars unless I am there. If they were to fall this minute and smash to smithereens she would be sad – the destruction of beauty is depressing – but she wouldn't miss them among all her little pots and pans and cups and saucers. Would it be stealing then? Taking away something Rosy doesn't want anyway?

I cannot bring myself to ask her to give them to me. She might refuse. It's an unthinkable risk. I know when you want something very much it gives people power over you. I will not give Rosy that power to withhold – or to grant. Too many people have it as it is.

Silently Rosy gets up and leaving a damp indentation of her dusty bottom on the bedspread goes out of the room.

My hands feel weak. I cannot stir out of my crouched position. I force my mind to be rational. Hundreds of thousands of people steal . . .

Suddenly my brain clicks. My eyes locate the fireplace. My hands spring to life, deft and obedient, and I bury the jars in a bed of ashes. It is almost summer. No one will kindle a fire for months. I can leave the jars there till Rosy forgets they ever existed.

Rosy returns bearing a saucer and my heart sinks. On the saucer are small mounds of sugar, rice and red pepper. It is an offering. A manoeuvre to shore up my shaky allegiance; and a silent testimony of her worth. She knows I love filling the jars, like their enormous counterparts in the kitchen, with sugar and rice.

There is no help for it. While Rosy fills the toy teapot with water from the bathroom I pry out the jars from the ashes and fill them with rice and sugar.

I could weep. Any time I manoeuvre a set of circumstances to suit me this happens. Fate intervenes. There is no other word for it. Fated! Doomed! No wonder I have such a scary-puss of a conscience.

* * *

Ayah has acquired two new admirers: a Chinaman and the Pathan.

Mother wonders why we are suddenly swamped with such a persistent display of embroidered bosky-silk and linen tea-cosies, tray-cloths, trolley sets, tablecloths, counterpanes, pillowcases and bedsheets.

Twice a week the Chinaman cycles up our drive, rattling and bumping over the stones, a huge khaki bundle strapped to the carrier.

Our drive is made of packed earth. Every year, worn by traffic and eroded by monsoons, the drive lays bare patches of brick rubble.

The Chinaman is dapper, thin, brusque and rude. He parks his bicycle in the porch, removes the cycle-clips from his khaki trousers and heaves his bundle to the veranda. 'Comeon, comeon, Chinaman come!' he shouts, squatting before his bundle and sorting out his wares for display. 'Comeon Mem-sahib, comeon Ayah. Comeon, comeon, Chinaman come!'

Mother yells from inside: 'Tell him to get out! What is this nonsense? Coming every day! Ayah? Yousaf? Is anyone there?'

Ayah comes to the veranda. 'Go, go!' she says in tart English. 'Besides Cantonese, the Chinaman speaks only a smattering of English.) 'Memsahib no want. Go, Go!'

But the Chinaman has sprung his trap with cunning. Ayah's attention is snared by the shimmering colours. Her eyes wander to the silks.

'Comeon, comeon,' he coaxes, getting up. He reaches for Ayah's arm and pulls her to his silks. 'See?' he says, stroking his free hand over the bosky and then over her arm. 'It silky like your skin. See? See?' he says burying her hand in the soft heap.

Ayah knows well how to handle his bold tilted eyes and

his alien rudeness. 'Oh-ho,' she says, all sing-songy. 'I have no munneeey – how I buy?'

'You sit,' coaxes the Chinaman, pulling Ayah to squat beside him and, retaining his hold, engages her in a staccato and desultory conversation. When Ayah's restiveness becomes uncontrollable he introduces a bribe: 'Now, what I can give you?' he muses. 'Let me see . . . Sit, sit,' he says and Ayah's restiveness succumbs to the dual restraints of hand and promises.

Although Ayah has been allotted quarters, she dwells and sleeps in our house. Soon the table tops, mantelpieces, sideboards and shelves in our rooms blossom with embroidered, bosky-silk doilies.

The attentions of Ayah's Pathan admirer also benefit our household. All our kitchen knives, table knives, Mother's scissors and paper-knife and Hari's garden shears and Adi's blunt penknife suddenly develop glittering razor edges. And it is not only our household the Pathan services. Gita Shankar's, Rosy-Peter's, Electric-aunt's and Godmother's houses also flash with sharp and efficient cutting implements. Even the worn, stubby knives in the servants' quarters acquire redoubtable edges: for the Pathan is a knife-sharpener.

I have often noticed him in the bazaar, plying his trade before street-side shops. He pushes a pedal on his machine and a large and slender wheel turns dizzily round and round. With great dexterity and judgement he brings the knife blades to the wheel, and in the ensuing conflagration of sparks and swift steel-screeches, the knives are honed to jewel edges. He wraps the loose end of his floppy turban about his mouth like a thug – to filter out the fine steel and whetstone dust.

It is only when I see him in a sidewalk brawl with the restaurant-wrestler, looking bewildered and furious, his face no longer covered like a thug's, that I recognise the face and connect it to the pink and tingly bottom we cycled past on our way to Imam Din's village.

The Pathan's name is Sharbat Khan. He too cycles up

our long drive, steel clattering and wheels wobbling over the rubble that sticks out of the mud. The cycle looks like a toy beneath the man from the mountains and involuntarily Adi and I grow tense, expecting the pistol-shot-like report of a punctured tyre. It is late in the afternoon and we stand on the veranda, hypnotised by his approach.

Sharbat Khan wears draw-string pantaloons so baggy they put to shame Masseur's shalwar – and over them a flared tunic that flaunts ten yards of coarse white homespun. He cycles past our bedroom and Gita Shankar's rooms to the back of the house. Adi and I scoot after him.

Sharbat Khan parks his cycle against a tree and squatting by it waits for Ayah.

Ayah comes.

Ayah is nervous in his presence: given to sudden movement; her goddess-like calm replaced by breath-stopping shyness. They don't touch. He leans across his bicycle, talking, and she shifts from foot to foot, smiling, ducking and twisting spherically. She has taken to sticking a flower in her hair, plucked from our garden. They don't need to touch. His presence radiates a warmth that is different from the dark heat generated by Masseur's fingers – the lightning-strikes of Ice-candy-man's toes.

Sharbat Khan tells her of his cousin who has a dry fruit and *naswar* (mixture of tobacco and opium) lean-to in Gowalmandi. It is a contact point for the many Pathans from his tribe around the Khyber working in Lahore. He gives Ayah news of the meat, vegetable, tea and kebab stall owners and of their families, whose knives he sharpens. He is doing well. And not only at sharpening knives.

Sharbat Khan cautions Ayah: 'These are bad times – Allah knows what's in store. There is big trouble in Calcutta and Delhi: Hindu-Muslim trouble. The Congress-wallahs are after Jinnah's blood . . .'

'What's it to us if Jinnah, Nehru and Patel fight? They are not fighting our fight,' says Ayah, lightly.

'That may be true,' says Sharbat Khan thoughtfully, 'but

they are stirring up trouble for us all.'

Sharbat Khan shifts forward, his aspect that of a man about to confess a secret. Ayah leans closer to him and I slide into her lap.

He glances at me dubiously, but at a reassuring nod from Ayah, says, 'Funny things are happening inside the old city . . . Stabbings . . . Either the police can't do anything – or they don't want to. A body was stuffed into a manhole in my locality . . . It was discovered this morning because of the smell: a young, good-looking man. Several bodies have been found in the gutters and gullies of the Kashmiri, Lahori and Bhatti Gates and Shalmi . . . They must have been dumped there from different neighbourhoods because no one knows who they are.'

'Are they Hindus?' asks Ayah, her carefree mood dispelled.

'Hindu, Muslim and Sikh. One can tell they are from prosperous, eating-drinking households . . .

'There have also been one or two fires . . . I don't like it . . .'

We fall into a pensive silence.

Ayah sighs, '*Arrey Bhagwan.*' She pushes me off her lap and unties a knot in her sari that serves as her wallet. She holds out a small bundle of tightly folded notes. 'Look,' she says, shaking her head to dispel the sombre mood. 'I've saved my whole salary this month . . . forty rupees!'

Sharbat Khan takes the money from her and, removing his turban, tucks it inside its rancid-smelling interior. His hair, matted to his head, is brown and falls from a centre parting to his ears.

Sharbat Khan loans money as a side business like most Pathans. He carries out transactions on Ayah's behalf and gives her the profits. Often he wears a gun. There are few defaulters.

I listen as Sharbat Khan talks to Ayah of the crops and sparse orchards in his mountain village. Now it is the apple season and the season for apricots. It is also time to cash the rice crop, the maize crop, and hoe the potatoes . . . He is going to his tribal village for a month or so to help his folk wrest the harvest from the gritty, unyielding soil of his land. There are leopards in the granite ravines and stony summits surrounding his village. He has encountered them on mountain trails, their eyes gleaming emerald by night, their spots camouflaged by the filtered sunlight dappling the underbrush by day.

'*Hai Ram!*' exclaims Ayah, her lips trembling with concern. 'Don't they attack?'

'Only if they're shown disrespect,' says Sharbat Khan. 'We mountain folk know what to do. We touch our foreheads and courteously say "*Salaam-alekum mamajee* [uncle]" and they let us alone.'

'I'd never have the nerve to say that!' says Ayah. 'I'd faint right away!'

'Then he'd think you very rude and eat you up!'

'*Arrey baba*, I'd never go to your village,' says Ayah firmly.

Sharbat Khan grins, his eyes shining with love. 'Then I must bring the mountains to you! What would you like?' he asks Ayah. 'Almonds? Pistachios? Walnuts? Dried apricots?' Sharbat Khan wears silver rings on his fingers, roughly embedded with turquoise and uncut rubies. 'Ah, the taste of those nuts!' he sighs, raising his fingers to his lips and smacking them, and sliding his warm tiger-eyes in a way that leaves Ayah so short of breath that she can barely say, 'Bring me pistachios.'

Sharbat Khan leans forward. 'What?' he asks, aware of his effect on her. 'I didn't hear you.'

Ayah shuffles her bare feet and fidgets with her sari. Her eyes are shy, full of messages. 'Bring me pistachios,' she says again. 'And almonds: they are good for the brain.'

'And what are pistachios good for?' asks Sharbat Khan knowingly, and Ayah lowers her head and fiddles with the scarlet rose anchored to the tight knot in her hair and says, 'How should I know?' And Sharbat Khan sighs again, and his eyes turn so radiant they shine like amber between his bushy lashes.

Something happens within me. Though outwardly I remain as thin as ever I can feel my stomach muscles retract to create a warm hollow. 'Take me for a ride – take me for a ride,' I beg and Sharbat Khan, tearing away his eyes from Ayah, places me on the cycle shaft. He gives me a turn round the backyard, grazing past the buffalo, the servants' quarters and the Shankars' veranda. He smells of tobacco, burnt whetstone and sweat. He brings me back and offers Ayah a ride.

'Sit in front: it's safer,' he says.

'*Aiiii-yo!*' she says in a long-drawn way, as if he has made an improper suggestion, and turning her face away covers her head with her sari.

Sharbat Khan coaxes her again, and with a great show of alarm Ayah wiggles on to the shaft in front and Sharbat Khan takes her off on a circuit of the backyard. He pretends to lose his balance: and as the front wheel swings wildly, '*Hai*, I'll die!' cries Ayah. The inhabitants of the servants' quarters pop out to watch the *tamasha* and applaud. Adi laughs and claps. Laughing, Sharbat Khan releases Ayah back under the trees.

He gives Adi a ride, and depositing him outside the kitchen, cycles down the drive like a mountain receding.

* * *

I hear the metallic peal of Father's cycle bell and rush out to welcome him. Mother rushes out of another door. It is almost three in the afternoon: Father is late for lunch. Together we slobber all over him as Father, with a phoney frown and a tight little twist of a smile beneath his moustache, places the cycle on its stand and removes the ledgers clamped to the carrier.

Mother removes his solar topi and slips off the handkerchief tied round his forehead to keep the sweat from his eyes. She brushes his wet curls back. As I reach up to kiss him Father bends and puts his arm round me. Mother relieves him of the ledgers and taking hold of his other arm winds it about herself, making little moaning sounds as if his touch fills her with exquisite relief. With me clinging to his waist and Mother hanging on to his arm Father labours up the veranda steps.

Making affectionate sounds we accompany Father to the bathroom. He washes his hands and empties his bladder and we accompany him to the dining table.

Mother and I sit with him. Mother talks while he chomps wordlessly on his food and looks at her out of the assessing and disconcerting eyes of a theatre critic. Mother chatters about friends and supplies political titbits filtered through their consciousnesses: Col. Bharucha says that Jinnah said . . . And Nehru said that . . . And oh, how I laughed when Mehrabai (that's the mirthsome Mrs Bankwalla) said this about Patel . . . and that about . . .

Unflagging, she gives a résumé of the anxious letters from sisters and sisters-in-law in Bombay and Karachi, who have heard all sorts of rumours about the situation in the Punjab and are exhorting us to come to them.

A little later, mention of Adi's hostile antics causes Father to scowl. Leaning forward to shovel a forkful of curried rice into his mouth he crumples his forehead up, and out of sharp and judgemental eyes gazes acutely at Mother.

Switching the bulletin immediately Mother recounts some observations of mine as if I've spent the entire morning mouthing extraordinarily brilliant, saccharinely sweet and fetchingly naïve remarks. 'Jana, you know what Lenny told me this morning? She said: "Poor Daddy works so hard for us. When I grow up, I will work in the office and he can read his newspaper all day!"'

Peals of laughter from Mother. A smile from Father.

And when Mother pauses, on cue, I repeat any remarks I'm supposed to have made: and ham up the performance with further innocently insightful observations.

Father rewards me with solemn nods, champing smiles, and monosyllables.

And as the years advance, my sense of inadequacy and

unworth advances. I have to think faster – on my toes as it were . . . offering lengthier and lengthier chatter to fill up the infernal time of Father's mute meals.

Is that when I learn to tell tales?

Chapter 10

Instead of school I go to Mrs Pen's. Her house is next to Godmother's on Jail Road – opposite Electric-aunt's – and I walk there with Ayah or with Hari. Channi, her slight but stately sweeper, takes out a small table and two chairs and we sit in the garden under bare February trees and lukewarm sunshine. Mr Pen lounges on the veranda in an easy chair.

A parrot might relish reciting tables. I do not.

> 'Two twos are four
> Two threes are six
> Two fours are eight
> Etc., etc.'

By the time I reach the five-times table I am resting my head on my arms stretched flat out on the table, peering sideways at Mrs Pen. My jaws ache – my mind wanders – I hear Mr Pen snore . . .

He is much darker than Mrs Pen. He is Anglo-Indian.

Mrs Pen is fair, soft, plump, English.

I have a trick. My voice drones on, my mind clicks off. I take time out to educate myself. I watch the trees shed their leaves and sprout new buds . . . and the predatory kites swoop on pigeons. And the crows, in ungainly clusters, attack the kites . . .

And I sniff a whiff off Mrs Pen as it drifts up from under the table, its mouldy reality percolating the dusting of cheap talcum powder.

Despite her efforts to clutter my brain with the trivia and trappings of scholarship I slip in a good bit of learning. The whiff off Mrs Pen enlightens me. It teaches me the biology of spent cells and ageing bodies – and insinuates history into my subconscious . . . of things past and of the British Raj . . . of human frailties and vulnerabilities – of spent passion and lingering yearnings. Whereas a whiff off Ayah carries the dark purity of creation, Mrs Pen smells of memories.

Mrs Pen reads aloud prosaic English history.

I turn my head the other way. I observe Mr Pen's fingers. They are long, fat and large. His legs are huge tubes encased in flannels and beneath them, visible through a hole in his socks, plops his mordant toe. I feel sorry for Mrs Pen. I can't imagine his fingers working the subtle artistry of Masseur's fingers – or his sluggish toe conveying the dashing impulses of Ice-candy-man's toes.

After Mrs Pen's I go to Godmother's.

Godmother rents rooms in the back of a bungalow. She has a large room, and a small room with a kerosene stove and a dangerous Primus stove. The small room serves as kitchen/pantry. And off it, a bathroom with three commodes.

I go straight to the kitchen. Slavesister, short and squat, is slaving over the kerosene stove. I follow her as she walks on painful bunions to the water-trough at the back of the compound and watch her scour the heavy pans and brass utensils with ash and mud. I help her carry them back.

Every now and then Slavesister serves Godmother strong half-cups of steaming tea which Godmother pours into her saucer and slurps. I too take an occasional and guilty sip. Drinking tea, I am told, makes one darker. I'm dark enough. Everyone says, 'It's a pity Adi's fair and Lenny so dark. He's a boy. Anyone will marry him.'

* * *

Yesterday I carried a gleaming image of the jars in my mind.

Something darker lurks in their stead today – fear and guilt.

The three jars are in my possession.

I glance about the room. There is not a single hiding place when I want one. When I don't need them they abound, secreting away things.

I tuck the jars in an old pair of felt slippers beneath a tangle of neglected toys in the bottom drawer of our dresser.

Adi breezes in and makes a beeline for the dresser. He opens and closes drawers, rummaging among the wrecked cars, trains, nursery books, gutless badminton rackets, and celluloid dolls. He grabs the deflated football he's looking for and I let my breath go. I need a safer hiding place.

Next morning I transport the jars to Mrs Pen's, wrapped in toilet paper and tucked in my school bag. After my tuition I transport them to Godmother's. She is propped up on three white pillows that are cement-hard and as heavy. I recline beside her on her cot, propped almost upright.

My eyes wander all over the room. Another string-cot, smaller and sagging, lies in front of the almirah with the three doors. Squeezed between two cupboards, fitting one into the other, are three more cots. Oldhusband sits hunched and still on a bentwood chair before a heavy mahogany desk. Chairs with cane seats, tin trunks and leather suitcases are stacked against the walls. My eyes, like happy roaches, crawl into the abundance of crevices and crannies.

Slavesister goes into the kitchen. When she calls Godmother to light the Primus I quickly slip the jars between two stacks of trunks covered by dhurries.

I hear Godmother pump the spirit stove: koochuck, koochuck, koochuck, koochuck. I see her, white-saried, bent forward in concentration, vulnerable and heroic.

The technology involved in starting the Primus is too complex for Slavesister to handle. Godmother exposes herself to grave risk every time she starts the stove. Like

Russian roulette, any one of the pumps might trigger the Primus to blow up in her face.

There is a fierce hissing. It is now safe to peek in. The ring of flame from the Primus is like a fierce blue storm.

I lie back on Godmother's pillows, absent-mindedly listening to her scold Slavesister. When she approaches I make room for her. She settles in the hollow of the bed and I wind myself about her like a rope.

She calls to Slavesister. Her voice is still stern from the scolding: 'I want that Japanese kimono Mehrabai brought me two years back. That red one. I want to give it to Bachamai's Rutti. Do you remember where it is?'

No answer.

She raps her punkah on the wall to attract her sister's attention, and raising her voice to accommodate the hissing stove, repeats the text, adding: 'Do you hear me?'

Still no answer.

'Oh? We are sulking, are we?'

No comment.

'We are getting all hoity-toity today?'

Godmother blinks exaggeratedly, and makes a haughty, naughty face and holds her long pointed fingers in such a supercilious and dainty manner that I burst into giggles. Godmother shakes with suppressed chuckles.

Catching her breath and sobering up, she says: 'Will you look for the kimono – or do I have to get up?'

The bed creaks as Godmother slowly heaves herself up and lowers her feet, and Slavesister comes in flapping her slippers noisily and saying, 'I'm coming, I'm coming . . . Really, Rodabai, you have no patience, have you? I can't cook and look for the kimono at the same time too, can I?'

Godmother caricatures her expression and pantomimes her martyred movements behind her rotund back.

'I know what you're doing. Go ahead: do it in front of the child! As it is she doesn't respect me. I have asked you so often not to. You never consider how you humiliate me, do you?'

Godmother continues her performance, pantomiming

Slavesister's gestures, opening and shutting her mouth in a dumb charade.

Godmother nudges me. Slavesister has commenced mumbling.

Godmother sets up an imitative hum. As Slavesister peers into boxes and suitcases looking for the kimono, she mumbles louder and Godmother says, 'Some people don't like being scolded. If they don't like being scolded they shouldn't hover around Primus stoves when I'm pumping them!'

'Mumble – grumble.' A lifting and shutting of trunk lids. A puzzled expression on Slavesister's face, a wad of toilet paper in her hands. 'What's this?'

'Careful! It's glass! It's mine,' I say, scampering off the cot.

Balancing her bifocals on the tip of her rubbery and shapeless nose, Slavesister examines the tiny jars admiringly. 'Where did you get them?'

'Rosy gave them to me.'

Perhaps I hesitate a fraction too long. Or my body signals contrarily. The moment the sentence is out I can tell Godmother knows I have stolen the jars. I leap back to my original roost, not able to meet her eyes, and hide my face in her sari.

'You have stolen the jars, haven't you?' she asks.

'No,' I say, shaking my head vehemently against her khaddar blouse.

'Don't lie. It doesn't suit you.'

There it is again! Lying doesn't become me. I can't get away with the littlest thing.

'Why not?' I howl. 'Why doesn't it suit me? No one says that to Adi, Ayah, Cousin, Imam Din, Mother, Father or Rosy-Peter!'

'Some people can lie and some people can't. Your voice and face give you away,' says Godmother.

'But I can't even curse,' I howl, sitting up.

Adi can swear himself red in the face and look lovable – Rosy can curse steadily for five minutes, going all the way from '*Ullu-kay-pathay*' to 'asshole', from Punjabi swear words to American, and still look cute. It's okay if Cousin swears – but if I curse or lie I am told it does not suit the shape of my mouth. Or my personality. Or something!

'Everybody in the world lies, steals and curses except me!' I shout, choked with self-pity. 'Why can't I act like everybody?'

'Some people can get away with it and some can't,' says Godmother. 'I'm afraid a life of crime is not for you. Not because you aren't sharp, but because you are not suited to it.'

A life sentence? Condemned to honesty? A demon in saint's clothing?

I was set firmly and relentlessly on the path to truth the day I broke a Wedgwood plate and, putting a brazen face on my mischief, nobly confessed all before Mother. I was three years old. Mother bent over me, showering me with the radiance of her approval. 'I love you. You spoke the truth! What's a broken plate? Break a hundred plates!'

I broke plates, cups, bowls, dishes. I smashed livers, kidneys, hearts, eyes . . . The path to virtue is strewn with broken people and shattered china.

* * *

Gandhijee visits Lahore. I'm surprised he exists. I almost thought he was a mythic figure. Someone we'd only hear about and never see. Mother takes my hand. We walk past the Birdwood Barracks' sepoy to the Queens Road end of Warris Road, and enter the gates of the last house.

We walk deep into a winding, eucalyptus-shaded drive: so far in do we go that I fear we may land up in some private recess of the zoo and come face to face with the lion. I drag back on Mother's arm, vocalising my fear, and at last Mother hauls me up some steps and into Gandhijee's presence. He is knitting. Sitting cross-legged on the marble floor of a palatial veranda, he is surrounded by women. He is small, dark, shrivelled, old. He looks just like Hari, our gardener, except he has a disgruntled, disgusted and irritable look, and no one'd dare pull off his dhoti! He wears only the loin-cloth and his black and thin torso is naked.

Gandhijee certainly is ahead of his times. He already knows the advantages of dieting. He has starved his way into the news and made headlines all over the world.

Mother and I sit in a circle with Gita and the women from Daulatram's house. A pink-satin bow dangling from the tip of her stout braid, Gita looks ethereal and content – as if washed of all desire. I notice the same look on the faces of the other women. Whatever his physical shortcomings, Gandhijee must have some concealed attractions to inspire such purified expressions.

Lean young women flank Gandhijee. They look different from Lahori women and are obviously a part of his entourage. The pleasantly plump Punjabi women, in shalwar-kamizes and saris, shuffle from spot to spot. Barely standing up, they hold their veils so that the edges don't slip off their heads as they go to and from Gandhijee. The women are subdued, receptive; as when one sits with mourners.

Someone takes Mother's hand, and hand in hand we go to Gandhijee. Butter wouldn't melt in our mouths. Gandhijee politely puts aside his knitting and uncreases his disgruntled scowl; and with an irrelevance I find alarming, says softly, 'Sluggish stomachs are the scourge of the Punjabis . . . too much rich food and too little exercise. The cause of India's ailments lies in our clogged alimentary canals. The hungry stomach is the scourge of the poor – and the full stomach of the rich.'

Beneath her blue-tinted and rimless glasses Mother's eyes are downcast, her head bowed, her bobbed hair – and what I assume is her consternation – concealed beneath her sari. But when Gandhijee pauses, she gives him a sidelong look of rapt and reverent interest. And two minutes later, not the least bit alarmed, she earnestly furnishes him with the odour, consistency, time and frequency of her bowel movements. When she is finished she bows her head again, and Gandhijee passes his hand over her head: and then, absently, as if it were a tiresome after-thought, over mine.

'Flush your system with an enema, daughter,' says Gandhijee, directing his sage counsel at my mother. 'Use plain, lukewarm water. Do it for thirty days . . . every morning. You will feel like a new woman.

'Look at these girls,' says Gandhijee, indicating the lean women flanking him. 'I give them enemas myself – there is no shame in it – I am like their mother. You can see how smooth and moist their skin is. Look at their shining eyes!'

The enema-emaciated women have faint shadows beneath their limpid eyes and, moist-skinned or not, they are much too pale, their brown skins tinged by a clayish pallor.

Gandhijee reaches out and suddenly seizes my arm in a startling vice. 'What a sickly-looking child,' he announces, avoiding my eye. 'Flush her stomach! Her skin will bloom like roses.'

Considering he has not looked my way even once I am enraged by his observation. 'An enema a day keeps the doctor away,' he crows feebly, chortling in an elderly and ghoulish way, his slight body twitching with glee, his eyes riveted upon my mother.

I consider all this talk about enemas and clogged intestines in shocking taste: and I take a dim and bitter view of his concern for my health and welfare. Turning up my nose and looking down severely at this improbable toss-up between a clown and a demon I am puzzled why he's so famous – and suddenly his eyes turn to me. My brain, heart and stomach melt. The pure shaft of humour, compassion, tolerance and understanding he directs at me fuses me to everything that is feminine, funny, gentle, loving. He is a man who loves women. And lame children. And the untouchable sweeper – so he will love the untouchable sweeper's constipated girl-child best. I know just where to look for such a child. He touches my face, and in a burst of shyness I lower my eyes. This is the first time I have lowered my eyes before man.

It wasn't until some years later – when I realised the full scope and dimension of the massacres – that I comprehended the concealed nature of the ice lurking deep beneath the hypnotic and dynamic femininity of Gandhi's non-violent exterior.

And then, when I raised my head again, the men lowered their eyes.

Chapter 11

The April days are lengthening, beginning to get warm. The Queen's Park is packed. Groups of men and women sit in circles on the grass and children run about them. Ice-candy-man, lean as his popsicles and as affable, swarming with children, is going from group to group doing good business.

Masseur, too, is going from group to group; handsome, reserved, competent, assured, massaging balding heads, kneading knotty shoulders and soothing aching limbs.

I lie on the grass, my head on Ayah's lap, basking in – and intercepting – the warm flood of stares directed at Ayah by her circle of admirers. The Falletis Hotel cook, the Goverment House gardener, a sleek and arrogant butcher and the zoo attendant, Sher Singh, sit with us.

'She is scared of your lion,' drawls Ayah, playfully tapping my forehead. 'She thinks he's let loose at night and he will gobble her up from her bed.'

Sher Singh, wearing an outsize blue turban and a callow beard, sits up. Delighted to be singled out by Ayah, he looks at me earnestly: 'Don't worry. I'll hang on to his leash,' he boasts, stammering slightly. 'He won't dare eat you!'

I'm not the least bit reassured. On the contrary, I am terrified. This callow youth with a stem-like neck hold the zoo lion?

'What kind of leash?' I ask.

'A-an iron ch-chain!'

It's much worse than I'd imagined. A lion roaring behind bars is bad enough. But a lion straining on a stout leash held by this thin, stuttering Sikh is unthinkable. I burst into tears.

'Now look what you've done,' says Ayah in her usual good-natured manner. Gathering me in her arms and hugging me she rocks back and forth. 'Don't be silly,' she tells me. 'The lion is never let out of his cage. The cage is so strong a hundred lions couldn't break it.'

'And,' says Ramzana the butcher, 'I give him a juicy goat every day. Why should he want to eat a dried up stick like you?'

The logic is irrefutable during daylight hours as I sit among friends beneath Queen Victoria's lion-intimidating presence. But alone, at night, the logic will vanish.

Masseur and Ice-candy-man drift over to us and join the circle. Masseur is raking in money. He has invented an oil that will grow hair on bald heads. It is composed of monkey and fish glands, mustard oil, pearl dust and an assortment of herbs. The men listen intently, but Masseur stops short of revealing the secret recipe. He holds up the bottle and Ayah reaches out to touch the oil.

'Careful,' says Masseur, whipping the bottle away. 'It'll grow hair on your fingertips.'

'*Hai Ram*!' says Ayah, quickly retracting her fingers, and rolling her eyes from one face to the next with fetching consternation.

We all laugh.

Not to be outdone, Ice-candy-man says he has developed a first-class fertility pill. He knows it will work but he has yet to try it out.

'I'll give it a try,' offers the Government House gardener.

'Your wife's already produced children, hasn't she?'

'Tch! Not for her, *yaar*. For myself. I feel old sometimes,' confesses the greying gardener.

'It is not an aphrodisiac. It's a fertility pill for women,' explains Ice-candy-man. 'It's so potent it can impregnate men!'

There is a startled silence.

'You're a joker, *yaar*,' says the butcher.

'No, honestly,' says Ice-candy-man, neglectful of the cigarette butt that is uncoiling wisps of smoke from his fist. He too will rake in money.

Masseur clears his throat and, breaking the spell cast by the fertility pill, enquires of the gardener: 'What's the latest from the English *Sarkar*'s house?'

The gardener, congenial and hoary, is our prime source of information from the British Empire's local headquarters.

'It is rumoured,' he says obligingly, rubbing the patches of black and white stubble on his chin, 'that Lat Sahib Wavell did not resign his viceroyship.'

He pauses, dramatically, as if he's already revealed too much to friends. And then, as if deciding to consecrate discretion to our friendship, he serves up the choice titbit.

'He was sacked!'

'Oh! Why?' asks Ice-candy-man. We are all excited by a revelation that invites us to share the inside track of the Raj's doings.

'Gandhi, Nehru, Patel . . . they have much influence even in London,' says the gardener mysteriously, as if acknowledging the arbitrary and mischievous nature of antic gods. 'They didn't like the Muslim League's victory in the Punjab elections.'

'The bastards!' says Masseur with histrionic fury that conceals a genuine bitterness. 'So they sack Wavell Sahib, a fair man! And send for a new Lat Sahib who will favour the Hindus!'

'With all due respect, malijee,' says Ice-candy-man, surveying the gardener through a blue mist of exhaled smoke, 'but aren't you Hindus expert at just this kind of thing? Twisting tails behind the scene . . . and getting someone else to slaughter your goats?'

'What's the new Lat Sahib like? This Mountbatten Sahib?' asks Ayah.

She, like Mother, is an oil pourer. 'I saw his photo. He is handsome! But I don't like his wife, *baba*. She looks a *choorail*!'

'Ah, but Jawaharlal Nehru likes her. He likes her *vaaary much*!' says Ice-candy-man, luridly dragging out the last two words of English.

'Nehru and the Mountbattens are like this!' the gardener concurs, holding up two entwined fingers. His expression, an attractive blend of sheepishness and vanity, reinforces the image of a seasoned inside tracker.

'If Nehru and Mountbatten are like this,' says Masseur, 'then who's going to hold our Jinnah Sahib's hand? Master Tara Singh?'

Masseur says this in a way that makes us smile.

'Ah-ha!' says Ice-candy-man as if suddenly enlightened. 'So that's who!' He slaps his thigh and beams at us as if Masseur has proposed a brilliant solution. 'That's who!' he repeats.

The butcher snorts and aims a contemptuous gob of spit some yards away from us. He has been quiet all this while and as we turn our faces to him he gathers his stylish cotton shawl over one shoulder and says: 'That non-violent violence-monger – your precious Gandhijee – first declares the Sikhs *fanatics*! Now suddenly he says: "Oh dear, the poor Sikhs cannot live with the Muslims if there is a Pakistan!" What does he think we are – some kind of beast? Aren't they living with us now?'

'He's a politician, *yaar*,' says Masseur soothingly. 'It's his business to suit his tongue to the moment.'

'If it was only his tongue I wouldn't mind,' says the butcher. 'But the Sikhs are already supporting some trumped-up Muslim party the Congress favours.' He has a dead-pan way of speaking which is very effective.

The Government House gardener, his expression wary and sympathetic, gives a loud sigh, and says: 'It is the English's mischief . . . They are past masters at intrigue. It suits them to have us all fight.'

'Just the English?' asks Butcher. 'Haven't the Hindus connived with the *Angrez* to ignore the Muslim League, and support a party that didn't win a single seat in the Punjab? It's just the kind of thing we fear. They manipulate one or two Muslims against the interests of the larger community. And now they have manipulated Master Tara Singh and his bleating herd of Sikhs!' He glances at Sher Singh, his handsome, smooth-shaven face almost expressionless.

Sher Singh shifts uncomfortably and, looking as completely innocent of Master Tara Singh's doings as he can, frowns at the grass.

'*Arrey*, you foolish Sikh! You fell right into the Hindus' trap!' says Ice-candy-man so facetiously that Sher Singh loses part of his nervousness and smiles back.

The afternoon is drawing to a close. The grass feels damp. Ayah stands up smoothing the pleats in her limp cotton sari. 'If all you talk of nothing but this Hindu-Muslim business, I'll stop coming to the park,' she says pertly.

'It's just a discussion among friends,' says Ice-candy-man, uncoiling his frame from the grass to sit up. 'Such talk helps clear the air . . . but for your sake, we won't bring it up again.'

The rest of us look at him gratefully.

* * *

There is much disturbing talk. India is going to be broken. Can one break a country? And what happens if they break it where our house is? Or crack it further up on Warris Road? How will I ever get to Godmother's then?

I ask Cousin.

'Rubbish,' he says, 'no one's going to break India. It's not made of glass!'

I ask Ayah.

'They'll dig a canal . . .' she ventures. 'This side for Hindustan and this side for Pakistan. If they want two countries, that's what they'll have to do – crack India with a long, long canal.'

Gandhi, Jinnah, Nehru, Iqbal, Tara Singh, Mountbatten are names I hear.

And I become aware of religious differences.

It is sudden. One day everybody is themselves – and the next day they are Hindu, Muslim, Sikh, Christian. People shrink, dwindling into symbols. Ayah is no longer just my all-encompassing Ayah – she is also a token. A Hindu. Carried away by a renewed devotional fervour she expends a small fortune in joss-sticks, flowers and sweets on the gods and goddesses in the temples.

Imam Din and Yousaf, turning into religious zealots, warn Mother they will take Friday afternoons off for the Jumha prayers. On Fridays they set about preparing themselves ostentatiously. Squatting atop the cement wall of the garden tank they hold their feet out beneath the tap and diligently scrub between their toes. They wash their heads, arms, necks and ears and noisily clear their throats and noses. All in white, check prayer scarves thrown over their shoulders, stepping uncomfortably in stiff black Bata shoes worn without socks, they walk out of the gates to the small mosque at the back of Queens Road. Sometimes, at odd hours of the day, they spread their mats on the front lawn and pray when the muezzin calls. Crammed into a narrow religious slot they too are diminished: as are Jinnah and Iqbal, Ice-candy-man and Masseur.

Hari and Moti-the-sweeper and his wife Muccho, and their untouchable daughter Papoo, become ever more untouchable as they are entrenched deeper in their low Hindu caste. While the Sharmas and the Daulatrams, Brahmins like Nehru, are dehumanised by their lofty caste and caste-marks.

The Rogers of Birdwood Barracks, Queen Victoria and King George are English Christians: they look down their noses upon the Pens who are Anglo-Indian, who look down theirs on the Phailbuses who are Indian-Christian, who look down upon all non-Christians.

Godmother, Slavesister, Electric-aunt and my nuclear family are reduced to irrelevant nomenclatures – we are Parsee.

What is God?

* * *

All morning we hear Muccho screeching at Papoo. 'I turn my back; the bitch slacks off! I say something; she becomes a deaf-mute. I'll thrash the wickedness out of you!'

'I don't know what jinn's gotten into that woman,' says Ayah. 'She can't leave the girl alone!'

I have made several trips to the back, hanging around the quarters on some pretext or other, and with my presence protecting Papoo.

Papoo hardly ever plays with me now. She is forever slapping the dough into chapatties, or washing, or collecting dung from the road and plastering it on the walls of their quarters. The dried dung cakes provide fuel.

In the evening she sweeps our compound with a stiff reed *jharoo*, spending an hour in a little cloud of dust, an infant stuck to her hip like a growth.

Though she looks more ragged – and thin – her face and hands splotched with pale dry patches and her lips cracked, she is as cheeky as ever with her mother. And forever smiling her handsome roguish smile at us.

Late that evening Ayah tells me that Muccho is arranging Papoo's marriage.

I am seven now, so Papoo must be eleven.

My perception of people has changed.

I still see through to their hearts and minds, but their exteriors superimpose a new set of distracting impressions.

The tuft of *bodhi*-hair rising like a tail from Hari's shaven head suddenly appears fiendish and ludicrous.

'Why do you shave your head like that?' I say disparagingly.

'Because we've always done so, Lenny baby, from the time of my grandfather's grandfathers . . . it's the way of our caste.'

I'm not satisfied with his answer.

When Cousin visits that evening I tell him what I think. 'Just because his grandfathers shaved their heads and grew stupid tails is no reason why Hari should.'

'Not as stupid as you think,' says Cousin. 'It keeps his head cool and his brain fresh.'

'If that's so,' I say, challenging him, 'why don't you shave your head? Why don't Mother and Father and Godmother and Electric-aunt and . . .'

Cousin stops my mouth with his hand and as I try to bite his fingers and wiggle free, he shouts into my ears and tells me about the Sikhs.

I stop wiggling. He has informed me that the Sikhs become mentally deficient at noon. My mouth grows slack under his palm. He carefully removes his hand from my gaping mouth and, resuming his normal speaking voice, further informs me: 'All that hair not only drains away their grey-matter, it also warms their heads like a tea-cosy. And at twelve o'clock, when the heat from the sun is at its craziest, it addles their brains!'

It is some hours before I can close my gaping mouth. Immediately I rush to Imam Din and ask if what Cousin says is true.

'Sure,' he says, pushing his hookah away and standing up to rake the ashes.

'Just the other day Mr Singh milked his cow without a bucket. He didn't even notice the puddle of milk on the ground . . . It was exactly two seconds past twelve!'

Cousin erupts with a fresh crop of Sikh jokes.

And there are Hindu, Muslim, Parsee, and Christian jokes.

* * *

I can't seem to put my finger on it – but there is a subtle change in the Queen's Garden. Sitting on Ayah's crossed legs, leaning against her chocolate softness, again the unease at the back of my mind surfaces.

I fidget restlessly on Ayah's lap and she asks: 'What is it, Lenny? You want to do soo-soo?'

I nod, for want of a better explanation.

'I'll take her,' offers Masseur, getting up.

Masseur leads me to the Queen's platform. Squatting beneath the English Queen's steely profile, my bottom bared to the evening throng, I relieve myself of a trickle.

'Oye! What are you gaping at?' Masseur shouts at a little Sikh boy who has paused to watch. His long hair, secured in a top-knot, is probably already addling his brain.

Masseur raises his arm threateningly and shouts: 'Scram!'

The boy flinches, but returning his eyes to me, stays his ground.

The Sikhs are fearless. They are warriors.

I slide my eyes away and, pretending not to notice him, stand up and raise my knickers. As Masseur straightens the skirt of my short frock I lean back against his legs and shyly ogle the boy.

Masseur gropes for my hand. But I twist and slip away and run to the boy and he, pretending to be a steam-engine, 'chook-chooking' and glancing my way, leads me romping to his group.

The Sikh women pull me to their laps and ask my name and the name of my religion.

'I'm Parsee,' I say.

'*O kee*? What's that?' they ask: scandalised to discover a religion they've never heard of.

That's when I realise what has changed. The Sikhs, only their rowdy little boys running about with hair piled in top-knots, are keeping mostly to themselves.

Masseur leans into the group and placing a firm hand on my arm drags me away.

We walk past a Muslim family. With their burka-veiled women they too sit apart. I turn to look back. I envy their children. Dressed in satins and high heels, the little Muslim girls wear make-up.

A group of smooth-skinned Brahmins and their pampered male offspring form a tight circle of supercilious exclusivity near ours.

Only the group around Ayah remains unchanged. Hindu, Muslim, Sikh, Parsee are, as always, unified around her.

I dive into Ayah's lap.

As soon as I am settled, and Ayah's absorption is back with the group, the butcher continues the interrupted conversation:

'You Hindus eat so much beans and cauliflower I'm not surprised your yogis levitate. They probably fart their way right up to heaven!' He slips his palm beneath his armpit and, flapping his other arm like a chicken-wing, generates a succession of fart-like sounds.

I think he's so funny I laugh until my tummy hurts. But Ayah is not laughing. 'Stop it,' she says to me in a harsh sombre whisper.

Sher Singh, who had found the rude sounds as amusing, checks himself abruptly. I notice his covert glance slide in Masseur's direction and, looking a little foolish, he suddenly tries to frown.

I twist on Ayah's lap to look at Masseur. He is staring impassively at the grinning butcher: and Butcher's face, confronted by his stolid disfavour, turns ugly.

But before he can say anything, there is a distraction. A noisy and lunatic holyman – in striking attire – has just entered the Queen's Garden. Thumping a five-foot iron trident with bells tied near its base, the holyman lopes towards us, shouting: *'Ya Allah!'* A straight, green, sleeveless shift reaches to his hairy calves. His wrists and upper arms are covered with steel and bead bangles. And round his neck and chest is coiled a colossal hunk of copper wiring. Even from that distance we can tell it's the Ice-candy-man!

I've heard he's become Allah's telephone!

A bearded man, from the group of Muslims I had noticed earlier, goes to him and deferentially conducts him back to his family. As Ice-candy-man hunkers down, I run to watch him.

A woman in a modern, grey silk burka whispers to the bearded man, and the man says, 'Sufi Sahib, my wife wants to know if Allah will grant her a son. We have four daughters.'

The four daughters, ranging from two to eight, wear gold high-heeled slippers and prickly brocade shirts over satin trousers. Frightened by Ice-candy-man's ash-smeared face and eccentric manner, they cling to their mother. I notice a protrusion in the lower half of the woman's burka and guess that she is expecting.

His movements assured and elaborate, eyeballs rolled heavenwards, Ice-candy-man becomes mysteriously busy. He unwinds part of the wire from the coil round his neck so that he has an end in each hand. Holding his arms wide, muttering incantations, he brings the two ends slowly together. There is a modest splutter, and a rain of blue sparks. The mad holyman says 'Ah!' in a satisfied way, and we know the connection to heaven has been made. The girls, clearly feeling their distrust of him vindicated, lean and wiggle against their mother, kick their feet up, and whimper. Their mother's hand darts out of the burka, and in one smart swipe, she spanks all four. Nervous eyes on Ice-candy-man, the girls stick a finger in their mouths and cower quietly,

Holding the ends of the copper wire in one hand, the holyman stretches the other skywards. Pointing his long index finger, murmuring the mystic numbers '7 8 6', he twirls an invisible dial. He brings the invisible receiver to his ear and waits. There is a pervasive rumble; as of a tiger purring. We grow tense. Then, startling us with the volume of noise, the muscles of his neck and jaws stretched like cords, the crazed holyman shouts in Punjabi: 'Allah? Do You hear me, Allah? This poor woman wants a son! She has four daughters . . . one, two, three, four! You call this justice?'

I find his familiarity alarming. He addresses God as 'tu', instead of using the more respectful 'tusi'. I'm sure if I were the Almighty I'd be offended; no matter how mad the holyman! I distance myself from him mentally, and observe him stern faced and rebuking.

'Haven't You heard her pray?' Ice-candy-man shouts. Covering the invisible mouthpiece with his hand, in an apologetic aside, he says: 'He's been busy of late . . . You know; all this Indian independence business.' He brings the receiver to his ear again.

Suddenly he springs up. Thumping his noisy trident on the ground, performing a curious jumping dance, he shouts: 'Wah Allah! Wah Allah!' so loudly that several people who have been watching the goings-on from afar, hastily get up and scamper over. Sikhs, Hindus, Muslims form a thick circle round us. I notice my little Sikh friend. I can tell from the reverent faces around me that they believe they are in the presence of a holyman crazed by his love of God. And the madder the mystic, the greater his power.

'Wah, Allah!' shouts Ice-candy-man. 'There is no limit to your munificence! To you, king and beggar are the same! To you, this son-less woman is queen! Ah! the intoxication of your love! The depth of your compassion! The ocean of your generosity! Ah! the miracles of your cosmos!' he shouts, working himself into a state. And, just as suddenly as he leapt up to dance before, he now drops to the ground in a stony trance. Our ears still ringing from his shouts, we assume his soul is in communion with God.

The woman in the burka, believing that the holyman has interceded successfully on her behalf, bows her body in gratitude and starts weeping. The bearded man fumbles in the gathers of his trousers and places two silver rupees – bearing King George's image – at the holyman's entranced toes.

Holding the holyman's pious finger, feeling privileged, I return to our group.

'*Aiiay jee, aiiay*! Sit, Sufi Sahib; sit! We are honoured!' exclaim the men in half awed, half mocking welcome, making room for Ice-candy-man between the Government House gardener and Masseur. Laying his trident aside, lighting a cigarette and assuming his customary, slouching pose on the grass, the holyman becomes Ice-candy-man.

The Government House gardener places his hand affectionately on Ice-candy-man's thigh, and says, 'Sufijee, have you heard the latest about the Lucknow Muslims?' In his quiet way, he is getting his own back for Butcher's wise-cracks about the levitating vegetarian Hindus.

The overly polite Lucknow Muslims are notorious for endlessly saying: 'After you, sir,' and 'No, sir, after you!' My attention is riveted. The Government House gardener relates his joke.

Two Muslim gentlemen arrive at a public toilet at the same time.

One insists, 'After you, sir.'

'No, sir, you first! After you!' insists the other.

Until, eventually, one of them resignedly says: 'You might as well go first, sir . . . I've been.'

Ayah becomes breathless laughing and almost rolls on the grass. Her sari slips off her shoulders and her admirers relish the brown gleam of her convulsed belly beneath her skimpy blouse, and the firm joggle of her rotund bosoms.

A clutch of Hindu children with caste-marks on their foreheads, curious at the burst of laughter, run up timidly and suddenly yell: 'Parsee Parsee, crow eaters! Crow eaters! Crow eaters!'

'We don't! We don't! We don't!' I scream.

The gardener, threatening to get up, throws his turban at them and they scamper in squealing disarray.

'Why do they say that?' I ask fiercely.

'Because y'all do "kaan! kaan!" at the top of your voices like a rowdy flock of crows,' says Ayah.

Ice-candy-man tucks his green shift between his legs as if he's wearing a dhoti, and acting like a timid Banya, declaims:

'We were only seventeen; they were a gang of four!
How we ran; how we ran; as we'd never run before!'

It is so apt to the occasion that my anger vanishes.

I have heard this couplet before. A glimpse of four Sikhs, Muslims or Parsees is supposed to send a mob of Banyas scurrying.

Chapter 12

A strange black box makes its appearance in my parents' bathroom.

It is Saturday and Cousin is visiting for the day. Mother, the indefatigably mirthsome Mrs Bankwalla, Mrs Singh and Maggie Phailbus, the schoolteacher who also lives on Warris Road, are sitting on the veranda. Having drawn their chairs close to the marble-topped coffee-table they talk in hushed voices that fade into silence when we pass. Even Mrs Bankwalla's explosive conviviality is subdued. I've noticed a lot of hushed talk recently. In bazaars, restaurants and littered alleys men huddle round bicycles or squat against walls in whispering groups.

We are playing kick-the-can in the garden. Cousin, Adi and Peter form one team and Rosy, Ayah, Papoo-with-babe-on-hip and I the other. It's girls versus boys, and having Papoo on our side compensates for Rosy's erratic play.

Abruptly Cousin puts his hand on his fly and, awkwardly shuffling his feet, dashes away. The game is suspended.

When Cousin returns we can tell by his studied nonchalance he has something to tell. We gather about him. After sliding his eyes this way and that he looks at us out of the wide and innocent eyes he displays whenever he has something to hide. He signals with a sly tilt of his head, and Adi, shoving Ayah from the back, rushes her out of the garden. Ayah good-naturedly disappears into the kitchen.

'I have seen something strange,' confides Cousin portentously. 'Follow me.'

In a furtive group we move past the portico to the side of the house. Cousin pushes open the bathroom door. We get a whiff of Dettol and, as we crowd the steps, I immediately see the black wooden box. It is heavy-looking, about a foot high, long and, narrow. Like a coffin for a very thin man. Rosy, turning pale, whispers, 'Someone is dead.'

We are agreed it is a coffin. It looks sinister enough. But the species of the corpse baffles us. Adi and Peter squat to examine the stays.

'It's locked,' says Cousin, who has already examined the locks. Without a word he attempts to lift the box. I give a hand. Rosy shies away. The box is heavy, and in the constricted space we are only able to lift it a foot or so. We try to shake it and tilt it. There is a very slight, heavy and dull movement.

'Definitely a corpse,' declares Peter.

'As if you can tell,' I say.

'What else can there be in a coffin, stupid!' says Adi.

We hear Mother's voice. Footsteps in the bedroom. We exchange alert glances and scamper into the garden to resume our game.

Cousin kicks the misshapen can distractedly, and our pursuit of him is half-hearted and abstracted.

But no one tells us what's in that box.

'A snake? A skeleton? A corpse?'

The servants don't know. The other adults maintain a maddening silence. We are not to be inquisitive: it belongs to Father and it's nobody's business but his.

We wander about with glazed, preoccupied eyes and pinched faces. We waste away.

Electric-aunt has begun to force-feed Cousin. She pinches his nostrils: and when he opens his mouth to breathe, pops in a tablespoon of food. She releases his nostrils only after he swallows the morsel.

Mother begins to sit with us at our small table with the oil-cloth and, beguiling us with fairy-tales, charming us with her voice, slips spoonfuls into our mouths.

Muccho chases Papoo with a broom shouting: 'Hai, my fate! If that accursed slut dies on me, how will I show my face to Jemadar Tota Ram?'

Tota Ram is Papoo's prospective husband . . . An almost mythical figure no one's seen.

Even Mrs Singh has begun to supervise her offspring's feed.

Gandhijee too is off his feed, we hear. There is a slaughter of Muslims in Bihar – he does not want it to spread to Bengal.

It doesn't.

Inspired by Gandhijee, we launch a more determined fast.

We turn sallow, hollow-eyed, pot-bellied. Electric-aunt's frenzied anxiety becomes chronic. Mother turns into a prophetess of doom. 'Mark my words,' she says eerily, 'you'll remain weaklings the rest of your lives!'

Muccho has taken to beating her hollow breasts and crying: 'What face will I show Tota Ram?' And Mrs Singh is moved to wring her hands!

Their strategies change. Cousin is force-fed chocolates and Carry-Home ice-cream by my resourceful aunt. They are easier to force-feed than food. He goes about with stuck nostrils and an open mouth. Mother's fairy-tales turn into horror-stories and every time we form our lips in an 'O' and suck in our horrified breaths, we unwittingly also suck in food. Their American mother is so upset when she sits before Rosy-Peter's hollow cheeks and full plates that she bursts into tears: and Rosy-Peter, astounded by this spectacle of maternal emotion, permit her to pour food into their gaping mouths. Muccho has started sweet-talking and spoon-feeding her stupefied and incredulous daughter.

Col. Bharucha gives us calcium-and-glucose injections.

If they want to get Gandhijee to eat the next time he fasts they should send for Muccho and Electric-aunt and Mother and Col. Bharucha. And even the unformidable Mrs Singh.

As mysteriously as it has appeared, the box disappears.

* * *

While I lead the life of a spoilt little brat with pretensions to diet, forty miles east of Lahore, in a Muslim village, Ranna leads the unspoilt life of a village boy shorn of pretensions. While Ayah shovels spoonfuls of chicken into my mouth as I doodle with Plasticine, Chidda, squatting by the clay hearth, feeds her son scraps of chapatti dipped in buttermilk. All day, baked by the sun, Ranna romps in the fields and plays with dung. And – when I close my eyes and I wish to – I see us squatting beneath the buffalo, our mouths open and eyes closed, as Dost Mohammad directs squirts of milk straight from the udder into our mouths – and I can still taste its foddery sweetness.

It is a little over a year since my visit to Ranna's village. Imam Din, who feels that the tension in the cities will spread to the villages, and is concerned for his numerous kin in Pir Pindo, decides to pay them another visit. When I excitedly protest and exclaim that I *will* go with him, he surprises me by agreeing at once, in a preoccupied way, that I can if Mother consents.

Mother consults Father, her friends, Ayah; and finally gives her hesitant permission – provided we go by train. Trains don't go to Pir Pindo, but we can get off at Thokar, and hire a tonga for the two remaining miles.

We have been in Pir Pindo for two days. On Baisakhi, the day that celebrates the birth of the Sikh religion and of the wheat harvest, we go to Dera Tek Singh. I ride on Imam Din's shoulders, Ranna on his father's – at the head of a procession of nephews, uncles, cousins, brothers, grandsons and great-grandsons. The women and girls – except for me, because I am insistent, and from the city – stay behind as always. The men go to the Baisakhi Fair every year: before Ranna was born – before his great-grandfather was born!

Dost Mohammad is walking in front of us. His head wrapped in a crisp white puggaree, his lungi barely clearing the mud behind his squeaky-new curly-toed shoes, a hookah swinging in his right hand, he looks like a prosperous landlord: and, riding atop his father's shoulders, Ranna imagined that the other villagers looked at them in awe and said among themselves (as Punjabis – even little ones – are want to imagine), 'Wah! There goes that fine-looking zemindar; walking at the head of his ramily with his handsome son on his head!'

It is the thirteenth of April. The wheat has been harvested; the spring rains have spent themselves, and the earth is powdery. From on top of Imam Din's head I see the other groups of villagers converging on Dera Tek Singh – Hindu, Muslim, Sikh – as they raise their own majestic trails of dust.

The festival is already in full swing when we arrive. A group of four fierce-looking Sikhs, their hair tied in turbans and wearing calf-length shirts over tight *churidar* pyjamas, perform the *Ghadka* before drifting waves of admirers. Wielding long swords and staves, clashing them to the beat of drums, the dancers lunge, parry, and twirl to the accompaniment of folk singers extolling the valour of ancient Sikh warriors. The singers shriek, their voices hoarse from the dust, and the effort to be heard above the uproar. There are several such groups.

Dost Mohammad leads us to the heart of the fair: to the rides and food stalls. Frying onion *pakoras*. A bubbling, spicy stew of chickpeas. Pink and yellow clouds of spun-sugar candy. Helium-filled balloons. Our every step deflected by aromas. The family scatters. Ranna and I spend most of our small allowance on food; stuffing ourselves on syrupy *gulab-jamans* and *jalebis*. We scramble for seats on the creaking ferris-wheel, its six wooden trays swaying from six wooden spokes. Each tray is jammed with children, and the stones that are juggled from one tray to another to balance them. Agile attendants scramble among the spokes like acrobats to turn the wheel with the weight of their bodies. Dost Mohammad lifts us into a tray. I don't trust the shallow railing guarding us; and as we orbit, our delighted limbs cramped, our eyes narrowed against the wind, I cling to Ranna. Holding the rickety edge of the swaying tray with one hand, he supports me with the other.

We ride the merry-go-rounds with metal seats and the seesaws. And despite the gaiety and distractions, Ranna senses the chill spread by the presence of strangers: their unexpected faces harsh and cold. A Sikh youth whom Ranna has met a few times, and who has always been kind, pretends not to notice Ranna. Other men, who would normally smile at Ranna, slide their eyes past. Little by little, without his being aware of it, his smile becomes strained and his laughter strident. 'What's the matter?' I ask him. 'Nothing,' he says, surprised.

In the afternoon Dost Mohammad takes us with him to visit Jagjeet Singh. He has his hookah with him so he waits outside the Gurdwara while we go in to summon the *granthi*. Jagjeet Singh is sitting cross-legged in front of an open Granth Sahib. It is resting on an elaborately carved walnut stand. I have never seen a book so large. Surely, if God dwells in books, He dwells in one as large! Later that night Ranna told me that he had wished that the holy Koran their mullah occasionally displayed was larger.

Jagjeet Singh leads us to his charpoy beneath a young banyan already spreading its tender shade over part of the temple wall. He shouts to a Sikh boy washing utensils at a well to fetch tea. Dost Mohammad asks the *granthi*'s permission to light his hookah.

Dost Mohammad has noticed the presence of strangers too. After the boy hands us our tea, and we settle down to blowing into and sipping from the steaming brass mugs, he asks: 'Jagjeet Singh-jee, you have a large number of visitors to the fair this year . . . All those stalwarts in blue turbans with staves and long *kirpans* . . .?'

The *granthi*'s genial face becomes uncommonly solemn. He rubs the puffy skin around his eyes and I notice how old and tired he looks. 'I don't know what to say,' he says, bowing his head. 'They are Akalis . . . The Immortals . . . Maharaja Ranjeet Singh formed the sect when he conquered the Punjab a hundred years ago.' And, though there is no one else that I can see — the Sikh boy is in any case too far away to hear — he moves closer to Dost Mohammad. Lowering his voice, he says: 'I visit the Golden Temple at Amritsar from time to time . . . The Akalis swarm around it like angry hornets in their blue turbans . . . I wish they'd remain there!' He pauses; then, scratching his curly beard and frowning he says: 'They talk of a plan to drive the Muslims out of East Punjab . . . To divide the Punjab. They say they won't live with the Mussulmans if there is to be a Pakistan. Owlish talk like that! You know, city talk. It's madness . . . It can't amount to anything . . . but they've always been like that. Troublemakers. You'll have to look out till this evil blows over.'

I don't know where Imam Din is. I wish to God he were here! It is, almost exactly, what he's been telling the villagers for the past two days. Dost Mohammad appears to have sunk lower into the charpoy. He is quiet for so long that the *granthi* turns to look at him anxiously. I feel Dost Mohammad's thigh twitch against mine. He raises his head slowly, and at last he says, 'We'll look out . . . Don't worry Jagjeet Singh-jee . . . We keep track of things on our *chaudhry*'s radio.'

'May the Ten Gurus help us,' the *granthi* sighs. '*Wah Guru!*'

A short while later, pressing the small of his back, and acting old, Imam Din lumbers up, sighing, '*Ya Allah! Ya Rahman! Ya Rahim!*' Seeing our mugs, he asks for tea. Other men, Sikh and Hindu friends and a few villagers from Pir Pindo, stroll up in twos and threes, and group around the *granthi*'s cot. They talk of everything but the intrusive presence of the Akalis. Before dusk Dost Mohammad's younger brother, Iqbal, joins us. He has bought some land in a village four miles west of Pir Pindo and had moved there. His wife is Ranna's favourite aunt. He loves going to their village to play with his cousins and to be spoilt by his Noni *chachi*. She always has something special for him to eat or wear, he tells me. His uncle tosses a knitted skull-cap into Ranna's lap, saying, 'Here's something from your Noni *chachi*, *pahailwan*!' He calls Ranna *pahailwan*, wrestler. It is an affectionate form of address. Ranna wears the cap at once and his uncle laughs and musses his hair.

'You'd better leave before it gets dark,' Jagjeet Singh says quietly to Dost Mohammad; the other men are talking among themselves. 'There's no telling who's about these days . . . and not all of them are your friends.'

The sun has set, but it is still light enough to see. Ranna was leaning against his father when the *granthi* spoke. The tone of the *granthi*'s voice, the sadness, and the resignation in it, turned the heaviness in Ranna's heart into the first stab of fear. Even in retrospect, these isolated impressions didn't add up to a reliable warning. Pir Pindo was too deep in the hinterland of the Punjab, where distances are measured in footsteps and at the speed of bullock-carts, for larger politics to penetrate.

The Sikhs of Dera Tek Singh escort us halfway to Pir Pindo.

That evening we crowd into the *chaudhry*'s courtyard to listen to his radio. The Congress and Muslim League spokesmen, the announcer says, warn the peasants not to heed mischievous rumours. Even Master Tara Singh, the leader of the Akali Sikhs, tells the peasants – especially the Muslims – to remain where they are. No one will disturb them.

* * *

A few days later, in Lahore, we hear of attacks on Muslim villages near Amritsar and Jullunder. But the accounts are contrary – and the details so brutal and bizarre that they cannot be believed. Imam Din tells Yousaf and Ayah that he is sure it is Akali propaganda, calculated to scare the Muslim peasants. And even if it does scare them, he asks, what good will it do the Akali Sikhs? Where can the scared Muslim villagers go? There are millions of them. Even suppose Dost Mohammad and his family leave Pir Pindo, which they can't . . . how can they abandon their ancestors' graves, every inch of land they own, their other kin? how will they ever hold up their heads again? Suppose every single person in Pir Pindo can hold his own someplace else – even then millions of Mussulmans will be left in East Punjab! Where will they go? No, he says, I have seen for myself; they cannot throw the Mussulmans out!

* * *

A fortnight after the Baisakhi Fair, late in the afternoon, an army truck disgorges a family of villagers outside our gate. Hearing the noise, I run to the kitchen. Imam Din is standing in the open door, staring at a string of men, women and children as they troop up our drive. I recognise some of the faces from Pir Pindo; they are distant kin – not of his immediate family – cousins, nephews or great-grandnephews thrice removed. I wonder how he will accommodate them all in his quarters. Ayah has one look at his face and says, 'Go, greet them. I'll prepare the tea and *parathas*.' Yousaf and Hari, followed by Imam Din, welcome the villagers and lead them to the quarters at the back.

The women and children are distributed among Imam Din and Ayah's quarters. The men will sleep in Hari and Yousaf's. There is a steep fall in the temperature at night, and it is still too cold to sleep out. It is difficult to count them; the babies all look alike. Excluding the tiny babies, there are at least fifteen guests. As the men squat in the courtyard, eating from a common tray as Muslims do, they tell us what happened the night before. They tell the story vividly, in the way of peasants, repeating the dialogue, presenting each detail of expression and movement, transporting us to the village.

Late in the evening three military lorries had lumbered into Pir Pindo gouging deep ruts in the fields and laying waste swathes of sugar cane. They were Gurkha soldiers come to evacuate them.

'Those Mussulmans who want to go to Pakistan had better get into the truck,' a soldier shouted through a megaphone. He was short and stocky like most of his race, and his small Tibetan features appeared frighteningly alien to the villagers. 'We will leave at dawn.'

'What?' the puzzled villagers asked. 'Is Pakistan already there?'

'Who knows,' said the Gurkha. 'I'm telling what I'm told to say.'

The villagers gathered in the open yard of their mosque. They squatted in a tight arc round the mullah and the *chaudhry*. I imagine their faces: obstinate, dazed. And the *chaudhry*'s as, smiling wryly, attempting with sarcasm and wisdom to mask his panic, he says: 'Do you expect us to walk away with our hands and feet? What use will they serve us without our lands? Can you evacuate our land?' he asks cunningly. And the villagers, as if they are at a debate where their *chaudhry*'s wit is scoring points, nod their heads and say: 'Wha! Wha! Well said! What answer do you have to that, *Hawaldar* Sahib?'

They peppered the Gurkhas with formidable questions. 'And what about our harvest?' they asked. 'And the crop we have just sown? And our cattle? Who will evacuate them?'

The soldiers, unimpressed by the sarcasm and indifferent to the villagers' confusion and troubles, shrugged and said, 'We're just here to evacuate you: hands, feet and heads. Nothing else. We've told you why we're here; the rest is up to you.'

'Do you expect us to leave everything we've valued and loved since childhood? The seasons, the angle and colour of the sun rising and setting over our fields are beautiful to us, the shape of our rooms and barns is familiar and dear. You can't expect us to leave just like that!'

The soldiers were weary. They stood up. 'You're not the only village we are to evacuate, you know,' one of them said.

The *chaudhry* remained quiet and the silence settled like a black cloud over their heads, blocking out the stars. At last the *chaudhry* said: 'If we have to go, if it's Allah's will, we will go when the time comes . . . The right time . . .'

'Yes . . . When the time comes, we shall see . . .' said the villagers.

The trucks left at dawn. Five families, who like our visitors were poor relatives and hired hands, with no land in the village, left Pir Pindo, not caring one way or the other where the sun rose or set.

Chapter 13

The times have changed; the world has changed its mind.
The European's mystery is erased.
The secret of his conjuring tricks is known:
The Frankish wizard stands and looks amazed.

(Iqbal)

Already it is winter. I am never warm. I feel coldest in the misty mornings when, holding Hari's calloused hand with my chilblained fingers, I walk on chilblained toes to Mrs Pen's.

The colder it gets the more reserved Hari becomes. I know he is secretly shivering. Cold turns me weepy and Hari secretive and Mrs Pen indulgent. She lets me off early.

At Godmother's I go straight to the kitchen. I am hungry. Slavesister warms some left-over curry and gives me the news that the Inspector General of Police, Mr Rogers, is dead. Murdered. His mutilated body discovered in the gutter.

For a moment I cannot breathe. I feel I might fall.

I know of death: a grandfather died in Karachi and his remains were consigned to the Tower of Silence. Moti's relatives are forever dying . . . But they weren't murdered. Or mutilated. And they weren't people I knew!

'How mutilated?' I ask, shocked.

'Never you mind,' says Slavesister.

I have seen goats slaughtered at the end of the Muslim fast on Eid. I've watched them being disembowelled and, with the other children, lined up to blow into their moist windpipes and inflate their lungs. But those were goats. Not tall men with moustaches and haughty voices and polished shoes and submissive wives . . .

'Will he go to heaven?' I ask breathlessly, clutching at straws.

'To hell!' says Mini Aunty with unexpected viciousness: giving me another shock. 'All Englishmen will burn in hell for the trouble they've started in the Punjab! And let me tell you. The Christian hell is for ever!'

The relish in her voice is ghoulish. I feel so upset at the awful fate awaiting Mr Rogers's mutilated carcass that I collapse on a stool. I cannot face the curry. I recall the police inspector's chilly blue eyes that so narrowly escaped mutilation by Mr Singh's fork and the spit-polished ears of his orphaned children.

I start sobbing. Godmother sits up in bed and calls: 'Hey! What's the matter?'

'Mr Rogers is dead,' I say choking on the words. 'He will burn in hell for ever!'

'Who said that?' demands Godmother, knowing very well who.

'Mini Aunty.' (That's Slavesister's pet-name. I've never heard her real name.)

'I know who's going to roast for ever if they don't watch out!' says Godmother. 'Don't listen to Mini. She has no more sense than a twit!'

'After the Mountbatten plan to tear up the Punjab . . . how can you . . .' mumbles Slavesister, shaking her head at the stove and looking martyred.

'If your mutilated body was discovered in the gutter then you'd know how it feels! Bad-mouthing a dead man!'

Slavesister clicks her tongue and peers into a steaming pan and extra sweetly smiles because she is on the verge of tears. Her pale brown lips, that despite their clear outline and generous width are flat, flatten further and stretch moistly.

'Will they put Mr Rogers into the Tower of Silence?' I ask, coming to the slave's rescue – and attempting to get the derailed conversation back on track.

'He's Christian. They'll bury him,' says Godmother.

It occurs to me that I don't know enough about the Tower. Perhaps I was too young when I first heard of it . . . The shock of Mr Rogers's demise makes me curious about all aspects of dying. 'What is the Tower of Silence?' I ask.

'We call it *Dungarwadi*: not Tower of Silence. The English have given it that funny name . . . Actually it is quite a simple structure: just a big round wall without any roof,' says Godmother.

'So?' I persist.

'So nothing!' interjects the ungrateful slave crankily. 'When little girls ask too many questions their tongues drop off!'

'I wasn't asking you,' I retort, and poking my tongue at her, pointedly turn to Godmother. Godmother never talks down to me like that.

'The dead body is put inside the *Dungarwadi*,' explains Godmother. 'The vultures pick it clean and the sun dries out the bones.'

I must look frightful because Godmother pats the bed and says, 'Come here.'

I sit down, facing her, and drawing me close she says: 'Mind you . . . It's only the body that's dead. Instead of polluting the earth by burying it, or wasting fuel by burning it, we feed God's creatures. The soul's in heaven, chatting with God in any case . . . Or broiling in hell like Mini's will.'

I feel curiously deprived. Here's an architectural wonder created exclusively by the charitable Parsees to feed God's creatures and I haven't even seen it. And I don't want to wait until I'm dead! Mr Rogers's murdered and mutilated body is forgotten and my eyes stop tearing.

'I want to see it,' I demand.

'We don't have one in Lahore,' says Godmother. 'There are too few Parsees: the vultures would starve. But when you go to Karachi or Bombay you can see it from the outside. Only pall-bearers can go in . . . We have a graveyard in Lahore.'

'Thank God!' says Mini Aunty so emphatically that Godmother – who views all emphatic statements from Mini Aunty as direct challenges to her authority – rears up from her pillows demanding: 'Why? What's there to thank God for?'

'I prefer to be buried.'

'Oh? Why?'

'You know why! It gives me the creeps . . . The thought of vultures smacking their beaks over my eyeballs!'

'You'd rather have your eyeballs riddled by maggots? Would you like me to post a sign over your body stating: Maggots only. No vultures allowed?'

'Really, Rodabai! I don't want to talk or think about it. Please forget I ever . . .'

'I don't know what you have against the poor vultures . . . favouring the maggots and worms over them! I'd be ashamed to call myself a Zoroastrian if I were you.'

'Being devoured by vultures has nothing to do with the religion . . . Surely Zarathustra had more important messages to deliver . . .'

'Since when have you become an authority on Zarathustra?' demands Godmother. 'Haven't you heard of Parsee charity? Only last month Sir Eduljee Adenwalla had his leg amputated in Bombay. Sick as he was, he sat in a wheelchair all through the ceremonies and had his leg deposited in the *Dungarwadi*! And what do you think happens when Parsee diabetics' toes are cut off? Do you think they discard them in the waste-basket and deprive the vultures?'

Holding the dripping ladle aloft Mini Aunty covers her ears with her plump and muscular arms and says: 'I don't want to know!'

Even I'm feeling queasy. Godmother looks at me and holds her peace; and Mini Aunty, pressing her advantage, says: 'I must say, you can be ghoulish sometimes. I wish you wouldn't talk such nonsense before the child . . .'

'What do you mean, nonsense?' challenges Godmother. 'Who was the one talking about eternal roastings in hell?'

'You know what I mean, Roda . . . Now don't . . .'

'Who's Roda? Who's permitted you to call me Roda? Since when have you become my elder sister?'

'You know I didn't mean it that way.'

'Which way did you mean it, then?'

Slavesister, almost on tiptoe, hovers quietly over the stove. Her wet smile is flattening. Her eyes do not dare to shift from the bubbling contents of the pan she is stirring.

'Some people are getting too big for their boots . . . Some people are becoming quite airy-fairy!'

Slavesister mumbles: 'Only my bunion's getting too big . . . I'll cut it off and mail it to the *Dungarwadi*.'

'What?' queries Godmother. 'What is your Highness mumbling?'

'Oh! All right, all right! Carry on . . . you must have everything your way, Rodabai . . . filling the child's mind with such notions . . . mumble, mumble.'

'Don't you all right, all right me! I'll have your carcass flown straight to the vultures!'

Slavesister doesn't answer. Only shakes her head and

mutters. She will not answer back now. She too has learned from experience.

'Small mouth, big talk!' grumbles Godmother as if to herself, but loud enough for Slavesister to hear. 'Little minds should not attempt to weigh in big fish!'

Still poised for attack, eyes bright, Godmother waits to see if Slavesister will respond.

But Slavesister's insurgence has been effectively squashed. She maintains a strategic silence, suppressing even her mumbles.

Godmother makes a magically triumphant face. She holds her pointy fingers in a 'V' for victory, winks at me and leans back on her concrete pillows.

I go into the kitchen to finish my curry but I cannot eat. Mr Rogers's English toes and kidneys float before my disembodied eyeballs . . .

And the vision of a torn Punjab. Will the earth bleed? And what about the sundered rivers? Won't their water drain into the jagged cracks? Not satisfied by breaking India, they now want to tear the Punjab.

Yousaf comes to fetch me. The sun has had time to warm the afternoon. It is balmy. 'Let's go through the Lawrence Gardens,' I urge, and Yousaf, unable to deny anyone, makes the detour through the gardens. We stop along a trimmed gardenia hedge to look at the sunken rose-garden; and we clamber up the slopes of artificial hills and run down bougainvillaea valleys ablaze with winter flowers. Casting long shadows we take a path leading to where Yousaf has parked his cycle.

Our shadow glides over a Brahmin Pandit. Sitting cross-legged on the grass he is eating out of a leaf-bowl. He looks at Yousaf – and at me – and his face expresses the full range of terror, passion and pain expected of a violated virgin. Our shadow has violated his virtue. The Pandit cringes. His features shrivel into arid little shrimps and his body retracts. The vermillion caste-mark on his forehead glows like an accusing eye. He looks at his food as if it is infected with maggots. Squeamishly picking up the leaf, he tips its contents behind a bush and throws away the leaf.

I am a diseased maggot. I look at Yousaf. His face is drained of joy, bleak, furious. I know he too feels himself composed of shit, crawling with maggots.

Now I know surely. One man's religion is another man's poison.

I experience this feeling of utter degradation, of being an untouchable excrescence, an outcast again, years later when I hold out my hand to a Parsee priest at a wedding and he, thinking I am menstruating beneath my façade of diamonds and a sequinned sari, cringes.

* * *

Late that evening there is a familiar pattern of sound.

Again they're after Hari's dhoti. But instead of the light, quick patter of bare feet there is the harsh scrape and drag of leather on frozen earth.

It doesn't seem quite right to toy with a man's dhoti when it is so cold. It is a summer sport.

Someone shouts, 'Get him before he gets into his quarters!' I hear Imam Din's bullying, bluff *barruk* as he bellows: *'Aha-hurrr! A-vaaaaaaay!'* And, closer to his quarry, Yousaf's provocative bubbly *'Vo-vo-vo-vo-vo-vo,'* as running he taps his mouth in quick succession. Curses! Hair all over my body creeps aslant as I hear Hari's alarmed cry.

Snatching me up and straddling me on her hip Ayah flings open the bathroom door and runs out. I am struck by the cold: and the approach of night casts uneasy shadows over a scene I have witnessed only in daylight. Something else too is incongruous. The winter shawl wrapped around Hari.

Yousaf is twirling his plume of hair and tugging at it as if he's trying to lift him. I feel a great swell of fear for Hari: and a surge of loathing for his *bodhi*. Why must he persist in growing it? and flaunt his Hinduism? and invite ridicule?

And that preposterous and obscene dhoti! worn like a diaper between his stringy legs – just begging to be taken off!

My dread assuming a violent and cruel shape, I tear away from Ayah and fling myself on the human tangle and fight to claw at Hari's dhoti.

Someone pulls off his shawl and it is trampled underfoot. Hands stretch and pull his unravelling mauve lady's cardigan (Mother's hand-me-down) and rip off his shirt. His dhoti is hanging in ragged edges and, suddenly, it's off!

Like a withered tree frozen in a winter landscape Hari stands isolated in the bleak centre of our violence: prickly with goose-bumps, sooty genitals on display.

With heavy, old-man's movements, Imam Din wrenches the shawl from under our feet and throws it at the gardener: and the tattered rag that was his dhoti. 'Cover up, you shameless bugger,' he says, attempting his usual bantering manner: but there is a gruff uncontrollable edge to his voice. He is not at ease with cruelty.

I look back. The Shankars stand on their veranda like fat shadows. Ayah has turned her face away. I run to her. I dig my face in her sari and stretch up my hands. Ayah tries to lift me but her fluid strength is gone. Her grip is weak. I hug her fiercely. Her heart beneath her springy breasts is fluttering like Ice-candy-man's nervous sparrows. She raises frightened eyes from my face and, turning to follow her gaze, I see an obscured shape standing by the compound wall. Stirred by a breeze, the shadows cast by a eucalyptus tree shift and splinter, and define the still figure of a man.

The man moves out of the darkness, and as he approaches I am relieved. It is only Ice-candy-man.

Chapter 14

Ayah is seeing more of Masseur. So, so am I. When Ayah's work is done, and she stretches out in the afternoon sun, massaging butter into her calves and smooth shins, she hums a new tune and sighs: *'Siski hawa ne lee: Har pati Kanp oothi*. The breeze sucked in his breath . . . The leaves trembled, breathless.' It's Masseur's song. He sings it in a rumbling, soulful baritone: and he sings often.

I am seeing more of Lahore, too. Ayah and I roam on foot and by bus: from Emperor Jehangir's tomb at Shahdara to Shahjehan's Shalimar Gardens. From the outskirts of the slaughter house to the banks of the Ravi in low flood. We amble through the tall pampas grass – purposefully purposeless – and sniffing the attar of roses, happen upon Masseur: his creamy bosky-silk shirt, his strong forearms and broad ankles stretched out on a dhurrie on the grey sand.

His cruet set of oils beside him, Masseur turns, making room for Ayah, and his eyes, full of honey, shower her with his maddening dreams. They lie, side by side, a stalk of grass stuck at a thoughtful angle between Masseur's teeth as he traces with a skilful finger Ayah's parted lips.

I get up and Masseur says, 'Lenny baby, don't go far.' His voice is gravelly with desire and it makes something happen in my stomach: as when Sharbat Khan, radiant with love, ogles Ayah.

I know Ayah is beyond speech – her will given over to a maestro's virtuosity. Masseur's consummate arm circles Ayah . . .

Caressing me through the pampas the breeze moans with love – and brings to me Masseur's song:

> 'Spring bloomed in moonlit wildernesses –
> Heady with sap the flowers swayed –
> And a rose, bubbling,
> Dancing in the breeze,
> Attracted a bumble-bee –

Floating, frolicking, the bumble-bee came –
Strutting among the flowers, strumming love.'

And so, the bumble-bee courts the rose. I listen to the words unfolding the rose's tragic story and wait intently for the change in Masseur's voice.

'And then one day [he sings in a very low and urgent key]
When all was hushed –
No stars, and in the sky no moon –
The bee stole the rose's youth –'

There it is. The fearful and tragic climax! The rose awakens, weeps, shrivels, swoons! And nature, in all its marvellous tenderness, commiserates:

'The breeze sucked in his breath –
The leaves trembled breathless –
Moist-eyed the stars winked out –

I wait a while, watching the shallow boats drift sluggishly on the shallow Ravi. The men in them, still as the dead, remain comatose as the boats, bumping along the shoals, right themselves and float slowly down stream.

* * *

We hear Masseur's song calling from the fountains, cypresses and marble terraces of the Shalimar Gardens. We hear him singing from the giddy heights of the minarets looming above Emperor Jehangir's tomb – directing his voice like a shower of petals to summon Ayah.

Ayah comes. And with her, like a lame limpet, come I.

We find Masseur waiting for us on the artificial hill behind the zoo lion's cage and by the chattering monkeys and among the peacocks. The heavy pleats of his Multani-silk lungi fall in slender folds to his ankles as leaning against the paling he waits for Ayah. And when she comes, the peacocks spread their tail feathers. And Masseur's movements unfold the rich pleats in his checked lungi.

Where Masseur is, Ayah is. And where Ayah is, is Ice-candy-man.

I sense his presence.

While Masseur's voice lures Ayah to the dizzy eminence of one minaret, it compels Ice-candy-man to climb the winding stairs to the other minaret. On the river bank I sense his stealthy presence in the tall clumps of pampas grass. He lurks in the dense shade of mangoes in the Shalimar Gardens and in the fearsome smells skirting the slaughter house . . . He prowls on the other side of the artificial hill behind the zoo lion's cage, and conceals himself behind the peacocks when they spread their tail feathers and open their turquoise eyes: he has as many eyes, and they follow us.

In the evenings he visits Ayah and squatting like an ungainly bird in his cotton shawl astounds her with his knowledge of our wanderings. And when his driven toes are too weary to perform their amazing seduction, his glib tongue takes over. Ayah, wide-eyed, wrapped in the silken web of his gossip, draws closer . . .

Ice-candy-man has an inexhaustible fund of gossip.

'Our lion tamer got rid of his tenants at last!' he announces one sultry afternoon in Electric-aunt's garden. He has followed us there. My aunt is busy inside filing her accounts in neat figures beneath the credit and debit columns. We are sitting outside so as not to disturb her while we wait for Cousin to return from school.

'How did he get rid of them? Did he win a case?' asks Ayah. 'Did he get the police to throw them out?'

'If you await court decisions, you wait for ever,' says Ice-candy-man with such contempt and authority that my faith in the judicial system is for ever shattered.

'I told Sher Singh to take matters in hand,' he continues. 'I told him: Why go through all the rigmarole of courts and notices when we have time-honoured remedies at hand?'

Ayah and I lean closer. Ayah is positively within striking distance. Ice-candy-man's toe twitches, but it is a weary, footsore little twitch and its impulse easily checked. I merely glance its way sternly and the twitch ceases.

'At first Sher Singh hemmed and hedged,' says Ice-candy-man. 'Then he said: "You're a Mussulman . . . The tenants are Mussulmans . . . Why should you help a Sikh?"'

His raconteur's gift places us in Sher Singh's shoes and we look at him with the same questions in our eyes.

'"Oye, you donkey," I told him. "So what if you're a Sikh? I'm first a friend to my friends . . . And an enemy to their enemies . . . And then a Mussulman! God and the politicians have enough servers. So, I serve my friends."'

Now he has us in his shoes. Ayah has an animated look on her rapt face. 'Tell us . . . what happened then?' she asks breathlessly.

'Lenny child, be a good girl,' says Ice-candy-man, snapping his fingers to flick the ash from his cigarette. 'Ask the cook to make me a strong cup of tea. Go: *putch-putch*.' (Kissing noises used to wheedle children dispatched on trivial errands.)

'No,' I say. 'I'm not going anywhere: I also want to listen to you.'

He glances at Ayah. Since Ayah appears content to have me stay, he says: 'Well, Sher Singh, his brothers Prem and Pratab, and one or two cousins – all strapping fellows . . . and I. Armed with hockey-sticks we went to their tenants' house while the men were at work. We made a bit of *hulla-goolla* outside the building. Waved our hockey-sticks and shouted: "Come to your windows, pretty ladies: don't hide. We have something to show you."'

Ayah and I, our eyes round, our lips parted, scarcely breathe.

'We attracted a crowd. There were quite a few dazzling eyes at some of the other windows in the building . . . But the ladies for whose benefit we were staging the show were more bashful.

'When I was sure we had their attention – and they were peeping at us through their reed blinds – as one man we opened our lungis! In such a way as to shield our rears: and in front our dangling dingdongs!'

Taking my cue from Ayah, I too wear a faintly scandalised, faintly amused expression.

'We exposed ourselves so that only they could see us. The crowd behind us guessed what was happening. There were one or two curses – one or two coarse remarks – but no interference. We made a few suggestive gestures . . . you know . . . It lasted only five minutes . . .

'But what a *hulla-goolla*! The women screamed and cursed . . . You'd have thought we'd raped them!

'We got wind the police were coming. By the time they appeared we'd wrapped our lungis back on and cleared out!' Ice-candy-man, half standing, moves his body and his arms like a magician conjuring images.

'I hear the men swore vengeance and what not. But this morning they cleared out!'

The triumph on his face is infectious: he sees it reflected in ours, and his teeth show increasingly white as his lips stretch and stretch into a smile in his narrow face. He crushes the stub of his cigarette into the grass – and I hear the school bus squeak to a halt as it deposits my cousin outside the gate.

* * *

Next evening when Ice-candy-man comes to our house I notice his toe is more vigorous. It is rested. We didn't wander far today. Only went to Godmother's.

Masseur massages Oldhusband every Thursday. Ayah was content to sit on her haunches and watch as, before our very eyes, beneath his supple fingers, Oldhusband acquired a youthful glow!

Later, when Electric-aunt and Cousin also came to Godmother's, Cousin informed me that Ice-candy-man's bicycle was parked outside Godmother's gate. In fact Cousin had purchased and devoured a raspberry popsicle. He showed me the inside of his raspberry-stained lower lip and drew my attention to a pale red stain on his khaki shorts.

Cousin is like that. Even when I believe him, he shows me, shows me, shows me things . . .

'Did you hear about Bhagwandas the tailor?' Ice-candy-man asks, settling down cross-legged on a mat on the servants' veranda outside Ayah's quarters. Ayah has just washed her long hair and, having brought it forward over her shoulder, is running a combative wooden comb through the wet tangles.

'Lenny baby,' Ice-candy-man tells me, almost burying his head in his cupped hands as he lights one of his smelly cigarettes, 'get me a glass of water. Tell Imam Din it's for me and he will put a bit of ice in it.'

'No,' I say, leaning firmly on his toe. 'I'm not going anywhere. I also want to know about the tailor. Tell me!'

'Let her be,' says Ayah, who is as curious as me. Bhagwandas is her tailor too.

'Well, he ran off with the Mission padre's wife!' Ice-candy-man pushes his pill-box cap forward rakishly and looks at Ayah out of the corners of his gleaming light brown eyes.

'*Hai!* No!' says Ayah, looking appropriately grave and scandalised and for a moment permitting the comb to cease its struggle with the tangles.

'Yes,' says Ice-candy-man, grinning into our avid faces. 'You know how it is when you women visit tailors . . . This is loose, that is tight. Alter this, alter that. The tailor's fingers touch here, smooth the cloth there . . .' Ice-candy-man's hand strays to Ayah's knees, and as he raises it to her shoulder his fingers brush her bosom. Ayah's eyes flash a warning and Ice-candy-man's serpentine arm floats away. He shifts his eyes from us and stares ingenuously into the fading day.

'The padre, poor fellow, still doesn't know what happened,' he says dreamily. 'He's a man of God. You know how they are. Simple. But the tailors are a sly lot. Never trust them, Lenny baby, with their measuring tapes, needles and threads – and smoothing fingers.'

'Where's your wife?' I ask. I've never thought to ask him before.

'In the village, with her mother.'

'What if she runs away?'

'She won't. They have no tailors in the village. No masseurs either . . . with their cunning fingers taking liberties!'

Ayah looks startled. So do I. This is the first time he has openly expressed his jealousy of Masseur. Although we have been conscious of the undercurrent of hostility between them, neither Ayah nor I realised its development into the acrimony Ice-candy-man's bitter voice has just expressed.

It changes the complexion of the evening. I become aware of the dusk that has gathered in shadows on the dung-plastered veranda and is thick behind the open door of Ayah's quarters. The earth floor, compressed and sprinkled with water and swept clean, and her small string-cot, large tin trunk, and pictures and statues of gods and goddesses in the niches are all obscured.

'Why don't you ever bring your wife here? I want to see her. Please bring her here,' I plead, fretting him, trying to talk away my misgivings.

And, having at the same time to restrain his refreshed toes, I sit on them.

'What'll she do here, Lenny baby?' says Ice-candy-man, once again far-away-eyed and in control. 'She's used to village ways, and to her folk there . . . She doesn't like to stay in the city . . . so I leave her there.'

'Is she your only wife?' I ask.

But Ayah is restive and clamps my mouth shut with her hand. 'Stop asking so many questions,' she says with unaccustomed irritability. 'Men don't like so much talk about their womenfolk.'

'Oh, I don't mind. Let her be,' says Ice-candy-man, pushing his cap back now that the impressive bit of gossip has been related. He musses my hair and, opening his thermos, reaches for a popsicle.

'Raspberry!' I demand, hoping there is still some raspberry left.

There is. Relinquishing my seat on his toes I stand up.

'Oof!' says Ayah suddenly, her comb caught painfully in her tangled hair.

Chapter 15

The periphery of my world extends to Mozang and Temple Road. Every Sunday we accompany the Shankars to the Daulatrams' two-storey brick house for an evening of classical Indian music. The singers all make faces and strange noises but Israr Ahmed is my favourite singing boy. We sit on carpets and the singers on white sheets facing us. The accompanists – a harmonium player and a tabla-drum player – wiggle their toes and chew betel-nut.

Israr Ahmed, a nondescript, unassuming, middle-aged clerk, is transformed into a dervish when he takes his turn on the white sheet. He flings his arms about, opens wide his mouth, displays *paan*-stained molars and makes noises that would turn the zoo animals green with envy. He gargles up and down the scale! He roars! He dislocates his jaw and hoists his mouth to one side – and then to the other.

Adi, Cousin and I cannot contain ourselves. In our fervour to acquire classical culture we copy his movements, contort our faces, twist our necks and are slapped and shushed for our pains.

* * *

Processions are becoming a part of the street scene. A youth holds aloft a stick with a green rag, bellows a slogan, and a group of rowdy urchins rally to the cry.

Adi and I slip past the attention of our vigilants and join the tiny tinpot processions that are spawned on Warris Road. We shout ourselves hoarse crying, *'Jai Hind! Jai Hind!'* or *'Pakistan Zindabad!'* depending on the whim or the allegiance of the principal crier. Within half an hour the processions disintegrate. The ragged flag holders, their trousers grey with washing, their singlets peppered with holes and grease spots, make a few desultory attempts to rally the stragglers. Then, lowering the banner, which reverts to becoming a lowly rag on a twig, the rabble-rouser usually climbs a mulberry tree for its fruit and we sneak back unnoticed.

* * *

We are gradually withdrawing from the shadow cast by the Queen's statue in the park. As the British prepare to leave we meet less and less at the park and more often at the wrestler's restaurant.

Adi and I climb the rickety wooden steps behind Ayah and pick our way between the empty tables to our crowd. It is still a bit early for the regular diners. Our friends are sitting at the back, on either side of two narrow tables joined together. They are arguing. Everybody appears to be quarrelling these days.

The wrestler shouts to Chotay, a skinny twelve-year-old in a skimpy lungi, to place wooden stools at either end of the tables. Adi and I sit on the stools, at the head and tail of the table, and Ayah sits down next to Masseur on the bench opposite the butcher.

Chotay hangs around, waiting for our order, and Ayah, with princessly authority and indulgence, orders three plates of vegetable biryani. 'See that it's hot,' she says, adopting Mother's tone with servants, 'or I'll see to you!'

Like all urchins apprenticed to such establishments

Chotay is bullied, teased and slapped around.

Continuing the conversation – and the feeding – our arrival has interrupted, Masseur says: 'If the Punjab is divided, Lahore is bound to go to Pakistan. There is a Muslim majority here . . .'

'Lahore will stay in India!' says the Government House gardener, cutting him short. He is sitting next to the butcher. 'There is too much Hindu money here,' he says in his quiet, seasoned way. 'They own most of the property and business in the city and . . .'

'But there are too many Mussulmans!' insists Masseur.

'So what? People don't matter . . . Money does!'

We look his way, startled by the unexpected cynicism, as he tucks a gob of rice into his mouth.

'It won't be hard to put the fear of God up the rich Hindus' dhoties – money or no money,' says the butcher in a coarse, harsh voice.

'It just might be the other way round,' murmurs the gardener.

In the tense silence that follows this exchange, only Adi and I look at them. The rest avert their eyes and appear to be preoccupied with their food.

Chotay appears with our plates, holding all three in one hand, and places them before us with a noisy clatter.

The butcher raps his plate on the table to indicate he wants another helping. The boy picks up the empty plate and the butcher, turning sharply, slaps his shaven head. It is a tempting target.

'Oye! You gone stupid?' says the butcher belligerently. 'D'you know what I want?'

'The same?' Chotay says, wincing. His bared, narrow chest makes him look frighteningly vulnerable.

The butcher spanks his head again. 'Did I ask for the same?'

Chotay stares at him foolishly.

'Bring me chops!' says Butcher as if he's just taught Chotay an invaluable lesson.

'You heard him, oye!' says the wrestler, also lightly

spanking the boy's head. 'What're you staring at our faces for? Hurry, or I'll break your bottom!' He exchanges a concurring glance with the butcher, showing his appreciation of the pains his friend has taken to smarten up the boy.

Chotay, ducking out of range of their hands, scampers away, dutifully saying, 'Be right back, *janab*!'

'What d'you mean, put the fear of God up the rich Hindus' dhoties?' says Ice-candy-man, turning his suspiciously innocent, olive-oil eyes on the butcher.

'You know what I mean, *yaar*,' says the butcher impassively.

I close my eyes. I can't bear to open them: they will open on a suddenly changed world. I try to shut out the voices.

All at once the Sikh zoo attendant shouts, 'And what about us?' so loudly that my eyes pop open. 'The Sikhs hold more farm land in the Punjab than the Hindus and Muslims put together!'

'They don't!' says the butcher flatly.

'Are you calling me a liar?' Sher Singh's voice cracks with excitement and his agitated fingers disperse bits of rice in his beard.

'The only way to keep your holdings, Sardarjee, is to arrive at a settlement with the Muslim League,' intervenes Masseur, smoothing the quarrel with his voice. He dusts the rice from Sher Singh's beard. 'If you don't, the Punjab will be divided . . . That will mean trouble for us all.'

'Big trouble,' concurs Sher Singh portentously: as if he has secret knowledge he could disclose.

'You're what? Only four million or so?' asks Masseur. 'And if half of you are in Pakistan, and the other half in India, you won't have much clout in either place.'

'You don't worry about our clout!' says Sher Singh offensively. 'We can look out for ourselves . . . You'll feel our clout all right when the time comes!'

'The British have advised Jinnah to keep clear of you bastards!' says the butcher just as offensively. 'The *Angrez* call you a "bloody nuisance"!'

'We don't want to have anything to do with you bastards either,' roars the puny Sikh, sounding more and more like the tiger in his name.

'History will repeat itself,' says the restaurant-owning wrestler phlegmatically. He slowly lowers his arm, and stretches it across the table. 'Once the line of division is drawn in the Punjab, all Muslims to the east of it will have their balls cut off!'

His quietly spoken words have the impact of an explosion. And, as in the aftermath of a blast, the silence excludes all extraneous sound . . . The shrill voices of the children in the gully, the noise of traffic from the Chungi. Only Ice-candy-man's voice as if from a distance, saying: 'Oye! You gone crazy? you son-of-an-owl!'

And the wrestler, quietly saying, 'My cousin's a constable in Amritsar District . . . he says the Sikhs are preparing to drive the Muslims out of East Punjab – to the other side of the Ravi.'

'But those are Muslim majority districts,' says Masseur.

'The Sikhs are the fighting arm of the Hindus and they're prepared to use it . . . like when they butchered every single Mussulman from Ambala to Amritsar a century ago, during the Mogul empire's break up.'

'Behold! The savage arm of the murderous Sikh!' says Masseur, holding aloft and dangling Sher Singh's puny arm; his fingertips showering curried rice. Masseur places his arm around the Sikh and hugs him affectionately.

'It's fit only for bangles now!' says the butcher contemptuously. He tosses the gnawed skeleton of a lamb chop over his shoulder. 'The Sikhs have become soft living off the fat of the land!'

'Don't fool yourself . . . They have a tradition of violence,' says the wrestler. 'Haven't you seen the portraits of the gurus holding the dripping heads of butchered enemies?'

'Shut up, *yaar*,' says Masseur, his face unusually dark with a rush of blood. 'It's all *buckwas*! The holy Koran lies next to the Granth Sahib in the Golden Temple. The shift

Guru Nanaik wore carried inscriptions from the Koran . . . In fact, the Sikh faith came about to create Hindu-Muslim harmony!' He looks around the table to see how we are taking his impassioned plea for reason. 'In any case,' he continues more mildly, 'there are no differences among friends . . . We will stand by each other.'

'Of course, *yaar*,' agrees the off-duty sepoy. (I can't tell what faith he belongs to.) 'Who are we to quarrel? Let the big shots fight it out!'

'You're right, brother,' says the Government House gardener. 'The politicians will say anything in times like these to suit their purpose . . . But the English *Sarkar* won't let anything like that happen . . . You saw how they clamped down on the Independence movement.'

There is an instant hum of agreement and disagreement.

'The English are not to be relied on, *yaar*,' interposes Ice-candy-man, pushing his empty plate away to show he's done with eating. 'They're too busy packing off with their loot to care what happens . . . But that Nehru, he's a sly one . . . He's got Mountbatten eating out of his one hand and the English's wife out of his other what-not . . . He's the one to watch!'

He should know. He's working in the Government House as a *chaprassi* these days. And given his inquisitive nature and wily ways –

'Don't underestimate Jinnah,' says the off-duty sepoy. 'He will stick within his rights, no matter whom Nehru feeds! He's a first-rate lawyer and he knows how to attack the British with their own laws!'

'Jinnah or no Jinnah! Sikh or no Sikh! Right law, wrong law, Nehru will walk off with the lion's share . . . And what's more, come out of it smelling like the Queen-of-the-*Kotha*!' Ice-candy-man speaks with an assurance that is prophetic.

They go on and on. I don't want to hear them. I slip into Ayah's lap and, closing my eyes, hide my face between her breasts. I try not to inhale, but I must; the charged air about our table distils poisonous insights. Blue envy: green avidity:

the grey and black stirrings of predators and the incipient distillation of fear in their prey. A slimy grey-green balloon forms behind my shut lids. There is something so dangerous about the tangible colours the passions around me have assumed that I blink open my eyes and sit up.

Some instinct makes me count us. We are thirteen.

I am not too young to know it is an uneasy number. I count us again, using my fingers like Mother does. There is Ice-candy-man, Masseur, Government House Gardener, Butcher, Sher Singh, the sepoy from the barracks, the wrestler, Yousaf and Hari who've been listening quietly, the Falletis Hotel cook, me, Adi and Ayah.

* * *

'Why is thirteen an unlucky number?' I ask Mother.

'Who told you it's unlucky? There are no unlucky numbers, dear – only lucky numbers.'

I ask Godmother.

'People say it's unlucky – I don't know. Ask Mini: she should know.'

'It's unlucky,' says Mini Aunty, promptly and definitely and nodding her head. 'I know. I was born on the thirteenth of March.'

I ask Cousin.

'Something to do with Jesus Christ . . . He had a farewell party, you know. Something to do with that.'

I ask Mrs Pen. She tells me that the farewell party was called the Last Supper. She tells me about Christ, the twelve apostles and about Judas's betrayal and Christ's crucifixion.

From the distance, drawing stridently nearer, clamours the 'tee-too, tee-too' of the dread siren. The sound shrivels time – the way Hari's genitals shrivelled. I am back in the factory filled with children lying on their backs on beds. Godmother sits by me, looking composed, as competent soldiers move about hammering nails into our hands and feet. The room fills with the hopeless moans of crucified children –

and with their collective sighs as they breathe in and out, in and out, with an eerie horrifying insistence.

I awaken to a distant, pulsating sound. The chant of slogans carried to me on gusts of wind.

Chapter 16

We leave early. Master Tara Singh is expected to make an appearance outside the Assembly Chambers, behind the Queen's Garden. Except for Muccho and her children, who remain behind in the servants' quarters, our house is deserted. Mother and Father left before us with the Singhs and the Phailbuses.

There is no room for us in the Queen's Garden. Seen from the roof of the Falettis Hotel – the Falettis Hotel cook has secured a place for us – it appears that the park has sprouted a dense crop of humans. They overflow its boundaries on to the roads and sit on trees and on top of walls. The crowd is thickest on the concrete between the back of the garden and the Assembly Chambers. Policemen are holding the throng from surging up the wide, imperious flight of pink steps.

There is a stir of excitement, an increase in the volume of noise, and Master Tara Singh, in a white *kurta*, his silken beard flowing creamily down his face, appears on the top steps of the Assembly Chambers. I see him clearly. His chest is diagonally swathed in a blue band from which dangles a decoratively sheathed *kirpan*. The folds of his loose white pyjamas fall above his ankles; a leather band round his waist holds a long religious dagger.

He gets down to business right away. Holding a long sword in each hand, the curved steel reflecting the sun's glare as he clashes the swords above his head, the Sikh soldier-saint shouts: 'We will see how the Muslim swine get Pakistan! We will fight to the last man! We will show them *who* will leave Lahore! *Raj karega Khalsa, aki rahi na koi!'*

The Sikhs milling about in a huge blob in front wildly wave and clash their swords, *kirpans* and hockey-sticks, and punctuate his shrieks with roars: '*Pakistan Murdabad!* Death to Pakistan! *Sat Siri Akaal! Bolay se nihaal!'*

And the Muslims shouting: 'So? We'll play Holi-with-their-blood! Ho-o-o-li with their blo-o-o-d!'

And the Holi festival of the Hindus and Sikhs coming up in a few days, when everybody splatters everybody with coloured water and coloured powders and laughs and romps . . .

And instead the skyline of the old walled city ablaze, and people splattering each other with blood! And Ice-candy-man hustling Ayah and me up the steps of his tenement in Bhatti Gate, saying: 'Wait till you see Shalmi burn!' And pointing out landmarks from the crowded tenement roof:

'That's Delhi Gate . . . There's Lahori Gate . . . There's Mochi Darwaza . . .'

'Isn't that where Masseur lives?' Ayah asks.

'Yes, that's where your masseur stays,' says Ice-candy-man, unable to mask his ire. 'It's a Muslim *mohalla*,' he continues in an effort to dispel his rancour. 'We've got wind that the Hindus of Shalmi plan to attack it – push the Muslims across the river. The Hindus and Sikhs think they'll take Lahore. But we'll surprise them yet!'

'*Hai Ram!* That's Gowâlmandi isn't it?' says Ayah. '*Hai Ram* . . . How it burns!'

And our eyes wide and sombre.

Suddenly a posse of sweating English tommies, wearing only khaki shorts, socks and boots, runs up in the lane directly below us. And on their heels a mob of Sikhs, their wild long hair and beards rampant, large fevered eyes glowing in fanatic faces, pours into the narrow lane roaring slogans, holding curved swords, shoving up a manic wave of violence that sets Ayah to trembling as she holds me tight. A naked child, twitching on a spear struck between her shoulders, is waved like a flag: her screamless mouth agape she is staring straight up at me. A crimson fury blinds me. I want to dive into the bestial creature clawing entrails, plucking eyes, tearing limbs, gouging hearts, smashing brains: but the creature has too many stony hearts, too many sightless eyes, deaf ears, mindless brains and tons of entwined entrails . . .

And then a slowly advancing mob of Muslim *goondas*: packed so tight that we can see only the top of their heads. Roaring: *'Allah-o-Akbar! Yaaaa Ali!'* and *'Pakistan Zindabad!'*

The terror the mob generates is palpable – like an evil, paralysing spell. The terrible procession, like a sluggish river, flows beneath us. Every short while a group of men, like a whirling eddy, stalls – and like the widening circles of a treacherous eddy dissolving in the mainstream, leaves in its centre the pulpy red flotsam of a mangled body.

The processionists are milling about two jeeps pushed back to back. They come to a halt: the men in front of the procession pulling ahead and the mob behind banked close up. There is a quickening in the activity about the jeeps. My eyes focus on an emaciated Banya wearing a white Gandhi cap. The man is knocked down. His lips are drawn away from rotting, *paan*-stained teeth in a scream. The men move back and in the small clearing I see his legs sticking out of his dhoti right up to the groin – each thin, brown leg tied to a jeep. Ayah, holding her hands over my eyes, collapses on the floor pulling me down with her. There is the roar of a hundred throats: *'Allah-o-Akbar!'* and beneath it the growl of revving motors. Ice-candy-man stoops over us, looking concerned: the muscles in his face tight with a strange exhilaration I never again want to see.

Ramzana the butcher and Masseur join us. Ayah sits sheathing her head and form with her sari; cowering and lumpish against the wall.

'You shouldn't have brought them here, *yaar*,' says Masseur. 'They shouldn't see such things . . . Besides, it's dangerous.'

'We are with her. She's safe,' says Ice-candy-man laconically. He adds: 'I only wanted her to see the fires.'

'I want to go home,' I whimper.

'As soon as things quiet down I'll take you home,' says Masseur reassuringly. He picks me up and swings me until I smile.

Ice-candy-man offers me another popsicle. I've eaten so many already that I feel sick. He gathers the empty tin plates strewn about us. The uneaten chapatti on Ayah's plate is stiff: the vegetable curry cold. Ice-candy-man removes the plate.

'Look!' shouts the butcher. 'Shalmi's started to burn!'

We rush to the parapet. Tongues of pink flame lick two or three brick buildings in the bazaar. The flames are hard to spot: no match for the massive growth of brick and cement spreading on either side of the street.

'Just watch. You'll see a *tamasha*!' says Ice-candy-man. 'Wait till the fire gets to their stock of arsenal.'

As if on cue a deafening series of explosions shakes the floor beneath our feet. Ayah stands up hastily and joins us at the parapet. The walls and balconies of a two-storey building in the centre of the bazaar bulge and bulge. Then the bricks start slowly tumbling, and the dark slab of roof caves into the exploding furnace . . .

People are pouring into the Shalmi lanes from their houses and shops. We hear the incredibly prompt clamour of a fire brigade. The clanking fire engine, crowded with ladders, hose and helmeted men, manoeuvres itself through the street, the truck with the water tank following.

The men exchange surprised looks. Ice-candy-man says: 'Where did those mother-fuckers spring from?'

The firemen scamper busily, attaching hoses, shoving people back. Riding on the trucks they expertly direct their powerful hoses at the rest of the buildings on either side of the road.

As the fire brigade drives away, the entire rows of

buildings on both sides of the street ignite in an incredible conflagration. Although we are several furlongs away a scorching blast from a hot wind makes our clothes flap as if in a storm. I look at Ice-candy-man. The astonishment on his features is replaced by a huge grin. His face, reflecting the fire, is lit up. 'The fucking bastards!' he says, laughing aloud, spit flying from his mouth. 'The fucking bastards! They sprayed the buildings with petrol! They must be Muslim.'

The Hindus of Shalmi must have piled a lot of dynamite in their houses and shops to drive the Muslims from Mochi Gate. The entire Shalmi, an area covering about four square miles, flashes in explosions. The men and women on our roof are slapping each other's hands, laughing, hugging one another.

I stare at the *tamasha*, mesmerised by the spectacle. It is like a gigantic fireworks display in which stiff figures looking like spread-eagled stick-dolls leap into the air, black against the magenta furnace. Trapped by the spreading flames the panicked Hindus rush in droves from one end of the street to the other. Many disappear down the smoking lanes. Some collapse in the street. Charred limbs and burnt logs are falling from the sky.

The whole world is burning. The air on my face is so hot I think my flesh and clothes will catch fire. I start screaming: hysterically sobbing. Ayah moves away, her feet suddenly heavy and dragging, and sits on the roof slumped against the wall. She buries her face in her knees.

'What small hearts you have,' says Ice-candy-man, beaming affectionately at us. 'You must make your hearts stout!' He strikes his out-thrust chest with his fist. Turning to the men, he says: 'The fucking bastards! They thought they'd drive us out of Bhatti! We've shown them!'

It is not safe to leave until late that evening. As the butcher drives us home in his cart the moonlight settles like a layer of ashes over Lahore.

* * *

In a rush I collect the dolls long abandoned in bottom drawers and toy chest and climb stools to retrieve them from the dusty tops of old cupboards. I line them up against the wall, on my bed, and Adi, intrigued by my sudden interest in dolls, stands by quietly watching.

I can't remember a time when I ever played with dolls: though relatives and acquaintances have persisted in giving them to me. China, cloth and celluloid dolls variously stuffed, sized, and coloured. Black golliwogs, British baby dolls with pink complexions, Indian adult dolls covered in white cloth, their faces painted on.

I pick out a big, bloated celluloid doll. I turn it upside down and pull its legs apart. The elastic that holds them together stretches easily. I let one leg go and it snaps back, attaching itself to the brittle torso.

Adi moves closer. 'What're you trying to do?' he enquires.

I examine the sari- and dhoti-clad Indian dolls. They are unreal, their exaggerated faces too obviously painted, their bodies too fragile. I select a large life-like doll with a china face and blinking blue eyes and coarse black curls. It has a sturdy, well-stuffed cloth body and a substantial feel.

I hold it upside down and pull its pink legs apart. The knees and thighs bend unnaturally, but the stitching in the centre stays intact.

I hold one leg out to Adi. 'Here,' I say, 'pull it.'

'Why?' asks Adi looking confused.

'Pull, damn it!' I scream, so close to hysteria that Adi blanches and hastily grabs the proffered leg. (He is one of the few people I know who is fair enough to blanch – or blush noticeably.) Adi and I pull the doll's legs, stretching it in a fierce tug-of-war, until making a wrenching sound it suddenly splits. We stagger off balance. The cloth skin is ripped right up to its armpits spilling chunks of greyish cotton and coiled brown coir and the innards that make its eyes blink and make it squawk 'Ma-ma'. I examine the doll's spilled insides and, holding them in my hands, collapse on the bed sobbing.

Adi crouches close to me. I can't bear the disillusioned and contemptuous look in his eyes.

'Why were you so cruel if you couldn't stand it?' he asks at last, infuriated by the pointless brutality.

* * *

How long does Lahore burn? Weeks? Months?

We climb to the roof of the Daulatrams' two-storey house to watch. The Daulatrams flee.

The Shankars, too, go. The back portion of our house is untenanted. The Shankars' abandoned belongings are stored by Mother in empty servants' quarters. Gita, with her short fat plait and satin bows, and her steamy, bellowing mate, have disappeared.

Still we go to the Daulatrams' abandoned house to see Mozang Chawk burn. How long does Mozang Chawk burn . . .?

Mozang Chawk burns for months . . . and months . . .

Despite its brick and mortar construction: despite its steel girders and the density of its terraces that run in an uneven high-low, broad-narrow continuity for miles on either side: despite the small bathrooms and godowns and corrugated tin shelters for charpoys deployed to sleep on the roof – and its doors and wooden rafters – the buildings could not have burned for months. Despite the residue of passion and regret, and loss of those who have in panic fled – the fire could not have burned for . . . Despite all the ruptured dreams, broken lives, buried gold, bricked-in rupees, secreted jewellery, lingering hopes . . . the fire could not have burned for months and months . . .

But in my memory it is branded over an inordinate length of time: memory demands poetic licence.

And the hellish fires of Lahore spawn monstrous mobs. These no more resemble the little processions of chanting urchins that Warris Road spawned – and that Adi and I shouted ourselves hoarse in – than the fires that fuse steel girders to mortar resemble the fires that Imam Din fans alive in our kitchen grates every morning.

Chapter 17

Playing British gods under the ceiling fans of the Falettis Hotel – behind Queen Victoria's gardened skirt – the Radcliff Commission deals out Indian cities like a pack of cards. Lahore is dealt to Pakistan, Amritsar to India. Sialkot to Pakistan. Pathankot to India.

I am Pakistani. In a snap. Just like that.

A new nation is born. India has been divided after all. Did tney dig the long, long canal Ayah mentioned? Although it is my birthday no one has time for me. My questions remained unanswered even by Ayah.

Mother makes a disappointing little fuss over me that lasts for about three minutes. She wishes me happy birthday and kisses me and instructs Imam Din to make sweet vermicelli with fried currants and almonds and hands Ayah a cup of milk afloat with rose petals to pour over my head before my bath.

Father hugs me, asks how old I am. I tell him I'm eight. (Yes, time has fiown forward. It will fly back yet.)

'Good, good,' says Father absent-mindedly. He doesn't even say, 'You're a big girl now,' as he did last year. I hang around him feeling bored, while he sits on the commode absorbed in newsprint.

I go to the kitchen and announce my birthday. 'So what?' says Adi, resuming his unseemly clamour for the sugar bowl. Imam Din and Yousaf say: 'How nice. How nice. Greetings, Lenny baby.' But they are preoccupied. Ayah hauls me off for a bath. I have to remind her to douse me with the milk-and-rose-petals.

It's the same at Godmother's. I get hugged and kissed, but insufficiently. Godmother is busy in the kitchen. She moves to and fro, looking like an upended whale in her white sari with her sloping shoulders and broadening torso and the sari narrowing round her ankles. She has the same noble bearing and alert, accommodating air of that intelligent mammal. As she moves to and fro, Godmother directs a nonstop stream of instruction and criticism at Slavesister. Just so's to keep her on her toes and in fair working order. Besides, Godmother is in a hurry. Left to her own assessment of priorities and speed, Slavesister can bog down to a stop.

'Have you soaked the rice yet?' Godmother enquires. 'After you've soaked it I want you to knead the chapatti dough. And I told you to tighten the cot strings yesterday ... Did you? Well then, you may have the pleasure of sleeping on it tonight! Give yours to Manek! Will you hurry up? Half the day's gone,' says Godmother, briskly putting Slavesister through her paces. 'If you don't pick up your feet you'll cut off my nose! Manek will be at our door any minute! I hate to think what he'll tell Piloo about the disorder in this house ... And I haven't even started preparing the halva for him.'

Dr Manek Mody is married to their middle sister, Piloo. Despite the loud-speaker in his throat, he is easy-going and genial and hardly the type to tattle to his wife about a disorderly house.

I am hurt. I thought the preparations for the sweet at least were on my account. I say so. 'Aren't you making the halva for my birthday?'

'Of course,' says Godmother pre-emptorily. 'It's for you. Who else?'

'Of course,' says Slavesister. Ever the opportunist, she adds, 'But we mustn't be selfish, must we? It's for you, and to sweeten Manek Uncle's mouth in welcome and, don't forget, we have to celebrate the new arrival yet!'

Godmother and I look at her blankly. 'Somebody has a baby I don't know of?' asks Godmother suspiciously.

'Have you forgotten already?' says Slavesister with reproof. 'We've all produced a baby . . . We've given birth to a new nation. Pakistan!'

'You *are* silly,' says Godmother crossly. But without the devastating artillery fire such an absurd way of putting things might be expected to provoke.

Godmother is a head taller than Slavesister. Standing on tiptoe she reaches for the semolina. 'Where is the rose-water?' she asks, peering into the top shelf. 'And where is the sugar? Can't anything ever be in place?'

'Everything is in place . . . If you'd only bother to look, Rodabai.'

'Is that so? The sugar and the rose-water jumped last night? And, now, where's the tea? Where's the tea?'

'Under your nose. Right under your nose. If you'd only look properly!' says the worm, turning!

Godmother locates the box of tea literally under her nose. She doesn't say anything. I can't believe it.

I am so astonished my jaw hangs open (ever since, I've had trouble with my mandibular). Hung-jawed I go to Oldhusband, and standing before him in a daze, say, 'It's my birthday.'

Oldhusband emerges from his habitually sour-faced stupor and kisses my forehead. Like a somnambulist I receive from him a small packet wrapped in tissue paper.

I open the packet. It is an autograph book with coloured pages, and it falls open on a yellow page with writing on it. I look at Oldhusband. He takes the book from my hand and reads aloud in resounding tones:

> 'To my dear Lenny,
> "The lives of great men all remind us
> How to make our lives sublime;
> And departing leave behind us
> Footsteps on the sands of time!"'

He must have been quite something when young! I am unutterably impressed! I've never seen him so animated.

'Will you leave your footsteps on the sands of time?' he asks.

I imagine a series of footsteps, obscured by litter, on the grey sand by the muddy Ravi. Ayah's, Masseur's and mine. I nod gravely, awed and overcome by the thunder of the words.

The only one who properly countenances my birthday is Cousin.

When Ayah takes me and Adi across the road from Godmother's to Electric-aunt's he comes galloping to the gate shouting, 'Happy birthday! Happy birthday!' And then, very seriously, like in films, he cautiously holds me by my shoulders and puckers his mouth. I read the intent in his eyes and, being theatrically inclined myself, I close my eyes and readily bunch my lips. I feel Cousin's wet, puckered mouth on my bunched-up lips. I know I'm supposed to feel a thrill, so, I muster up a little thrill.

The thrill comes and goes but Cousin's mouth remains in exactly the same position, exerting exactly the same pressure as at the moment of impact. The muscles of my mouth begin to ache. I open my eyes: and discover Cousin's bewildered eyes gazing directly into mine. He doesn't know if he is doing it right. Or when to stop. The kissing scenes in the films go on much longer. But I can tell at that alarming proximity that the muscles in Cousin's jaws are trembling. My neck, too, is beginning to ache at that awkward angle. Kissing, I'm convinced, is overrated. Trust Cousin to enlighten me. When our mutual agony becomes unbearable, Ayah suddenly slaps Cousin hard on his back, thereby ungluing our stalemate, and scolds: 'Oye! What is this badmashi? Shame on you!'

Cousin totters off balance and looks sheepish. And becomes defensive when Ayah casually spanks him again. I think she is repaying me for minding Ice-candy-man's toes.

Electric-aunt appears on her veranda and holding hands we gallop up to her, trailed unenthusiastically by Adi and good-naturedly by Ayah.

'What? No party?' says Electric-aunt, raising her scanty eyebrows and rubbing it in. She bares a white row of tiny teeth, as neatly packed and even as a goat's, in a bright smile.

Cousin looks at me pityingly: 'We'll have one right here!' he volunteers gallantly.

While Ayah makes hard-boiled-egg sandwiches Cousin tears Electric-aunt's cook away from the radio. They take off on their cycles to buy a cake and potato chips. Electric-aunt, compensating for her lack of charm with an abundance of energy and thrift, briskly opens a locked cupboard in her store and removes paper napkins, plates, party hats and streamers that have already served Cousin's birthdays on two occasions. She counts out eight little candles from an economy-sized box of fifty.

Cousin returns with brown paper bags and a dented cardboard cake box. I blow out the candles and cut the squashed cake. And then we sit around the radio listening to the celebrations of the new Nation. Jinnah's voice, inaugurating the Constituent Assembly sessions on 11 August, says: 'You are free. You are free to go to your temples. You are free to go to your mosques or any other place of worship in the State of Pakistan. You may belong to any religion or caste or creed, that has nothing to do with the business of State . . . etc., etc., etc. *Pakistan Zindabad!*'

Chapter 18

Mr Singh, long hair knotted on top of his head, on long hairy legs, in his yellow pyjama-shorts and wearing his *kirpan*-dagger, carrying a hockey-stick and trailed by his modest American wife and two sweaty and subdued children, comes up our drive just as the huge red sun rests on the top of the house opposite ours.

The family settles in wicker chairs on the veranda beneath the slowly squeaking ceiling fan. Mother, her young face grave and composed behind her tinted glasses, greets them with a stylish handshake – which Mr Singh stands up to receive. Mother's touch ignites men. Mr Singh's beard glows and his forehead turns incandescent.

Mr Singh is obviously uncomfortable perched on the dainty wicker chair. He would prefer to sit cross-legged but manages to keep both dusty, slippered feet firmly on the floor. I signal to Rosy-Peter to come inside but they shake their heads and sit listlessly on their chairs.

'The Mehtas have gone! The Malothras have gone! The Guptas have gone!' says Mr Singh, coming straight out with what is uppermost in his mind. He is not a man for preliminary niceties.

'The Guptas too? When?' asks Mother, her voice throbbing with concern.

'About two hours back. They are joining an escorted convoy of cars.'

Mother's eyes grow moist. Mrs Singh discreetly wipes the tears that have rolled into the recently acquired indigo smudges beneath her eyes. Rosy gets up and, exposing her damp cotton knickers, which look absurd on her eight-year-old bottom, scrambles on to her mother's lap. Mrs Singh smooths her daughter's hair.

Mr Singh clears his throat. 'I don't think there are any Hindu families left on Warris Road,' he says.

'There aren't,' Mother agrees.

'Just two Sikh families. The Pritam Singhs and us.'

We hear a cycle rattle up the drive and the continuous peal of a cycle-bell as Father pedals slowly and laboriously into the portico. Smiling and nodding at our visitors, he parks the cycle on its stand next to the Morris and locks it. Father has reverted to going to work on his cycle, leaving the Morris for Mother.

Mr Singh, noticeably relieved by Father's presence, shakes hands affably and Father, tucking his shirt into his flaring knee-length khaki shorts, sits down with a questioning countenance.

Alerted by the cycle-bell Yousaf brings Father a frosted glass of water on a tray and takes away his khaki solar topi. There is silence as Father tips his head and drains the glass. He pushes back a short fringe of curls plastered to his forehead and removing his spectacles wipes the perspiration from the deep indentations on either side of his nose.

Gurdaspur's gone to India,' he remarks, settling into his chair and cleaning his glasses with a damp handkerchief.

'Yes! That's a surprise,' says Mrs Singh unexpectedly. The fact she has spoken out her thoughts indicates the measure of her inner turmoil. 'I hear they had hoisted the green Pakistani flag and all. There's bound to be trouble,' she says, making what is for her a remarkably pertinent statement.

Father nods significantly. He snaps his fingers to summon Yousaf, and turning his thumb down mutely indicates his wish for more water.

Now that Father is here Mr Singh spreads his thighs comfortably and, placing his hands on his knees, leans forward: 'Sethi Sahib, we have just received orders from our leaders . . . We are to leave Lahore for ever!'

Father raises surprised, questioning eyebrows and Mr Singh continues: 'I'm meeting them tonight. They've worked out plans for a complete Sikh evacuation. We'll form our own armed escort. I'll take our buffaloes . . . And whatever essentials we can pile into a truck. Each family is allotted a truck.'

Father's sharp eyes grow severely comprehending and sympathetic. He frowns and clears his throat. 'Is there anything we can do?'

'Can you store a few things for us? Furniture and what we can't take?' says Mr Singh. 'You know, houses are being looted. Empty ones especially. They haven't come to the better neighbourhoods yet, but who knows? I'll come back for them later. Things have to subside.' Mr Singh spreads his hands in a confused and helpless gesture.

'Sure,' Father nods.

As always economical, Father makes the single word

work on both counts: that he will be glad to store anything for Mr Singh; and that things must subside.

'Of course!' says Mother warmly. 'Bring anything! We'll keep it with the Shankars' things. You can leave it with us for as long as you want!'

Mr Singh's and Father's eyes glisten in the dusk. The sun has disappeared. Mr Singh hawks and directs his spit in a long arc into the portico, near some flowerpots with ferns. Father directs a commiserating gob of spit to nestle next to Mr Singh's.

A sob escapes Mrs Singh. Mother's mouth twitches and she sniffs. 'Go and play outside! Or inside!' she says sternly to me, indicating Rosy and Peter with her quivering chin. She gets up to switch on the lights.

We go into the kitchen to Imam Din for chapatties with sugar and butter. Imam Din sprinkles a more generous helping of sugar than usual, and flapping his arms and crowing pretends to be a rooster to amuse Rosy-Peter. They are amused.

They follow me to the back of the house where I go looking for Ayah.

* * *

Things have become topsy-turvy. We've stopped going to the Queen's Garden altogether. We've also stopped going to the wrestler's restaurant. There is dissension in the ranks of Ayah's admirers. In twos and threes, or singly, they come instead to our house and sit with Ayah on the patch of lawn at the back or, as on this evening when Rosy-Peter and I join them, on the Shankars' neglected veranda. Ayah comes and goes, as duty or Mother calls, and the visitors talk among themselves. Butcher and the restaurant wrestler have ceased to visit.

Tonight, illuminated by the dusty yellow veranda light, we are grouped around a radio. Masseur is there. Also Hari, Sher Singh and the Government House gardener. Imam Din and Yousaf are still catering to the demands of my parents and their visitors. Adi is clinging to Ayah's back, rocking her to and fro and pulling strands of hair out of her bun. Rosy, Peter and I settle down on the brick floor to listen. The broadcast is fragmented by static.

'So! Gurdaspur's gone to India after all,' says the zoo attendant, shaking his outsize, turbaned head.

'Shush!' says the Government House gardener, cupping his hand behind his hoary ear to listen better.

The radio announces through the crackling: 'There have been reports of trouble in Gurdaspur. The situation is reported to be under control.'

'Which means there is uncontrollable butchering going on in Gurdaspur,' says the gardener flatly, reflecting the general opinion. 'It is the Kali-*yuga*, no doubt about it,' he says to a collective and resigned sigh of assent.

Masseur turns the radio off. Moti and his untouchable wife Muccho have silently joined the group. They sit on the veranda steps, just a little bit apart.

'If the worst comes to the worst, you can go to Gurdaspur – or to Amritsar,' says Masseur to the Sikh youth.

'I'm not going anywhere,' says Sher Singh, bristling. But he sounds more obstinate than determined.

'I said, if the worst comes to the worst,' says Masseur mildly.

'Whoever must go, will go,' says the Government House gardener, leaning forward laboriously to pick up his curly-toed slippers. He taps them on the floor to shake off the dried manure and picks off bits of grass adhering to the sides.

'*Aeeee!* You rascal!' groans Ayah, tugging her hair out of Adi's fists and tumbling him forward on her lap. 'I'll teach you to behave, you badmash!' She grins and holds Adi struggling in the powerful vice of her thighs. Raising her arms she calmly plaits her hair.

We stir and stretch, preparing to break up for the evening. And just then, in the muted rustle, we hear the rattle of a bicycle hurtling up our drive at an alarming speed. We grow still, expectant. And emerging from the night like a blundering and scraggy bird, scraping his shoe on the veranda step to check the heedless velocity of his approach – Moti and Muccho scramble out of his way – Ice-candy-man comes to an abrupt and jolted halt. He is breathless, reeking of sweat and dust, and his frantic eyes rake the group. They rest for an instant on the Sikh, and flutter back to us. 'A train from Gurdaspur has just come in,' he announces, panting. 'Everyone in it is dead. Butchered. They are all Muslim. There are no young women among the dead! Only two gunny-bags full of women's breasts!' Ice-candy-man's grip on the handlebars is so tight that his knuckles bulge whitely in the pale light. The kohl lining his eyes has spread forming hollow, skull-like shadows: and as he raises his arm to wipe the perspiration crawling down his face, his glance once again flits over Sher Singh. 'I was expecting relatives . . . For three days . . . For twelve hours each day . . . I waited for that train!'

What I've heard is unbearable. I don't want to believe it. For a grisly instant I see Mother's detached breasts: soft, pendulous, their beige nipples spreading. I shake my head to focus my distracted attention on Ice-candy-man. He appears to have grown shades darker, and his face is all dried up and shrivelled-looking. I can see that beneath his shock he is grieving.

Instinctively I look at the zoo attendant. Sher Singh is staring at the popsicle man. His pupils are black and distended. His checked shirt is open at the throat: and his narrow pigeon-chest is going up and down, up and down, in the eerie veranda light.

* * *

A crowd has gathered in the narrow alley in front of the tobacco-*naswar* shop. If it is one thing I am, it's inquisitive. I slip away from Ayah, and sliding between the thicket of legs ease my way into the centre. I see the Pathan. Sharbat Khan has returned from the mountains!

I shout, '*Saalam ailekum*, Khan Sahib!' But busy pushing the pedal on his scraping and sparking machine he doesn't hear me. People are holding out to him their knives, choppers, daggers, axes, staves and scythes. And in the clamour, nose to the grindstone, Sharbat Khan sharpens one blunt edge after the other.

The crowd swells as more and more people get to know that Sharbat Khan is back. Children, sent by their mothers and grandmothers, run up with an assortment of kitchen knives and meat-cleavers and circle the crowd trying to squeeze in. Some are good-naturedly picked up and passed through, but for the most part the men appear nervous – and so anxious to get their own implements sharpened that they threaten and abuse the children. They must have a lot of wood to chop. A lot of meat to cut. A lot of grass to mow with their scythes.

I spot Sher Singh. He is struggling towards Sharbat Khan with a tangled armload of daggers and swords. He has to be carrying the entire stock of his family's religious arsenal! He has a touchy, defensive look that I have noticed on his face of late. It makes me want to bring him into our house and ask everybody to be nice to him. Ayah too is very careful how she talks to him. He bristles even at her mildly flirtatious teasing. She handles him with the caution Sher Singh lavishes on the nervous little lion cubs in the zoo. He has taken us to see the cubs. It's all very well to see them romp and mew, but within a year they will roar their way into my nightmares and sink their fangs in me. Kittens are drowned. Why not them?

A hand suddenly grips my arm and yanks me out. It is Masseur's unerring hand. 'What are you doing in this crowd?' he asks. 'You could get hurt.'

We spot Ayah. She appears panicked. And when she sees us she rushes up to me and picks me up and fusses over me as if I've been lost and found.

'It's all right,' I say, wishing to reassure her, 'I was only looking at Sharbat Khan.'

'Oh,' she says. 'He's back?'

'Yes,' I say, pointing at the crowd. 'He's sharpening their knives.'

That evening Sharbat Khan visits us, bringing Ayah almonds, pistachios and dried apricots tied in a square of red satin. 'How long've you been back?' asks Ayah, undoing the knots in the bundle with her teeth and examining the contents with her fingers.

'Two days,' he says, his voice honeyed with adoration. 'I would've come earlier but there was such a rush of business. I never knew there were so many daggers and knives in Lahore!'

'If you'd waited much longer my presents would have rotted,' says Ayah.

I am surprised. Ayah appears to have lost her sense of awe and excitement in Sharbat Khan's presence. She is not the least bit awkward. Instead of hiding her face and fidgeting with her sari she looks at him out of calm and bemused eyes.

Masseur, perfumed and primed, comes half an hour later. He is wearing a long creamy silk shirt over his heavy linen lungi and his moustache is oiled and gleaming. The men appraise each other with cautious suspicion as Masseur, hitching up his lungi, hunkers down on the floor.

'You've been away for quite some time,' drawls Masseur, twirling the pointed tips of his moustache with a significance I miss. 'Three months or so?'

'Yes,' says Sharbat Khan, pensively smoothing the thick growth of hair, cropped like a rug, on his upper lip. 'And you've been here all that time?'

'Obviously,' says Masseur coolly.

They look as if each is a whiskered dog circling the other – weighing in and warning his foe.

Ayah, meanwhile, is cracking the almonds with her small strong teeth and chewing them with appreciative smacks. She offers the kernels to me and then to Masseur. Masseur smiles and shakes his head, no. He lifts his shirt and withdraws from a knot tied in his elegant lungi a small packet of prepared *paan*. He holds the betel-leaf out to Ayah. Ayah looks at the succulent *paan*, plump with cardomom, and then at Masseur's mouth. Her face reflects an answer. And Sharbat Khan turns away his face, honourably conceding the round.

Enough is enough! They have stared at each other and secretly communicated until Ayah's mouth is red with *paan*, and I am fit to scream. Sharbat Khan carefully places the gold *kulla* – around which his turban is wrapped – on his head and stands up. Without a word he mounts his bicycle and wobbles away with his machine clattering dejectedly behind him.

His departure brings to mind the Chinaman. It occurs to me that I haven't seen him for a long time. 'Where is he? Tell me. Tell me,' I shout into Ayah's ears, and holding her by them, force her to turn to me.

'The Chinaman?' she asks absently. 'Oh, he went away at the first smell of trouble,' she says, with melodious indulgence for the cowardly Chinaman.

'What trouble?'

'This Pakistan–Hindustan business . . .'

'Where did he go?' I ask.

'Oh, I don't know,' says Ayah. 'Probably back to his China.'

Masseur's been with Ayah practically all evening, yet there's no sign of Ice-candy-man. I wonder about it.

The next evening Masseur has Ayah all to himself. And the next. Still no sign of the popsicle vendor.

I am disturbed. So is Ayah. 'Where is everybody?' she asks Masseur: meaning the Government House gardener, the wrestler, the butcher, the zoo attendant, Ice-candy-man and the rest of the gang. Even Yousaf and Imam Din appear to have become less visible.

Chapter 19

Papoo and I are helping Hari bathe the buffalo in the afternoon when Adi walks up in the slush and, manoeuvring himself between me and the buffalo, stands absolutely, intensely still. As if this alone is not enough to rivet my attention, he murmurs in my ear: 'Follow me!'

He turns and casually walks away. I can tell he is wild with excitement and has exercised all his self-control not to break into a run. I'd follow him to the ends of the earth to discover the cause of his excitement.

When we are outside the Shankars' empty rooms, he turns to me his shining eyes. He has no right to look like this . . . As if lit up from within. Regardless – I'd follow him to the ends of the earth.

'What is it?' I whisper in a frenzy.

'The black box is back in the bathroom.'

It is a rare occasion: Adi-made-of-mercury standing still, and confiding in me.

Not only is the black box back, says Adi, but he also knows what's in it.

'What? What? Tell me,' I plead.

But Adi, like a cat playing with the poor tail-less mousey, says: 'See for yourself.'

I tiptoe up the bathroom steps and approach the long box. It is as sinister as ever. I take Adi's word for it that it is open – but I dare not lift the lid. I have no wish to be scared out of my wits: What if it's a grinning, skeletal corpse?

Adi puts a cautioning finger on his lips and lifts the lid. Nestled in scarlet velvet, in a depression specially carved for it, like a dark jewel in its setting, is an enormous double-barrel gun. I feel its smooth barrels and its polished wood.

No wonder we couldn't carry the box. The gun is heavy. Between us we carry the gun, Adi cautiously leading at the barrel end, and me at the other. Nervous that we might be discovered, or that the gun might fire its double barrels into Adi's behind, we at last reach the gate.

Adi takes first turn. I help him stand up the gun and he looks like a diminutive Gurkha with a cannon.

I don't know how long we take turns holding the gun. An hour – perhaps two. We hear the ubiquitous chanting of the mobs in the distance: '*Allah-o-Akbar!*' comes the fragmented roar from the Muslim *goondas* of Mozang. '*Bole so nehal: Sat siri akal!*' from the Sikh *goondas* of Beadon Road. Standing at attention with the gun I feel ready to face any mob.

There is little traffic; a few tongas, half a dozen cyclists. A group of prisoners, the chains along their arms and legs clanking, eye the gun speculatively and the policeman shepherding them prudently crosses the road. No one talks to us. The presence of the dual barrels is intimidating.

Luckily it's not my turn when Father cycles up and comes to a grim halt in front of Adi. Not loquacious at his calmest, Father is rendered speechless. He glares at Adi. 'Put it back at once!' he says at last. He slaps Adi for the first time in his life.

Pushing the cycle with one hand Father comes to me and thumps my back. As thumps go it is a half-hearted thump – unlike Mother's whole-hearted whacks that cause us to stagger clear across rooms – but no beating of Mother's every hurt so much.

After dinner Father sits us on his lap and explains: 'Your lives weren't worth two pice when you showed off with that gun.'

The black box again disappears.

* * *

Ice-candy-man visits at last. Once again we are gathered on the Shankars' abandoned veranda. I cannot believe the change in him. Gone is the darkly grieving look that had affected me so deeply the evening he emerged from the night and almost crashed into us with the grim news of the train-load of dead Muslims.

Ice-candy-man has acquired an unpleasant swagger and a strange way of looking at Hari and Moti. He is full of bravado – and still full of stories. 'You remember Kirpa Ram? That skinflint we all owe money?' he asks, barely bothering to greet anyone as he settles among us, chomping on a *paan*. His mouth, slimy and crimson with betel-juice, bloated – as if he's become accustomed to indulging himself.

'That money-lender would squeeze blood from a fly!' he says, bending over to spit betel-juice into a flowerpot holding a delicate tracery of ferns. 'Well,' he continues, 'Kirpa Ram's packed his family off to Delhi. But can he bear to part from those of us he's been fattening on? No! So, he stays. He thinks he's that brave!' Ice-candy-man's mouth curls in a contemptuous sneer. 'But the instant we entered his house I saw his fat dhotied tail slip out of the back door! Ramzana the butcher noticed a damp patch on one of the walls. It had been hastily whitewashed. He scraped the cement and removed a brick. What d'you think he found? Pouches with nine hundred guineas sewn into them! Nine hundred golden guineas!'

Ice-candy-man studies us, moving his swaggering eyes triumphantly from face to face.

Ayah, the Government House gardener, Hari and Moti stare back with set, expressionless faces. Masseur frowns. Yousaf scowls at the naked veranda bulb. Imam Din gets up, leaning heavily on the Government House gardener, and invoking Allah's mercy and blessings and sighing, heads for the kitchen.

'Show me your hand,' says Ice-candy-man to Ayah.

Ayah, surprised into thinking he wants to read her future, opens her plump palm and shows it to Ice-candy-man. I also think he is initiating seduction through palmistry. Instead he places a gold coin in her hand. Ayah studies it minutely and bites it to test the gold.

It is bitten and passed from hand to hand and on to me. I examine Queen Victoria's embossed profile with fascination. Despite the difference in the metals it is the same profile she displays in her statue.

Ayah returns the coin to Ice-candy-man.

'Keep it. It's for you,' he says grandly, folding her fingers over it.

'No,' she says, shaking her head and hiding her hands behind her back.

She's like me. There are some things she will not hold.

'But I brought it specially for you! Please accept it,' pleads Ice-candy-man, for the first time sounding like his old ingratiating self.

Ayah averts her face. 'Where's Sher Singh?' she suddenly asks. As if the zoo attendant is somewhere he ought not to be.

There is no reply.

'He's left Lahore, I think,' says Yousaf at last, glancing at Ice-candy-man.

Ice-candy-man makes a harsh, crude sound. 'There's natural justice for you!' he says, spitting the red juice into the ferns again. 'You remember how he got rid of his Muslim tenants? Well, the tenants had their own back! Exposed themselves to his womenfolk! They went a bit further . . . played with one of Sher Singh's sisters . . . Nothing serious – but her husband turned ugly . . He was killed in the scuffle,' says Ice-candy-man casually. 'Well, they had to leave Lahore sooner or later . . . After what one hears of Sikh atrocities it's better they left sooner! The refugees are clamouring for revenge!'

'Were you among the men who exposed themselves?' asks the Government House gardener. His tone implies more a mild assertion than a question.

'What's it to you, oye?' says Ice-candy-man raising his voice and flaring into an insolent display of wrath. 'If you must know, I was! I'll tell you to your face – I lose my senses when I think of the mutilated bodies on that train from Gurdaspur . . . that night I went mad, I tell you! I lobbed grenades through the windows of Hindus and Sikhs I'd known all my life! I hated their guts . . . I want to kill someone for each of the breasts they cut off the Muslim women . . . The penises!'

In the silence that follows, the gardener clears his throat.

'You're right, brother,' he says. I feel he cannot meet Ice-candy-man's eyes. He is looking so deliberately at the floor that it appears as if he is hanging his head. 'There are some things a man cannot look upon without going mad. It's the mischief of Satan . . . Evil will spawn evil . . . God preserve us.' His voice is gruff with the burden of disillusion and loss. 'I've sent my family to Delhi. As soon as the *Sarkar* permits I will join them.' The gardener turns his weary gaze upon Hari. 'Have you made plans to go, brother?' he asks.

'Where to?' says Hari, shaking his head and wiping his eyes with his arm. 'I'll ride the storm out. I've nowhere to go.'

'You'll find some place to go,' says the Government House gardener. 'When our friends confess they want to kill us, we have to go . . .' He makes no move to wipe the tears running in little rills through his grey stubble and dripping from his chin. The red rims of his eyes are blurred and soggy and blend into the soft flesh as if he has become addicted to weeping.

Moti and Papoo are sitting bowed and subdued on the veranda steps. 'What about you two?' Masseur asks. 'Are you leaving?'

After a pause, during which we hear Moti's knuckles crack as he presses his fingers against his palm, speaking hesitantly and so low that I can barely hear him, he says, 'I talked to the padre at the Cantonment Mission . . . We're becoming Christian.'

Ice-candy-man, appearing restless, nods casually. 'Quite a few of your people are converting,' he says. 'You'd better change your name, too, while you're at it.'

The longer I observe Ice-candy-man the more I notice the change wrought in him. He seems to have lost his lithe, cat-like movements. And he appears to have put on weight. Perhaps it's just the air of consequence on him that makes him appear more substantial.

'The Falettis Hotel cook has also run away with his tail between his legs!' he informs us, unasked. And once again he appears bloated with triumph . . . and a horrid irrepressible gloating.

It is very late. The frogs are croaking again. We might have some rain yet. Except for Masseur, everyone has gone. We move to the patch of grass near the servants' quarters. There is a full moon out but it is pitch-dark where we sit under a mulberry tree. There is no breeze. And except for the occasional rustle in the leaves caused by a restless bird, or the indiscernible movement of a frog, the night is still.

Ayah is crying softly. 'I must get out of here,' she says, sniffing and wiping her nose on her sari-blouse sleeve. 'I have relatives in Amritsar I can go to.'

'You don't need to go anywhere,' says Masseur, so assuredly possessive that I feel a stab of jealousy. 'Why do you worry? I'm here. No one will touch a hair on your head. I don't know why you don't marry me!' he says, sighing persuasively. 'You know I worship you . . .'

'I'm already yours,' says Ayah with disturbing submission. 'I will always be yours.'

'Don't you dare marry him!' I cry. 'You'll leave me . . . Don't leave me,' I beg, kicking Masseur.

'Silly girl! I won't leave you . . . And if I have to, you'll find another ayah who will love you just as much.'

'I don't want another ayah . . . I will never let another ayah touch me!'

I start sobbing. I kiss Ayah wherever Masseur is not touching her in the dark.

Chapter 20

Rosy-Peter have gone. The Government House gardener has gone . . .

And the gramophones and speakers mounted on tongas

and lorries scratchily, endlessly pouring out the melody of Nur Jehan's popular film song that is now so strangely apt:

> *Mere bachpan ke sathi mujhe bhool na jana –*
> *Dekho, dekho hense na zamana, hanse na zamana.*
> Friends from our childhood, don't forget us –
> See that a changed world does not mock us.

Instead, wave upon scruffy wave of Muslim refugees flood Lahore – and the Punjab west of Lahore. Within three months seven million Muslims and five million Hindus and Sikhs are uprooted in the largest and most terrible exchange of population known to history. The Punjab has been divided by the icy card-sharks dealing out the land village by village, city by city, wheeling and dealing and doling out favours.

For now the tide is turned – and the Hindus are being favoured over the Muslims by the remnants of the Raj. Now that its objective to divide India is achieved, the British favour Nehru over Jinnah. Nehru is Kashmiri; they grant him Kashmir. Spurning logic, defying rationale, ignoring the consequence of bequeathing a Muslim state to the Hindus: while Jinnah futilely protests: 'Statesmen cannot eat their words!'

Statesmen do.

They grant Nehru Gurdaspur and Pathankot, without which Muslim Kashmir cannot be secured.

Nehru wears red carnations in the buttonholes of his ivory jackets. He bandies words with Lady Mountbatten and is presumed to be her lover. He is charming, too, to Lord Mountbatten. Suave, Cambridge-polished, he carries about him an aura of power and a presence that flatters anyone he compliments tenfold. He doles out promises, smiles, kisses-on-cheeks. He is in the prime of his Brahmin manhood. He is handsome: his cheeks glow pink.

Jinnah is incapable of compliments. Austere, driven, pukka-sahib accented, deathly ill: incapable of cheek-kissing. Instead of carnations he wears a karakuli cap, sombre with tight, grey lamb's-wool curls: and instead of pale jackets, black *achkan* coats. He is past the prime of his elegant manhood. Sallow, whip-thin, sharp-tongued, uncompromising. His training at the Old Bailey and practice in English courtrooms has given him faith in constitutional means, and he puts his misplaced hopes into tall standards of upright justice. The fading Empire sacrifices his cause to their shifting allegiances.

Mother shows me a photograph: 'She is Jinnah's wife,' she says. 'She's Parsee.'

The woman in the photograph is astonishingly beautiful. Large eyes, liquid-brown, radiating youth, promising intelligence, declaring innocence, shining from an oval marble-firm face. Full-lipped, delighting in the knowledge of her own loveliness: confident in the knowledge of her generous impulses. Giving – like Ayah. Daring – like Mother. 'Plucky!' Mother says.

For the lady in the photograph is daring: an Indian woman baring her handsome shoulders in a strapless gown in an era when such unclothing was considered reprehensible. Defying, at eighteen, her wealthy knighted father, braving the disapproval of their rigid community, excommunicated, she marries a Muslim lawyer twenty-two years older than her. Jinnah was brilliant, elegantly handsome: he had to be to marry such a raving beauty. And cold, too, he had to be – to win such a generous heart.

'Where is she?' I ask Mother.

Mother's eyes turn inwards. Her lips give a twitch: 'She died at twenty-nine. Her heart was broken . . .'

Her daring to no account. Her defiance humbled. Her energy extinguished. Only her image in the photograph – and her innocence – remain intact.

But didn't Jinnah, too, die of a broken heart? And today, forty years later, in films of Gandhi's and Mountbatten's lives, in books by British and Indian scholars, Jinnah, who for a decade was known as 'Ambassador of Hindu-Muslim Unity', is caricatured, and portrayed as a monster. The man about whom India's poetess Naidu Sarojini wrote:

. . . the calm hauteur of his accustomed reserve masks, for those who know him, a naïve and eager humanity, an intuition quick and tender as a woman's, a humour gay and winning as a child's – pre-eminently rational and practical, discreet and dispassionate in his estimate and acceptance of life, the obvious sanity and serenity of his worldly wisdom effectually disguise a shy and splendid idealism which is of the very essence of the man.

Chapter 21

Hari has had his *bodhi* shaved. He has become a Muslim.

He has also had his penis circumcised. 'By a barber,' says Cousin, unbuttoning his fly in Electric-aunt's sitting room. Treating me to a view of his uncircumcised penis, he stretches his foreskin back to show me how Hari's circumcised penis must look.

I recall Hari's dark genitals, partially obscured by the dust and dusk and crumpled with fear as he stood in the circle of his tormentors. My imagination presents unbearable images. I shake my head to dispel them and revert my attention to Cousin's exposed flesh.

His genitals have grown since I last examined them – three years ago – after he'd had his hernia operation. The penis is longer and thicker and gracefully arched – and it seems to be breathing.

'Feel it,' offers Cousin.

I like its feel. It is warm and cuddly. As I squeeze the pliant flesh it strengthens and grows in my hand.

'Hey!' I say. 'What's this!'

Cousin has a funny look in his eyes that I don't trust.

'I have become a honey-comb,' he says. 'Lick me, here, and see what happens.'

I lick the tip gingerly. Nothing. No honey.

'You've got to suck out the honey.' Cousin arches his back and manoeuvres his penis to my mouth.

'Suck it yourself!' I say, standing up.

'I can't,' says Cousin.

I see the absurdity of my suggestion. I shrug away.

I like Cousin. I've even thought of marrying him when we grow up: but this is a side of him I'm becoming aware of for the first time, and I don't like it.

'All right, I'll show you anyway,' says Cousin in a conciliatory voice. 'Just look: I'll show you something.'

Cousin pumps and pumps his penis and it becomes all red and I think he will tear himself and I say, 'Stop it! You'll bleed,' but he pumps and pumps and I begin to cry.

Cousin too is close to crying. He mopes around for the rest of the afternoon with his fly looking stuffed. I haven't been able to keep my eyes off flies since: intrigued by the fleshy machinery.

Hari has adapted his name to his new faith: he wants us to call him Himat Ali. He has also changed his dhoti for the substantial gathers of the draw-string shalwar.

* * *

I spend the night after my birthday at Godmother's. Late in the evening her room resembles the barracks dormitory we peep into from the servants' quarters roof. Five cots are laid out at all angles and there is hardly any space to walk.

I lie on my cot, between Godmother and Dr Manek Mody. Oldhusband is already snoring gently from the direction of our feet. Only the kitchen light is on and Slavesister is softly laying out the cups and saucers for the morning's tea.

'Hurry up and go to sleep, Lenny,' says Dr Mody, so gleefully that I become suspicious and ask, 'Why?'

'Because I want to pounce on your Roda Aunty and eat her up. I'm hungry.'

There he goes again.

Godmother is silent. I reach out my hand and tap the wooden frame of her charpoy in the dark and she holds my hand tight.

Dr Mody makes a 'slurp-slurp' sound and rubs his hands together in the dark.

'Don't be silly. You can't eat people,' I say.

'Go to sleep, can't you?' he says, ignoring my comment. 'Now, where do I start? . . . Roast leg of Aunty or barbecued ribs? Of course! I'll make a nice jelly from her trotters! Seasoned with cinnamon and orange juice – slurp-slurp. Just like Imam Din's jelly.'

Imam Din makes a delicious jelly – but out of sheep's trotters.

Dr Mody's cot creaks as he sits up, and I see his pyjama-suited silhouette and bald head shining menacingly in the faint light from the kitchen. I spring out of bed and wrap my limbs about Godmother. She lies within my small arms and legs like a trusting and tremulous whale in her white garments. 'If you touch her, I will kill you!' I scream. 'I have a double-barrel gun!'

'I think I will start with crumbed chops à la Roda,' says the doctor undeterred.

The light is blocked briefly as Slavesister comes through the door, carefully balancing a saucer of hot tea for Godmother. She notices the seated doctor and asks, 'Can I get you a night-cap?'

'Yes, please. I'd love a hot cup of blood à la Roda: with salt and pepper.'

I have a brilliant idea. 'You can have Mini Aunty. She is fatter.'

'Thank you very much!' says Mini Aunty.

'I don't want Mini. I'm in the mood for a tough old thing I can chew on.'

'You're a ghoul!' I screech sternly.

'Oh, no. I'm only a vampire.'

'Now, now. No more of that,' intervenes Slavesister. 'Someone will have nightmares . . . And then someone might wet her bed.'

'Someone will not wet her bed!' I say firmly, using the tone Godmother uses to squash her.

'Never mind your cheek. Get back to your charpoy. You should be fast asleep,' says Slavesister, completely unabashed, and patiently holding out Godmother's saucer of hot tea.

'Chi, chi, chi! She wets her bed?' says Dr Mody holding his nose. 'Chi, chi, chi! Don't sleep next to me.'

'She does not wet the bed,' says Godmother, rising gallantly to the occasion – and to take her saucer of tea.

'You wouldn't know. You don't wash the sheets,' says Slavesister recklessly. She's probably counting on the inch Godmother allowed her when, bemused by the events of that historic day, she let Slavesister get away with insubordination on my birthday. But her lucky break has gone the way of all such breaks and Godmother, rearing up on her pillows, retaliates: 'Don't think I've not been observing your tongue of late! If you're not careful, I'll snip it off! Then you'll probably learn not to be rude in front of guests. I hate to think what Manek will tell our middle sister about your behaviour before your elders!'

'Really, Rodabai! How long will you treat me like a child?'

'Till you grow up! God knows, you've grown older – and fatter – but not up! This child here has more sense than you. Now stop eating our heads. Say your prayers and go to sleep.'

Slavesister retreats to the kitchen and commences mumbling.

Dr Manek Mody represses his cannibalistic prowling and lies down quietly.

It's lovely to have someone fight your battles for you.. Specially when you're little. I adore Godmother. I latch on to her tighter, and kiss her rough khaddar nightgown. The pantry light goes out. Slavesister gropes her way to her sagging charpoy and continues her mumbles in the vicinity of our heads.

'Um! Um!' warns Godmother.

The mumbles stop.

I know Dr Mody is only teasing. After all, I'm eight!

When will they stop treating me like a baby? And I'm fed up of being called Lenny baby, Lenny baby, Lenny baby . . .

When Godmother comes out of her bath the next morning, clattering into the kitchen on wooden thongs, her dolphin shape wrapped in only her sari, one shoulder bare, hair dripping – all dewy and fresh – she looks like a dainty young thing. As if the water has whittled away her age.

By the time Slavesister emerges from her bath, looking like melting tallow and oozing moisture from powdered pores, Godmother has put on her bodice and blouse and velvet slippers and pumped alive the hissing Primus stove. She appears accepting of life. Conscious of her irrepressibly youthful spirit – raring to go.

'What took you so long in the bath?' she says, getting the day off to a flying start. 'You know Manek has to go out early. You know there's so much to be done – the boys are coming in the evening – and you retire to splash from the bucket like Cleopatra!'

Slavesister is too sedated from her bath to react. Oozing moisture, she moves about gathering the ingredients for the omelettes and begins chopping the onions and green peppers.

Dr Mody, anxious not to miss the chatter, bursts into the kitchen in his striped pyjamas. And as if his loud voice were not enough, he claps hands to gain attention: 'Where's breakfast? Where's breakfast? I'm so hungry I could eat Rodabai! Such a pity Lenny's here . . .' he says, grinning from ear to ear – and nicely fanning banked fires.

'If Bathing Beauty didn't take hours wallowing in her bath like Cleopatra, you'd have breakfast! Come on. Come on. Move your fingers!'

'Yes, Mini! Move it. Move it,' says the doctor putting his short arms round Slavesister's heavy shoulders and hugging her affectionately.

'Mind you don't cut yourself,' cautions Godmother.

'It's not the first time I'm using a knife, Rodabai,' says Aunt Mini reasonably.

'I said "mind". I have enough worries without your adding to them!'

'Yes, yes! Mind you don't chop off your fat little fingers,' says Dr Manek Mody, echoing Godmother.

'Now, don't you go joining hands with her,' says Mini Aunty.

'Her? Her?' asks Godmother, looking confusedly at her brother-in-law and at me. 'Who's her? Where's her?'

Slavesister chops the tomatoes silently.

'Yes? Who's her?' asks her brother-in-law.

Oldhusband emerges from the bathroom. He is, as always, dry and brittle, and irritated.

'His Sourship's had his bath. Manek, you'd better take your turn before Cleopatra decides to settle down to her business on the commode.'

'Really, Rodabai . . . I hate to say it, but you really are going too far,' says Slavesister.

'Oh? Where to? Where am I going?'

'Don't make me say something you'll regret . . .'

'Come on. Out with it! I'd like to know where I'm going . . . and where I stand!'

'Yes. Out with it! Where are you packing my Rodabai off to?'

'Manek, you'd be wise to keep out of this,' says Slavesister solemnly. 'Don't aggravate the situation . . . It's bad enough without your encouraging her.'

'Is that so?' Godmother is in good form. 'May I ask who you are to tell Manek not to meddle? Are you somebody? Queen Cleopatra of Jail Road, perhaps?'

'You know! I'm nothing . . . nobody . . .'

'Then who does your Nobodyship think she is ordering about? You meddle all you want, Manek! You are married to our sister. You have every right to encourage whom you wish to in this house!' Godmother turns to face her stoic kid sister. 'And he's only asking what I wish to know! How far, exactly, am I going?'

'I hate to say it . . . but, you are becoming . . . vulgar!'

'Oh? Is that so? And what do you think you are becoming . . . when you loll on the commode all morning spreading perfumes?'

'Chi, chi, chi!' says Dr Mody, holding his fleshy nose.

'I'll chop off your nose, you *chi-chi-chiwalla!*' says Mini Aunty. She often acts the spoilt sis-in-law with him.

'No wonder Mrs Pen asked the other morning if the garbage cart had been to us. No wonder! I feel so embarrassed . . .' says Godmother batting her eyes.

'If it's constipation, I can help her out,' says the professional medicine-man.

'Is that what it is?' asks Godmother, all intelligent and alert and concerned. 'Is she constipated, do you think? Could you prescribe her a strong purgative?'

'I can give her a horse's dose, if you wish.'

'So good of you, Manek,' says Godmother. 'People will stop taking us for the neighbourhood manure dump.'

Slavesister wipes her face on her sleeve. Her lips are moist and flattened: they appear to be moving.

'Are you muttering?' demands Godmother. 'Kindly permit us to share your mutters.'

'No . . . it's just the onions . . .' Slavesister manages to say. 'The omelette *masala* is ready. Where do you want me to make the omelette?'

Slavesister has wisely elected to sound docile and matter-of-fact.

Oldhusband shuffles out of the kitchen and settles with his prayerbook in the bentwood chair. The white stubble on his cheeks quivers as he silently mumbles his prayers.

Godmother has invited four students from the King Edward Medical College dorms to tea. Their parents, who have at some point in time known either Godmother or one of her kin, have requested her to keep an occasional eye on them.

Godmother invites them whenever her brother-in-law visits Lahore. She feels it is good for the fledglings to be in the company of a fully-fledged doctor. Though, as far as I can tell, they diligently compete in setting each other a bad example.

Only two students, Yakoob from Peshawar and Charles Chaudhry, an Indian Christian from Multan, show up that evening.

'Prakash and his family have migrated to Delhi,' says Yakoob, explaining the absence of the Hindu boy.

We are sitting on the drive in a rough circle; Godmother in her easy chair and I on her lap.

'Roshan Singh left for Amritsar only last Monday,' says Yakoob explaining the absence of the Sikh student. 'Some *goondas* from Bhatti were after his sisters. We escorted them, and the whole family, to a convoy.'

Slavesister, sitting on her low stool with her podgy knees spread beneath her sari, clucks mournfully and shakes her head.

'It's to be expected, I suppose,' says Godmother sighing.

'Pretty girls?' enquires Dr Manek Mody. 'Sikh girls have beautiful eyes,' he states, airing his eye-fetish.

'Oh yes!' says Charles Chaudhry with bated breath. 'Light eyes. Hazel. Greenish . . . You can get lost in them, man!'

Ayah helps Mini Aunty serve tea.

'Your a-y-a-h has the most enormous eyes I've ever seen,' says the doctor to me in English. 'Gorgeous! Ravishing!'

People spell out the letters thinking Ayah will not understand the alphabet. This occurs so frequently that she'd have to be a real nitwit not to catch on.

Ayah, aware she is the star attraction, rolls and slides her thickly fringed eyes to glamorous effect as she passes the tea. She goes in and fetches a plate of almond fudge and sweet lentil *ladoos*.

'Look out! There's a fly on the *ladoos*,' says Dr Mody.

Being a doctor he is more agitated by the fly's presence than we are.

'Are you bothered by such a little fly?' says Ayah, peeking at the bald doctor from the corners of her teasing eyes. 'Let it be: it will hardly eat anything.'

Dr Mody looks at her, surprised: too taken aback to comment.

Then he springs out of his chair and flutters his small hand over the *ladoos*, saying: 'Shoo, shoo!' The disturbed fly lifts sluggishly and the doctor, in a swift brown movement, catches it in his fist. He puffs up and surveys us as if he's caught a lion.

'Well done!' says Mini Aunty: ever the sycophant.

'Why don't you eat it,' I tell him. 'You're always hungry!'

Dr Mody slaughters the fly with a loud clap. 'No, I'll save it for you,' he says, stepping up to me and shoving his hand with the dead fly towards my mouth.

I scream and bury my face in Godmother's blouse. She fends him off with one hand and holds me protectively with the other. I feel her movements as she chuckles and flays.

Dr Mody sits down laughing; and when I turn to look at him he makes a straight face and pretends to eat the fly.

'You're a pig!' I say.

But once launched, Dr Mody cannot be distracted long from his fetish. He peers at me acutely: 'Why do you have such an unfortunate pair of eyes?' he enquires. 'You're a bit cross-eyed, aren't you?'

'No. I'm not!' I protest loudly.

'Not cross-eyed,' says Slavesister, and treacherously adds, 'She only squints.'

'No!' I shout. 'I don't!'

'Don't shout,' says my traitorous aunt, covering her ears. 'We're not deaf.'

'I don't understand it,' says the spiteful cannibal. 'Your mother has such sweet chinky little eyes – such a pity her daughter's eyes are like this.' He crosses his index fingers.

I ignore him.

'What about your Rosy-Peter's American mother? How is she?' the doctor suddenly asks. It's hard to keep track of his abrupt shifts in conversation.

'They left long ago,' I say. Caught off guard, I'm civil.

'Another set of green eyes gone!' laments the doctor, sadly shaking his head. 'I'd follow them to the ends of the earth!'

If one keeps his single track in mind the doctor is not so hard to follow after all. The woolly, ruminative silence that succeeds the doctor's soulful sighs is abruptly shattered by Oldhusband.

'What's all this business about eyes! eyes! eyes!' he explodes. 'You can't poke the damn thing into their eyes!'

Slavesister gasps, shocked out of her hostess smile. The boys titter sheepishly. Dr Manek Mody looks completely confounded.

I have never seen Oldhusband so awesome – not even when he thundered Longfellow at me.

'He's quite right!' says Godmother, standing by her matter-of-fact spouse.

Oldhusband has been hauled through the book, zombie-like, in his cane-bottomed chair, white-stubbled, unprepossessing . . . He has been dragged, disgruntled, from the earliest pages to sit mute on the drive with Godmother and Slavesister while they chatter and fight and clap hands and sing: 'Lame Lenny! Three for a penny!' He has been compelled to snore at our feet – and to spout verse and shuffle his feet. All so that he may in the end confound the carnivorous doctor with his testy outburst!

Now that he's had his say, he can peaceably pass away . . .

Of course, I only appreciated what Oldhusband had said years later.

Chapter 22

Mother develops a busy air of secrecy and preoccupation that makes her even more remote. She shoots off in the Morris, after Father drudges off on his bicycle; and returns late in the afternoon – and scoots out again. Electric-aunt often accompanies her, her thin lips compressed in determined silence, her efficient eyes concentrated on inward thoughts.

Our bewildered faces again grow pale as we ponder their absences. We eat less. We are fretful.

They aren't the least bothered.

'What can they be up to?' wonders Cousin on a warm April afternoon, lying face down on the cool living-room floor of the Singhs' empty rooms.

'Why don't they take us?' I say, hurt at being deprived of drives while my mother and my aunt gallivant God knows where.

'I know where they go. I know everything,' says Adi, with a transparence that convinces us he knows absolutely nothing.

Ayah, almost as mystified as us, volunteers an intriguing bit of information. 'Get a look in the car's dicky sometime.'

'Why?' I demand, surprised.

'Because it is full of petrol cans!' she confides. And on this dramatic note attempts to slip away.

But Cousin grabs the end of her sari. And I jump up to block her exit. And as she tries to escape, the sari unravels. Giggling, turning giddily on the balls of her feet like a gaudy top, she wraps herself back in and bounces down among us. '*Toba, toba!*' she says, and touching the tips of her ears in quick succession saying, 'I've never seen such badmash children! Who's going to iron your mother's sari? You?'

Mother and Father are going out to dinner later. Four hours later! The sari can wait. Matters of more moment – like the dickyful of petrol – have to be considered first.

The car dicky is always locked. I accept Ayah's statement on faith, but Cousin is suspicious. 'How do you know about the petrol?' he asks, permitting mistrust to shade his voice.

'I know!' says Ayah, buttoning up.

Cousin can be silly sometimes. Here we are, on the brink of a revelation, and he insults Ayah.

'If Ayah says there is petrol in the car's dicky, there *is* petrol in the car's dicky!' I say.

Adi holds Ayah by her ears and, shaking her head like a coconut, says: 'Come on, tell more. Please, please!'

'We won't tell anybody. I swear!' I say. And to establish faith, pinch the skin on my throat.

'I swear I won't either! You know you can trust me,' says my mistrustful Cousin, adequately humbled and at his most adult and charming. He too pinches the skin on his Adam's apple, and on his knees moves closer to Ayah.

Ayah turns her head this way and that and rolls her eyes about the room. Cousin quickly gets up and peers into the other uninhabited rooms of the annexe to make sure there are no eavesdroppers.

When Cousin returns, Ayah says: 'If your mothers get to know I told you this . . . Hare Krishna! They'll kill me!'

Again we take an oath of silence, and further reassure her by our solemn faces.

'Look into the godown next to my quarters sometime,' she says. 'It's full of gallons and gallons of petrol!'

We are stupefied. Petrol is rationed. It is an offence to store it.

'Your mother brings the cans in the car,' she says, guiltily removing her eyes from mine, 'and takes them out again! I help her carry them in . . . and I help her carry them out!'

'Doesn't anyone else know about it?' enquires my stupefied, mystified and circumspect Cousin.

'Only your mothers,' says Ayah. 'We do the loading and the unloading when everyone's asleep. We cover the cans with sheets and table-cloths.'

I am so shocked that my jaw drops. I look at Adi and

Cousin. They, too, have been struck by similar thoughts. Their eyes are crossed in dismay and their jaws, too, are unhinged.

'What are you gaping like that for? Close your mouths!' says Ayah sharply – looking bewildered – sensing that we are incriminating our mothers. 'If they do something we don't understand, they have a good reason for it!'

I'm astonished she has not caught on. We clam our mouths shut.

We now know who the arsonists are. Our mothers are setting fire to Lahore!

Back and forth, back and forth, go our mothers on their secret missions, carrying their sinister freight in the dicky of our Morris Minor. And the more they absent themselves, the higher rise the flames in the walled city, and all over Lahore – and the quicker they return, the closer swirl the angry billows of sooty smoke.

And by our silence we commit ourselves to complicity. We're sure Father knows. Why else would he leave the Morris for Mother?

My heart pounds at the damnation that awaits their souls. My knees quake at the horror of their imminent arrest. In ominous dreams they parade Warris Road. In high heels: in chiffon saris: escorted by soldiers: in single file: handcuffed, legcuffed, clanking chains . . . Their mournful eyes seeking us as they are marched into Birdwood Barracks.

For the first time, unbidden, I cover my head with a scarf and in secluded corners join my hands to take the 101 names of God. The Bountiful. The Innocent. The Forgiver of Sin. The Fulfiller of Desire. He who can turn Air into Ashes: Fire into Water: Dust into Gems! The angle of the walls deflects the ancient words of the dead Avastan language and the prayer resounds soothingly in my ears. Often I notice Cousin with his skull-cap on his head lurking in locked bathrooms and I feel my concern is shared. And at night when Adi whips the darkness with his *kusti*, as he goes through the ritual of the sacred thread, I know what evil he prays to banish from our mother and aunt's thoughts.

At the end of the month when Ayah conducts her bi-yearly search for nits on our heads, she discovers we have each sprung one white hair!

I'm surprised our hair hasn't all turned white.

* * *

Himat Ali holds my school satchel, and I hold his finger, as we walk down Warris Road to Mrs Pen's.

At the Salvation Army wall I tug on Hari-alias-Himat-Ali's finger to cross the road. I have become increasingly fearful of the tall brick wall with its wire-veined eyes. Today the slit vents emanate a steely reek that sets my teeth on edge – and fills me with a superstitious dread.

Himat Ali, too, is uneasy. He pulls back saying: 'Stay here. There is something on the other side.'

But my fear of the wall and my congenital curiosity prevail. It is only a bulging gunny-sack. We cross the road.

The swollen gunny-sack lies directly in our path. Hari pushes it with his foot. The sack slowly topples over and Masseur spills out – half on the dusty sidewalk, half on the gritty tarmac – dispelling the stiletto reek of violence with the smell of fresh roses.

He was lying on one side, the upper part of his velvet body bare, a brown and white checked lungi knotted on his hips, and his feet in the sack. I never knew Masseur was so fair inside, creamy, and his arms smooth and distended with muscles and his forearms lined with pale brown hair. A wide wedge of flesh was neatly hacked to further trim his slender waist, and his spine, in a velvet trough, dipped into his lungi.

The minute I touched his shoulder, thinking he might open his eyes, I knew he was dead. But there was too much vigour about him still . . . and his knowing tapering fingers with their white crescents and trimmed nails appeared pliant and ready to assert their consummate skill.

Himat Ali, trembling, suddenly buckles and squats by Masseur as if settling to a long vigil by a sick friend. He removes his puggaree, revealing his shaven *bodhi*-less head, and placing it on his knee wipes a smudge of dust from Masseur's shoulder.

'Oye, *pahialwan*. Oye, my friend,' he whispers. 'What have they done to you?' And he strokes Masseur's arm with his trembling hand as if he is massaging Masseur.

Faces bob around us now. Some concerned, some curious. But they look at Masseur as if he is not a person.

He isn't. He has been reduced to a body. A thing. One side of his handsome face already buried in the dusty sidewalk.

Chapter 23

Beadon Road, bereft of the colourful turbans, hairy bodies, yellow shorts, tight pyjamas, and glittering religious arsenal of the Sikhs, looks like any other populous street. Lahore is suddenly emptied of yet another hoary dimension: there are no Brahmins with caste-marks – or Hindus in dhoties with *bodhis*. Only hordes of Muslim refugees.

Every bit of scrap that can be used has been salvaged from the gutted shops and tenements of Shalmi and Gowalmandi. The palatial bungalows of Hindus in Model Town and the other affluent neighbourhoods have been thoroughly scavenged. The first wave of looters, in mobs and processions, has carried away furniture, carpets, utensils, mattresses, clothes. Succeeding waves of marauders, riding in rickety carts, have systematically stripped the houses of doors, windows, bathroom fittings, ceiling fans and rafters. Casual passers-by, urchins and dogs now stray into the houses to scavenge amidst spiders' webs and deep layers of dust, hoping to pick up old newspapers and cardboard boxes, or any other leavings that have escaped the eye and desire of the preceding wave of *goondas*.

In Rosy-Peter's compound, and in the gaunt looted houses opposite ours, untended gardenia hedges sprawl grotesquely and the lawns and flower beds are overrun with weeds. There are patches of parched cracked clay in which nothing grows. Even the mango and banyan trees look monstrous, stalking the unkempt premises with their shadows.

We still wander through the Singhs' annexe but the main bungalow, the Hindu doctor's abandoned house behind theirs, and parallel to ours, shows surreptitious signs of occupation. A window boarded with newspaper, a tattered curtain, a shadow of someone passing and the murmur of strangers' voices keep us away.

Months pass before we see our new neighbours. Frightened, dispossessed, they are coping with grief over dead kin and kidnapped womenfolk. Grateful for the roof over their heads and the shelter of walls, our neighbours dwell in shadowed interiors, quietly going about the business of surviving, terrified of being again evicted.

Rosy-Peter's house and the house opposite still remain unoccupied. These are to be allotted to refugees who can prove they have left equally valuable properties behind.

It is astonishing how rapidly an uninhabited house decays. There are cracks in the cement floor of the Singhs' annexe and big patches of damp on the walls. Clouds of mosquitoes rise in dark corners and lizards cleave to the ceilings. It looks like a house pining for its departed – haunted – like Ayah's eyes are by memories of Masseur. She secretly cries. Often I catch her wiping tears.

The glossy chocolate bloom in her skin is losing its sheen.

* * *

Ayah has stopped receiving visitors. Her closest friends have fled Lahore. She trusts no one. And Masseur's death has left in her the great empty ache I know sometimes when the muscles of my stomach retract around hungry spaces within me . . . but I know there is an added dimension to her loss I cannot comprehend. I know at least that my lover lives somewhere in the distant and possible future: I have hope.

She haunts the cypresses and marble terraces of the Shalimar Gardens. She climbs the slender minarets of Jehangir's tomb. We wander past the zoo lion's cage and past the chattering monkeys and stand before the peacock's feathery spread. We sit among the rushes on the banks of the Ravi and float in the flat boats on its muddy waters . . . And as Masseur's song, lingering in the rarefied air around the minarets and in the fragrance of gardens, drifts to us in the rustle of the pampas grass, Ayah shivers and whispering croons:

> 'The bumble-bee came –
> Strutting among the flowers, strumming love . . .'

And holding the end of her sari in her hands like a supplicant, she buries her unbearable ache in her hands. I stroke her hair. I kiss her ears, feeling my inadequacy.

While Masseur's voice haunts Ayah, it impels Ice-candyman to climb the steep steps of the minarets after us. He prowls the hills behind the zoo lion's cage and lurks in the tall pampas grass. He follows us everywhere as we walk, hand in hand, two hungry wombs . . . Impotent mothers under the skin.

* * *

Mother's jaunts in the Morris are becoming less frequent, and fires all over Lahore are subsiding. Or having become so much a part of the smoking skyline they no longer claim our attention.

Does one get used to everything? Anything?

Processions still chant from various distances and varying directions, but they have lost their urgency: sounding more like the cries of merchants hawking wares. Closer, we hear the rumble of carts as horses canter down Queens Road to Mozang Chungi, accompanied by receding cries of '*Allah-o-Akbar!*' and '*Pakistan Zindabad!*'

We shrug. They probably have wind of some abandoned house that has not been properly ransacked. These merchant-looters have bypassed our street for some time.

And then one morning we again hear the rumble of carts and the roar of men shouting slogans on Warris Road.

From the very first instant I sense danger: we all do. Perhaps it is the speed of their approach: perhaps the aim of their intent buffeting us in threatening waves. There is a heightening in the noise and a shift in the clatter of horseshoes on the tarmac: a slowing that defines their target. It is either the house in front of ours, or ours. The house opposite, with gaping holes where once there were doors and windows, has nothing left to loot.

Mother comes out and joins Ayah, Adi and me on the veranda. The inhabitants of the servants' quarters run to the front and gather before the kitchen and in the vacant portico. Father has taken the Morris to work. Apparently unperturbed, Imam Din beats eggs in the kitchen.

Mother, voluptuous in a beige chiffon sari, is alert. In charge. A lioness with her cubs. Ayah, with her haunted, nervous eyes, is lioness number two. Our pride on the veranda swells as Moti's wife and five children join us.

There is a stamping and snorting of horses and scraping of wooden wheels on the road as the cart-cavalry comes to a disorderly halt outside our gate. We see the carts milling about in the dust they have raised, the men standing in them. We hear them asking questions; debating; shouting to be heard above the noise.

And, suddenly, the men roar again: '*Allah-o-Akbar!*' And ride into the house opposite ours.

Ayah is not on the veranda. She has disappeared.

'Where's Ayah?' I ask. I'm hushed by a hiss of whispers. Mother communicates a quick, secret warning that is reflected on all faces. Ayah is Hindu. The situation with all its implications is clear. She must hide. We all have a part to play. My intelligence and complicity are taken for granted.

Then they are roaring and charging up our drive, wheels creaking, hooves clattering as the whipped horses stretch their scabby necks and knotted hocks to haul the load for the short gallop. Up the drive come the charioteers, feet planted firmly in shallow carts, in singlets and clinging linen lungis, shoulders gleaming in the bright sun. Calculating men, whose ideals and passions have cooled to ice.

They pour into our drive in an endless cavalry and the looters jump off in front of the kitchen as the carts make room for more carts and the portico and drive are filled with men and horses; some of the horses' noses already in the feed bags around their necks. The men in front are quiet – like merchants going about their business – but those stalled in the choked drive and on the road chant perfunctorily.

The men's eyes, lined with black antimony, rake us. Note the doors behind us and assess the well-tended premises with its surfeit of pots holding ferns and palm fronds. A hesitancy sparks in their brash eyes when they look at our mother. Flanked by her cubs, her hands resting on our heads, she is the noble embodiment of theatrical motherhood. Undaunted. Endearing. Her cut-crystal lips set in a defiant pucker beneath her tinted glasses and her cropped, waved hair.

Men gather round Yousaf and Hari asking questions, peering here and there. Papoo and I, holding hands, step down into the porch. Mother doesn't stop us.

Still beating eggs, aluminium bowl in hand, Imam Din suddenly fills the open kitchen doorway. He bellows: 'What d'you *haramzadas* think you're up to?' There is a lull in the processionists' clamour. Even the men on the road hear him and suspend their desultory chanting. The door snaps shut and Imam Din stands on the kitchen steps looking bomb-bellied and magnificently *goondaish* – the grandfather of all the *goondas* milling about us – with his shaven head, hennaed beard and grimy lungi.

'Where are the Hindus?' a man shouts.

'There are no Hindus here! You *nimak-haram* dogs' penises . . . There are no Hindus here!'

'There are Hindu name-plates on the gates . . . Shankar and Sethi!'

'The Shankars took off long ago . . . They were Hindu. The Sethis are Parsee. I serve them. Sethi is a Parsee name too, you ignorant bastards!'

The men look disappointed and shedding a little of their surety and arrogance look at Imam Din as at an elder. Imam Din's manner changes. He descends among them, bowl and fork in hand, a Mussulman among Muslims. Imam Din's voice is low, conversational. He goes into the kitchen and brings out a large pan of water with ice-cubes floating in it. He and Yousaf hand out the water in frosted aluminium glasses.

'Where's Hari, the gardener?' someone from the back shouts.

'Hari-the-gardener has become Himat Ali!' says Imam Din, roaring genially and glancing at the gardener.

Himat Ali's resigned, dusky face begins to twitch nervously as some men move towards him.

'Let's make sure,' a man says, hitching up his lungi, his swaggering gait bent on mischief. 'Undo your shalwar, Himat Ali. Let's see if you're a proper Muslim.' He is young and very handsome.

'He's Ramzana-the-butcher's brother,' says Papoo, nudging me excitedly.

I notice the resemblance to the butcher. And then the men are no longer just fragmented parts of a procession: they become individual personalities whose faces I study, seeking friends.

Imam Din is standing in front of the gardener, his arms outstretched. 'Get away! I vouch for him. Why don't you ask the barber? He circumcised him.'

Someone yells in loud Punjabi: '*O yay, nai!* Did you circumcise the gardener here?'

From out on the road, transmitted by a chain of raucous voices, comes the reply: 'I did a good job on him . . . I'll vouch for Himat Ali!'

The handsome youth, cheated out of his bit of fun, tries to lunge past Imam Din.

'Tell him to recite the *Kalma*,' someone shouts.

'Oye! You! Recite the *Kalma*,' says the youth.

'La Ilaha Illallah, Mohammad ur Rasulullah.' (There is no God but God, and Mohammad is His prophet.) Astonishingly, Himat Ali injects into the Arabic verse the cadence and intonation of Hindu chants.

The men let it pass.

'Where is the sweeper? Where's Moti?' shouts a hoarse Punjabi voice. It sounds familiar but I can't place it.

'He's here,' says Yousaf, putting an arm round Moti. 'He's become a believer . . . A Christian. Behold . . . Mister David Masih!'

The men smile and joke: 'O ho! He's become a black-faced gen-tle-man! Mister *sweeper* David Masih! Next he'll be sailing off to Eng-a-land and marrying a memsahib!'

And then someone asks, 'Where's the Hindu woman? The ayah!'

There is a split-second's silence before Imam Din's reassuring voice calmly says: 'She's gone.'

'She's gone nowhere! Where is she?'

'I told you. She left Lahore.'

'When?'

'Yesterday.'

'He's lying,' says the familiar voice again. 'Oye, Imam Din, why are you lying?'

I recognise the voice. It is Butcher.

'Oye, *Baray Mian!* Don't disgrace your venerable beard!'

'For shame, old man! And you so close to meeting your Maker!'

'Lying does not become your years, you old goat.'

The raucous voices are turning ugly.

'Call upon Allah to witness your oath,' someone says.

'Oye! Badmash! Don't take Allah's name! You defile it with your tongue!' says Imam Din losing his geniality.

'Ha! So you won't take an oath before Allah! You're a black-faced liar!'

'Mind your tongue, you dog!' shouts Imam Din.

Other voices join in the attack and, suddenly, very clearly, I hear him say: '*Allah-ki-kasam*, she's gone.'

I study the men's faces in the silence that follows. Some of them still don't believe him. Some turn away, or look at the ground. It is an oath a Muslim will not take lightly.

Something strange happened then. The whole disorderly mêlée dissolved and consolidated into a single face. The face, amber-eyed, spread before me: hypnotic, reassuring, blotting out the ugly frightening crowd. Ice-candy-man's versatile face transformed into a saviour's in our hour of need.

Ice-candy-man is crouched before me. 'Don't be scared, Lenny baby,' he says. 'I'm here.' And putting his arms around me he whispers, so that only I can hear: 'I'll protect Ayah with my life! You know I will . . . I know she's here. Where is she?'

And dredging from some foul truthful depth in me a fragment of overheard conversation that I had not registered at the time, I say: 'On the roof – or in one of the godowns . . .'

Ice-candy-man's face undergoes a subtle change before my eyes, and as he slowly uncoils his lank frame into an upright position, I know I have betrayed Ayah.

The news is swiftly transmitted. In a daze I see Mother approach, her face stricken. Adi and Papoo look at me out of stunned faces. There is no judgement in their eyes – no reproach – only stone-faced incredulity.

Imam Din and Yousaf are taking small steps back, their arms spread, as three men try to push past. 'Where're you going? You can't go to the back! Our women are there, they observe purdah!' says Imam Din, again futilely lying. The men are not aggressive, their game is at hand. It is only a matter of minutes. And while the three men insouciantly confront Imam Din and Yousaf, other men, eyes averted, slip past them.

I cannot see Butcher. Ice-candy-man too has disappeared.

'No!' I scream. 'She's gone to Amritsar!'

I try to run after them but Mother holds me. I butt my head into her, bouncing it off her stomach, and every time I throw my head back, I see Adi and Papoo's stunned faces.

The three men shove past Imam Din and something about their insolent and determined movements affects the proprieties that have restrained the mob so far.

They move forward from all points. They swarm into our bedrooms, search the servants' quarters, climb to the roofs, break locks and enter our godowns and the small store-rooms near the bathrooms.

They drag Ayah out. They drag her by her arms stretched taut, and her bare feet – that want to move backwards – are forced forward instead. Her lips are drawn away from her teeth, and the resisting curve of her throat opens her mouth like the dead child's screamless mouth. Her violet sari slips off her shoulder, and her breasts strain at her sari-blouse stretching the cloth so that the white stitching at the seams shows. A sleeve tears under her arm.

The men drag her in grotesque strides to the cart and their harsh hands, supporting her with careless intimacy, lift her into it. Four men stand pressed against her, propping her body upright, their lips stretched in triumphant grimaces.

I am the monkey-man's performing monkey, the trained circus elephant, the snake-man's charmed cobra, an animal with conditioned reflexes that cannot lie . . .

The last thing I noticed was Ayah, her mouth slack and piteously gaping, her dishevelled hair flying into her kidnappers' faces, staring at us as if she wanted to leave behind her wide-open and terrified eyes.

Chapter 24

The evenings resound to the beat of drums. Papoo is getting married. In the wake of my guilt-driven and flagellating grief and pining for Ayah the drums sound mournful, and the preparations for the wedding joyless.

For three days I stand in front of the bathroom mirror staring at my tongue. I hold the vile, truth-infected thing between my fingers and try to wrench it out: but slippery and slick as a fish it slips from my fingers and mocks me with its sharp rapier tip darting as poisonous as a snake. I punish it with rigorous scourings from my prickling toothbrush until it is sore and bleeding. I'm so conscious of its unwelcome presence at all times that it swells uncomfortably in my mouth and gags and chokes me.

I throw up. Constantly.

For three days, as I scour my tongue, families of sweepers, huddled in bunches, in gaudy satins and brocades, drift up our drive, and past the bathroom window. The women shade their dusky faces beneath diaphanous shawls with silver fringes, their glass bangles and silver anklets jingling as they shuffle their feet, the men strutting amidst them like cocks in tall, crisply crested turbans.

At the back, on the servants' verandas, two old crones with missing teeth take turns beating a sausage-shaped drum with both hands and droning ribald ditties. Papoo, cowed by all the unwonted attention, sits glowering in a corner of their quarters like a punished child, her skin glowing from mustard-oil massages and applications of turmeric and Multani mud-packs. Sometimes, when I sit listlessly by her holding her hand, smiling politely at the remarks and wisecracks of the women, drawing courage from my fingers Papoo's eyes regain their roguish sparkle and she snaps and lunges at the women, and flinging herself on the dirt floor enacts temptestuous tantrums of protestation. Infuriated by her daughter's intractable behaviour before her kinswomen Muccho lashes out and is withdrawn cursing, while the remaining women, wheedling, cajoling and bribing Papoo with sweets, restore her to a precarious semblance of docility.

Ayahless and sore-tongued I drift through the forlorn rooms of my house, and back and forth from the festive quarters. The kitchen has become a depressing hell-hole filled with sighs as Imam Din goes about his work spiritlessly. Even Yousaf cracks his smiles less frequently. Mother is out all day. And when she is home she has such a forbidding expression on her exhausted face that Adi and I elect to keep out of her way.

With no one to awaken me I sleep late on the morning of Papoo's wedding. It is Saturday: exactly a week from the day Ayah was carried off. Adi tugs my toe so it hurts and says: 'Aren't you getting up? The guests have come . . . the bridegroom's *baraat* will be here soon!'

I quickly slip into a stiffly starched and frothy frock and put on my white socks and buckled shoes and run to the back.

The caterers have already lit log fires beneath two enormous cauldrons and the sultry air is permeated by the aroma of biryani and spicy goat korma. I weave through the male guests squatting like patient sheep outside the scant lemon hedge that demarcates the servants' courtyard. The yard itself is thronged by women in bright satins edged with gold and silver *gota*. The crowd is thick outside the sweeper's quarters and I have to squeeze my way through the knot of women at the door. But even after my eyes get accustomed to the dingy light in the small, square dung-plastered room it takes me a while to realise that the crumpled heap of scarlet and gold clothes flung carelessly in a corner is really Papoo. I squat by her, smiling and awkward, and, lifting her *ghoongat*, peer into her face. She has an enviable quantity of make-up on. Shocking-pink lipstick, white powder, smudged kohl: and she is fast asleep.

There is a stir among the seated women and a sudden air of excitement. Someone outside shouts: 'Tota Ram's *baraat* has come!'

I shake Papoo: 'Wake up . . . Come on!' Papoo sits up, shoving her *ghoongat* back drowsily, and looks at me with a strange cock-eyed grin, as if she is drunk.

I run out with the rest of the immediate kin to receive the *baraat* just as the bridegroom's party enters our gates and the six-man band, in faded red uniforms with tarnished gold braid, bursts into brassy clamour. I glimpse the short bridegroom behind the musicians, bobbing among the men in the entourage. The women, some on foot, some crammed into tongas with their babies, follow. The groom is wearing a purple satin lungi and a long, whitely gleaming satin shirt. His chest is bristling with garlands centred with gold-beribboned cardboard hearts and strung with crisp, new one-rupee notes and flowers. His head is covered by a thick white turban with a gold *kulah* and beneath it hangs the *sehra*, veiling his face with chains of marigolds. Judging by his height, Tota Ram must be Papoo's age – about eleven or twelve. I am confused. The distraught way Muccho carried on when Papoo was off her feed led me to believe that Tota Ram was an important, frightening and grown man.

The groom is led into Hari's quarters, which have been cleared of their meagre belongings to receive him. Now the curious women surge to see the *doolha*. I fight my way in with them. He is sitting straight on a high-backed chair, his legs dangling brand-new two-tone shoes.

Something about his gestures disturbs me: the way he shifts in the chair, the manner in which he inserts his hand behind the tickling flowers to scratch his nose. He sneezes – an unexpectedly violent sound – and, snorting wetly, clears his throat. For a moment I wonder if someone older is responsible for the sounds. They don't belong behind the *sehra*. Again the bridegroom sneezes: so mightily that the *sehra* swings out. Then he parts the curtain of flowers hanging from his head and I see his face!

He is no boy! He is a dark, middle-aged man with a pockmark-pitted face and small, brash, kohl-blackened eyes. He has an insouciant air of insolence about him – as though it is all a tedious business he has been through before. I cannot take my eyes off him as he scrutinises the women with assertive, assessing directness. There is a slight cast in the close set of his eyes, and the smirk lurking about his thin, dry lips gives an impression of cruelty. The women in the room become hushed. He shifts his insolent eyes to the ceiling, as if permitting the women to gape upon his unsavoury person, and then lowers his *sehra*.

After the initial shock, two or three older women from Papoo's family pull themselves together and move forward to greet and bless him as is ritually required. The elderly and cynical dwarf permits their embraces and then sits back, his spread legs swinging carelessly, and the women, some of them tittering in a shocked way behind the fingers screening their mouths, resume their chattering. I remain rooted to the dirt floor, unable to remove my eyes from him, imagining the shock, and the grotesque possibilities awaiting Papoo.

* * *

I sit quietly beside the bride. The women from the groom's family lift her *ghoongat* and comment indulgently on the innocence that permits the child-bride to sleep through her marriage. Bending frequently, stepping over the satiny spread of legs and thighs of about twenty women jammed together on the floor, they exhibit an impressive display of the clothes and the tawdry jewellery they have brought for the bride and her mother.

A little after noon two enormous round copper platters, heaped with fragrant pilaf and goat curry, are brought into the room. The women gather around them and silently fall to eating. The caterers provide a separate china plate for the bride. Muccho shakes her daughter awake, urging: 'Come, doll, sit up and eat, doll.' I study Muccho's face with curious eyes. There is a contented smile on her lips – smug and vindicated.

As Papoo struggles groggily to sit up, her eyes swivel weakly under her half-open lids. Muccho shakes her roughly again, and forming small morsels of rice with her fingers, stroking Papoo's back, feeds her. Papoo chews slowly, absently, her childish, lipsticked mouth slack. 'Oi, dopey. *Ufeemi!* Wake up!' says Muccho affectionately. And though the tone of voice calling her an opium-addict is disarmingly facetious, it suddenly strikes me that Papoo has in fact been drugged. I have seen enough opium addicts to realise this. Mr Bankwalla's and Col. Bharucha's cooks are both addicted.

Towards evening the *doolha* is brought into the room and made to sit by his comatose bride. He keeps his face covered by the *sehra*, but by the way his head shifts I can tell he is slyly ogling me and the young women moving about the room.

Later in the afternoon the Mission padre stands in the door in his long black cassock with a high, white collar. His heavy laced-up boots appear incongruous with his flowing garments. His hair is cropped very short and he has a well-bred and timid expression on his humble face. I wonder if he is the padre whose wife absconded with the seductive tailor.

The women hug their knees and shuffle back to make room for his passage as the padre, accustoming his eyes to the dark, steps hesitantly into Moti's quarters. Holding his gilt-edged Bible and rosary deferentially he makes the sign of the cross and squats before the couple. Papoo is shaken awake and surreptitiously propped up by Muccho as the padre recites the Christian marriage litany in Punjabi.

Chapter 25

There are mysterious developments afoot in the servants' quarters behind the Hindu doctor's house paralleling ours. The courtyard has been walled off and a very tall and burly Sikh with curling hair on his legs stands guard outside a high, tin-sheet gate, criss-crossed with wooden beams. There is a padlock the size of a grapefruit on the gate, and a large key hangs from the steel bangle around the Sikh's wrist. He unlocks the gate sometimes to pass the women inside sacks of grain and baskets of vegetables.

The servants evade questions as if there is something shameful going on. Cousin, Adi and I are agog. And on a Sunday afternoon – it is already October – we sneak up the stairs and, minding the holes in the roof, tiptoe to look into the enclosed courtyard. Our servants' quarters' roof runs in a continuous line of clay to their roof, demarcated only by a foot-high brick wall.

We assume it's a women's jail, even though they look innocent enough – village women washing clothes, crossing the courtyard with water canisters, chaffing wheat and drying raw mangoes for pickling. There is very little chatter among the women. Just apathetic movements to and fro.

The Sikh guard squats in front of a small water tank in his white cotton drawers, scouring his teeth with a walnut twig. He must have just washed his hair because it is flung round his neck like a coarse scarf to keep it from trailing in the mud.

The guard spots us on the roof and glowers ferociously. As he stands up his hair uncoils and hangs down almost to his knees. We scamper from his view like scared spiders, careful not to fall through the holes where the mud has given way between the decaying rafters.

After a while, taking care to tread quietly and not daring to talk, we peer between the rafters into the dim, smoke-filled cubicles. I feel a nervous, nauseous thrill, as I make out the dark shapes of women in shalwar-kamizes moving lethargically between their cots. In one of the cubicles a thin long face looks up unseeing through the veil of smoke and the eerie desolation of that pallid face remains stamped on my mind.

* * *

The Hindu doctor's house so unobtrusively occupied by our new refugee neighbours sprawls in an ungainly oblong block between the women's jail and Rosy-Peter's annexe. Its cement plaster shows beneath scabs of peeling white-wash. I don't know how many people dwell in the abandoned bungalow, but the number of its occupants appears to be increasing. There is more movement behind the windows boarded up with cardboard and newspaper, a greater frequency and laxity in the sudden shouting and subdued chatter.

We still don't know anything about them. Who they are, where they're from. They keep to themselves, unobtrusively conducting their lives, lurking like night animals in the twilight interiors of their lairs, still afraid of being evicted from property they have somehow managed to occupy.

* * *

The woman is pulling a faded kamize that is too short for her over a wash-greyed shalwar. Her head is covered by a frayed voile *chuddar* and she is standing before Mother, awkward and uncomfortably tall. I recognise her the moment I see her. Her eyes are downcast and a nervous, apologetic smile – that is more like a twitch – jerks about her lips. I feel a surge of panic. Does Mother know she's interviewing a criminal to replace Ayah? But there is a quality so anxious and despairing about the narrow pallid face that I conceal my knowledge. I would rather trust myself to the dangerous care of the jailbird than betray her: so strong is the drag of guilt and compassion she has exerted on me. She looks at Mother out of appealing eyes. Docile. Ready to please. So in need. Servilely murmuring: 'Yes, *jee*, I will do everything . . . Anything you want.'

'These are decent folk, mind you! They're not the kind that let fly dog-and-cat abuses,' interjects Imam Din gruffly, leaning against Mother's bedroom door with the proprietory air of an elderly and pampered flunkey. 'You'll be looked after if you work properly.'

He is as transparent as me. He cannot hide his pity.

'I am not frightened of work, brother,' says the woman in thickly accented, village Punjabi. 'I will sweep, clean, milk the buffalo, churn the butter, wash clothes, clean out latrines, make chapatties . . . After all, I've been a housewife.'

She stops speaking abruptly and looks unaccountably guilty and even more bashful. Suddenly, folding her knees, she hunkers down on the bedroom floor and draws her *chuddar* forward over her face.

'You won't need to do any of that!' says Mother. She indicates me with her glance. 'Here's your charge. All I want you for is the care of the children . . . Don't let them out of your sight.'

The woman swivels on her heels and gazes into my eyes so intensely that I feel it is I, and not Mother, who is empowered to employ her. The jerky smile about her lips distends fearfully. 'I will guard her like the pupils in my eyes,' she says. 'Don't I know how careful one has to be with young girls? Especially these days!' Her tone of voice and choice of words – as of village women uttering platitudes – is grotesque in the obviously straitened and abnormal circumstances of her life.

We call her by her name, Hamida. We can't bear to call her Ayah.

* * *

Looking for Ayah. We are all looking for Ayah. Mother and Electric-aunt, heads together, go goos-goosing and whispering, contorting their faces in strange and solemn ways. And when they see us they hush and dramatically alter their fierce expressions. Their reassembled, we-were-just-talking-of-this-and-that features frighten me more than the news they are attempting to spare me.

Father once again cycles to work, leaving the Morris for Mother. Electric-aunt and Mother drive off, come back, and are off again with such frequency and urgency that I ache with expectation and shattered hope each time I anxiously look into the returning Ayah-less car.

Sharbat Khan returns from the hills and Hari, alias Himat Ali, squatting on his trembling haunches and weeping shamelessly, tells him: 'He sprang at me out of a gunny-sack, dead!' And wiping his tearing eyes says, 'The dead bastard! Didn't he know she'd be alone?'

Wrapped in a blanket, turban wound round his mouth, Sharbat Khan cycles up for low-voiced conversations with Imam Din and Yousaf. He rattles away – sometimes accompanied by Yousaf – and the way their legs pedal, and the way they lean into the wind, I can tell they are looking for Ayah.

Sharbat Khan looks different. His tiger eyes are grim and bloodshot. He drives his foot hard on the pedal of his machine and examines the edges of the knives he sharpens as though he will use them to kill us all. Sometimes he looks at me as if he is trying to probe my soul and search out the aberrations in my personality that made me betray Ayah. Then he shakes his head and bitterly says: 'Children are the Devil . . . They only know the truth.'

I can no longer look into his eyes.

* * *

Hamida keeps her bowed head covered and her eyes averted from Father. She shuffles and pivots awkwardly on her long legs, hunching her narrow shoulders meekly, careful not to offend anyone by her unusual height.

Hamida has to be trained from scratch. Yousaf teaches her how to make beds the way Mother likes. Mother shows her how to stack clothes in tidy piles in cupboards, how to wash woollens and dry them on spread towels. Hamida has never used an iron. She never does. She is so terrified of electricity that she doesn't even switch on the lights – until Cousin shows her how to with a wooden clothes hanger, which, it is dinned into her head, makes her shock-proof.

We tell her where our things go and Mother shows her how to bathe us and massage my legs.

I barely limp now.

Hamida has to be restrained from latching on to Mother and massaging and pummelling her limbs whenever she finds Mother sitting, sewing or reading in bed. Hamida doesn't know what to do with her hands in Mother's presence. And, when idle, in fluttering panic they reach out and massage whoever is at hand. Adi wiggles and slips away from her grasp. Or, if she is too insistent, kicks out. I let her hands have their will with me and tolerate her irksome caress. She is like a starved and grounded bird and I can't bear to hurt her.

Sometimes her eyes fill and the tears roll down her cheeks. Once, when I smoothed her hair back, she suddenly started to weep, and noticing my consternation explained: 'When the eye is wounded, even a scented breeze hurts.'

* * *

Hamida comes to fetch me from Mrs Pen's. When we are close to the house, she casually says: 'Imam Din has guests . . . Poor things: they have suffered a lot . . . The Sikhs attacked their village.'

'Where are they from?' I ask, my pulse quickening.

'Pir Pindo . . . or some such village.'

I leave her hand and as I run towards the house I hear her voice trying to restrain me. 'Be careful, Lenny baby,' she cries. 'Wait for me!' And she runs after me. My heart beating wildly, I run into the servants' courtyard.

A small boy, so painfully thin that his knees and elbows appear swollen, is squatting a few feet away concentrating on striking a marble lying in a notch in the dust. He is wearing ragged, draw-string shorts of thin cotton and the dirty cord tying them in gathers round his waist trails in the mud. His aim scores, and he turns to look at me. His face is a patchwork of brown and black skin; a wizened blemish. He starts to get up, showing his teeth in a crooked smile; and with a shock I recognise Ranna. His limbs are black and brittle; the circular protrusion of his windpipe and ribs so skeletal that I can see the passage of air in his throat and lungs. He is covered with welts; as if his body has been chopped up, and then welded. He sees my horror and winces, turning away. 'Ranna,' I say, moving quickly to touch him. 'Ranna! What happened to you?' I can't help it; I look at the ugly scab where his belly-button used to be. He stares at me his face crumbling. And, as wheeling abruptly, he runs into Imam Din's quarters, I see the improbable wound on the back of his shaved head. It is a grisly scar like a brutally gouged and premature bald spot. In time the wound acquired the shape of a four-day-old crescent moon.

I almost live in the quarters. Hamida sits with us for short periods, and when she pulls Ranna to her lap and he presses against her, her disorderly hands grow tranquil. I only go to the house to sleep. I eat my meals in Imam Din's quarters, relishing everything Ranna's Noni *chachi* cooks. That's when they talk – using plain Punjabi words and graphic peasant gestures – Ranna, bit by bit, describing the attack on Pir Pindo, Noni *chachi* recounting her part in the story, and Iqbal *chacha* intervening with clarification, conjecture and comment. It is hard to grasp that the events they describe took place only a couple of months ago . . . that, like Ranna, Pir Pindo is brutally altered . . . that his family, as I knew it, has ceased to exist . . .

* * *

No one realised the speed at which the destruction and the rampage advanced. They didn't know the extent to which it surrounded them. Jagjeet Singh visited Pir Pindo under cover of darkness with furtive groups of Sikhs. A few more families who had close kin near Multan and Lahore left, disguised as Sikhs or Hindus. But most of the villagers resisted the move. The uncertainty they faced made them discredit the danger. 'We cannot leave,' they said, and, like a refrain, I can hear them say: 'What face will we show our forefathers on the day of judgement if we abandon their graves? Allah will protect us!'

Jagjeet Singh sent word he was risking his life, and the lives of the other men in Dera Tek Singh, if he visited Pir Pindo again. The Akalis were aware of his sympathies for the Muslims. They had threatened him. They were in control of his village.

Jagjeet Singh advised them to leave as soon as they could: but it was already too late.

Ranna's story

Late that afternoon the clamour of the monsoon downpour suddenly ceased. Chidda raised her hands from the dough she was kneading and, squatting before the brass tray, turned to her mother-in-law. Sitting by his grandmother Ranna sensed their tension as the old woman stopped chaffing the wheat. She slowly pushed back her age-brittle hair and, holding her knobby fingers immobile, grew absolutely still.

Chidda stood in their narrow doorway, her eyes nervously scouring the courtyard. Ranna clung to her shalwar, peering out. His cousins, almost naked in their soaking rags, were shouting and splashing in the slush in their courtyard. 'Shut up. Oye!' Chidda shouted in a voice that rushed so violently from her strong chest that the children quietened at once and leaned and slid uneasily against the warm black hides of the buffaloes tethered to the rough stumps. The clouds had broken and the sun shot beams that lit up the freshly bathed courtyard.

The other members of the household, Ranna's older brothers, his uncles, aunts and cousins were quietly filing into the courtyard. When she saw Khatija and Parveen, Chidda strode to her daughters and pressed them fiercely to her body. The village was so quiet it could be the middle of the night: and from the distance, buffeting the heavy, moisture-laden air, came the wails and the hoarse voices of men shouting.

Already their neighbours' turbans skimmed the tall mud ramparts of their courtyard, their bare feet squelching on the path the rain had turned into a muddy channel.

I can imagine the old mullah, combing his faded beard with trembling fingers as he watches the villagers converge on the mosque with its uneven green dome. It is perched on an incline; and seen from there the fields, flooded with rain, are the same muddy colour as the huts. The mullah drags his cot forward as the villagers, touching their foreheads and greeting him sombrely, fill the prayer ground. The *chaudhry* joins the mullah on his charpoy. The villagers sit on their haunches in uneven rows lifting their confused and frightened faces. There is a murmur of voices. Conjectures. First the name of one village and then of another. The Sikhs have attacked Kot-Rahim. No, it sounds closer . . . It must be Makipura.

The *chaudhry* raises his heavy voice slightly: 'Dost Mohammad and his party will be here soon . . . We'll know soon enough what's going on.'

At his reassuring presence the murmuring subsides and the villagers nervously settle down to wait. Some women draw their veils across their faces and, shading their bosoms, impatiently shove their nipples into the mouths of whimpering babies. Grandmothers, mothers and aunts rock restive children on their laps and thump their foreheads to put them to sleep. The children, conditioned to the numbing jolts, grow groggy and their eyes become unfocused. They fall asleep almost at once.

Half an hour later the scouting party, drenched and muddy, the lower halves of their faces wrapped in the ends of their turbans, pick their way through the squatting villagers to the *chaudhry*.

Removing his wet puggaree and wiping his head with a cloth the mullah hands him, Dost Mohammad turns on his haunches to face the villagers. His skin is grey, as if the rain has bleached the colour. Casting a shade across his eyes with a hand that trembles slightly, speaking in a matter-of-fact voice that disguises his ache and fear, he tells the villagers that the Sikhs have attacked at least five villages around Dehra Misri, to their east. Their numbers have swollen enormously. They are like swarms of locusts, moving in marauding bands of thirty and forty thousand. They are killing all Muslims. Setting fires, looting, parading the Muslim women naked through the streets – raping and mutilating them in the centre of villages and in mosques. The Bias, flooded by melting snow, and the monsoon, is carrying hundreds of corpses. There is an intolerable stench where the bodies, caught in the bends, have piled up.

'What are the police doing?' a man shouts. He is Dost Mohammad's cousin. One way or another the villagers are related.

'The Muslims in the force have been disarmed at the orders of a Hindu Sub-Inspector; the dog's penis!' says Dost Mohammad, speaking in the same flat monotone. 'The Sikh and Hindu police have joined the mobs.'

The villagers appear visibly to shrink – as if the loss of hope is a physical thing. A woman with a child on her lap slaps her forehead and begins to wail: '*Hai! Hai!*' The other women join her: *'Hai! Hai!'* Older women, beating their breasts like hollow drums, cry, 'Never mind us . . . save the young girls! The children! *Hai! Hai!*'

Ranna's two-toothed old grandmother, her frail voice quavering bitterly, shrieks: 'We should have gone to Pakistan!'

It was hard to believe that the decision to stay was taken only a month ago. Embedded in the heart of the Punjab, they had felt secure, inviolate. And to uproot themselves from the soil of their ancestors had seemed to them akin to tearing themselves, like ancient trees, from the earth.

And the messages filtering from the outside had been reassuring. Gandhi, Nehru, Jinnah, Tara Singh were telling the peasants to remain where they were. The minorities would be a sacred trust . . . The communal trouble was being caused by a few mischief-makers and would soon subside – and then there were their brothers, the Sikhs of Dera Tek Singh, who would protect them.

But how many Muslims can the Sikh villagers befriend? The mobs, determined to drive the Muslims out, are prepared for the carnage. Their ranks swollen by thousands of refugees recounting fresh tales of horror they roll towards Pir Pindo like the heedless swells of an ocean.

The *chaudhry* raises his voice: 'How many guns do we have now?'

The women quieten.

'Seven or eight,' a man replies from the front.

There is a disappointed silence. They had expected to procure more guns but every village is holding on to its meagre stock of weapons.

'We have our axes, knives, scythes and staves!' a man calls from the back. 'Let those bastards come. We're ready!'

'Yes . . . we're as ready as we'll ever be,' the *chaudhry* says, stroking his thick moustache. 'You all know what to do . . .'

They have been over the plan often enough recently. The women and girls will gather at the *chaudhry*'s. Rather than face the brutality of the mob they will pour kerosene around the house and burn themselves. The canisters of kerosene are already stored in the barn at the rear of the *chaudhry*'s sprawling mud house. The young men will engage the Sikhs at the mosque, and at other strategic locations, for as long as they can and give the women a chance to start the fire.

A few men from each family were to shepherd the younger boys and lock themselves into secluded back rooms, hoping to escape detection. They were peaceable peasants, not skilled in such matters, and their plans were sketchy and optimistic. Comforted by each other's presence, reluctant to disperse, the villagers remained in the prayer yard as dusk gathered about them. The distant wailing and shouting had ceased. Later that night it rained again, and comforted by its seasonal splatter the tired villagers curled up on their mats and slept.

The attack came at dawn. The watch from the mosque's single minaret hurtled down the winding steps to spread the alarm. The panicked women ran to and fro screaming and snatching up their babies, and the men barely had time to get to their posts. In fifteen minutes the village was swamped by the Sikhs – tall men with streaming hair and thick biceps and thighs, waving full-sized swords and sten-guns, roaring, '*Bolay so Nihal! Sat Siri Akal!*'

They mowed down the villagers in the mosque with the sten-guns. Shouting '*Allah-o-Akbar!*' the peasants died of sword and spear wounds in the slushy lanes and courtyards, the screams of women from the *chaudhry*'s house ringing in their ears, wondering why the house was not burning.

Ranna, abandoned by his mother and sisters halfway to the *chaudhry*'s house, ran howling into the courtyard. Chidda had spanked his head and pushed him away, shrieking, 'Go to your father! Stay with the men!'

Ranna ran through their house to the room the boys had been instructed to gather in. Some of his cousins and uncles were already there. More men stumbled into the dark windowless room – then his two older brothers. There must be at least thirty of them in the small room. It was stifling. He heard his father's voice and fought his way towards him. Dost Mohammad shouted harshly: 'Shut up! They'll kill you if you make a noise.'

The yelling in the room subsided. Dost Mohammad picked up his son, and Ranna saw his uncle slip out into the grey light and shut the door, plunging the room into darkness. Someone bolted the door from inside, and they heard the heavy thud of cotton bales stacked against the door to disguise the entrance. With luck they would remain undetected and safe.

The shouting and screaming from outside appeared to come in waves: receding and approaching. From all directions. Sometimes Ranna could make out the words and even whole sentences. He heard a woman cry, 'Do anything you want with me, but don't torment me . . . For God's sake, don't torture me!' And then an intolerable screaming. 'Oh God!' a man whispered on a sobbing intake of breath. 'Oh God, she is the mullah's daughter!' The men covered their ears – and the boys' ears – sobbing unaffectedly like little children.

A teenager, his cracked voice resounding like the honk of geese, started wailing: 'I don't want to die . . . I don't want to die!' Catching his fear, Ranna and the other children set to whimpering: 'I don't want to die . . . Abba, I don't want to die!'

'Hush,' said Dost Mohammad gruffly. 'Stop whining like girls!' Then, with words that must have bubbled up from a deep source of strength and compassion, with infinite gentleness, he said, 'What's there to be afraid of? Are you afraid to die? It won't hurt any more than the sting of a bee.' His voice, unseasonably light-hearted, carried a tenderness that soothed and calmed them. Ranna fell asleep in his father's arms.

Someone was banging on the door, shouting: 'Open up! Open up!'

Ranna awoke with a start. Why was he on the floor?

Why were there so many people about in the dark? He felt the stir of men getting to their feet. The air in the room was oppressive: hot and humid and stinking of sweat. Suddenly Ranna remembered where he was and the darkness became charged with terror.

'We know you're in there. Come on, open up!' The noise of the banging was deafening in the pitch-black room, drowning the other children's alarmed cries. 'Allah! Allah! Allah!' an old man moaned non-stop.

'Who's there?' Dost Mohammad called; and putting Ranna down, stumbling over the small bodies, made his way to the door. Ranna, terrified, groping blindly in the dark, tried to follow.

'We're Sikhs!'

There was a pause in which Ranna's throat dried up. The old man stopped saying 'Allah'. And in the deathly stillness, his voice echoing from his proximity to the door, Dost Mohammad said, 'Kill us . . . Kill us all . . . but spare the children.'

'Open at once!'

'I beg you in the name of all you hold sacred, don't kill the little ones,' Ranna heard his father plead. 'Make them Sikhs . . . Let them live . . . they are so little . . .'

Suddenly the noon light smote their eyes. Dost Mohammad stepped out and walked three paces. There was a sunlit sweep of curved steel. His head was shorn clear off his neck. Turning once in the air, eyes wide open, it tumbled in the dust. His hands jerked up slashing the air above the bleeding stump of his neck.

Ranna saw his uncles beheaded. His older brothers, his cousins. The Sikhs were among them like hairy vengeful demons, wielding bloodied swords, dragging them out as a sprinkling of Hindus, darting about at the fringes, their faces vaguely familiar, pointed out and identified the Mussulmans by name. He felt a blow cleave the back of his head and the warm flow of blood. Ranna fell just inside the door on a tangled pile of unrecognisable bodies. Someone fell on him, drenching him in blood.

Every time his eyes open the world appears to them to be floating in blood. From the direction of the mosque come the intolerable shrieks and wails of women. It seems to him that a woman is sobbing just outside their courtyard: great anguished sobs – and at intervals she screams: 'You'll kill me! *Hai Allah* . . . Y'all will kill me!'

Ranna wants to tell her, 'Don't be afraid to die . . . It will hurt less than the sting of a bee.' But he is hurting so much . . . Why isn't he dead? Where are the bees? Once he thought he saw his eleven-year-old sister, Khatija, run stark naked into their courtyard. her long hair dishevelled, her boyish body bruised, her lips cut and swollen and a bloody scab where her front teeth were missing.

Later in the evening he awoke to silence. At once he became fully conscious. He wiggled backwards over the bodies and slipping free of the weight on top of him felt himself sink knee-deep into a viscous fluid. The bodies blocking the entrance had turned the room into a pool of blood.

Keeping to the shadows cast by the mud walls, stepping over the mangled bodies of people he knew, Ranna made his way to the *chaudhry*'s house. It was dark inside. There was a nauseating stench of kerosene mixed with the smell of spilt curry. He let his eyes get accustomed to the dimness. Carefully he explored the rooms cluttered with smashed clay pots, broken charpoys, spilled grain and chapatties. He had not realised how hungry he was until he saw the pile of stale bread. He crammed the chapatties into his mouth.

His heart gave a lurch. A woman was sleeping on a charpoy. He reached for her and his hand grasped her clammy, inert flesh. He realised with a shock she was dead. He walked round the cot to examine her face. It was the *chaudhry*'s older wife. He discovered three more bodies. In the dim light he turned them over and peered into their faces searching for his mother.

When he emerged from the house it was getting dark. Moving warily, avoiding contact with the bodies he kept stumbling upon, he went to the mosque.

*

For the first time he heard voices. The whispers of women comforting each other – of women softly weeping. His heart pounding in his chest he crept to one side of the arching mosque entrance. He heard a man groan, then a series of animal-like grunts.

He froze near the body of the mullah. How soon he had become accustomed to thinking of people he had known all his life as bodies. He felt on such easy terms with death. The old mullah's face was serene in death, his beard pale against the brick plinth. The figures in the covered portion at the rear of the mosque were a dark blur. He was sure he had heard Chidda's voice. He began inching forward, prepared to dash across the yard to where the women were, when a man yawned and sighed, '*Wah Guru!*'

'*Wah Guru! Wah Guru!*' responded three or four male voices, sounding drowsy and replete. Ranna realised that the men in the mosque were Sikhs. A wave of rage and loathing swept his small body. He knew it was wrong of the Sikhs to be in the mosque with the village women. He could not explain why: except that he still slept in his parents' room.

'Stop whimpering, you bitch, or I'll bugger you again!' a man said irritably.

Other men laughed. There was much movement. Stifled exclamations and moans. A woman screamed, and swore in Punjabi. There was a loud cracking noise and the rattle of breath from the lungs. Then a moment of horrible stillness.

Ranna fled into the moonless night. Skidding on the slick wet clay, stumbling into the irrigation ditches demarcating the fields, he ran in the direction of his Uncle Iqbal and his Noni *chachi*'s village. He didn't stop until deep inside a thicket of sugar-cane he stumbled on a slightly elevated slab of drier ground. The clay felt soft and caressing against his exhausted body. It was a safe place to rest. The moment Ranna felt secure his head hurt and he fainted.

Ranna lay unconscious in the cane field all morning. Intermittent showers washed much of the blood and dust off his limbs. Around noon two men walked into the cane field, and at the first rustle of the dried leaves Ranna became fully conscious.

Sliding on his butt to the lower ground, crouching amidst the pricking tangle of stalks and dried leaves, Ranna followed the passage of the men with his ears. They trampled through the field, selecting and cutting the sugar-cane with their *kirpans*, talking in Punjabi. Ranna picked up an expression that warned him that they were Sikhs. Half buried in the slush he scarcely breathed as one of the men came so close to him that he saw the blue check on his lungi and the flash of a white singlet. There was a crackling rustle as the man squatted to defecate.

Half an hour later when the men left, Ranna moved cautiously towards the edge of the field. A cluster of about sixty Sikhs in lungis and singlets, their carelessly knotted hair snaking down their backs, stood talking in a fallow field to his right. At some distance, in another field of young green shoots, Sikhs and Hindus were gathered in a much larger bunch. Ranna sensed their presence behind him in the fields he couldn't see. There must be thousands of them, he thought. Shifting to a safe spot he searched the distance for the green dome of his village mosque. He had travelled too far to spot it. But he knew where his village lay and guessed from the coiling smoke that his village was on fire.

Much later, when it was time for the evening meal, the fields cleared. He could not make out a single human form for miles. As he ran again towards his aunt's village the red sun, as if engorged with blood, sank into the horizon.

All night he moved, scuttling along the mounds of earth protecting the waterways, running in shallow channels, burrowing like a small animal through the standing crop. When he stopped to catch his breath, he saw the glow from burning villages measuring the night distances out for him.

Ranna arrived at his aunt's village just after dawn. He watched it from afar, confused by the activity taking place around five or six huge lorries parked in the rutted lanes. Soldiers, holding guns with bayonets sticking out of them, were directing the villagers. The villagers were shouting and running to and fro, carrying on their heads charpoys heaped with their belongings. Some were herding their calves and goats towards the trucks. Others were dumping their household effects in the middle of the lanes in their scramble to climb into the lorries.

There were no Sikhs about. The village was not under attack. Perhaps the army trucks were there to evacuate the villagers and take them to Pakistan.

Ranna hurtled down the lanes, weaving through the burdened and distraught villagers and straying cattle, into his aunt's hut. He saw her right away, heaping her pots and pans on a cot. A fat roll of winter bedding tied with a string lay to one side. He screamed: 'Noni *chachi*! It's me!'

'For a minute I thought: Who is this filthy little beggar?' Noni *chachi* says, when she relates her part in the story. *'I said: Ranna? Ranna? Is that you? What're you doing here!'*

The moment he caught the light of recognition and concern in her eyes, the pain in his head exploded and he crumpled at her feet unconscious.

'It is funny,' Ranna says. *'As long as I had to look out for myself, I was all right. As soon as I felt safe, I fainted.'*

Her hands trembling, his *chachi* washed the wound on his head with a wet rag. Clots of congealed blood came away and floated in the pan in which she rinsed the cloth. *'I did not dare remove the thick scabs that had formed over the wound,'* she says. *'I thought I'd see his brain!'* The slashing blade had scalped him from the rise in the back of his head to the top, exposing a wound the size of a large bald patch on a man. She wondered he had lived; found his way to their village. She was sure he would die in a few moments. Ranna's *chacha*, Iqbal, and other members of the house gathered about him. An old woman, the village *dai*, checked his pulse and his breath and, covering him with a white cloth, said: 'Let him die in peace!'

*

A terrifying roar, like the warning of an alarm, throbs in his ears. He sits up on the charpoy, taking in the disorder in the hastily abandoned room. The other cot, heaped with his aunt's belongings, lies where it was. He can see the bedding roll abandoned in the courtyard. Clay dishes, mugs, chipped crockery, and hand-fans lie on the floor with scattered bits of clothing. Where are his aunt and uncle? Why is he alone? And in the fearsome noise drawing nearer, he recognises the rhythm of the Sikh and Hindu chants.

Ranna leapt from the cot and ran through the lanes of the deserted village. Except for the animals lowing and bleating and wandering ownerless on the slushy paths there was no one about. Why hadn't they taken him with them?

His heart thumping, Ranna climbed to the top of the mosque minaret. He saw the mob of Sikhs and Hindus in the fields scuttling forward from the horizon like giant ants. Roaring, waving swords, partly obscured by the veil of dust raised by their trampling feet, they approached the village.

Ranna flew down the steep steps. He ran in and out of the empty houses looking for a place to hide. The mob sounded close. He could hear the thud of their feet, make out the words of their chants. Ranna slipped through the door into a barn. It was almost entirely filled with straw. He dived into it.

He heard the Sikhs' triumphant war cries as they swarmed into the village. He heard the savage banging and kicking open of doors: and the quick confused exchange of shouts as the men realised that the village was empty. They searched all the houses, moving systematically, looting whatever they could lay their hands on.

Ranna held his breath as the door to the barn opened.

'Oye! D'you think the Musslas are hiding here?' a coarse voice asked.

'We'll find out,' another voice said.

Ranna crouched in the hay. The men were climbing all over the straw, slashing it with long sweeps of their swords and piercing it with their spears.

Ranna almost cried out when he felt the first sharp prick. He felt steel tear into his flesh. As if recalling a dream, he heard an old woman say: He's lost too much blood. Let him die in peace.

Ranna did not lose consciousness again until the last man left the barn.

* * *

And while the old city in Lahore, crammed behind its dilapidated Mogul gates, burned, thirty miles away Amritsar also burned. No one noticed Ranna as he wandered in the burning city. No one cared. There were too many ugly and abandoned children like him scavenging in the looted houses and the rubble of burnt-out buildings.

His rags clinging to his wounds, straw sticking in his scalped skull, Ranna wandered through the lanes stealing chapatties and grain from houses strewn with dead bodies, rifling the corpses for anything he could use. He ate anything. Raw potatoes, uncooked grains, wheat-flour, rotting peels and vegetables.

No one minded the semi-naked spectre as he looked in doors with his knowing, wide-set peasant eyes as men copulated with wailing children – old and young women. He saw a naked women, her light Kashmiri skin bruised with purple splotches and cuts, hanging head down from a ceiling fan. And looked on with a child's boundless acceptance and curiosity as jeering men set her long hair on fire. He saw babies, snatched from their mothers, smashed against walls and their howling mothers brutally raped and killed.

Carefully steering away from the murderous Sikh mobs he arrived at the station on the outskirts of the city. It was cordoned off by barbed wire, and beyond the wire he recognised a huddle of Muslim refugees surrounded by Sikh and Hindu police. He stood before the barbed wire screaming, '*Amma! Amma!* Noni *chachi!* Noni *chachi!*'

A Sikh sepoy, his hair tied neatly in a khaki turban,

ambled up to the other side of the wire. 'Oye! What're you making such a racket for? Scram!' he said, raising his hand in a threatening gesture.

Ranna stayed his ground. He could not bear to look at the Sikh. His stomach muscles felt like choked drains. But he stayed his ground: '*I was trembling from head to toe*,' he says.

'*O, me-kiya!* I say!' the sepoy shouted to his cronies standing by an opening in the wire. 'This little mother-fucker thinks his mother and aunt are in that group of Musslas.'

'Send him here,' someone shouted.

Ranna ran up to the men.

'Don't you know? Your mother married me yesterday,' said a fat-faced, fat-bellied Hindu, his hairy legs bulging beneath the shorts of his uniform. 'And your *chachi* married Makhan Singh,' he said, indicating a tall young sepoy with a shake of his head.

'Let the poor bastard be,' Makhan Singh said. 'Go on: run along.' Taking Ranna by his shoulder he gave him a shove.

The refugees in front watched the small figure hurtle towards them across the gravelly clearing. A middle-aged woman without a veil, her hair dishevelled, moved forward holding out her arms.

The moment Ranna was close enough to see the compassion in her stranger's eyes, he fainted.

With the other Muslim refugees from Amritsar, Ranna was herded into a refugee camp at Badami Baug. He stayed in the camp, which is quite close to our Fire Temple, for two months, queuing for the doled out chapatties, befriended by improvident refugees, until chance – if the random queries of five million refugees seeking their kin in the chaos of mammoth camps all over West Punjab can be called anything but chance – reunited him with his Noni *chachi* and Iqbal *chacha*.

Chapter 26

Cousin's cook drops hints. He tells Cousin he suspects where Ayah is. Yes, he thinks she's in Lahore.

Then he clams up. And no matter how much Cousin threatens or cajoles him, doesn't add one illuminating word. I dare not question the cook. In front of me he clams up. And in private threatens Cousin he won't tell him anything if he blabs to me.

I roam the bazaars holding Himat Ali's wizened finger, Hamida's glutinous hand. I visit fairs and *melas*, riding on Yousaf's shoulders, looking here and there. And when I ride on the handlebar of his bicycle, peering into tongas, buses, bullock-carts and trucks, I sometimes think I spot Ayah and exclaim! But it always turns out to be someone who only resembles Ayah.

* * *

Godmother is influential. Even Col. Bharucha visits her. Neighbours of all faiths drop in to talk: and to pay their respects. But Godmother seldom ventures out. She only visits if someone is very sick or in extreme need of her.

Or if she feels the call to donate blood.

The call nags her this stifling July morning. Godmother tucks a cologne-watered handkerchief into a little pocket in her sari-blouse, puts on her maroon velvet going-out slippers, pins her going-out beige silk sari to her hair and armed with a black umbrella sets off in a tonga to bequeath blood. I accompany her. Schools and tuitions are suspended for summer vacations and I am spending the week with her. Hamida and Adi spend most evenings with us. Mother visits occasionally and I feel distanced from her – like with a guest.

Godmother lies down on a hard hospital bench covered only with a white sheet. A nurse bends her arm back and forth and rubs the crease in her arm with cotton wool that smells just like the muzzle did when Col. Bharucha operated on my leg. The lady-doctor approaches with a hideous injection syringe and sick to my stomach I turn my face away and squeeze Godmother's hand. Her answering grip remains steady.

When I look at her again, the blood-sucking needle withdrawn, she appears to have grown longer – as if the noble deed has added stature to her horizontal form. I am certain her blood will save many wounded lives.

Perspiring and half dead from the heat, we return from the hospital. Mini Aunty hands Godmother a precious half-glass of iced water from a thermos and says she would also like to donate blood.

Godmother is firm with her middle-aged kid sister. 'No,' she says, 'you may kindly not donate your blood! I can't afford to have you go all faint and limp on me.'

Slavesister looks unutterably deprived. 'All right,' she says, sagging against the kitchen door jamb. 'Go to heaven all by yourself, then. Deny me even good deeds!'

Godmother is truly astonished.

'Is that what you believe?' she asks, staring at Slavesister slack-jawed and open-mouthed; for once at a complete loss.

At last, shaking her head, Godmother rotates her thumb against her temple: 'A screw loose somewhere,' she says, looking dazed. 'What's to become of her, I don't know . . . In heaven or in hell!'

* * *

Over the years Godmother has established a network of espionage with a reach of which even she is not aware. It is in her nature to know things: to be aware of what's going on around her. The day-to-day commonplaces of our lives unravel to her undercurrents that are lost to less perceptive humans. No baby – not even a kitten – is delivered within the sphere of her influence without her becoming instantly aware of its existence.

And this is the source of her immense power: this reservoir of random knowledge, and her knowledge of ancient lore and wisdom and herbal remedy. You cannot be near her without feeling her uncanny strength. People bring to her their joys and woes. Show her their sores and swollen joints. Distilling the right herbs, adroitly instilling the right word in the right ear, she secures wishes, smooths relationships, cures illnesses, battles wrongs, solaces grief and prevents mistakes. She has access to many ears. No one knows how many. And, when talking incessantly about my resurrected friend I relate to her the rigours of Ranna's experience, she achieves for him a minor miracle! Ranna is suddenly siphoned into the Convent of Jesus and Mary as a boarder.

It surprises me how easily Ranna has accepted his loss; and adjusted to his new environment. So . . . one gets used to anything . . . If one must. The small bitternesses and grudges I tend to nurse make me feel ashamed of myself. Ranna's ready ability to forgive a past none of us could control keeps him whole.

The Convent is on the outskirts of Shahdara, about halfway between Imam Din's village and Lahore. Barricaded by tall brick walls the girls' school accepts boys up to a certain age. Getting a poor refugee child admitted to a Convent school is as difficult as transposing him to a prosperous continent: and as beneficial. Not only for him, it is said, but for seven succeeding generations of the Ranna progeny. Ranna visits us on the weekends he can get a cycle ride into Lahore.

Godmother can move mountains from the paths of those she befriends, and erect mountainous barriers where she deems it necessary.

She is on to something. I can tell. When I catch her goos-goosing with Slavesister and they stop whispering abruptly, I know they are talking of Ayah. Slavesister behaves as if they are not hiding anything from me. But Godmother, to her credit, looks guilty as hell.

She has never let me down yet. I have more faith in her

investigative capacities than I have in Mother's and Electric-aunt's sorties.

* * *

The mystery of the women in the courtyard deepens. At night we hear them wailing, their cries verging on the inhuman. Sometimes I can't tell where the cries are coming from. From the women – or from the house next door infiltrated by our invisible neighbours.

There is a great deal of activity by day: of trucks going to and from the tin gates sealing the courtyard; of women shouting; but no hint of the turmoil and suffering that erupts at night.

And closer, and as upsetting, the caged voices of our parents fighting in their bedroom. Mother crying, wheedling. Father's terse, brash, indecipherable sentences. Terrifying thumps. I know they quarrel mostly about money. But there are other things they fight about that are not clear to me. Sometimes I hear Mother say, 'No, Jana; I won't let you go! I won't let you go to her!' Sounds of a scuffle. Father goes anyway. Where does he go in the middle of the night? To whom? Why . . . when Mother loves him so? Although Father has never raised his hands to us, one day I surprise Mother at her bath and see the bruises on her body.

And at dawn the insistent roar of the zoo lion tracking me to whatever point of the world I cannot hide from him in my nightmares.

It gets so that I cannot sleep. Adi is asleep within moments but I lie with my eyes open, staring at the shadows that have begun to haunt my room. The twenty-foot-high ceiling recedes and the pale light that blurs the ventilators creeps in, assuming the angry shapes of swirling phantom babies, of gaping wounds forming deformed crescents – and of Masseur's slender, skilful fingers searching the nightroom for Ayah.

And when I do fall asleep the slogans of the mobs reverberate in my dreams, pierced by women's wails and shrieks – and I awaken screaming for Ayah.

Mother rushes to my side and bends over me. In the faint glow from the nigh-light I see her hand sweep my body as she symbolically catches mischievous spirits and banishes them with a loud snap of her fingers. At the same time she blows on me, making a frightening noise like moaning winds: Whooooo! whoooooo! The sound is eerie enough to banish any presence: natural or supernatural. She places a six-inch iron nail, blessed by the Parsee mystic Mobed Ibera, the disciple of Dastur Kookadaru, under my mattress to ward off fear.

Sometimes Mother lies beside me, her touch as fresh and soothing as daylight, and tells me the old story of the little mouse with seven tails. Mother has wisely changed the ending. 'And then there was only one tail left,' she says, 'and the little mousey came home laughing: "Ha, ha, ha, ha!"' Mother's artificial laugh bounces off the walls so heartily that it dispels fear and I too laugh. 'And the little mousey said,' says my mother, '"Mummy, mummy, no one teased me. They said, 'Little mousey with one tail. Nicey mousey with one tail!'"'

I have outgrown the story – but the intimacy it recalls lulls the doubts and fears in my growing mind.

Mother asks Hamida to sleep on a mat in our room. Hamida squats by my bed and we talk in whispers till I fall asleep.

One cold night I am awakened by a hideous wail. My teeth chattering, I sit up. I must have just dozed off, because Hamida is still sitting by my bed.

'Shush,' she says. 'Go to sleep . . . It's just some woman.'

I lie down and Hamida patiently strokes my arm.

'Why do they wail and scream at night?' I ask.

It is not a subject I have broached till now, mindful of Hamida's sensibilities.

'Poor fate-smitten woman,' says Hamida, sighing. 'What can a sorrowing woman do but wail?'

'Who are those women?' I ask.

'God knows,' says Hamida. 'Go to sleep . . . there is nothing we can do . . . She'll be all right in the morning.'

My heart is wrung with pity and horror. I want to leap out of my bed and soothe the wailing woman and slay her tormentors. I've seen Ayah carried away – and it had less to do with fate than with the will of men.

'Did you cry?' I ask Hamida.

'Who doesn't? We're all fate-smitten . . .'

'I mean, when you were there?'

Her hand on my leg goes still.

'I saw you before you came to us, you know. I saw you in the jail next door.' I speak as gently as I know how.

'What nonsense you talk . . .'

'I looked down at you from a hole in the roof. You couldn't see me – but I saw you. I recognised you straightaway when you were talking to Mother about the job . . . But I didn't tell her!'

After a pause, breathing heavily in the dark, Hamida says, 'Your mother knows I was there.'

The woman in the jail has stopped wailing. It is so quiet – as it must be at the beginning of time.

'Why were you in jail?' I ask at last.

'It isn't a jail, Lenny baby . . . It's a camp for fallen women.'

'What are fallen women?'

'*Hai!* The questions you ask! Your mother won't like such talk . . . Now keep quiet . . .'

'Are you a fallen woman?'

'*Hai*, my fate!' moans Hamida, suddenly slapping her forehead. She rocks on her heels and makes a crazy keening noise, sucking and expelling the air between her teeth.

'What's the matter? Don't do that . . . please don't do that,' I whisper, leaning over to touch her.

'If your mother finds out this is how you talk, she'll throw me out! *Hai*, my fate!'

Again she slaps her forehead and makes that strangling nasal noise.

'I won't tell her . . . I promise! Stop it. Please don't do that!'

I get out of bed and press her face into my chest. I rock her, and Hamida's tears soak right through my flannel nightgown.

I won't mention her fall ever again. I can't bear to hurt her: I'd rather bite my tongue than cause pain to her grief-wounded eye.

But this resolve, too, goes the way of all resolutions.

'What's a fallen woman?' I ask Godmother.

'A woman who falls off an aeroplane.'

Godmother can be like that sometimes. Exasperating. She can't help it.

'Wouldn't she break her head and die?' I say patiently.

'Maybe.'

'But Hamida didn't break her head . . . She says she's a fallen woman.'

'Oh?' Godmother's expression changes.

As I tell her of my conversation with Hamida, Slavesister loiters about the room. She pretends to arrange papers on the desk. The letters and papers are already sorted out and neatly stacked. Although she has her back to me, I can tell her ears are switched on.

'Hamida was kidnapped by the Sikhs,' says Godmother seriously. On serious matters I can always trust her to level with me. 'She was taken away to Amritsar. Once that happens, sometimes, the husband – or his family – won't take her back.'

'Why? It isn't her fault she was kidnapped!'

'Some folk feel that way – they can't stand their women being touched by other men.'

It's monstrously unfair: but Godmother's tone is accepting. I think of what Himat-Ali-alias-Hari once told me when I reached to lift a tiny sparrow that had tumbled from its nest on our veranda.

'Let it be,' he'd stopped me. 'The mother will take care of it. If our hands touch it, the other sparrows will peck it to death.'

'Even the mother?' I asked.

'Even the mother!' he'd said.

It doesn't make sense – but if that's how it is, it is.

'That's why your mummy tells you to stay with Hamida all the time – or with us,' says Slavesister unctuously. 'When your mother tells you something, it's for your own good.'

There she goes again: butting in and making serious matters trivial.

'Her mother's not here,' says Godmother. 'It won't do you any good buttering her up in her absence.'

'And I'm not married either! It doesn't matter if I'm kidnapped,' I speak up.

'Oh yes? And who'll marry you then? It'll be hard enough finding someone for you as it is.'

'Mummy says: my husband will search the world with a candle to find me!'

'Poor fellow . . . He won't know you the way we do, will he? Your husband will clutch his head in his hands and weep!'

'Cousin wants to marry me!' I'm surprised how smug I feel saying it. I don't think I particularly want to marry Cousin – but though he has not actually asked me to, I think he has implied it. It's a comforting thought. If only as a last resort.

'He hasn't seen any girls besides our Lame Lenny, Three For a Penny. Wait till he sees the world!' says Mini Aunty.

What an asinine thing to say about my worldly Cousin! Even Godmother suppresses a smile.

'Kindly go about your business,' she tells her sister. 'And stop messing with those papers! As it is, I can't find anything when I want it.'

'What is the mtter with you?' Cousin asks.

'Nothing.'

I'm feeling despondent. When something upsets me this much I find it impossible to talk. It used not to be so. I wonder: am I growing up? At least I've stopped babbling *all* my thoughts.

This idiocy of bottled-up emotions can't be a symptom of growing up, surely! More likely I'm reverting to infancy the way old people do. I feel so sorry for myself – and for Cousin – and for all the senile, lame and hurt people and fallen women – and the condition of the world – in which countries can be broken, people slaughtered and cities burned – that I burst into tears. I feel I will never stop crying.

'Is your stomach hurting?' Cousin asks cautiously, afraid of a rebuff.

I'm grateful that he has stayed his ground at least and not gone tearing off on some pretext to avoid my irrational outburst.

'No.' I shake my head. 'I'm not hurting.'

And then, of its own accord, my mouth blurts, 'No one will marry me. I limp!' Almost at once I feel less aggrieved.

'But I'll marry you,' volunteers my gallant cousin.

I search his face through my tears. Thank God, he doesn't sound the least martyred. I couldn't bear it. He looks fond and sincere. I find it hard to recall my multitudinous anguishes of a moment before. I even feel a little foolish. And alarmed – lest I irrevocably commit myself to Cousin.

'A slight limp is attractive,' says Cousin, solemn and authoritative.

'Oh yes?' I say, airing my doubt.

'I like the way it makes your bottom wiggle.' He waves two fingers back and forth.

I twist strenuously and, tugging my short dress taut across my buttocks, peer down. There is very little bottom to see.

'When you grow up, you'll have a much bigger bottom,' asserts my solicitous and perceptive cousin. 'It will look very attractive, then . . .' he says somewhat uncertainly.

My deepening scepticism has infected him too.

'I read a story,' he continues gravely, 'in which the heroine limped. Her one leg was shorter. She didn't even have a pretty face. But her limp was so sexy, everybody wanted to marry her!'

I don't care for Cousin's second-hand consolations. In any case, I don't want him harping on my limp.

'Col. Bharucha says I'll stop limping by the time I grow up.'

'A pity,' says Cousin. 'I find it attractive.'

'I can always keep it, if you like,' I say politely, and further guarding my options I add: 'Let's see how I feel about marrying you when I grow up.'

'Do you find me attractive?' Cousin suddenly asks, gazing compellingly into my eyes.

'Yes,' I say courteously, and avert my eyes.

'How attractive?' Cousin is insistent. 'Do you think you could love me passionately? Die for me?'

I reflect a moment. Cousin certainly does not arouse in me the rapture Masseur aroused in Ayah . . . I recall the bewildering longings the look on Masseur's face stirred in me when he looked at Ayah . . . And other stirrings . . .

'I don't find you that attractive,' I say truthfully.

'I suppose you're too young,' says Cousin. 'You haven't known passion.'

I open my eyes wide and look demurely at Cousin, and let it pass.

But Cousin can't: 'Do you find anyone more attractive than me?'

'Yes,' I say, 'I think I found Masseur more attractive . . .'

I surprise myself. Mouthing the words articulates my feelings and reveals myself to me.

'But he was old!' says Cousin equally surprised.

I suddenly feel shy and Cousin looks unutterably dejected. I think my sudden shyness convinces him of my wayward heart more than any protestations would.

'Who else do you find attractive?' Cousin asks, managing to wipe his face and voice of all expression.

'Oh I don't know . . . There was a little Sikh boy . . .'

'Do me a favour,' Cousin says. 'Think about all the people you find more attractive than me – and let me know.'

I have been so engaged by my reaction to the names named that I fail to notice the bitterness and sarcasm that have crept into his voice.

I look about me with new eyes. The world is athrob with men. As long as they have some pleasing attribute – height, width, or beauty of face – no man is too old to attract me. Or too young. Tongawallahs, knife-sharpeners, shopkeepers, policemen, schoolboys, Father's friends, all exert their compelling pull on my runaway fantasies in which I am recurringly spirited away to remote Himalayan hideouts; there to be worshipped, fought over, died for, importuned and wooed until, aroused to a passion that tingles from my scalp into the very tips of my fingers, I finally permit my lover to lay his hands upon my chest. It is no small bestowal of favour, for my chest is no longer flat.

Two little bumps have erupted beneath my nipples. Flesh of my flesh, exclusively mine. And I am hard put to protect them. I guard them with a possessive passion beside which my passion for possessing Rosy's little glass jars pales. Only I may touch them. Not Cousin. Not Imam Din. Not Adi. Not anybody. I can't trust anyone.

Not even Mother who has taken to bathing me; and with her characteristic prim and solemn expression bunches her fingers round them and goes: 'Pom-pom.'

'Let me, let me . . .' says Cousin and pokes his hand out every-which-way every chance he gets. I find it fatiguing to maintain my distance from him.

And from Adi, who resolutely materialises whenever I'm bathing and glues his eye to a crack in the bathroom door. When Hamida blocks it, Adi shifts to another crack: and when that too is plugged, he jumps up and down on a ledge outside the bathroom window with a rapt determination that is like an elemental force. Hearing Hamida's twittering remonstrances and my shrill screams, Imam Din emerges roaring: 'Wait till I catch you, you shameless bugger,' and carries Adi, wiggling and kicking, towards the kitchen. I peer out of the window and Adi's face, flushed with a cold rage, bodes ill for any ideas Imam Din might have of sitting him on his lap. Even Imam Din could not handle that frustrated cobra fury.

As the mounds beneath my nipples grow, my confidence grows. I tell Imam Din to hold Adi in the kitchen, push Hamida out of the bathroom and lock the door. I examine my chest in the small mirror hanging at an angle from the wall and play with them as with cuddly toys. What with my limp and my burgeoning breasts – and the projected girth and wiggle of my future bottom – I feel assured that I will be quite attractive when I'm grown up.

Cousin walks with me and Hamida to the bazaars and gardens, rides with us in tongas, and I dutifully point out to him all the men and boys I find appealing. 'See the boy with the cute little buck teeth?' I ask. 'I could die for him!' and 'Look-look-look,' I say physically turning Cousin's head. 'Look at that fellow in the tonga with his feet up!'

'I'm keeping tabs,' says Cousin mournfully after this has gone on for some days. 'You are attracted by roughly ten per cent of the male population in Lahore.'

'Is that too much?' I enquire.

'Why not me?' Cousin demands, ignoring my question. 'What's wrong with me?'

'You're too young, maybe.'

'But some of the boys you liked are younger . . . I'll grow up!'

My heart sinks sadly for my Cousin. Why don't I feel all suffocated and shy when I'm with him? I try to fathom my emotions.

'Maybe I don't need to attract you. You're already attracted,' I say.

It is like that with Cousin. He even shows me ME!

I've admitted it before: I have a wayward heart. Weak,

susceptible and fickle. But why do I call it my heart? And blame my blameless heart? And not blame instead the incandescence of my womb?'

Chapter 27

I spend hours on the servants' quarters' roof looking down on the fallen women. The turnover, as they are rescued, sorted out and restored to their families, is so rapid that I can barely keep track of the new faces that appear and so soon disappear. The camp is getting crowded. If this is where they bring kidnapped women, this is where I'll find my Ayah.

Hamida knows where to find me when Mother asks for me – or when someone is going to Godmother's on an errand and thinks of taking me along. Sometimes, furtively climbing the stairs, Hamida sits quietly with me and together we look at the dazed and dull faces. If they look up we smile, and Hamida makes little reassuring gestures; but the women only look bewildered and rarely smile back.

I wonder about the women's children. Don't they miss their mothers? I pray that their husbands and families will take them back. Hamida seldom mentions her children. All I've been able to get out of her is that she has two teenage sons and two daughters, one as old as me and one younger.

'The youngest was just beginning to walk,' says Hamida one crisp afternoon as we sun ourselves on the roof. Hamida has come to fetch me for lunch, but she is willing to stay for a while.

'Don't you miss your children?' I ask.

'Of course,' says Hamida.

'Then why don't you go to see them?'

'Their father won't like it.'

'They must miss you. You could see them secretly, couldn't you?'

'No,' says Hamida turning her face away. 'They're better off as they are. My sister-in-law will look after them. If their father gets to know I've met them he will only get angry, and the children will suffer.'

'I don't like your husband,' I say.

'He's a good man,' says Hamida, hiding her face bashfully in her *chuddar*. 'It's my kismet that's no good . . . we are *khut-putli*, puppets, in the hands of fate.'

'I don't believe that,' I say. 'Cousin says we can change our kismet if we want to. The lines on our palms can also change!'

Hamida gives me a queer quizzical look. 'Have you heard of the prince who was eaten by a tiger?' she asks.

'No,' I say, shaking my head and settling comfortably against the roof wall to listen.

It is the perfect day for a story. The sun is warm on our skins, casting a quiet, lazy spell on the afternoon. It is the first story Hamida tells me. Later I discover she has a fund of unusual and depressing little tales.

Once upon a time there was a king who had no children, says Hamida. Night and day the king and his queen prayed for a son. They travelled afar, visiting one holy-man after another, and visited all the shrines of saints in their kingdom. The queen wove temple saris for the various goddesses, stuck flowers in their images and covered the goddesses with gold.

One night the king had a dream. In his dream a ragged noly-man with wild hair said: 'O, king, your dearest wish will be granted. Before the year is out you will have a son. But you have accumulated an unfavourable karma. In your past life you were disobedient to your guru and, at times, even irreverent. You will be punished for your insolence. Your son will be eaten by a tiger in his sixteenth year.'

As foretold, the royal couple was blessed with a beautiful son. The king and queen rejoiced and diligently distributed food and money among their poorer subjects to improve the condition of their karmas and earn blessings.

The king decreed that all tigers be hunted and killed. He organised tiger hunts and rode at the head of the elephant cavalry to decimate the beasts rounded up by the drummers. He offered handsome rewards for the pelts brought by the hunters.

The prince grew tall and beautiful. He was compassionate and filled with laughter. The more they loved him the more his subjects feared the prophecy.

By the time the prince was ten years old they had killed all the tigers and, as an added precaution, all the domestic and alley cats: for what is a cat if not a miniature tiger? The tigers in the surrounding kingdoms were also killed.

As the prince grew older he yearned to hunt: and at last the king was satisfied that it was safe for the prince to venture into the forest. Most people had forgotten what a tiger even looked like!

The fateful year dawned. The prince turned sixteen.

Once again the wild-haired holy-man appeared in the king's dream. 'The tiger who will eat the prince is already near,' he said to the trembling king.

Again the hunters beat the bushes and searched the woods. There were no pug marks or droppings even – no trace to show that tigers had once inhabited the forests.

The prince was confined to the palace. He was never left unattended. Huntsmen patrolled the forests and armed guards the palace gates.

The king and queen prayed more, fasted oftener, and did all manner of penance. The king gave his fine robes to the beggars and wore the coarse garments of the fakirs. He distributed large portions of his wealth among the poor and donated fortunes to shrines, mosques, temples and churches. He undertook vows and oaths that would bind him to a lifetime of penitence if his son was spared.

The year was almost past. The king, in his penitent's sackcloth, was discussing affairs of state in the *darbar* when the prince walked in. The king made room for his son on the marble *takth*, covered with silk rugs. The assembly bowed till the prince settled amidst the velvet cushions and signalled them to sit. He lay back on the bolsters and after a while he fell asleep.

The *darbar* was almost over when the prince awakened from a terrifying dream. His frightened eyes opened on a finely wrought hunting scene painted on the ceiling. Royal huntsmen, spears poised in varying attitudes of attack, surrounded a fierce tiger, bare-fanged and richly striped. Suddenly the prince screamed and cried: 'Oh! The tiger! The tiger! He's got me!' He fell back and writhing in agony died.

In the pandemonium that followed, the king's eyes quickly traced the path of his son's congealed stare: and, horrified, he saw the lifelike glow on the rich pelt dim, and the tiger's shining eyes revert to yellow paint!

Hamida, who has been gawking skywards like the horrified monarch, returns halfway to earth and looks at me.

But I'm in no mood to countenance tragedy. Despite the unnatural angle of my upended hairs, despite the accelerated beat of my heart, despite the gloaming images of the screaming prince and the chill on my skin I rend the story with savage logic. If the king's karma was so lousy how come he was king? And why should the poor prince suffer for his father's . . .? And how can a painted tiger . . .?

'Perhaps it's not so unreal as it is unfair!' I conclude.

'What does Fate care?' says Hamida with placid and omniscient certainty. 'That's why it is fate!'

We become still: cocking our ears to a din and uproar coming from the kitchen.

'Imam Din's caught the *billa*!' says Hamida, her narrow face lighting up. And just as Ayah and I ran to the back at the sounds of struggle with Hari's dhoti, we now run towards the kitchen: Hamida holding me by the hand and my feet flying to match her long strides.

Neighbours and the servants already form a small crowd. Imam Din, one leg on the ground and one on the kitchen steps, has a huge black and battle-scarred cat trapped in the screen door and is pressing his whole weight on the frame to hold the slippery intruder. The cat, caught below its ribs, is suspended a foot off the floor. Frantically twisting, its teeth bared, the panicked creature is spitting wildly.

Imam Din roars: 'That'll teach you to sneak into the kitchen, you one-eared monster! Make all the noise you want! I'm not letting go of you, you badmash *billa*!'

The crowd outside the kitchen grows as more people run up from the road. Someone shouts: 'That tom sneaks into our kitchen too! Teach the fellow!' and someone else yells: 'He sure won't poke his snout into your pans again!' And Yousaf yells, 'That's enough, *yaar! Bas kar!*' and Imam Din says, 'This time I'm going to teach him . . . It's the third time I've caught the thug! Poke your nose into the milk will you?'

'Let him go,' I scream. 'He'll die.'

'He's not about to die,' says Hamida. 'He's a tough old alley cat!'

The Morris rolls up the drive and comes to a stop in the porch. Mother beeps the horn and shouts: 'What's going on?'

Imam Din is so intent on chastising the cat that he doesn't hear her, and oblivious of her presence roars invective at the caterwauling animal.

'Let her go at once!' screams Mother, slamming shut the door of the car. She cannot see the cat's gender – it is secreted behind the door – but the rest of us seem to know it's a *him*.

Mother grabs hold of Imam Din's shirt and pulls but I don't think he even notices.

'Get the fly-swat, Lenny!' screams Mother in an absolute frenzy.

I dash in and fetch the fly-swat with a long reed handle and a wire-mesh flap. Mother snatches it from my hand and, waving her arms in an awkwardly feminine and energetic way, swats Imam Din with it. She strikes his legs, arms, shoulders, and even his shaven head.

All at once Imam Din lets go the door and grips his arm.

The surprised cat bounds down the steps and spitting and bouncing like a charred fire-cracker streaks zigzagging past the startled crowd.

Imam Din turns to face Mother. Glasses dramatically awry, face flushed, she continues to whack him. Imam Din looks bewildered – and searches confusedly for the flies she is swatting on his person. When he realises her fury is directed at him, his bewilderment turns to incredulity, and then to shock. He holds out his hand and like a man taking away a dangerous toy, snatches the fly-swat from Mother. He examines it as if he's never seen a fly-swat before.

Surprised at being so peremptorily disarmed Mother yells: 'Get out of my sight! *Duffa ho!*'

Large tears welling from his old eyes, Imam Din turns his broad back on her, and followed by my excited mother walks zombie-like into the crowd. Absorbed and protected by the crowd Imam Din scrutinises the tears in his shirt and the fine lines of blood congealing on his forearms.

'Shame on you! Tormenting a small cat! Get out of my sight!' Mother shouts once more, and whirling around in her silk sari and tinted glasses marches inside.

'Look!' says Imam Din to the sympathetic crowd. 'I can't believe it . . . She drew blood!'

'It was only a fly-swat, *yaar*,' says Yousaf taking hold of his arm. He shouts at the gawkers: 'What's there to see? Go on, push off!'

Muttering and laughing among themselves the crowd breaks up. Some vault the walls to neighbouring houses and some walk down the drive to the road.

Yousaf leads Imam Din into the kitchen. Hamida and I follow. Hamida saying in her conciliatory and submissive manner: 'What if *Baijee* had a whip, brother? What would you've done then? Oh, ho! Look at the tears in your clothes,' she exclaims. 'Tch-tch-tch! Don't worry. I'll sew them so they'll look like new!'

Imam Din refuses to have his clothes mended and remains sullen all afternoon.

When Father returns late in the evening Imam Din presents himself before Father's bicycle and with a most injured countenance says: '*Baijee* struck me with a fly-swat! I bled!'

Father places his cycle on its stand and raising his brows in a clutch of surprised wrinkles looks at us out of baffled eyes.

'Imam Din caught the *billa* in the kitchen door, and wouldn't let him go. And Mummy hit him with the fly-flapper,' I explain.

Father turns his astonished eyes upon Imam Din.

Turning and twisting, Imam Din displays a scattered and spidery mesh of wounds where the wire scratched him. 'This . . . And this. And see this!' he says stretching the small tears in his lungi and shirt.

Father locks his cycle. Making a few clucking noises of insincere sympathy he prepares to go in, when Mother bursts out of banging springdoors shouting: 'Stop snivelling in front of Sahib, you big idiot! You're lucky it was only a fly-flap! Go in, someone, and get him bangles. If he whines like a woman he must wear bangles!'

Despite her shouting Mother sounds good-humoured and we release our suppressed laughter. Even Father cannot suppress his tight little smile.

Shaking his head sheepishly Imam Din ambles off towards the kitchen and Mother laughs and clings to Father and Father continues to smile, despite her clinging, and says: 'The fly-flap's upset him. If you'd used a stick he wouldn't have minded so much.'

Adi and I laugh and laugh and hug Father and our clinging mother. I feel deliriously light-hearted. So does Adi. Father has spoken directly to Mother: addressing her instead of the walls, furniture, ceiling – or using us as deflecting conduits to sound his messages off. It is becoming an increasingly rare occurrence – this business of his talking to our mother: out of public or party view that is.

* * *

And suddenly, the hunt for Ayah is off. I sense it. So does Adi.

They only pretend to look for her. Mother still takes off in the Morris but I know it is not to look for Ayah. I can tell by the way the car's wheels flatten on the stones and by the determined angle of Skinny-aunt's chin – that the car's dicky is loaded with petrol. They can set fire to the world for all I care! I want my Ayah.

Chapter 28

It is a bad phase in my life. Even Cousin is avoiding me. I haven't seen him for a week. I must talk to him about my concerns or I'll crack up. Adi and I go over to Electric-aunt's. Cousin is studying for his exams.

'I don't know where the sun rises these days,' says Electric-aunt in awed and perplexed pleasure, holding the screen door open and ushering us in. 'Your cousin doesn't wish to be disturbed even by you!' She looks at me archly and flashes all her little goat's teeth in a conceited smile.

Electric-aunt parts the navy-blue curtains and, poking only her head through, quietly whispers: 'Lenny and Adi are here, dear. Won't you see them for just five minutes?'

Since I can't hear his response, and I'm determined to see him, I throw him a line: 'All work and no play makes Jack a dull boy!'

I know he'll bite. Imagine getting away with calling Cousin *dull*.

Cousin drifts into the sitting room in his long shorts and short socks, looking all stand-offish and preoccupied, and greets us unenthusiastically. He perches on the edge of the three-piece sofa, tilting his legs primly to one side and, as if he's a grown man masquerading in short legs, makes desultory small talk with Adi. He doesn't even look at me. Except when I force him to by addressing him insistently – and then he glances my way briefly and coldly, before again bestowing his attention on Adi. To leave no doubt of his tedium at our presence he folds the newspaper into a stiff bat and, with nerve-racking springs and explosive whacks, swats flies on the sofas, tables and radio top.

Electric-aunt covers her ears. 'Oh! Do stop being so jumpy, dear,' she exclaims and, like an angular streak of zigzag lightning, darts from the room.

Cousin perches on the sofa again, elegantly crossing his ankles this time and hastily, before he has a chance to spring up and swat more flies, I whisper: 'They've stopped looking for Ayah!'

'Have they?' says Cousin, looking down at me coolly, and turns to Adi as if I've said something as uneventful and uncomplicated as: 'Godmother rapped Mini Aunty's knuckles with her punkah!'

I can't understand it. I'm furious. 'Let's leave him to his dreary studies,' I say witheringly. But Adi, who has not received such singular attention from Cousin since the time he was almost kidnapped and basked for two days in glory, is reluctant to leave. I have to drag him away.

* * *

It is unnerving. The more aloof Cousin becomes, the more I think about him. I find my day-dreams, for the first time, occupied by his stubby person and adenoidal voice. They are pedestrian and colourless compared to my caveman and kidnapper fantasies, but they are as completely engrossing. I thrill. I feel tingles shoot from my scalp to my toe tips. And Cousin's proximity, compared to the remoteness of imagined lovers tucked away in unseen wildernesses, drives me to reckless excess.

Against all my instincts and sense of dignity, I chase Cousin. I hang around Electric-aunt's house and around Cousin – when he tolerates my presence. I fetch him glasses of water and bunches of grapes and sharpen his pencils and copy out his homework and follow him wherever he goes. If he goes into the bathroom I wait patiently outside the door – hungering for any crumbs he might throw by way of aloof comment or observation. These he restricts – like my father with Mother – to impatient and disparaging monosyllables, mute signals and irate scowls.

And while I hang about Cousin, my eyes hang on him, and I shamelessly and eloquently ogle Cousin.

'Are you in love with him or something?' Adi asks artlessly, but I catch a sly glitter at the edge of his eyes when he turns away. I don't care. Let him think what he likes.

Ranna still visits us on Sundays, if he gets a ride on a bicycle or in a cart. But this Sunday when he comes, his scars covered by crisp white cotton, his bruised face eager; though my heart goes out to him, my mind is filled with thoughts of Cousin. My time consumed in his pursuit. Ranna tags along. But after this he visits less frequently. He goes to Imam Din's village instead, to be with his uncle and Noni *chachi* and his cousins. In any case we are growing apart. It is inevitable. The social worlds we inhabit are too different; our interests divergent.

* * *

Cousin is restored to me on a great surge of excitement when he bursts into my room and bolting the door breathes into my ear, 'I saw Ayah!'

My heart pounds so wildly I cannot speak. Where? Here? In our house? But then Cousin wouldn't have bolted the door. Ayah must be at the Recovered Women's Camp!

'Where is she – in the camp?' I ask, voicing my assumption. And feeling weak-kneed, I sit on the bed.

'I saw her in a taxi. At Charing Cross,' says Cousin, breathing so close I'm forced to lie back. Looking annoyingly complacent and placing an arm on either side of me, Cousin, the bearer of great good news, the restorer of withheld warmth, bears down on me: and in that instant I realise that his aloofness was only a sham calculated to arouse my ardour. Bent on further pleasuring me, squashing his panting chest on my flattened bosom, Cousin gives me a soggy kiss. Poor Cousin. His sense of timing is all wrong. The news about Ayah has cooled my passion. Pushing him back and holding him at arm's length, I say, 'If you don't tell me everything at once, I'll knee your balls!' (I have grown up!) 'Who was she with? Where is she?'

Cousin, resuming his aloof stance, examines his nails and snottily says: 'I said, I saw her in a taxi. You know . . . pass by.'

'You could have followed the taxi,' I howl.

'How? I have engines in my legs?'

I'm not perturbed by his sarcasm or his disdain. His coldness is a hoax anyway.

'Did she see you? How did she look? Did you wave?'

'I don't think she saw me,' says Cousin, thawing before my importunate queries. 'She was all made up!'

'Really? Tell me! What do you mean, made up?'

I scramble across the bed on my knees and grab Cousin by his curly hair.

'Like a film actress,' he says.

Cousin turns in order to accommodate the rest of his body to his twisted neck and, focusing his eyes on my chest, carefully places his hands on my breasts. I draw back, slapping his hands till my palms sting, feeling sick and all shrivelled up.

Cousin looks at me, lovesick and sheepish, his spanked fingers quivering guiltily on his thighs.

'If you ever do that again, I'll break your fingers, knuckle by knuckle,' I say severely. (The previous threat appears to have had no effect – hence the changed perspective.)

'But I love you,' says Cousin. As if that condones his lascivious conduct.

'Well I don't!'

'Then why did you hang around me? And make all those funny eyes and stare at me?'

'I won't anymore. You were only pretending to be stand-offish! You're a phoney!'

'Ha! It worked, didn't it? I had you panting with passion!'

'You didn't!'

'Oh, yes? Look,' says Cousin, conciliatory: 'I love you. But I can't pretend not to all my life just so you'll run after me.'

'You're supposed to chase me!' I say. 'Boys are supposed to chase girls!'

'But you run away!'

'It's only when you put your hands here and there and everywhere.'

'Even before you grew your breasts you didn't love me,' says Cousin bitterly. 'You find everybody but me attractive!'

'I can't help it. If that's the way I feel – that's how it is.'

The next day, angrily hauling me by my organdy sleeve before Godmother, Cousin complains, 'She loves approximately half of Lahore . . . Why can't she love me?'

Godmother, in her wisdom, says: 'It's simply a case of *Ghar ki murg; dal barabar*. A neighbour's beans are tastier than household chickens.'

'But she's just a household chicken, too! Still I love her!' wails Cousin, his nasal voice cracking and squeaking. Passion does make one silly . . . I should know! I feel awfully sorry for him.

'Don't worry,' says the slave, waddling up and mussing his hair. 'It's only puppy love. Wait'll you start noticing your neighbouring chicks!'

'So?' demands Godmother. 'What about the young cocks Lenny will notice?'

'Yes? What about them?' I repeat.

If Cousin wasn't trying so hard to be manful, he'd be crying.

We arrive at a compromise, a finely delineated covenant: I will keep an open mind and let bygones be bygones, and

Cousin will stop wooing me and wait a couple of years before touching my breasts again. We shall see how I feel about it then.

In the meantime Cousin sensibly sets about becoming indispensable. Knowing the way to my heart, he scurries about trying to find out the whereabouts of Ayah. He brings me rumours, and acting on the misleading leads, wastes energy on futile forays into the remotest, seediest and most dangerous parts of the congested city.

Chapter 29

And then, late one evening, I, too, see Ayah. It doesn't register at once. It is only after the taxi has driven past, slowing at the corner of Mozang Chawk and Temple Road, that I realise that the flashy woman with the blazing lipstick and chalky powder and a huge pink hibiscus in her hair, and unseeing eyes enlarged like an actress's with kohl and mascaraed eyelashes, sitting squashed between two thin poets, was Ayah.

In the evening I pester Hamida to take me to the Queen's Garden. She has never taken us there. She says she feels shy sitting among all those strangers.

When I finally get her to agree to take us, Mother announces that Godmother wants Adi and me to spend the night with her.

Dr Manek Mody is visiting again, and he wishes to see us.

* * *

'It's the third time I've told you to put the water to boil!' scolds Godmother from her bed. 'What's the matter with you? The Demon of Laziness finally get you?'

'I'm going, I'm going.' Slavesister's string-bed creaks as she stands up in her crumpled nightie. 'Rodabai, you are so impatient. Really . . .'

'I'm impatient? Do you know what time it is? Do you know Manek attended to the milkman while your Lazyship snored?'

Dr Manek Mody peeps alertly from behind his rustling newspaper. Having been awake for an hour, he's ready for excitement.

Adi stirs beside me and sits up sleepily. I prop myself up on my elbows.

'Even the children awake before you,' says Godmother sternly.

'Shame, shame,' says Dr Mody fastidiously holding the tip of his nose. 'Poppy shame!'

Slavesister's rat-tail braid has come loose and untidy strands of greying hair plaster her neck and back. Although it is only the middle of April we require the ceiling fan that is groaning round and round. Slavesister wipes her moist face on her sleeve.

'I think the demon has found permanent lodging in her!' mutters Godmother.

Abandoning the newspaper, the doctor springs out of his chair, saying, 'I'll exorcise the demon. I know how!'

Tilting forward and extending his index finger he says to Mini Aunty: 'Here, pull it.'

'Don't be silly, Manek,' says Mini Aunty.

'Come on, pull,' coaxes the doctor, looking like a brown-domed elf. 'I swear, you'll hear the demon leave.'

The flaps of Adi's ears move forward. He's that curious. So am I.

Godmother, propped on her pillows, displays a solemn face. But curiosity and amusement quiver in the tension of her restrained muscles.

'Do as Manek says,' she orders, as if instructing a child to drink Milk of Magnesia.

Ignoring her and shaking her head, Slavesister carries her drowsy, martyr's smile into the kitchen.

Dr Mody rushes in after her and, listing forward once again, points his finger.

'Please, Mini Aunty, please pull it,' Adi and I clamour, crowding into the kitchen.

Godmother lowers her feet to the floor and, sitting forward on her cot, peers at us. 'Your hand won't fall off you know,' she calls. 'Here's someone perfectly willing to exorcise your demons and what do you do? Insult him!'

'He's a doctor, not a magician!' says Slavesister.

'I practise exorcism in my spare time – didn't you know? Try it . . . My finger won't explode.'

'Stubborn as a donkey!' decrees Godmother through the door.

'Please, Mini Aunty, be a sport,' I beg. Adi is so excited, and so nervous that the exorcism may not materialise – or take place in his absence – that he dances from foot to foot and has tears in his eyes.

'Oh, all right!' says Slavesister, suddenly capitulating. She tugs at the doctor's finger and, acquiring an air of intense concentration, the gifted doctor farts.

He stands up straight and looks as startled as us. 'Some demon! Did you hear him? He almost tore my ass!'

'Much obliged to you, Manek,' calls Godmother from her bed.

'What d'you have in your stomach? Atom bombs?' enquires Mini Aunty, giving the doctor a whack on his chest.

'That's no way to treat an exorciser,' the doctor says, staggering back a step and looking at her with a slighted countenance.

'It is,' says Mini Aunty, giving him another whack.

'Behave yourself, Mini!' shouts Godmother from the bedroom. 'The poor man risked his life for you!'

'How did you do that?' asks Adi, his legs perfectly still, his face agog.

'Prayer and practice,' says Dr Mody. 'Here, pull my finger.'

He tilts forward and Adi tugs at his pointing finger. With

compressed lips and quivering chin the doctor lets loose a crackling battery of crisp wind. Again Adi pulls and again he farts.

'Me too, I clamour.

The doctor obligingly directs his finger at me. When I pull nothing happens. I'm disappointed.

'Too bad,' says the doctor. 'You have no demons today. We'll try tomorrow.'

In the next three days Cousin, Adi and I are possessed by a posse of demons so numerous that the doctor is hard pressed to exorcise them. He directs Mini Aunty to feed him huge quantities of what he calls anti-demon potions: and Godmother's rooms reek of cabbage, beans and hard-boiled eggs.

Since we all ingest the same nourishment, I fall asleep to a medley of winds: the doctor's magnificent explosions, Godmother's and Slavesister's muted put-putterings, Oldhusband's bass bubblings and Adi's and my high-pitched and protracted eeeeeeeps.

Oldhusband? He's still inhabiting the pages?

Clearly, he has not, as I'd thought, passed away.

Let him stay, as we all stay, in Godmother's talcum-powdered and intrusive wake.

* * *

I cannot believe my eyes. The Queen has gone! The space between the marble canopy and the marble platform is empty. A group of children, playing knuckles, squat where the gunmetal queen sat enthroned. Bereft of her presence, the structure looks unwomaned.

The garden scene has depressingly altered. Muslim families who added colour when scattered among the Hindus and Sikhs, now monopolise the garden, depriving it of colour. Even the children, covered in brocades and satins, cannot alleviate the austerity of the black burkas and white *chuddars* that shroud the women. It is astonishing. The absence of the brown skin that showed through the fine veils of Hindu and Sikh women, and beneath the dhoties and shorts of the men, has changed the complexion of the queenless garden. There are fewer women. More men.

Hamida, her head and torso modestly covered by her coarse *chuddar*, holding her lank limbs close, sits self-consciously on the grass by herself. There is little comfort in laying my head on her rigid lap.

Adi and I wander from group to group, peering into faces beneath white skull-caps and above ascetic beards. The Azan must have sounded. Some women spread prayer mats on the grass and kneeling start to pray. I feel uneasy. Like Hamida, I do not fit. I know we will not find familiar faces here.

* * *

'I saw Ayah! It was her!'

It is cool outside. The sun has set – and in the protracted dusk I am straddling Godmother and clutching her face in my hands. My legs have grown so long I can touch the ground with my toes.

'It must be someone who looks like Ayah. With all that make-up on it's hard to tell.'

Godmother is being intractable.

'I saw her with my own eyes,' I say, pulling down the skin beneath my eyes.

'Sometimes we only see what we wish to see,' says Mini Aunty, issuing the nugget of wisdom as if she's an oracle. 'And don't do that,' she adds, 'you'll grow pouches under your eyes.'

'I know the difference between what I see and what I only want to see,' I shout. I wish she wouldn't intrude. As it is, it's harder to convince Godmother than I'd expected. She must believe me. She's the only one who takes me seriously – except Cousin – and he hasn't been able to unearth anything yet.

'But Cousin also saw her,' I say.

'It can't be her. Ayah is with her family in Amritsar!'

Godmother conveys a certainty that for an instant undermines mine. It can only mean that her network has failed her. I am dismayed.

'How can you be so sure?' I ask.

Godmother hesitates, then she says, gravely, 'Ask your mother.'

'What's she got to do with it?'

I'm surprised. It's not like Godmother to pass the buck. 'What's happening?' I cry. 'Why isn't anyone telling me anything?'

'Lenny, there's some things best left alone,' says Godmother.

'You should send for the family exorcist, Rodabai,' says Mini Aunty. 'Manek will rid her of her stubbornness.'

'If you can't keep your mouth shut, go inside,' Godmother says sharply. Her nostrils are twitching. I've seldom heard her talk to Slavesister like this – totally without her tongue in her cheek.

I feel hopeless. I rub my runny nose and my tears on Godmother's blouse. I'm horribly frightened that Godmother, despite all her canny and uncanny resources, might be misled.

And Godmother, unable to bear my confusion and anguish, and guilty because of her own deviousness, says, 'Lenny, have you noticed how busy your mummy's been all year? Going out all the time?'

I nod.

'I'll tell you a secret,' says Godmother, 'but I want to be sure you won't tell anyone. It could get your mother into real trouble.'

I draw back and permit Godmother to search my solemn face and my honourable eyes. She trusts what she sees because she says:

'Mummy and your aunt rescue kidnapped women. When they find them, they send them back to their families: or, to the Recovered Women's Camps. She arranged for Ayah to be sent to her relatives. She didn't want you to know. She felt you had accepted her absence – you'd only start fretting again.'

Don't I know they went on futile Ayah hunts? Or were they just pretending to look for Ayah, using it as a cover for more sinister activities? Doesn't Godmother know about the petrol in the dicky? Doesn't she know that Electric-aunt and Mother were dashing off armed with petrol-cans and tinted glasses long before anyone had even heard of kidnapped women?

Obviously Godmother does not know. I'm dumbfounded. Godmother, who makes it her business to know everything about everybody, doesn't know about the arsonists! I still live in dread of my mother and aunt's imminent arrest. Hand-and-leg-cuffed and jangling chains! And Godmother's naïvety compounds my fear. She is slipping dangerously, just when her capabilities are most needed. I am tempted to tell her the truth, but I bite my wretched truth-infected tongue just in time. One betrayal is enough. I, the budding Judas, must live with their heinous secret.

It is getting quite dark. Already the dew is settling on our clothes. I shiver on Godmother's lap. Godmother says, as if musing aloud: 'Come to think of it, we haven't seen that popsicle-man in a long time.'

Mini Aunty calls from within, 'You'd better get in, or someone will be sneezing her head off tomorrow.'

* * *

Cousin, too, binds me to secrecy. Crowding me into a corner of Rosy-Peter's still deserted room he whispers into my ear: 'Want to know why Ayah was all made up?'

I respond with a breathless nod.

'Because she has converted her profession!'

'She's become Christian?' I enquire tentatively, not knowing what to make of the revelation.

'Not her religion, silly! Her profession. D'you think Virgin Mary'd be caught dead wearing all that make-up?'

'I don't know,' I confess. What does Virgin Mary have to do with Ayah?

'She wouldn't!' declares my knowing Cousin. 'Ayah has become the opposite of Virgin Mary. She's become a dancing-girl!'

'An actress!' I exclaim, enthralled. That would explain the make-up. The only dancing-girls I've seen are in Indian films.

'Well,' says Cousin, a trifle uncertain. 'Dancing girls do grow into actresses sometimes . . .'

'Oh?' I say, and wait patiently.

'Ayah is just a dancer in the Hira Mandi . . . The red-light district.'

Hira Mandi means Diamond Market. Cousin is being deliberately obtuse. He knows how important any news of Ayah is to me. I would like to shake him. Instead, like stepping on eggshells, I ask, 'Where is this Diamond Mandi with the red light?'

'Behind the Badshahi mosque. It's where dancing-girls live.'

'And the diamonds? Who sells the diamonds?' I prod gingerly.

'There are no real diamonds there, silly. The girls are the diamonds! The men pay them to dance and sing . . . and to do things with their bodies. It's the world's oldest profession,' says Cousin as if he's uttering profundities instead of drivel.

My patience is wearing thin. Still, 'What things?' I ask.

Although I'm cautious with Cousin, wary of surprises, the gullibility that made me climb a stool to insert my finger into the AC current remains.

Ever ready to illuminate, teach and show me things, Cousin squeezes my breasts and lifts my dress and grabs my elasticised cotton knickers. But having only the two hands to do all this with he can't pull them down because galvanised to action I grab them up and jab him with my elbows and knees: and turning and twisting, with my toes and heels.

Becoming red in the face, Cousin lets me be. And standing apart, and with exasperation, says: 'How do you expect me to tell you what? If you don't let me show you how?'

And Cousin starts all over again to show me, and pulling my kicking feet from under me, succeeds in de-knickering me. And putting his hand there, trembles and trembles . . .

Until I punch his ears and shout: 'You're breaking your promise!'

'Who told you all this?' I demand, pulling my knickers up and scowling, my sharp elbows bristling like dangerous quills as I settle down warily in the corner.

'My cook told me.'

'Which men do such things to her?' I demand to know.

'Oh, any man who has the money . . . My cook, wrestlers, Imam Din, the knife-sharpener, merchants, pedlars, the governor, coolies . . .'

If those grown men pay to do what my comparatively small Cousin tried to do, then Ayah is in trouble. I think of Ayah twisting Ice-candy-man's intrusive toes and keeping the butcher and wrestler at arm's length. And of those strangers' hands hoisting her chocolate body into the cart.

That night I take all I've heard and learnt and been shown to bed and by morning I reel dizzily on a fleetingly glimpsed and terrible grown-up world.

I decide it's time to confront Mother.

* * *

I hound Mother with a mute and dogged sullenness. It is Friday, the day to invoke the great Trouble Easers, the angels Mushkail Assan and Behram Yazd. (In troubled times they are frequently evoked by the Parsees.) As Mother prepares for the ceremony, spreading a white sheet on the bedroom floor and placing the small fire altar and photographs of the saints on it, she casts perplexed eyes my way. The less I am able to speak out, the more turbulent grows the temper of my pent-up accusations. Mother kneels on the floor and strikes a match to light the joss-sticks. She arranges the sandalwood shavings on the fire altar and places a criss-cross of small sandalwood sticks on top of them. She holds out the box and says: 'Here, Lenny, would you like to light the fire?'

I whip my hands behind my back as if she has offered me a scorpion. I shake my churlish head.

'What's the matter?' she enquires, on her knees before the unlit altar.

In a harsh, squeaky rush of words I can hardly believe are issuing from me I hear myself say: 'Don't think we don't know what you're up to with the petrol-cans and matches!'

Mother looks so bewildered and alarmed that I wonder for an instant if Cousin, Adi and I are not mistaken. The twinge of doubt passes.

'I know about the petrol in the car's dicky!' I accuse, once again steadfast in my righteous and indignant conviction.

'Oh?' says Mother looking, if anything, more perturbed and baffled. 'I didn't think it necessary you children should know about it . . . It could be dangerous . . .'

'But we do know!' I cry. 'We aren't dumb! You and Aunty should be ashamed of yourselves! Deceiving everybody! Pretending to look for Ayah and instead burning Lahore!' I can no longer hold back my tears or prevent the tragic break in my voice.

'Oh my God!' Mother exclaims. 'Is that what you think?'

And as understanding slowly replaces the astonishment on her face, she pulls me to her lap. Wiping my tears with her soft hands, speaking simply and gravely, she says, 'I wish I'd told you . . . We were only smuggling the rationed petrol to help our Hindu and Sikh friends to run away . . . And also for the convoys to send kidnapped women, like your ayah, to their families across the border.'

'You should have trusted me!' I cry, trying to stay the threatening surge of self-loathing and embarrassment from annihilating me.

'Yes,' she says, solemnly shaking her head up and down. 'I should have!'

How could she have? How can anyone trust a truth-infected tongue?

* * *

On Monday I come straight to Godmother's from Mrs Pen's. I remove my satchel, kick off my shoes and I am peeling off my damp socks when Godmother abruptly says:

'You were right. Ayah is still in Lahore.'

I feel goose-bumps erupt all over. My body feels drained of strength. I totter across the cool cement to Godmother's bed. 'How did you find out?' I ask, when I am able to get my breath back.

'I have my sources,' she says.

I realise the question was redundant.

'What did you find out?' I ask.

'She's married.'

'I heard she's converted into a dancing-girl,' I say.

Godmother is taken aback. 'Who told you that?'

'Cousin told me,' I say. 'His cook told him.'

'She isn't a dancing-girl any more: she's a wife. Her husband is coming to see me this evening.'

'Is Ayah coming?' I ask at once.

'He isn't bringing her.'

'Who's her husband?' I ask eagerly.

'You'll see.'

* * *

I can't wait for evening. When's evening? Four? Six? Eight o'clock? It is already three. The waterman is spraying the drive from the leather pouch slung on his back and the fine dust clings in little balls to drops of water. I can see him through the screen door and smell the steam off the parched earth.

'Let's sit out,' I say impatiently.

'We'll go outside at five o'clock. Like we do every day,' says Mini Aunty.

'Can't I take the chairs out at least?' I say impatiently.

'My, my! One would think someone was expecting her own bridegroom! He'll come when he comes and your sitting outside will not hurry him the tiniest bit!'

'When you've finished laying your eggs of wisdom,' says Godmother, 'you can make me some tea.'

Mini Aunty, sitting in her petticoat and blouse, fans herself harder. Her face is beaded with sweat. 'Let me cool off a bit,' she says: 'I haven't had a moment's respite all day.'

She is exaggerating of course. She has been flopped in that armchair for the past half-hour.

'If you think you have too much to cope with you can live someplace else,' says Godmother.

'I didn't say that, now, did I?' says Mini Aunty placidly.

'Oh? I need to oil my ears?' says Godmother. 'I thought I heard you say you were overworked.'

Mini Aunty gets up with a sigh and, shifting her weight from one bulging bunion to the other, waddles into the kitchen.

By five o'clock we are seated outside, waiting. It is oppressively hot. The thin, pointed leaves of the eucalyptus droop in brittle clusters over our heads and rattle as the sparrows, twittering feverishly, settle for the evening. The table-fan is ineffectual against the dust suspended in the air.

'We're bound to have a dust-storm. It's too still,' Mini Aunty remarks. Raising her petticoat above her spread knees she flaps a punkah before her modestly averted thighs.

'I wish you wouldn't chatter so witlessly,' says Godmother, sounding unduly irascible. 'Predicting dust-storms in the season for dust-storms is not very bright.'

I stall my restless movements on Godmother's lap. I realise how tense she is. We are all tense, waiting. It is almost six o'clock . . . then behold! The bridegroom comes. Lean, lank and loping, in flowing white muslin, raising dust with his sandalled feet, the poet approacheth.

Only now do I realise that one of the lean and languid poets flanking Ayah was Ice-candy-man.

*

Ice-candy-man acknowledges our presence through dreamy kohl-rimmed eyes and removing his lamb's-wool Jinnah-cap, touching his forehead in a mute and protracted salaam, squats bowed before Godmother. He has grown his hair and long oily strands curve on his cheeks. He smells of jasmine attar.

'Live long,' says Godmother, leaning forward to stroke his shoulder – and crushing me in the process.

Ice-candy-man shuffles back and, pushing his hair behind his ears, draws us into the orbit of his poetic vision. He waits quietly while we absorb his incredible transformation. He has changed from a chest-thrusting *paan*-spitting and strutting *goonda* into a spitless poet. His narrow hawkish face, as if recast in a different mould, has softened into a sensuous oval. He is thinner, softer, droopier: his stream of brash talk replaced by a canny silence. No wonder I didn't recognise him in the taxi.

'Where have you been all these months?' exclaims Godmother pleasantly. 'It was impossible to trace you. I was worried. God forbid, I thought you died in the riots!'

For a startled instant Ice-candy-man's eyes lose their poetic mist and focus as clearly as an eagle's on Godmother. But quickly retrieving his composure he says: 'I'm truly sorry. Had I known you wished to see me I would have presented myself earlier.' He recites Faiz:

> '*Tum aye ho na shab-e-intezar guzri hai –*
> *Talash main hai seher baar baar guzri hai!*
> You never came . . . The waitful night never passed –
> Though many dawns have passed in the waiting.'

Astonishingly, we are not amazed at the surge of words pouring from him: so well do they suit the poetic mould of his metamorphosed character.

'*Shabash!* Well said!' says Godmother.

With a start, I scrutinise her face. Except for a thin smile it is clear of all expression. Yet, in some indefinable way, ominous.

'You have become a gifted poet! And not, as rumoured,

a Mandi pimp!' The thrust of her words is still smooth. 'But tell me,' she says, 'why do you live in the Hira Mandi? It's the red-light district, isn't it? No wonder tongues wag. It is not a suitable place for a family man.'

The lines on the poet's face trace his hurt feelings. 'Not a suitable place? No place could be more suitable,' he says, settling lower on his heels. 'Why do you think the Mandi lies in the shadow of the Old Mogul Fort?'

'How should I know? I don't frequent brothels,' says Godmother.

An uncertain smile flickers on Ice-candy-man's face. But then he casts his eyes down: he doesn't know what to make of Godmother's remark.

'*Baijee*, I don't want you to misjudge me,' he says circumspectly. 'You know how deeply I respect you . . . I want to explain something almost no one remembers anymore . . . I want very much that you understand . . . Then judge me!'

Godmother nods slightly, gravely, her face deadpan.

'The Mogul princes built Hira Mandi – to house their illegitimate offspring and favourite concubines,' says Ice-candy-man, speaking with less assurance than before. 'But you know our world . . . Who cares for orphans? Each emperor provided only for his own children, and neglected the sons of his father. The girls, left to fend for themselves, danced, and themselves became royal concubines. And the boys became musicians, singers and poets. Royal indulgences – in those days at least.'

Had I not been looking at Ice-candy-man as he spoke, I would not have believed it was him. Not only has his voice changed, but his entire speech. His delivery is flawless, formal, like an educated and cultured man's. And, continuing in that same confiding manner, he murmurs, 'You are my mother and father . . . I've told no one this – they wouldn't understand . . . You see, I belong to the *Kotha* myself . . . It is the cradle of royal bastards.'

Ice-candy-man's eyes shine with a curious, prickly mixture of shame and pride as he glances at Godmother.

Godmother's eyes on his face remain impassive.

'My mother was from the *Kotha*,' he says. 'She moved to Bhatti Gate when she married my father. He died when I was very young . . . He was a well-known puppeteer.

'My mother belonged to the old stock – she came from the House of Bahadur Shah. There's a strict distinction – the old families from distinguished houses don't mix with the new girls and their set-up. They are nothing but prostitutes – young girls kidnapped by pimps! Anything goes where they're concerned. Poor girls . . . Their lot is pitiful and hideous, I admit. They are forced into all kinds of depravities on pain of death . . . and often die. But we protect our women. We marry our girls ourselves. No one dare lay a finger on them! They are artists and performers . . . beautiful princesses who command fancy prices for their singing and dancing skills!

'Because of my family connection my wife and I live in the old quarter of the Mandi. They have accepted her. For my sake . . . and for the sake of her divine gifts! She has the voice of an angel and the grace and rhythm of a goddess. You should see her dance. How she moves!' And then in another poetic outburst Ice-candy-man declaims:

> 'She lives to dance! And I to toast her dancer's grace!
> Princes pledge their lives to celebrate her celebrated face!'

I am hypnotised by the play of emotion on Ice-candy-man's elastic face: by the music in his voice conjuring voluptuous images of smitten Mogul princes and of Ayah dancing as statues of Hindu goddesses come to life. Considering his revealed lineage it is little wonder he sounds like a cultured courtier. His face, too, has acquired the almond-eyed, thin-lipped profile of the handsome Moguls portrayed in miniatures.

So carried away am I by the virtuosity of his performance that I don't notice Godmother's reaction until she speaks.

'Have you said all you wish to say?' she asks: and I turn on her lap to look at her again. Knowing her as I do I can tell by the hooded droop of her wrinkled lids, by the sombre shape of her tongueless cheeks, that she is in a cold rage: and God help Ice-candy-man.

But Ice-candy-man doesn't know her as well. Quoting Wali, misjudging her fury, and as if presenting credentials, he declares:

> *'Kiya mujh ishq ne zalim ko aab ahista ahista*
> *Ke aatish gul ko karti hai gulab ahista ahista.*
> Slowly, my love has compelled her, slowly –
> The way the sun touches open the rosebud, slowly.'

Affected at last by Godmother's stony silence, Ice-candy-man lowers his eyes. His voice divested of oratory, he says, 'I am her slave, *Baijee*. I worship her. She can come to no harm with me.'

'No harm?' Godmother asks in a deceptively cool voice – and arching her back like a scorpion its tail, she closes in for the kill. 'You permit her to be raped by butchers, drunks, and *goondas* and say she has come to no harm?'

Ice-candy-man's head jolts back as if it's been struck.

'Is that why you had her lifted off – let hundreds of eyes probe her – so that you could marry her? You would have your own mother carried off if it suited you! You are a shameless badmash! *Nimakharam!* Faithless!'

'Yes, I'm faithless!' Stung intolerably, and taken by surprise, Ice-candy-man permits his insolence to confront Godmother. 'I'm a man! Only dogs are faithful! If you want faith, let her marry a dog!'

'Oh? What kind of man? A royal pimp? What kind of man would allow his wife to dance like a performing monkey before other men? You're not a man, you're a low-born, two-bit evil little mouse!'

Ice-candy-man is visibly shaken. His hazel eyes dart frantically – like the sparrows he once trapped for the mems – as he glances at Mini Aunty, the road, me, for sympathy or a means of succour. And then, his yellow eyes narrowed, he stares at Godmother with naked malevolence.

I see him now as Godmother sees him. Treacherous, dangerous, contemptible. A destructive force that must be annihilated.

'You have permitted your wife to be disgraced! Destroyed her modesty! Lived off her womanhood!' says Godmother as if driven to recount the charges before an invisible judge. 'And you talk of princes and poets? You're the son of pigs and pimps! You're not worth the two-cowries one throws at lepers!'

Struck by the naked power and fury of her attack, Ice-candy-man's body twitches. His head jerks forward and his long fingers gouge the earth between his sandals. And, as if committed against his will to witness the litany of his transgressions, his gaze clings to Godmother's. 'I s-saved her,' he stammers. 'They would've . . . killed her . . . I married her!'

'I can have you lashed, you know? I can have you hung upside down in the Old Fort until you rot!'

Ice-candy-man shifts his eyes to the ground. And in the pause that follows, tears, and a long strand of mucus from his nose, drip into the fissures at his feet.

'It's no good crying now. You'll be shown as little mercy as you showed her.'

'I don't seek mercy,' he says, his voice so muffled and blocked that it registers like an afterthought. 'If I deserve to be hung, then hang me!'

It is frightening to watch the silent tumult of Ice-candy-man's capitulation. The back of his neck is stretched in a long, shallow arch and his head hangs between his knees. His arms move helplessly, not knowing where to rest.

'Get out of my sight, you whining *haramzada*!' says Godmother.

Ice-candy-man just squats there, excreting his pain and tears, and as I look at him, I realise there is more to his turmoil than the rage and terror generated by Godmother's attack.

'It's too late to repent,' says Godmother with a magnitude of grief that makes my eyes smart with sudden tears.

'You have trapped her in the poisonous atmosphere of the *Kotha.*'

'Allah is my witness, I'm married to her,' he says in a horrible, gruff voice.

'There is no God for the likes of you *shaitans*!' Godmother says remorselessly. 'You are no more married to her than I am.'

'What do you want me to do? Slit my throat? Stab my heart?' His cap lies on the ground. His dusty hands, the nails dark with dirt, tremble on his knees.

'Restore her to her family in Amritsar.'

'What if she refuses to leave me?' says Ice-candy-man, as if dredging from a deep doubt in his chest a scrap of hope. 'I have been a good husband . . . Ask her. I've covered her with gold and silks. I'd do anything to undo the wrong done her. If it were to help to cut my head off, I'd cut my head and lay it at her feet! No one has touched her since our *nikah.*'

'When did the marriage take place?' asks Godmother, unmoved.

'In May.'

'She was lifted in February and you married her in May? What were you doing all that time?'

Ice-candy-man remains silent.

'Why don't you speak? Can't you bring yourself to say you played the drums when she danced? Counted money while drunks, pedlars, sahibs, and cut-throats used her like a sewer?' Godmother's face is slippery with sweat. Her thighs beneath me are trembling. I have a potent sense of her presence now. And when I inhale I can smell the formidable power of her attack.

'Did you marry her, then, when you realised that Lenny's mother had arranged to have her sent to Amritsar?'

Ice-candy-man, his muddied hair falling forward from his bowed head, remains still.

'Why don't you speak? A little while back you couldn't stop talking!'

Suddenly Ice-candy-man clenches his hair in his fists. His

eyes are bloodshot. His face is a puffy patchwork of tears and mud. He tugs his hair back in such a way that his throat swells and bulges like a goat's before a knife, and in a raw and scratchy voice he says: 'I can't exist without her.' Then, rocking on his heels in his strange, boneless way, he pounds his chest and pours fistfuls of dirt on his penitent's head. 'I'm less than the dust beneath her feet! I don't seek forgiveness . . .'

There is a suffocating explosion within my eyes and head. A blinding blast of pity and disillusion and a savage rage. My sight is disoriented. I see Ice-candy-man float away in a bubble and dwindle to a grey speck in the aftermath of the blast and then come so close that I can see every pore and muddy crease in his skin magnified in dazzling luminosity. The popsicle man, Slavesister and we and our chairs and the table with the fan skid at a tremendous angle to dash against the compound wall and the walls bulge and fly apart. Godmother's house and Mrs Pen's house sway crazily, the bricks tumbling.

The images blur and I try desperately to suck the air into my deflated lungs and Godmother holds my violently shivering body tight and I hear her say as if from far away, 'Look how you have upset the child! You've turned us all insane!' And she pats my breathless face and sharply says, 'Stop it! Stop it! Take a deep breath! Come on, inhale. Everything is going to be all right!'

She must have signalled to Slavesister because the slave heaves herself off her stool and, anxiety quickening her movements, stoops to lift me. Her face, too, is streaked with tears and her eyes red and she is muttering: 'Finish it now, Rodabai, that's enough. Pack him off.' And I cling to Godmother. And stretch like bubble-gum when Slavesister tries to pull me away. And at a signal from Godmother she lets me be. And I, rubbing my face in Godmother's tightly bound bosom, grind the cloth between my teeth and shake my head till the khaddar tears and I smell blood and taste it.

'Ouch! Stop it! You've turned into a puppy have you?' says Godmother pushing my face away.

And when my teeth are pried away from her bloodied blouse and I at last look into her shrewd, ancient eyes, I can tell her tongue is once again in her cheek.

Everything's going to be all right!

Jinnah-cap in hand, Ice-candy-man stands before us. His ravaged face, caked with mud, has turned into a tragedian's mask. Repentance, grief and shock are compressed into the mould of his features . . . And his inflamed eyes are raw with despair.

The storm that has been gathering all day rushes up the drive, slamming open the doors and windows. The three-pronged eucalyptus dips threateningly above our heads. As we scurry to shut the windows and carry the chairs inside, waves of mud obscure the drive and swallow the poet's fluttering white clothes.

The innocence that my parents' vigilance, the servants' care and Godmother's love sheltered in me, that neither Cousin's carnal cravings, nor the stories of the violence of the mobs, could quite destroy, was laid waste that evening by the emotional storm that raged round me. The confrontation between Ice-candy-man and Godmother opened my eyes to the wisdom of righteous indignation over compassion. To the demands of gratification – and the unscrupulous nature of desire.

To the pitiless face of love.

Chapter 30

Just as Godmother feels the urge to donate blood she is impelled by an urge to pop up at the right place in the hour of a person's need. Yet I am surprised when fingering her grey silk sari and matching blouse laid out on the stack of trunks I ask, 'Where are you going?' and she, after an unintended and dramatic pause, replies, 'I'm going to see Ayah.'

My heart stops. I feel as if I've run all the way from Warris Road instead of walking here, holding Hamida's finger. If I don't hold her finger Hamida turns hysterical and babbles, '*Hai!* We'll be run over by the cars and tongas.'

It is Saturday morning. Adi and Cousin have gone to the grassless Warris Road park to play cricket. That is, Cousin will play and Adi will probably be forced to spectate. Mother is out.

I cannot speak. Godmother holds my twiggy arm beneath my starched and puffed-out sleeve and pulls me to the cot. Oldhusband, sitting before his desk on the bentwood chair, is reading his prayer book. Sibilant hisses flutter between his lips and every short while he clears his phlegmy throat. And, in a voice that sounds inaudible, and quivers with anxiety, I finally ask, 'Can I come with you?'

Godmother stares sombrely before her and remains quiet.

'Please.' I swallow on a lump in my throat.

'I can't take you,' Godmother says. 'It's no place for children.'

'I want to see Ayah,' I say, my longing making me sigh between the words.

'I really wish I could take you.'

'Why don't you ask her to come here? Won't her husband bring her?'

'He is willing to. But she refuses to come.'

I cannot believe Ayah wouldn't want to see me. See us.

'Her husband is lying,' I say fiercely. 'He's making excuses.'

'No, she is ashamed to face us,' says Godmother.

'Ashamed?' I say surprised. And even as Godmother says: 'She has nothing to be ashamed of,' I know Ayah is deeply, irrevocably ashamed. They have shamed her. Not those men in the carts – they were strangers – but Sharbat Khan and Ice-candy-man and Imam Din and Cousin's cook and the butcher and the other men she counted among her friends and admirers. I'm not very clear how – despite Cousin's illuminating tutorials – but I'm certain of her humiliation. Sensing this I more than ever want to see Ayah: to comfort and kiss her ugly experiences away.

'I want to tell her I am her friend,' I say sobbing defencelessly before Godmother. And remembering Hamida's remarks, I cry, 'I don't want her to think she's bad just because she's been kidnapped.'

I have never cried this way before. It is how grown-ups cry when their hearts are breaking.

* * *

Mini Aunty returns, silently bearing grocery bags and ice, looking like a fat and elderly sari-clad wax doll melting.

Godmother greets her. 'I thought the tongaman had run off with you! What took you so long?'

It is a purely rhetorical salutation and Mini Aunty need not reply if she doesn't want to. Ignoring Godmother, looking neither guilty nor annoyed, Slavesister is preoccupied with stashing the groceries and splintering and stuffing the ice into a thermos.

We hear a horse snort, and the creak of tonga wheels outside the door. Then a steady liquid noise, as of water gushing from a hose under pressure.

Oldhusband raises his praying voice in forbidding censure.

'Ummm, umM, uMM, UMM!' hums Godmother in a rising crescendo of disapproval, and breaking into speech she says, 'My God! How do you expect us to sit outside this evening?'

'It will evaporate . . . You can't imagine how hot it is!' says Slavesister, unperturbed.

'Can't I? Where do you think I live? In the North Pole?' and then, reverting to the matter in hand: 'What if the horse decides to perform on a grander scale? Will that evaporate too? How often must I tell you not to let the tonga come in?'

'I've told the tongawallah to take care of that.'

'Oh? What will he do? Diaper the horse?'

Mini Aunty continues placidly to unwrap her sari, and turning mildly pleading eyes to Godmother says, 'The tongawallah said the poor horse really had to get some water or he'd collapse.'

We hear the tongaman cluck his tongue and lead his horse and tonga to the trough at the back.

'You'd better remember to sprinkle the evaporated puddle with rose-water before we sit out,' says Godmother sarcastically, but in a softer tone, thereby conceding Mini Aunty a reprieve on compassionate grounds.

'I've arranged for the tonga to take you to –' In deference to my youthful presence Mini Aunty abruptly checks herself. She ends by enigmatically saying, 'You-know-where, at two o'clock.'

'Then you'd better set about getting lunch ready,' says Godmother.

* * *

Godmother's fingers are slightly trembling. Not with the tremor of age but with nervous concentration as she drapes her sari, with its finely embroidered floral border, before a slender half-mirror embedded in the cupboard. Her concentration is a tribute to the six yards of heavy grey silk, and to the occasion for which it is being worn. Normally, not bothered with their appearance, both she and Slavesister wrap their saris without the aid of mirrors. Unlike Mother, who pivots fastidiously in high heels in front of a full-length mirror to adjust the hem of her sari and precisely arrange the dainty fall of her pleats. It wouldn't be fitting if Mother dressed with less circumspection. In her case I feel adorning and embellishing her person is an obligatory rite and not a vanity.

Godmother moves closer to the mirror. As she carefully begins to pin the border to her hair, Mini Aunty, looking as if she has arrived at a decision, suddenly and gravely declares: 'I think I'd better come with you. You'll need my support!'

Her teeth clamped on a tangle of U-shaped hair pins Godmother turns abruptly. Facing Slavesister she says: 'Since when have I started needing your support in such matters?'

'You can't go there alone, Roda. You must have someone with you.'

Notice the unembellished Roda? Mini Aunty uses this form of address to sidle into a more dominant role. This has been occurring with alarming frequency of late: and the slave gets away with it – and the meagre Roda – with alarming frequency.

'Oh, all right! If it makes you feel any better, I'll take Lenny along,' says Godmother, attempting to appear reasonable but only managing to sound devious.

'You can't be serious!' exclaims Mini Aunty.

'Why not? She won't be contaminated – if that's what you're afraid of.'

'How can you even dream of taking the child there!' says Mini Aunty, her eyes brimming with reproach, the chubby disc of her cheeks lengthening in solemn consternation.

'I'm not taking her *there*,' says Godmother. 'We are only visiting a simple housewife in her simple house. The house merely happens to be *there*.'

'But what will her mother say?'

'That's between me and her mother. You know perfectly well she trusts my judgement . . . Not like some ungrateful brats I could name!'

'I know you . . .' says Slavesister, pale and hangdog. 'The more I say the more stubborn you become. One can't tell you anything. Have your way . . .'

'Have I ever done otherwise?'

'Oh, I know! You always have your way . . .'

'Then why are you wasting my time?'

'But have you given a thought to what people might say?'

'That I've become a dancing-girl? With bells on my ankles? Or worse?'

It is too much for Slavesister. Blinking tears she goes into the kitchen and commences mumbling.

Come to think of it, I'm hearing her mumbles after a long time.

At two o'clock the tongaman taps on the door with the bamboo end of his whip and shouts: 'I've arrived, *jee*. I'm parked by the gate.'

Godmother quickly compresses her lips and daubs her face with talcum powder. She peers at me through the chalk storm and, almost shyly, winks into my awed and smitten countenance. She looks grand. Her noble ghost-white face and generous mouth set off to advantage by the slate-grey sari and its pretty border. She is my very own whale – and her great love for me is plain in her shining eyes.

'We are going. Lock the door,' Godmother calls, and hand in hand we step into the abrasive heat.

The increasing congestion and uproar in the streets as we pass Data Sahib's tomb and approach the Badshahi mosque barely registers as leaning against Godmother I fall into a stupor induced by the heat and glare and the jolting rhythm of the tonga.

When Godmother gently shakes me awake we are already parked beneath a straggling *sheesham*, its small leaves brittle with the heat and dust, in front of a narrow alley. The tongaman has placed the feed sack in front of his horse and is tying the reins to the shaft. The sweat-darkened animal just stands there, its neck hanging, too exhausted to feed. Preceded by the tongaman we walk into the blessed shade of the constricted gullies of the old city.

Godmother is nervous. I can tell from the pressure of

her grip. After the clamour of the streets the silence in the alleys is vaguely discomforting. There are few people about and too few children. The naked babies tottering about the drains and doorsteps whimper listlessly and are scolded by irritable mothers from inside who sound as if it's dawn instead of three in the afternoon.

We emerge on a broader lane which has the appearance of a bazaar with rows of shops at the ground level and living quarters with frail arched windows and decaying wooden balconies teetering above. Still half asleep and drugged by the oppressive humidity and heat, I look for a tin can, or anything else to kick as I walk, but there is hardly any litter.

We walk past two young women, yawning and stretching in front of a stall overflowing with garlands of scarlet roses, jasmine and mounds of marigolds. The owner, wearing only a lungi, is perched like a contented and contemptuous deity amidst his wares.

Coming suddenly upon the fragrance of sprinkled flowers and the blaze of colours freshens my senses. The women chatting with the flower-man look tousled, as if they have just awakened and are still loitering in the shalwar-kamizes they have slept in. Except for the betel-leaf and cigarette stalls and a few eating places where meat and *pakoras* are being fried, there is very little sign of commerce. The ancient, roughly carved doors are shut for the most part. And the few that are open reveal steep flights of narrow steps or twilit interiors I cannot see into.

My previous excursions inside the old city had been enlivened by the cries of shop-keepers and hawkers and the bawling and shrieking of urchins; the lanes teeming with men and burka-veiled women and littered with the discarded newspaper bags used by vendors. I miss the mounds of rotting fruit and vegetables and the bones picked clean by the kites, their enormous wings stirring in the garbage: and the sudden yelp of kicked mongrels and raucous flights of crows and scraps of cardboard and rusted iron and the other debris even the poor have no use for.

Godmother pinches her sari austerely beneath her chin and maintaining her eyes straight in front of her marches regally behind the tongaman. Her sari, catching the breeze the cunningly structured alleys miraculously generate in an otherwise windless city, billows greyly about her shoulders and back. None of the women here is veiled. The bold girls, with short, permed hair, showing traces of stale make-up, stare at us as if we are freaks. They whisper and burst into giggles when we pass and bury their faces in each other's shoulders and necks. Their crumpled kamizes are too short and the *pencha*-bottoms of their shalwars too wide. Even I can tell they are not well brought up. I have never seen women of this class with cropped and frizzed hair: nor using the broad and comfortable gestures of men. The few men, in singlets and faded lungis, scratch their carelessly bared stomachs as they loiter in the lane, or pause to joke with the girls. Some have their hands inside their lungis and are cleaning themselves after urinating as prescribed, unconsciously indulging in what I've heard snidely described as 'the national pastime'.

Our tongaman halts before a weathered door with deep grooves. I glimpse the chain holding the panels closed from inside. 'This is the address, *Baijee*,' he says, and at a nod from Godmother, batters the door with his hand.

There is an instant shout: 'Coming!' followed by the lightfooted patter of a lightweight poet hastening down the steps. The door opens and the poet blinks his kohl-rimmed eyes in the glare. Ice-candy-man looks subdued, flustered, honoured. Displaying the exquisite courtesy of Mogul courtiers, spouting snatches of felicitous verse, picking me up with one hand and supporting Godmother with the other as we slowly mount the steps – Godmother pausing to catch her breath – Ice-candy-man ushers us into the sitting room. Guiding Godmother to a sofa covered in glossy green velvet, he adjusts the cushions behind her and draws a peg table conveniently close. Then he breathlessly says: 'I'll fetch Mumtaz,' and disappears behind the pink and white checked curtains.

'So!' whispers Godmother, blinking and nodding impishly. 'He has christened our ayah Mumtaz!'

'I like the name,' I say.

I think it fitting that a courtier's wife be named after a Mogul queen. And the room, too, is befitting: long and narrow, filled with ornate chairs covered in velvet, sporting little tables with crocheted doilies and thick glass and brass vases crammed with red paper poppies. The arched windows are shaded by reed screens and the walls are a gleaming pink. The room has the gratifying appeal of a cool and delicious tutti-frutti ice-cream.

And then Ayah comes: teetering on high heels, tripping on the massive divided skirt of her *garara*, jangling gold bangles. Her eyes are lowered and her head draped in a gold-fringed and gauzy red *ghoongat*. A jewelled tika nestles on her forehead and bunches of pearls and gold dangle from her ears. Ice-candy-man guides his rouged and lipsticked bride to sit beside Godmother. Godmother lightly strokes Mumtaz's covered head and says: 'Bless you my daughter . . . Live long.'

I feel frightfully shy. I had expected to leap on Ayah and hug her to bits. But now that she is here, in the awesome shape of a bride, I can do no more than shift uneasily in my chair and stare at her. I notice the tiny pieces of tinsel glitter stuck on her chin and cheeks.

'Lenny baby, aren't you going to embrace my bride?' Ice-candy-man asks.

And Ayah raises her eyes to me.

Where have the radiance and the animation gone? Can the soul be extracted from its living body? Her vacant eyes are bigger than ever: wide-opened with what they've seen and felt: wider even than the frightening saucers and dinner plates that describe the watchful orbs of the three dogs who guard the wicked Tinder Box witches' treasures in underground chambers. Colder than the ice that lurks behind the hazel in Ice-candy-man's beguiling eyes.

At last Ayah casts her lids down: and bowing her head, extends her hennaed hands to me. I move awkwardly into the voluminous skirt of her brocade *garara*. And through the prickling brocade and silver lamé of her kamize at last feel the soft and rounded contours of her diminished flesh. She buries her head in me and buries me in all her finery; and in the dark and musky attar of her perfume.

Leaving Mumtaz to sit awkwardly with us Ice-candy-man goes inside to make the tea.

Godmother moves to the edge of the sofa and tenderly raises Mumtaz's chin, saying, 'Let me have a good look at our bride.'

Ayah's face, with its demurely lowered lids and tinsel dust, blooms like a dusky rose in Godmother's hands. The rouge and glitter highlight the sweet contours of her features. She looks achingly lovely: as when she gazed at Masseur and inwardly glowed. But the illusion is dispelled the moment she opens her eyes – not timorously like a bride, but frenziedly, starkly – and says: 'I want to go to my family.' Her voice is harsh, gruff: as if someone has mutilated her vocal cords.

Even Godmother can't bear the look in her eyes. She gently removes her hand, and Ayah's unsupported face collapses and is again half hidden in the *ghoongat*. Godmother composes herself with a visible effort. And the look of shock and pity fading, sitting taut on the edge of the sofa, she at last says: 'Isn't he looking after you?'

Mumtaz nods her head slightly.

'What's happened has happened,' says Godmother. 'But you are married to him now. You must make the best of things. He truly cares for you.'

'I will not live with him.' Again that coarse, rasping whisper.

I have moved to my chair across the room but I hear Ayah's discordant murmurs clearly. (It is not without reason Mini Aunty has designated my talented ears 'cricket ears'.)

'Does he mistreat you . . . in any way?' Godmother asks with uncharacteristic hesitancy.

'Not now,' says Mumtaz. 'But I cannot forget what happened.'

'That was fated, daughter. It can't be undone. But it can be forgiven . . . Worse things are forgiven. Life goes on and the business of living buries the debris of our pasts. Hurt, happiness . . . all fade impartially . . . to make way for fresh joy and new sorrow. That's the way of life.'

'I am past that,' says Mumtaz. 'I'm not alive.'

Godmother leans back and withdraws the large cambric handkerchief tucked into her blouse. She wipes her forehead.

'What if your family won't take you back?' she asks.

'Whether they want me or not, I will go.'

We hear the clatter of ill-fitted cups and saucers. The curtain bulges and Ice-candy-man comes through, carefully bearing a tray. He pauses in front of the curtain and manifesting an awed and felicitous aspect, sweeping his dramatic eyes from Godmother to the pink walls of his house, recites Ghalib's famous couplet:

''Tis a miracle wondrous that you have come:
Marvelling, I look from you to the walls of my house . . .'

He places the tray on a small table near Godmother and, interminably stirring the tea with a spoon to dissolve the sugar, deferentially hands her the cup. 'Is it strong enough?' he enquires. 'More milk? Sugar?'

Godmother takes a sip. 'It's all right,' she says tersely.

Turning to me, flourishing an autumnal forest of popsicles, Ice-candy-man says, 'Look what I have for my Lenny baby.'

I take two sticks. One for each hand.

Ayah refuses her tea with a shake of her lowered head. Ice-candy-man stoops and, holding the cup close to Ayah's fingers, coaxes, 'Have some, *meri kasam*. Drink it for *Baijee*'s sake at least . . .'

'I don't want any,' she says harshly. While he passes the pastry with the little dabs of jam, his anxious courtier's eyes keep alighting on Mumtaz. Assuming the role of the misused lover so dear to Urdu poets, he quotes Mir:

> *'Hai ashiqi ke beech sitam dekhna hi lutf*
> *Mar jana ankhe moond ke kuch hunar nahin.*
> 'Tis nothing . . . to roll up one's eyes and die.
> I endure my lover's tyranny wide-eyed.'

Ice-candy-man appears to have sensed the content of the exchange between Godmother and his bride. Maintaining a nervous stream of chatter, quoting snatches of poetry, pressing us to eat and drink, he attempts to conceal his misgiving.

'I'll get the kebabs,' he says after a while, looking at our faces hesitantly, seeking our approval. 'They should be done by now.'

Godmother nods briefly.

Ice-candy-man leaves the room and, slipping to the floor like a floating bundle of crumpled silk, Ayah grasps Godmother's legs. 'Please – I fall at your feet, *Baijee* – please get me away from him.'

'Are you sure that's what you want?' says Godmother, bending to look into her face. 'You might regret your decision . . . You should think it over.'

'I have thought it over . . . I want to go to my folk.'

'Let's see what I can do,' Godmother says gently. 'I'll try my best.'

Ayah is sniffing and rubbing her face on Godmother's legs.

'Get up, my daughter . . . Have faith . . . Have patience,' says Godmother holding her and trying to pull her to the sofa.

Stepping on and getting entangled in her enormous skirts, Mumtaz scrambles to rise just as the poet enters with a fragrant dish of kebabs. He quickly reaches for Ayah and helps her to sit on the sofa.

The poet's manner is subdued, his face drawn, apprehensive: and his eyes, red with the strain of containing his tears, hover caressingly on Ayah. They flit to Godmother in mute appeal.

Godmother strokes Ayah's back. Ayah is huddled over,

silently weeping, her body trembling. 'Have patience, daughter, have faith. Go. Go and wash your face,' says Godmother, helping Ayah to stand up. Gathering her skirt with both hands, Ayah clumsily staggers out of the room on her unnatural heels.

Godmother's mouth is set. She turns her austere eyes on Ice-candy-man.

'How long has she been like this?'

'Like how?'

'Emptied of life? Despairing?'

In a slow, coiling movement Ice-candy-man squats directly in front of Godmother. 'The past is behind her,' he says. Taking the kitchen rag from his shoulder he wipes his face. It is as if he has wiped off all artifice, all pride: his humility and despair are manifest. 'I cannot help the past,' he says. 'But now she has everything to live for.'

Godmother's eyes on the poet's exposed face are dispassionate. Cold. And gliding forward on his haunches Ice-candy-man clasps her hands in both his and places them on his bowed, penitent's head.

'Please. Please persuade her . . . explain to her . . . I will keep her like a queen . . . like a flower . . . I'll make her happy,' he says, and succumbing to the pressure of his pent-up misery starts weeping.

'We shall see,' says Godmother: and in a coldly significant gesture withdraws her hands from Ice-candy-man's head. He remains like that, stranded, crouched forward, his face hidden by long black strands of falling hair. After what seems like hours he turns to me, swivelling on his haunches, and his beguiling eyes, weighed with insupportable uncertainties, plead his cause.

The longer I look at him the more willing I am to be beguiled by those tearing, forlorn eyes. How long have they been like that? When I think of Ayah I think she must get away from the monster who has killed her spirit and mutilated her 'angel's' voice. And when I look at Ice-candy-man's naked humility and grief I see him as undeserving of his beloved's heartless disdain.

He is a deflated poet, a collapsed pedlar – and while Ayah is haunted by her past, Ice-candy-man is haunted by his future: and his macabre future already appears to be stamped on his face.

* * *

I am feverish to see Cousin. I haven't told anyone about our visit with Ayah. Not even Adi. I sit on Electric-aunt's veranda waiting for the school bus to deliver my cousin. Hamida is in the kitchen talking to the cook. Electric-aunt is inside, whirling herself into her sari, issuing a battery of instructions to her sweepress and at the same time listening to the four o'clock news.

The minute I see the bus I run to the gate to receive my cousin. The school bus, windows crammed with boys' faces, lurches away spewing exhaust smoke and Cousin scowls at me. He doesn't like me seeing all those boys – or all those boys looking at me. Besides he's embarrassed to be seen associating with such a skinny girl.

Cousin is flushed and sweaty and weighed down by his school bag. I relieve him of the precariously bulging geometry box in his hand and say, 'I went to see Ayah and Ice-candy-man yesterday!'

Cousin comes to a dead stop just inside the gate.

'Where?'

'At their house.'

Cousin looks amazed. Then pale, and very serious, he leads me into the shade of the gardenia hedge in front of the garden wall. We sit on the warm and dusty grass and Cousin enquires, grimly: 'Who took you there?'

'Godmother.'

'Godmother?' Cousin is incredulous. He is also disconcerted.

'She didn't want to take me. But I cried . . . and she took me along.'

'She shouldn't have,' says Cousin, in a tone of voice that suggests he is Godmother's age, and Godmother a naughty little girl.

'Okay,' he continues, in the same censorious tone. 'Tell me what you saw in the Hira Mandi. Tell me what happened. Tell me everything.'

I tell him everything. I tell him the details of Ayah's despair and the spurned courtier-poet's anguish.

'Is that all?' Cousin appears disappointed, and at the same time mollified. 'You would have seen a lot more if you'd gone there after dark.'

'Like what?' I say feeling that either he is deliberately aggravating me, or we are at cross purposes.

'Girls dancing and singing – and amorous poets. And you would have been raped.'

'What's that?'

(I never learn, do I?)

'I'll show you someday,' says Cousin giving me a queer look.

I don't press the point. 'What do you think will happen now?' I enquire instead.

'If Godmother says she'll help Ayah get away, she'll get her away.'

You see? Everyone has confidence in Godmother.

'What did you say Ayah's new name was?' Cousin asks.

'Mumtaz.'

'That's a nice name for a dancing-girl,' says Cousin, rolling the words and rolling his eyes and leering horribly.

'Can't you talk straight?' I say, ready to hit him.

'You've been to the *Kotha*! You visit the dancing-girls! and you want *me* to talk straight?'

'I think the heat has scrambled your brains,' I declare, standing up in disgust.

Cousin yanks the hem of my skirt and I thud back on the scratchy grass.

'If you want me to stay,' I say, 'you'd better mind how you talk!'

'Okay,' says Cousin changing his tone and composing

his features. 'You want me to tell you what goes on there?'

He knows he has me hooked.

'As long as you tell me and don't start demonstrating,' I say, warning him with my voice and also a wagging finger.

I wait for my message to sink in, and then I ask, 'What's *Kotha*?' Godmother had used the word when talking to Ice-candy-man: and now Cousin.

'The Hira Mandi,' explains Cousin, 'is also known as the *Kotha*. Roof. Because the dancing-girls carry on their main business upstairs.'

As Cousin talks a fascinating picture emerges.

The *Kotha* is the cultural pulse of the city. It is where poets are inspired, where their songs are sung and made famous by the girls, and singing-boys. It is also a stepping stone to film stardom for the nautch-girls. The girls are taught to sing and dance and talk elegantly and look pretty and be attractive to men. It sounds very much like a cross between a Swiss finishing school a female cousin of mine in Bombay was sent to and a School for the Fine and Performing Arts.

After mulling over the complexities of the discourse on the cultured *Kotha* – which I know is also the cradle of royalty, I enquire: 'But what are pimps?' Another word that arouses peculiar reactions in people.

'They look after the dancing-girls,' says Cousin.

'A kind of male ayah?'

'No,' says Cousin, sounding condescending and painfully adenoidal. 'They protect the girls from drunks and look after money the girls get. They bring men and introduce them to the dancing-girls.'

I'm beginning to understand. The pimps are a kind of adult and mercantile cupid.

I also have an insight into the potent creative force generated within the *Kotha* that has metamorphosed Ice-candy-man not only into a Mogul courtier, but into a Mandi poet. No wonder he founts poetry as if he popped out of his mother's womb spouting rhyming sentences.

But all this still doesn't explain the twittering flap and the hush-hush any mention of the Hira Mandi evokes. Or the contempt in which everybody appears to hold this Institute of Culture.

. . . Or the girls who looked too at ease loitering in the Mandi gullies and lacked the docile modesty of properly brought up Muslim women.

I have many questions, but Cousin appears to have had his fill of enlightening me. He is hungry and thirsty and we go inside.

Chapter 31

'Dr Selzer! Come here. Come here,' Mother yells cheerfully from the veranda: summoning him also with a snappy wave of her hand. She is pouring tea for Mr Phailbus, his daughter Maggie, and his son Theo. Since they are Indian Christians they are among the few remaining neighbours we still know.

The Shankars' rooms at the back have been let to Dr Selzer. The German doctor does not inhabit the rooms as much as possess them. He lives alone and he padlocks the rooms when he goes out. He has only one servant.

The doctor's steps, deflected from their course by my Mother's voice, falter. And turning round politely he approaches us from the drive.

'I was just this minute talking about you!' warbles Mother enthusiastically, flashing all her beautiful teeth in a magical smile.

Dr Selzer is taller than Col. Bharucha. Taller even than the murdered Inspector General of Police, Mr Rogers. But he is much less intimidating. He lacks Col. Bharucha's charge of thunder and the departed policeman's I'm-in-charge-here air of haughtiness. He is polite: and assured in a subdued, understated way. And though he doesn't talk much I can tell from the expression on his face that he is a gentle gentleman. He keeps so much to himself I think because he's shy.

Dr Selzer practises his calling in two rooms he has rented on Birdwood Road, behind Warris Road. One room is occupied by a self-trained and indigenous chemist who deciphers and dispenses the prescriptions.

The doctor walks to and from his office. He says he needs the exercise. He says he will buy a car when his wife comes from Germany. Even Father likes him. Mother is so impressed by his doctoring that she has transferred my diminishing limp – and sundry colds, coughs and attacks of diarrhoea – to his care and taken it upon herself to promote his practice. Between his permanent presidency of the Parsee Anjuman and his thronging patients Col. Bharucha has become too busy in any case.

Mr Phailbus, who is a retired magistrate – and a budding homeopath besides – stands up to shake hands. Mr Phailbus's kindness and congeniality twinkle in his dark eyes. His sere shock of cropped white hair barely clears the German doctor's shoulders. Theo, lean, reserved and dark as a thundercloud, also shakes Dr Selzer's hand.

'Mrs Sethi was just telling us all about you,' says Maggie affably. She is comfortably ensconced in the chair, one slipperless foot resting jauntily on her red-satin-shalwared thigh. She wiggles her dusty toes invitingly and Dr Selzer, with quiet resignation, settles down beside her.

'Look at Lenny!' Mother exclaims, yanking me closer to the Phailbuses for better observation. 'Isn't she looking better already?'

'Much better. Much better,' murmur the three Phailbuses, nodding their heads.

'Eat and run! Eat and run! That's all she's done all year!'

says Mother, lovingly and graphically squeezing both my bottoms. 'It's a wonder she has any bottom left.'

'Tch, tch, tch,' says Maggie Phailbus sympathetically.

'Look,' says Mother. Jacking up the skirt of my starched pink frock and the rim of my knickers she points out a small incision and bump in my groin. 'He inserted the pill here: right under the skin: and overnight her dysentery was finished! Have you ever heard of amoebic dysentery being cured just like that?' She snaps her fingers.

Heads nod again and eyes widen in wonder as the spell of my mother's voice conjures the Jewish doctor into a savage wizard and my cure into a feat of unparalleled sorcery.

'He's excellent! I tell you, he's excellent!' asserts Mother exuberantly. 'Lenny, walk!' commands Mother, and like a performing poodle I parade up and down before the Phailbuses, taking care to place my awkward heel on the floor.

'See?' says Mother triumphantly. 'He's cured her limp!'

Dr Selzer stretches his lips in a mild smile and his eyes, assured yet shy, search her face for a clue to his release.

But Mother has no mind to let him go yet. In her zeal as promoter and town-crier of Dr Selzer's genius she has neglected Mr Phailbus's accomplishments: and being scrupulously fair she informs Dr Selzer – in an awed whisper that portends revelations – that Mr Phailbus is a homeopath: another miracle worker! Holding her shapely lips and chiselled chin in the refined and mannered way she assumes when talking to Englishmen and others of the white species, she says: 'God bless our Mr Phailbus. Do you know I had a cyst that big inside here?' She gathers her fingers into a fist and waves the fist discreetly and vaguely in the direction of her lower abdomen. 'Even the date for the operation was fixed. It was just by chance that I told Mr Phailbus about it. He said: "Let me have a try. If my powders work you may spare yourself an operation." I know homeopathy is harmless. So I had one of those sweet powders of his before going to bed. The next morning the cyst had melted! I couldn't feel it: just a little bit of discharge. Col. Bharucha was amazed! He said he had never seen a cyst vanish like that!'

Mr Phailbus's gentle eyes beam and twinkle above his half-moon glasses and Dr Selzer looks mildly and suitably impressed.

At this point I become aware of a sudden commotion in Rosy-Peter's compound. Mingled with the thud of hooves and the creaking of wooden wheels are the raised voices of men squabbling and cursing and the sounds of running feet and of combat. We cock our ears and exchange alert glances. And taking advantage of our momentary inattention Dr Selzer, discreetly murmuring his goodbyes, slips away.

Mother and I, followed by the Phailbuses, run down the veranda steps. Imam Din is already standing on the handy kitchen stool looking over the wall and Hari and Yousaf are scrambling on to it for a ring-side view.

'What happened?' Mother shouts.

Hamida, her head covered, is hovering excitedly near the men. She directs a squeaky stream of sentences at us that we cannot make anything out of.

'Oye, Sardarjee, stop it! You'll kill him!' shouts Imam Din.

Moti-alias-David-Masih is running up from the back, followed by his wife and progeny and parents and sisters and the other inhabitants of the servants' quarters. The sounds of combat increase. A man bellows in pain and then belts out a breathless string of vintage Punjabi curses in a hoarse, wailing voice. Hari-alias-Himat-Ali and Yousaf jump the wall and disappear on the other side.

'Will someone tell me what's going on?' Mother shouts in an imperious frenzy.

I climb aboard the kitchen stool and clamour to be picked up by Imam Din and he lifts me up and sits me on the wall.

Three horse-drawn carts are crowded any old how to

the far side of our neighbours' compound and in front of them, quite close to the wall, is the scene of battle: an entwined jumble of arms and legs and torn clothing tumbling through a mesh of snarled hair. Yousaf, Himat Ali and the other men in the forefront are trying to restrain and lift the hefty Sikh guard. The Sikh is entwined with someone on the floor and is viciously attacking and bellowing: 'Dog! Mother-fucker! Son of an owl!'

Just then the men succeed in pulling the fighters apart and slowly, assisted by several pairs of hands and dusting his clothes, a man arises from the dust. His face and arms are grimed with blood and dirt and his hand is twisted at an unnatural angle. Someone wipes his face with a wet rag and as the man, in obvious pain, pushes the rag away, I see frantic amber eyes.

'It's the Ice-candy-man,' I scream to Mother. 'They've beaten him up!'

A group of men hastily bundle him into a cart and three scruffy-looking *goondas* in singlets and lungis jump in after him. One of them, standing up in the carriage, whips the horse savagely and the cart, followed by the other carts, groans and creaks down the rutted drive.

The remaining men group around the outraged Sikh who is hollering: 'I'll break the bastard's neck next time! I've never had trouble before! Let anyone touch the women . . . See what I'll do to their cocks and balls! They are my sisters and mothers!' He thumps his massive chest. His knee-length hair, mauled by Ice-candy-man, is in dramatic, spiky disarray. The men stare at him in wonderment and nod their heads.

Imam Din plucks me off the wall and deposits me near Hamida. Mother is yelling at the gate. Trailed by Hamida I run to her as Mother screams after the departing cart, '*Duffa ho!* Show your blackened faces at someone else's door! That scoundrel! He can't deceive me again! If he dares show his face I'll call the police and have him hung upside down!'

She is flushed and fuming and panting in a fierce way.

Her penetrating voice I am sure can be heard by the men in the disappearing carts.

Maggie and Mr Phailbus try to soothe Mother. Mr Phailbus, who has the power to heal and calm in his hands, strokes Mother's head and shoulders and Mother's rage subsides somewhat. The Phailbuses say goodbye at the gate and saunter away, talking in subdued voices, and Mother marches up our drive with a preoccupied expression that betrays the battle she is still engaged in with the object of her recriminations.

Hamida and I run to the back and rush up the stairs to the servants' roof. The women and children from the quarters are already looking over the short parapet wall into the courtyard. Since it would be improper for Moti and Hari to look at the women, they are squatting at a polite distance, anxious for whatever news of Ayah they can acquire second-hand. The women in the courtyard appear agitated. They flutter in and out of the rooms and answer our insistent queries with more animation than they have ever displayed before. Their voices rise up to us from upturned faces: Ayah is exhausted. She's all right. She doesn't wish to see you . . . best leave her alone. She's being registered.

'Let her be. It'll take hours if she's being registered,' says Hamida, slapping her forehead in a gesture of sympathy, and talking from experience. 'They'll be asking her a hundred-and-one questions, and filling out a hundred-and-one forms.' She is referring to the clerks from the Ministry for the Rehabilitation of Recovered Women. 'Yes, sister, let her do as she wishes . . .' say the women on the roof.

And I chant: 'Ayah! Ayah! Ayah! Ayah!' until my heart pounds with the chant and the children on the roof picking it up shout with all their heart: 'Ayah! Ayah! Ayah! Ayah!' and our chant flows into the pulse of the women below, and the women on the roof, and they beat their breasts and cry: *'Hai! Hai! Hai! Hai!'* reflecting the history of their cumulative sorrows and the sorrows of their Muslim, Hindu, Sikh and Rajput great-grandmothers who burnt themselves alive rather than surrender their honour to the invading hordes besieging their ancestral fortresses.

The Sikh guard, noisily splashing himself at the tap outside the gate, stands up to look at us – and when he beholds only the women and children on the roof, he holds his peace – and once again settles to wash the blood and mud from his clothes and hair.

'Ayah! Ayah! Ayah!' we chant and *'Hai! Hai! Hai!'* the weeping women: and supported by two old women Ayah appears in the courtyard. She looks up at us out of glazed and unfeeling eyes for a moment, as if we are strangers, and goes in again.

I institute a vehement and importunate enquiry. After a great deal of painstaking probing and prying I ferret out a fairly accurate account of the events that led to Ayah's extradition from the Hira Mandi.

The long and diverse reach of Godmother's tentacular arm is clearly evident. She set an entire conglomerate in motion immediately after our visit with Ayah and single-handedly engendered the social and moral climate of retribution and justice required to rehabilitate our fallen Ayah.

Everything came to a head within a fortnight. Which in the normal course of events, unstructured by Godmother's stratagems, could have been consigned to the ingenious bureaucratic eternity of a toddler nation greenly fluttering its flag – with a white strip to represent its minorities – and a crescent and star – from the National Assembly building behind the unqueened garden and its eviscerated marble marquee.

Brand-new flags flutter, too, from the filigreed turrets of the pink High Court and the General Post Office and other government offices and the new fronts of bazaar shops in the Shalmi and Gowalmandi and the oil and engineering companies – those ubiquitous visitants from foreign lands – and the domes and minarets of new mosques erupting all over Lahore . . . some beautiful as poems and some bedraggled.

And armed with the might of a small and fluttering green flag a posse of policemen in a jeep – and a wired black van – squeezed their way right into the constricted, drain-divided heart of the Hira Mandi and stopped before the popsicle-man's splintered door. The police, waving signed papers and batons, swarmed through the rooms of Ice-candy-man's *Kotha* and finding Ayah there took her away, a willing accompanist, to the black van. And all the Mandi pimps and poets and musicians . . . and all the flower-sellers, prostitutes, butchers, cigarette and *paan* vendors, wrestlers and toughs of the cultured *Kotha* could do nothing about it. Nor do Ice-candy-man's threats, pleading, remonstrance, bellows, declamations, courtly manners, resourcefulness or wailing impede the progression of the van in its determination to deposit Ayah, with her scant belongings wrapped in cloth bundles and a small tin trunk, at the Recovered Women's Camp on Warris Road. To be followed there in three galloping carts by Ice-candy-man and his cronies – all their outrage and broken bones and pimpy influence to no avail.

Chapter 32

> Give me the (mystic) wine that burns all veils,
> The wine by which life's secret is revealed,
> The wine whose essence is eternity,
> The wine which opens mysteries concealed.
> Lift up the curtain, give me power to talk.
> And make the sparrow struggle with the hawk.
>
> (Iqbal)

Ice-candy-man has taken to patrolling Warris Road: his broken left arm supported in a sling and pressed to his chest as if affirming a truth.

Sometimes he squats across the road from our wall and sometimes inside Rosy-Peter's compound – patiently, and from a distance, watching the tin-sheet gates. Occasionally he recites Zauq:

> 'Why did you make a home in my heart?
> Inhabit it. Both the house and I are desolate.
> Am I a thief that your watchman stops me?
> Tell him, I know this man. He is my fate.'

The guard is getting used to his presence; and to his poetic outbursts. When he first spied him the Sikh advanced threatening to tear him limb from limb and stuff his genitals every which where. Our household, attracted to the wall by the shouting, saw Ice-candy-man's splintered arm raised to defend himself from the blows, and his tearing eyes, and Imam Din and Yousaf shouted: 'Let him be, *yaar*, he's harmless.'

The Sikh merely pulled the popsicle-man to his feet by his unbroken and frail arm and Ice-candy-man meekly walked away.

Even the Sikh has given way to his indefatigable persistence and now eyes him with a certain awe. For Icy-candy-man is acquiring a new aspect – that of a moonstruck fakir who has renounced the world for his beloved: be it woman or God. Repeating a couplet by Faiz as if it is a prayer, he murmurs:

> 'There are other wounds besides the wounds of love –
> Other nights besides passionate nights of love –'

Driven more, I suspect, by private demons than by fear of Mother's threats, Ice-candy-man has not stepped inside our gates. Sometimes he brings with him his thermos of popsicles and does business in a desultory fashion, giving away more ices than he sells. And sometimes, when the Sikh guard accompanies our unseeing and unfeeling Ayah to Mr Phailbus for homeopathic treatment, Ice-candy-man squats patiently outside the Phailbuses' wall.

Often I accompany Ayah to Mr Phailbus's; and when we

walk past the candy-man, he greets us courteously and does not stare at Ayah, but casts his eyes down. Ayah behaves as if he is invisible. And, his overgrown hair shading his eyes, he sometimes murmurs a couplet by another romantic poet, Ghalib:

> 'My passion has brought me to your street –
> Where can I now find the strength to take me back?'

Ayah behaves as if he is inaudible too.

He has become a truly harmless fellow. My heart not only melts – it evaporates when I breathe out, leaving me faint with pity. Even the guard lets down his guard and at times, when in the mood for company, squats by Ice-candy-man, gleaning wisdom from his comments on life and its ways and the wayward ways of God and men and women, until it's time to accompany Ayah back. Then, Zauq's poems and Ice-candy-man's voice humming in our minds, we murmur:

> 'Don't berate me, beloved, I'm God-intoxicated!
> I'll wrap myself about you; I'm mystically mad.'

Each morning I awaken now to the fragrance of flowers flung over our garden wall at dawn by Ice-candy-man. The courtyard of the Recovered Women's Camp too is strewn with petals; and sometimes with the added glitter of cheap candy wrapped in cellophane. And after Himat Ali sweeps up the red roses crushed by the sun, and the camp women the petals scattered near the tin gates in their courtyard as if they were no more than goat droppings, Ice-candy-man's voice rises in sweet and clear song to shower Ayah with poems.

> 'Bewitching faces don't remain buried
> They reappear in the shapes of flowers.'

Until, one morning, when I sniff the air and miss the fragrance, and run in consternation to the kitchen, I am told that Ayah, at last, has gone to her family in Amritsar.

. . . And Ice-candy-man, too, disappears across the Wagah border into India.

walk past the candy-man, he greets us courteously and does not stare at Ayah, but casts his eyes down. Ayah considers it [illegible]. And for once [illegible] his eyes [illegible] a couplet by another romantic poet, Ghalib:

My passion has brought me to your street
Where can I [illegible]

Ayah [illegible] as if he [illegible]

He [illegible] becomes [illegible] fellow [illegible] girls [illegible] when [illegible] leaving [illegible] play. [illegible] when in the mood for company, [illegible] candy-man, gleaning wisdom from his comments on [illegible] and its ways and the wayward ways of God and men and women, until it's time to accompany Ayah [illegible]. Then, [illegible] poems [illegible] we [illegible]

Don't tease me, [illegible] God [illegible]
I'll [illegible] myself about you, I'm [illegible]

Each morning I awaken now to the [illegible] over our garden wall at [illegible]. The courtyard of the Recovered Women's Camp [illegible] with [illegible] and [illegible] with the [illegible] candy wrapped in cellophane. And after [illegible] up the [illegible] by the sun and [illegible] women [illegible] yard as if they were no more than [illegible] candy-man's [illegible] and [illegible] Ayah with poems:

The [illegible] faces don't [illegible]
They [illegible] of flowers.

Until, one morning, when I [illegible] and [illegible] in conversation [illegible] told that Ayah, at last, has gone to her family in Amritsar.

And the candy-man, [illegible] disappears across the Wagah border into India.